I kicked off my slippers and lifted the quilt, climbing in at the end of Cissy's bed and there, with my back pressed against the brass bars, with my arms wrapped round knees drawn up to my breast, I looked at my aunt again. Her hair was spread loose on the pillow, her eyes were wide open, glistening and dark, and so lovely she was, so fragile that night, and I honestly thought she'd never so much resembled that girl in the painting, in the Millais that hung in our hall. And with that in mind, I suddenly asked, 'Cissy, why did you give up the stage? Why have you only come back to it now? And why did you never marry . . . always living with Mama and me? Did you never fall in love?'

'I did love someone . . . once.'

That was my chance. At last I could ask. 'Was it that man from Wilton's?'

'Yes. I was only thirteen when we met. Now, it seems like a lifetime ago.' Cissy paused and gazed up at the ceiling where firelight was dancing over the mouldings, all the elegant plaster flowers and shells. 'I never wanted anyone else.'

Essie Fox divides her time between Windsor and Bow in the East End of London. She is the author of *The Virtual Victorian*: www.virtualvictorian.blogspot.com.

Find out more at www.essiefox.com.

THE SOMNAMBULIST

ESSIE FOX

An Orion paperback

First published in Great Britain in 2011
by Orion
This paperback edition published in 2012
by Orion Books Ltd,
Orion House, 5 Upper St Martin's Lane,
London WC2H 9EA

An Hachette UK company

3 5 7 9 10 8 6 4

Image of *The Somnambulist* by Millais reproduced
by kind permission of Bolton Museum.

A CIP catalogue record for this book
is available from the British Library.

ISBN 978-1-4091-2119-0

Typeset at The Spartan Press Ltd,
Lymington, Hants

Printed and bound in Great Britain by Clays Ltd,
St Ives plc

The Orion Publishing Group's policy is to use papers
that are natural, renewable and recyclable products and
made from wood grown in sustainable forests. The logging
and manufacturing processes are expected to conform to
the environmental regulations of the country of origin.

www.orionbooks.co.uk

The Somnambulist by John Millais

Acknowledgements

The publication of *The Somnambulist* has been like a dream come true – a dream that could not have been realised without my agent, Isobel Dixon. And, with the book being sold to Orion, I could not have asked for a more generous and astute editor than Kate Mills who, along with her assistant Jade Chandler, has shown un-erring patience and tact when faced with my questions and foibles.

By its very nature an author's life can be isolated and over the past few years the advice of Margaret Gray and the friendship offered to me by members of the online writing group, Write Words, has been a great source of support. My Facebook and Twitter associates have also provided a virtual 'community': the perfect blend of fact and frivolity. You all know who you are!

In real life I must mention the encouragement pro-vided by my dear friend, Rachel Ward. And not forget-ting Rhian Pack and Elizabeth Herkstroker – always there to keep me sane with a coffee and a smile.

But the biggest appreciation of all must go to my husband and daughter who, at times, must surely have wondered if I would ever re-emerge from my world of dreams and fantasy.

For my husband,
who first lured me to the East End.

For my mother,
who first led me into the woods,
and the memories that those trees still hold,
that live on in the hearts of each one of us.

PART ONE

If he comes suddenly, do not let him find you
sleeping. What I say to you I say to everyone:
Watch!

Mark 13:36–37

WILTON'S MUSIC HALL

GEORGE FRIDERIC HANDEL'S FAMOUS OPERETTA,

THE STORY OF

ACIS AND GALATEA

Polyphemus desired the nymph Galatea. Seduced by her beauty and singing, the giant wooed her with precious shells and stones. He offered her delicacies; the sweet flesh of newly born children, red wines fortified with their blood. He followed whenever she left the shore, wandering through the meadows or woods. But, when spying her naked, entwined in the arms of the shepherd boy Acis, his fury drew down dark and thunderous clouds. He flung bolts of lightning, great rocks and boulders, cruelly murdering his usurper.

Galatea fled back to the oceans, buried beneath the waves, never singing or showing her face again. But where her tears mingled with the blood of Acis, bubbling up from the stones that had crushed him, that liquid became a sparkling stream that flowed down the hillside and into the sea, so that Acis's spirit could join with his love, to follow where Polyphemus could not.

That cutting was pasted in Cissy's scrapbook. The date she'd written underneath was November 13th, 1881; the very last time she ever sang.

Cissy had the voice of an angel. But then, she was closer to Heaven than any of us could know. It used to

3

make me shiver inside, hearing those notes so clear and pure, like crystal, like rippling water, until – just like water – she slipped through our hands.

Some nights I still dream of her as Galatea, her face streamed with liquid ribbons of light, her eyes gazing up from the depths of the sea. And she sees Polyphemus: the giant who still grieves, who still waits on the shore for his nymph to return, who is doomed to view nothing but shifting waves.

They say passion is sweet, and it may be for some. But a love unrequited must taste dry as ashes. It must be as bitter as gall.

1

I'd been to Wilton's Hall before. I would have been seven or eight at the time, and somehow Aunt Cissy persuaded Mama to allow me a trip to the pantomime. *Ali Baba and the Forty Thieves* it was, and as we rushed off to climb in a cab, Mama called after us down the front steps, 'You watch that child . . . there'll be forty thieves in the audience!'

I heard Cissy's sudden intake of breath as she paused to look back from the pavement edge, 'Oh, Maud . . . you know we'll be perfectly safe. I promise to bring Phoebe home by ten.'

And we were quite safe, and home by ten, though perhaps Mama's fears had been justified because something was stolen – and that was my heart; coming home in a giddy excitement, unable to eat or sleep that night for thinking of all the sights and sounds, the thick smells of greasepaint, tobacco and sweat. That show had been mayhem, like nothing I'd ever seen before, with Alf Merchant's 'astonishing, leaping, juggling' dogs, and the high-stepping dancers, and the swaggering swell who got the whole crowd singing along with 'Burlington Bertie from Bow'.

I thought that was wonderful, happening to live in Bow myself, humming the chorus all the way home, though when the cab pulled up for a while, caught in a jam on the Mile End Road, Cissy leaned closer, touching my arm, saying, 'Best we don't sing that in front of Maud . . . I don't think your mama would approve.'

'I know,' I answered with sad resignation, repeating my mama's favourite chant, ' "The halls are all seething with drunkards and sin". But Cissy . . .' I frowned, biting down on my lip, staring up at my aunt in confusion, 'you're not a sinful drunk, and you used to work in the theatre too.'

'Yes,' Cissy sighed, her face slowly lighting up in a smile, 'and you know, there were nights when the opera house closed, when we all stayed in costume and jumped into broughams, driven at breakneck speed across town . . . performing at Wilton's all over again.'

I squeezed my eyes shut to think of that, wishing I could have seen her then, wishing that I could go back in time. But as it turned out, several years would pass by before I returned to Wilton's Hall.

When I did it was everything I remembered. Brass barley-twist pillars. A balcony fronted with friezes of roses, and the walls painted pink with gilt plasterwork, full of arched niches and sparkling mirrors. The ceiling was crowned by a glass chandelier with thousands of crystals and burning jets, and when Aunt Cissy came onto that stage the light shimmered like blessings all over her face. Her brown eyes were splintered with gold. Her turquoise gown gleamed in watery twists, and the emeralds wound at her arms and throat were glinting green flashes of fire.

My mama, inclined as something of a prude, had been scandalised when that costume was made, complaining the silk 'clung indecently' to every curve of her sister's body. But on the night of the performance her morals were spared any humiliation for, confined with the flu to her bedroom in Bow, snuffling over a menthol bowl, Mama was in no state to go anywhere – not even the short drive to Whitechapel. And, though I'm ashamed to admit it, I was glad of her illness that night. It meant I might actually have some fun. It meant I had Cissy all to myself.

Well, almost all. Old Riley, her dresser, was bustling around in the backstage room, threading some pearls into Cissy's hair, curling it up with the irons. But as Cissy had hardly performed in years, Old Riley's main occupation those days was that of a seamstress – making up other people's theatrical costumes, making up most of our dresses and hats. And she threw in a bit of palm reading too, though Mama insisted she never told mine, threatening with dark looks of reproach: 'The Devil comes as a soothsayer, a sorcerer, a conjurer of spells. Never trust those who call up the dead for such things are abominations to God.'

While watching her deft fingers working the needle, I was trying to imagine Old Riley as Satan – with horns, cloven feet and a long forked tail – when I suddenly jumped at the sound of some knocking, like a thundering drum roll outside on the door, and a freckled bald head was poking round, and Old Riley was beaming, 'Oh look, here's Bill Wright come to see us. Phoebe, have you met Bill before? He's a good friend of mine . . . the stage manager here.'

Old Riley might have been widowed for years, but she never went short on male company and Bill blew her a kiss as he stepped in the room, big sausagey fingers held out to shake mine. 'I've certainly heard of Miss Turner.

7

Charmed to meet you at last, I'm sure. Perhaps we'll see more of you, after the show? Mr Wilton's ordered in the champagne and there's none of the usual rabble tonight. The whole place is heaving with West End toffs, with it being an operatic event. But there's a slight problem.' He turned to my aunt. 'I was wondering, Mrs Stanhope' – though unmarried, and really a Miss like me, professionally Cissy was called *Mrs* Stanhope – 'whether your niece, Miss Turner here, might consider getting herself decked up as one of our shepherdesses tonight? We're already four down, what with this wretched ailment that's going around. She'll only need smile, be one extra body to stand on the stage, to make up our depleted numbers.'

'Well, Phoebe, what do you think?' Cissy looked back through the foxed, blackened glass, still holding a cup in front of her mouth. She'd been gargling with port wine and vinegar, hoping to ward off Mama's contagion: any ill effects it might have on her voice.

I laughed nervously, and then blurted out, 'Oh . . . I'd love to . . .' though soon growing reticent. 'But what do you think Mama would say?'

'How old are you, dearie?' Old Riley set down her box of pearls, her one good eye fixed hard on me. The other was covered up by a patch, and I never did get to see underneath. Cissy told me she'd lost the sight when a cart had thrown up a stone in the street, putting her eye clean out. And, just what were the chances of that! But she saw well enough with what was left. Very green it was, with laughter lines crinkling all round the edge, though right then it was narrowed in stern concentration, and I felt embarrassed to be so appraised, and I wondered why she'd asked my age, when surely she knew that perfectly well, so often visiting round at our house; practically one of the family.

Meanwhile, glancing back at Cissy, I saw myself in the mirror, the glimpse of a dim and distorted reflection in which I might be her shadowy wraith. But where my aunt's hair was a waving soft brown, mine was straight as a poker and very much darker, the same with my eyes which, when finally free of that silvery spell, looked back at Old Riley again to say, 'I'll be seventeen, next February.' And then, to Bill Wright, still hovering there by the open door, 'I *can* sing a little. I know all the words from Cissy's rehearsing but . . .' I paused for a moment, and despite a fire crackling away in the hearth, I started to shiver. When I swallowed my throat felt gritty and sore, and my voice sounded queerly hoarse when I said, 'It's . . . well, what Mama would think.'

'Nearly seventeen! Our little Phoebe! My, my . . . where have all the years gone?' Old Riley let out a wistful sigh. 'Well, a shame for the show not to be a success, and you know what I think of Maud Turner . . . always too protective with you! I'm surprised she's let you come out tonight, considering what she thinks of the halls. But it's only this once and where's the harm? Come on, dearie. I think you'll enjoy it. We'll get you fixed up in no time at all. A quick dash of powder to give you some colour and—'

'And no need to sing,' Bill Wright assured. 'Smile and follow the other girls' actions. You're pretty enough. You've a natural grace, and there's no denying it's in the blood!'

'Why not give it a go?' Cissy looked over her shoulder, giving me one of those mischievous smiles, just as she used to when I was small, when she would arrive back home very late, when Mama was sleeping soundly next door and Cissy would stand beside my bed, lifting a finger up to her lips, whispering 'Ssh' as she climbed on in, then snuggling close as she held me tight and told me all of those wonderful stories – stories about her singing days when she travelled to faraway places – places like Paris, or even Vienna, from times long before I had even been born.

And the proof of her fame was right there in our hall where, halfway up the stairs on the little half landing, the copy of a Millais was hung. That painting was called *The Somnambulist*, and it showed a young woman with flowing dark hair, wearing no more than a thin cotton gown as she walked at the perilous edge of a cliff. She carried a candle, but no flame had been lit, and I always feared she might slip to her death, dashed on the rocks in a cold grey sea.

Some thought it was based on a popular novel, the one called *The Woman in White*. Others said that an opera inspired it, and that woman the very spit of Aunt Cissy when she was singing the part of Amina, in Bellini's *La Sonnambula*. The production in Covent Garden had sold out on every night. I know, because I saw the cuttings, all of them pasted up in her scrapbook. I loved to stroke that book's leather covers and look through the pages inside. Cissy saved some of my drawings there too, and the daisy chains from our days in the park – all those withered and fragile links of our love. Whenever I wove them I used to pray – and my prayer was this, and always the same – that if none of those tiny stems were to break then God might grant my secret wish: for Cissy to be my mother, not Maud.

You see, Maud, my mama, was so ordered and strict you'd hardly think them related at all. I used to feel like a frayed piece of string caught up in an endless tug of war, being torn between Cissy, all music and light, and Mama with her stern and daunting frown as she sat there embroidering quotes from the Bible, or reciting from that old book of hers, the one full of *Moral Advice for Young Ladies*. It felt like a penance. Not that I'd ever done anything wrong, but if my mama could have her way we'd spend half our lives on our knees in church, or marching along the Mile End Road, singing hymns and banging on tambourines.

It was on account of her being in with that Mr Brown's Hallelujah crowd, all very much against alcohol. But Mama was a woman of strange contradictions and if Cissy's friends were visiting – particularly Mr Collins, a wonderful pianist who still played the halls – we might have a bit of a sing-song, and Cissy would pour out glasses of port, and though Mama looked on with a scowl, she still used to sneak a sip now and then. And, come every Christmas, Old Riley would tease her by waving a sherry glass under her nose while Mama looked peevish and ranted back, 'Mrs Riley, if you were not Cissy's good friend, I would ask you to go back home, right now. Mr Turner would be spinning round in his grave if he knew of the demon drink in this house.'

Mr Turner, that is my dead father, had once been a soldier in Mr Brown's Army. I believe that was how he and Mama first met. He died when I was no more than a baby, but the way Mama constantly spoke his name you'd think it was her, not Old Riley at all, who was trying to summon up the dead. Though, going by that photograph propped by her bed – a young man, a pith helmet on top of his head, a white band round the front daubed with strident black letters: PREPARE TO MEET THY GOD – well, you'd wonder Mama could have liked him at all.

And I know it must sound disrespectful to speak so of my very own father, but if you could have seen that picture – those glowering eyes, and the dark bristled growth sprouting around a miserable mouth – then I think you would know what I mean. He was not what you'd call the most handsome man.

Anyway, with him being 'promoted to Glory', Mama took me out on the streets in his place, marching with the Hallelujah crowd, dressing me up like the rest of the women, in blue capes and blue bonnets with big red rosettes. I hated that hat. It was always too hot, sticky and itchy under my chin. I hated the way the drunkards leered or spat out great gobbets of black congealed blood and how, once, when we handed out Temperance tracts, a ragged old man with a scabby cracked face caught hold of my arm and dragged me into an alley where he slammed me hard against a slimed wall, where he tried to fumble under my skirts, and his breath on my face stank of fish and decay, and though I was repulsed, quite terrified, his glittering eyes transfixed me. I thought they were burning right into my soul. I thought they looked just like my father's.

At some point, I must have come to my senses, screaming and kicking until Mama appeared, and then I was retching and sick on the pavement, and then I was crying all the way home. Once we were back, she ran me a bath with the water so hot that it scalded my skin. She scrubbed out my mouth with the carbolic soap, and then set to work with the rubbing below, so rough I was stinging and sore for days, and later while I lay in my bed a terrible row got up downstairs, with Aunt Cissy shouting that it was a disgrace to send a child out on the streets like that, and what was Maud Turner trying to prove?

After that day, if Mama went out with her banners and flags, I stayed at home in the care of my aunt and instead of the Bible Cissy would read from her poetry books, or romantic novels with thrilling, mysterious stories that Mama called lurid and lewd. Mind you, if she happened to be in the room I knew she was listening to every word. You could practically see her ears flapping.

Still, I have to admit, she looked fit to explode the time when Old Riley was at the house, saying that Cissy should write her own novel, and what a sensation that would be – filled with famous musicians, a French marquis, even a rogue prince from nearer home. No matter I'd heard it all before, and I'm sure only half of those stories were true, but I loved to imagine that glamorous world, always wondering why, for all her admirers, and all of the presents of jewellery and flowers, Aunt Cissy had never decided to marry – and why she had given up the stage.

I did ask Mama about it once but she only dithered and stammered excuses, first saying that Cissy had been taken ill, then that Jesus had led her to see the light, coming at last to realise how immoral her life in the theatre had been. But I wasn't convinced by any of that, always sensing there must have been something more; something that might have caused Cissy remorse.

Perhaps that's why I never did pluck up the courage to ask my aunt about it directly. Perhaps, that's why I felt so pleased when Cissy decided to work again – to play Galatea at Wilton's Hall. And how thrilling it was to be there that night because even though the passing of years had begun to trace lines on my aunt's lovely face, when Old Riley was done with her box of tricks, Cissy looked flawless, she looked like a goddess; eyes sparkling, lips reddened with carmine paste. When she walked out onto that stage, something magical happened. She grew shiny and sleek. She exuded an aura of golden light. And when Aunt Cissy opened her mouth, when all of those lovely notes issued out, I think everyone in the audience sighed – as if they were already mourning her loss.

A firm nudge in my back, and Bill Wright was hissing, 'Go on then, Miss Turner, you'll be all right. What are you waiting for?'

Straight away, I felt trapped, my limbs stiff as a corpse, my fingernails digging into my palms. At the stage front, beyond the flare of the lights, hundreds of eyes peered up through the gloom. At the back was a painted oilcloth, a glorious pastoral scene where woodlands and meadows sloped down into rivers, where a grotto was strewn with seaweed and shells. On the floor, a mirror was set as a pool, reflecting the azure skies above with its fluffy-winged cherubs in cotton wool clouds. Around it were grasses and flowers, all most realistic, cut out from board, over which I almost stumbled and fell when dragged on by another shepherdess. I followed her lead, with both arms flung wide, very nearly colliding with a stuffed lamb when she stopped at a mossy hillock, where she sat and reclined upon the green velvet, where I also attempted a graceful pose, though soon realising that it was one thing to observe from the wings, quite another to act naturally on the stage. I felt like some gauche automaton, unable even to open my mouth, never mind being able to mime the words:

Oh the pleasure of the plains!
Happy nymphs and happy swains

14

Oh, there was no pleasure, however lovely the flights of the voices and orchestra strains that were swirling all around the hall. That baroque masque might be an idyll for some, but for Phoebe Turner there was nothing but cringing embarrassment. I tried to smile as instructed. I tried to hold my crook elegantly, but the flowers and ribbons were all of a tremble, and the garland of roses set on my head began to slip forward alarmingly. My nose was itching. I wanted to sneeze, was finding it harder and harder to breathe, and those flouncy skirts and petticoats, the corset Old Riley had laced so tight, were made for a much smaller Bo Peep than me. And, there I was, stuck on Wilton's stage, shuffling my way across the boards until I was safely concealed once more – where I belonged – right next to the ropes, the winches and pulleys; the clumsy backstage mechanisms – where Bill Wright stared out from the opposite wing, his big bald dome all shiny with sweat, his hands flung up in frustration. But the best I could do was to shake my head, to offer a mute apology before my attention diverted elsewhere, hearing the crowd's collective gasp – watching as Cissy walked onto the stage. Her arm rested on that of the shepherd boy, Acis, a young tenor whose hair was a crown of gold curls, who looked over and smiled, and gave me a wink! The hot rise of my blush must have matched his cheeks, powdered very pink and much too effete to make a convincing Acis for me. But who in that hall would not believe, or be entranced when Cissy sang:

> *Oh, didst thou know the pains of absent love,*
> *Acis would ne'er from Galatea rove.*

Looking back out at the audience, all thoughts of pretty boy Acis were lost when my eye came to rest on somebody else – a man who was sitting in the front row. Though in late middle age he was strikingly handsome, with thick silver hair swept back from his brow, a waxed grey moustache above sensual lips and, beneath hooded lids, his eyes were so dark they might have been black. I wondered if those eyes had me mesmerised, for a watery rushing sound filled my ears, all the mellow woodwind arpeggios becoming strangely discordant and slow, until nothing was left but one long blurring note during which I was wondering who he could be, and whether he'd ever been to our house – perhaps a musician, or another singer – because I felt sure I'd seen him before, and yet, I couldn't—

My ears filled up with the music again, and that was the moment when Cissy's voice faltered, when I looked over and saw that her gaze had fixed upon the very same man. It was only a slight hesitation. Her composure was soon regained – except for one thing, and perhaps no one else even noticed it there, that glistening silver trail on her cheek.

2

Back at the house in Tredegar Square, Cissy was hushing for me to be quiet as we tiptoed past Mama's bedroom door. I held my breath and then sighed with relief to hear only snores from the other side. There would be no inquisition that night.

Once I'd kissed Cissy, once my own door was shut, I sat with a thump on the dressing stool, slumping forward, two elbows propped on the table, two palms cupped under my chin as I stared straight ahead at the looking glass. Behind me the fire had burned down low, the odd yellow flame darting out from red coals, and with no candle lit my reflection was dim. My face looked clean enough, but I still took a handkerchief out of the drawer, rubbing hard at my cheeks in the hope that no smearing of greasepaint remained; no telltale sign that Mama might see in the morning.

But what if she looked too long in my eyes? Would she be able to see that I'd changed? And what could I say about Wilton's that night without betraying, not only myself, but whatever secret Cissy held?

I saw him again, twice more that night, the man who'd been in the audience, who'd stared so intently at Cissy, who – I felt sure – brought that tear to her eye. The second occasion was later on, when the show was done, when a bit of a party was getting up, and me with a bird's eye view of it all, looking down as I was from the balcony. The third time was when we were leaving, when Bill Wright and Old Riley saw Cissy and me safely into a waiting cab, though it was a while before we set off, with Old Riley creating such a kerfuffle, with all of that hugging and whispering, and Cissy looking like misery, as if someone had gone and died.

Shivering there inside the cab, I felt drawn to look out of the window, back down to the other end of the alley where the air was dark and thick with fog. Despite this I saw him beneath the trees that bordered the church mission gardens, and there wasn't a moment of doubt in my mind for he really had such a distinctive look, and I had the distinct impression that he was only waiting there in the hope of seeing Cissy again. Not that she seemed to have noticed him, and with those others shuffling round I thought it best not to say anything. And when, at last, our cab drove off, it was in quite the other direction.

Cissy was staring down at her lap, her mood still very glum indeed, and we'd gone quite a way down Commercial Road before she suddenly stirred from her trance, reaching forward to touch my cheek, her fingers cool on the warmth of my flesh. With a sad sort of smile on her lips she said, 'You gave Mr Wright quite a turn. He thought you were going to collapse of sheer fright, right out there, right in front of the audience.'

'I'm sorry, Cissy. I let you all down.'

'We should have known better, expecting you to go on like that, without having any rehearsal at all.'

'The thing is . . .' I wasn't quite sure how to frame the question, the one that kept nagging away in my mind. 'I noticed a man in the audience. I was wondering who he might have been?'

She laughed, a little too gaily. 'Which *one* of the hundreds in Wilton's did you particularly have in mind?'

'The one who almost made you stop singing. The one who made you cry. The one you were speaking with after the show, who was hanging around again outside.'

'Was he?' She glanced back down at her lap, her fingers twisting back and forth, until she looked up, looked me straight in the eye.

'Have you been spying on me?'

'No,' I protested, though I couldn't help feeling some itch of guilt, 'not spying, not exactly that, only I couldn't help seeing, and then I couldn't help wondering if . . .'

'Oh, Phoebe,' she broke in. 'I didn't think he would be there. I'd rather not talk about it now. It's too late. I'm too tired . . . tired of it all. I didn't sing well. I didn't . . .'

She sighed, pressed the heel of a hand to her brow, setting her mouth in a tight resigned line, a little too pinched, too much like Mama, and not wanting to cause any further distress, I drew up my knees, nestling into the corner of the cab, gathering coat folds around like a blanket before plunging both hands deep into my pockets. And while staring silently out of the window I found myself almost hypnotised by the fog-muted glow of the street lamps – *black into yellow, black into yellow* – the creaking, rolling sway of the carriage, the muffled clopping beat of the hooves.

Oh, I wished I'd never mentioned that man. I hated to see my aunt upset. It happened so rarely, which only made those moments all the more unsettling. And the fact was I already knew his name, and whether or not my suspicions were right, and whether or not he and Cissy were lovers who'd had some sort of tiff, I wasn't as sympathetic as I probably should have been because, to tell you the truth, that night I'd found a romance of my own.

When the final curtain fell such a stamping and cheering was going on, with everyone clapping and shouting 'bravo'. Galatea – Aunt Cissy – was centre stage, Polyphemus and Acis on either side, while the rest of the chorus gathered behind, and alone, from my place of disgrace in the wings, I watched everything in a pensive mood, thinking how Cissy's fellow stars represented the two distinct forms of desire. The shepherd boy stood for innocence, being handsome and fresh-faced and golden-haired. Polyphemus was a vision of jealous lust, with that gruesome false eye painted over his brow with which he had spied on the nymph, Galatea, until her life ended, or might just as well have, sinking down under the waves like that – and never coming up again.

A while later, still pondering the nymph's sad fate, I found my way back to the dressing room where the atmosphere was equally bleak. Cissy was sitting in front of the mirror, the glass misted over with all of the steam rising up from a battered tin bath in the corner. Old Riley was flipping a coin at the boy who'd been lugging the buckets to fill up the tub and, once he'd pushed past me and made himself scarce, she gave me a serious look and said, 'Ssh! Cissy's still lost in the part. It was always like this in the old days. She'll soon come back to her senses again.'

But the thing was, Cissy never did come back, never really the same as she'd been before. Perhaps it was Bill Wright's thunder effects, that big metal board he'd been wobbling backstage, or the crashing of cymbals and acrid grey smoke from the phosphorous flares when the giant appeared. Perhaps they'd made Cissy go deaf, dumb and blind, because she sat there, not saying a word, not even flinching when – *bang* – the door slammed in a sudden draught, and Old Riley gasped, clutching a hand to her matronly breast, and I turned abruptly, seeing no more than a thin bloom of dust, and the cobwebs and cracks on plaster-blown walls, and the mice droppings, and the balls of hair that formed a small mound in the corner. And that was the moment it seemed to me that a blind-fold had suddenly dropped from my eyes, and Wilton's was losing its magic allure – all the glamour and colour fading away, and my voice very dull when I answered Old Riley, 'It must be my fault. I never should have gone on that stage.'

'I'd swear on my life it's no such thing.' Old Riley smiled – a little bit forced, but still a smile, after which she held out her arms and said, 'Come on, dearie. Let's get you out of that costume. You don't suit frills and flounces and that's a fact.'

With the corsets unlaced and the puffings of chintz puddled like little waves at my feet, I was never so glad to breathe easy again. Phoebe Turner's real life might be dull as her gown, the fabric a stiff and rusty black, and I might not like it very much, but at least when I was wearing that I knew exactly who I was – which right then was someone very cold, who wished she'd thought to bring a shawl, folding her arms and trembling while watching Old Riley's vigorous efforts at poking the coals in the hearth.

The old woman straightened with a groan. 'I'd say we're in for another big freeze. Mind you, it could always be worse. When I was a girl, my old ma used to tell of that time when the Thames froze right over. Imagine that, Phoebe, skating from Tower Bridge to Richmond and back. What a lark that must have been!' With hardly a breath, she prattled on. 'Look at you, shaking there like a leaf. Come and sit on this stool, get warmed up by the fire while I brush out your hair. Oh, if only my own bit of grey shone like that, Bill Wright might show some interest again.' She heaved a great sigh, before going on, 'I'm planning on dying it red, you know.'

'Red?' Wondering what Mama would say about that, I sat down as instructed, one side of me very nearly scorched, the other remaining as cold as ice. Old Riley slapped rose cream over my cheeks, chiding while wiping away at the rouge, 'Can't you stop fidgeting? And look at this garland stuck on your head, the state of those petals.' She clicked her tongue. 'I knew it. They should have got silk ones instead . . . still good for something after a show, what with trimming up hats, and . . .'

She broke off mid-sentence, her arms darting forward, hands brushing at fizzing sparks on my knees. 'Phoebe, wake up. Can't you see those logs spitting? That's the very last thing Mr Wilton wants now . . . the whole place going up in flames!'

Reluctantly scraping the stool to one side, I muttered a somewhat surly reply, 'Would it matter so much if this dress did burn? I hate these dark colours . . . always dressing in mourning.'

'Mmm, what's that ducky? Who's that in mourning?' Old Riley was distracted, not listening to me, looking over her shoulder at Cissy again – Cissy the statue, still not moving a muscle, not saying a single word.

'Me! In this dress. This dress that you made that I wear for a man I can't even remember!'

Old Riley turned back with a snort. 'Well, I tend to agree. As you know, I'm a widow myself, but I don't spend my life crying over what's gone. Maud Turner's a fine-looking woman. She should worship some real flesh and blood for a change. She should give up her grieving before it's too late, and stop wasting the good life God gave her. If that's not a sin, I don't know what is!'

And then, out of nowhere, she suddenly asked, 'What do you reckon to our Eddie Collins?'

'Mr Collins!'

'He's still handsome enough. He's still got ambition, and talented too. You look in his eyes. You'll see a couple of twinkling stars.'

'Mama thinks him too bohemian by far. She's more likely to fancy that Mr Brown, always preaching away on his sermon box, prophesying damnation, and fire and brimstone.'

Old Riley harrumphed and then stepped towards her costume rack, smoothing down the cream satin of the gown that Cissy had planned to wear after the show. I thought of Mama, always dressing in black. I thought of when Mr Collins came round and how, if Mama was to enter the room, his fingers might stumble over the keys when playing on Cissy's piano. But really, I'd never considered romance. Mr Collins must be in his forties. My mama was forty-nine! And who could say what Old Riley might be – perhaps she was fifty, perhaps she was sixty. And then, as if she could read my mind, she glanced over her shoulder and gave a wry smile. 'You've still got a lot to learn about love. Now, why don't you run off while Cissy gets changed? Go and find Mr Collins or ask Bill Wright for a glass of that bubbly he promised before. Maud Turner need never know.'

Old Riley might have winked. With one eye it wasn't that easy to tell, but I guessed that she wanted me gone, wanting to speak with Cissy alone, and I had no argument with that, only relieved to escape that room, what with the chill and my aunt's black mood, and the hanging cloud of steamy gloom that still had not lifted one inch from her head.

Very soon, I peered out from the side of the stage. The hall's enormous chandelier had been dimmed down, burning very low, and with most of the audience having gone, a party of sorts was starting up. Some waiters were pushing back chairs, clearing a space near the front of the stage, draping tables with long white cloths, upon which some flickering candles were set. I heard the soft sucking pop of corks as bottles were opened and glasses were filled and, despite feeling sorely in need of a drink – only some water to ease my parched throat – I was far too embarrassed to show my face; not after that dire performance of mine.

I did see Mr Collins, standing quite near, in an alcove screened off from the rest of the hall where the show's musicians had been concealed. I was about to say hello when I noticed him talking with somebody else, a man half hidden behind the big curtain, and it must have been a heated discussion because Mr Collins looked all bothered and pink, every now and then giving a shake of his head.

Thinking it best not to interrupt, I made my way out of the hall itself and into the entrance corridor. There, a wide central staircase was rising, straight up to the balcony floor above, and down near the end that led out to the street was a door to the Prince of Denmark bar where punters could purchase their drinks for the show and have them topped up again afterwards. I'd only ever been in one bar, and that under Mama's most stern supervision, but the Devil must have been in me that night, for I was intrigued to step nearer and take a sneaking glance at all of the glistening bottles and glasses, the gleaming brass and mahogany fittings and everything so warm and inviting, glowing with red from a blazing fire. But through the roar of those leaping flames, I'm sure I heard Mama hissing her warnings of Satan and Sin and Inebriation, of Lust and other such Wickedness, and it may have been the effect of the show, but I imagined that door to be a giant's mouth, exhaling hot gusts of beery breath. From inside came deep rumbles of masculine laughter, some slurred conversations, and then, through the fug of tobacco smoke, I saw the Shepherd Boy Acis again, his arm draped around a little Bo Peep; neither one of them having changed out of their costumes. Her fingers twirled through his golden curls, moving on down to caress his thigh which extended beneath scanty tunic skirts. But what had seemed appropriate when parading about on the stage was anything but in such a place, and that man, that Acis, whoever he was, well, he could have put his trousers on!

I didn't know what to think, where to look. I was feeling – what – disgust, or allure? It swiftly turned into embarrassment, when his eyes lifted to meet my gaze, when I glanced away in a state of confusion only to find myself face to face with some weaselly, grinning character. A grog-blossom nose. Two eyes like black buttons that narrowed to slits when he croaked, 'Why don't you come in and join the fun? Come on, missy . . . don't pretend to be shy.'

I thought of when I was a little girl – dragged into an

alley – a foul-breathed old man, and I worried that Mama was right all along, that drink only led to one thing in the end, and that was ruin and debauchery.

Ducking back into the corridor, I hoisted my skirts and ran up the stairs, and loitered a while by a pillar there, hoping black shadows might keep me safe, much relieved to see no one following. A cracked laugh, a crude oath being sworn, and then the bar door was closed again, and the shaft of fiery light from within became no more than a thin line of red – the line over which I *must not pass*.

When my drumming heart had slowed, when I was able to breathe again, I crept on to the end of the passage-way, pushing against some double doors beyond which I heard music and laughter rising from the hall below, and leaning against the balcony rail, I crossed my arms and rested a cheek on the backs of my hands – like one of those painted cherubs spying down from up high in the clouds.

Directly beneath was Old Riley. She was having a chat with Bill Wright. Mr Collins was at the piano, while another man played a violin, and three or four couples were starting to dance – until the music came to a halt when an elderly man walked onto the stage, clapping his hands for attention, shouting out in a gravelly voice, 'I'm sure I don't need to be introduced. If you don't know me, you shouldn't be here. But, in case you've forgotten, my name is John Wilton. I hope you've enjoyed this even-ing's performance. I hope that you'll join with me right now in thanking Cicely Stanhope, who has graced us with her considerable charms.'

Polite applause rippled round the hall and following Mr Wilton's gaze I saw Cissy down at the side of the stage, her cheeks very flushed; either from the warmth of his praise or else the hot water in her bath. She was wearing her ivory satin gown, and where the black silk of her evening gloves ended, the pale flesh of her upper arms was exposed. Stripped of its pearls, her hair was coiled back, a few damp curls hanging loose at the neck, and I was thinking how lovely she looked when something else distracted my eye – a movement behind the stage curtain, a long leg sticking out and a polished black shoe that was circling slowly through the air.

Mr Wilton laughed and then announced, 'Now for some of the fare we're more famous for, a bit less of the cultured and tragic, a bit more of the common or garden fun. Ladies and gentlemen, let's have a warm welcome for another favourite act of mine. Introducing the king of British burlesque . . . our very own Champagne Charlie!'

A great cheer went up when 'Charlie' strode out, wearing his topper and fancy striped pants, and his whiskers resembling walrus tusks. His stage name was really George Leybourne, and very famous he was in those days, driving around in his carriage and four, always waving a bottle of Moët champagne: a living and breathing endorsement for his generous sponsors' brand. There'd been a time, a few years before, when he'd taken a fancy to my aunt, turning up in the square at all hours of the night, serenading her from our front porch. Cissy always used to ignore him but Mama would come rushing into my room – which happened to be at the front of the house – insisting I cover my ears with my hands, before raising the sashes and shouting out that George was a scandalous libertine. The last time it happened, she ran down the stairs, opened the door and flew down the steps, trying to hit George on the head with a poker while screaming at the top of her voice for someone to fetch the constabulary.

I don't know if any policemen came but after that George kept well away, and on that night in Wilton's Hall Cissy ignored him all over again, too busy looking at somebody else – that older man I'd seen from the stage, who'd had such a strange effect on me. He was standing close at her side, inclining his face to speak in her ear, and when Cissy nodded he took her arm, leading her off through the rest of the crowd, only to stop at the edge of the hall where, no doubt, he assumed the balcony's shadows obscured them from all other eyes. But not mine.

I saw they were very absorbed in each other, and I noticed how grave was Cissy's expression, and how she listened intently to every word that gentleman said. Of course, I couldn't hear a thing, only able to watch as her shoulders slumped, as one of his hands then cupped her chin, lifting it, bringing it close to his lips – so close that I had to hold my breath, hardly daring to move and quite convinced that he was about to give her a kiss.

Such disappointment when she pushed him off, turning and walking back through the crowd, towards where Bill Wright and Old Riley were standing. And there, Cissy acted as if nothing had happened, but I knew she was only pretending. She kept glancing over her shoulder, towards where that man was still standing, and he was staring back at her, as if there was nothing else in the room. And so deeply immersed had I become in watching their little drama that I very nearly jumped out of my skin to feel the warm brush of breath on *my* cheek and a stranger's voice softly murmuring, 'You don't have a drink? Can I offer you one?'

Dreading it might be that drunk from the bar, I spun

around and then lashed out, his offering knocked to the floor with a crash.

While stooping down to collect broken shards, a young man raised his eyes to mine. 'I'm sorry.' He made his apology. 'I didn't mean to alarm you. I noticed you standing up here. I thought you looked lonely, in need of a friend.'

I thought: *You don't need to apologise. I might forgive you anything.*

I said, 'Oh . . . it's spilled!' stating the blindingly obvious, staring down at the fizzing puddle of bubbles spreading all over the boards. Meanwhile he was standing again, lifting a bottle from one of the benches placed a little way behind, from which he filled another glass, the foam rising all the way up to the rim. But this time no wine spilled onto the floor, and when the bottle was set back down he smiled his invitation to me. 'Won't you come and sit down? You're quite safe. I won't bite.'

'I'm not sure I want to. I'm not sure I should.'

With my back pressed hard to the balcony rail, I felt shy and confused all over again. If Mama could see she'd be horrified. Not only had I appeared on a stage, not only had I looked into a bar, then seen Cissy caught in some secret liaison, but here I was, all alone with a man, and what's more a man proffering alcohol. And what if she saw what caught my eye, looking over his shoulder to view those three murals painted high up on the wall? I knew she would think them decadent. But then, we were very near to the docks, with the trade in Eastern tea and cloth, and so many *infidel immigrants* – well, that's what Mama always called them.

The paintings depicted some Indian women, one strumming what looked like a mandolin, one holding a flute up to her lips, one waving her elegant arms in the air as if she was dancing or singing a song. All wore the most exotic gowns, with pantaloons exposed beneath, with golden hoops piercing their noses and ears, with bangles adorning bare ankles and wrists, and below the veils that covered their heads, each brow had been daubed with a little red spot.

Mama would call those 'the red stains of sin', and thinking it best not to stare any more, I lowered my face demurely – though not so low that I couldn't sneak another good look at my new friend. I already liked his voice, the tones being soft and refined. I liked his elegant evening attire and guessed that he must be in his mid-twenties. His face, with its regular features, still held the ghost of youth's bloom, the bones not as angled as they might become. Straight brows framed a pair of clear grey eyes, above which fair hair was short and oiled, and he wore no moustache, nothing to mar the sweet curve of those lips – those lips that had touched my cheek, which were parting once again to ask, 'Little shepherdess, are you always so shy, hiding away from the world like this?'

He drew nearer and lifted the glass to my lips, and I really don't know what came over me but I suddenly snatched it right out of his hand and swallowed it down – every single last drop – only afterwards feeling mortified at such a display of bad manners.

He laughed. 'I suppose it's thirsty work, standing on stage, looking petrified . . . though I must say you carried it off very well.'

The indignation I felt at his teasing was diffused by the sting of my tears. 'How can I go down and mix with the others? They must all think me such a fool.'

'I'm sorry.' His hand touched my wrist. 'I didn't mean

to upset you. Really, I doubt anyone even noticed, all entranced by the divine Mrs Stanhope. But, I have to say when *you* fled the stage, hiding behind that side curtain, I felt quite a pang of loss. You really are very pretty you know.'

'Stop mocking me!' I grew bolder; perhaps because of that wine, to which I was not accustomed at all. My breaths were coming too shallow and fast, and taking a moment to ground myself I heard the trill of piano notes. Looking back over the balcony rail, I saw George Leybourne jump down from the stage, beginning to strut his way through the crowd, to target a simpering shepherdess – the same one I'd seen with Acis in the bar, now giggling and shrieking when George took her hand, planting his kisses, starting to sing:

> *I've seen a deal of gaiety throughout my noisy life,*
> *With all my grand accomplishments, I never could get a*
>   *wife . . .*
> *The thing I most excel in is the PRFG game,*
> *A noise all night, in bed all day and swimming in*
>   *champagne . . .*

At that point he paused and drew the girl closer, and everyone raised their glasses and cheered, laughing and joining in the refrain:

> *For Champagne Charlie is my name, Champagne Charlie*
>   *is my name . . .*

'They say he's quite the ladies' man.' The younger man was at my side, and without even lifting my eyes from the scene, I said, 'Yes he is. Though I'm only surprised he hasn't gone mad, singing that same song again and again. Mind you, it's so very popular. Why, even the

Hallelujah crowd have decided to take it up these days. Mr Brown says the Devil has all the best tunes, and why shouldn't he use a few of them too . . . only with different words, of course. You must have heard them out on the streets?'

At that, I gave a brief rendition of 'Bless His Name, He Sets Me Free', going on to repeat some of Old Riley's gossip, though to tell you the truth I didn't know what I was talking about.

'They say George earns hundreds of guineas every week . . . that he lives in a mansion in Mayfair, that he's grown very fond of the libertine's life . . . but the air in the bubbles of all that champagne can only deflate his ability.' And while taking no heed of my friend's shocked expression I carried on digging into my hole. 'Mind you, I've always wondered about that "PRFG game". I've racked my brain, and everyone tells me it's nothing but nonsense . . . but what do you suppose it could mean?'

'Well,' he gave a small cough, 'I always imagined you theatre girls to be a little more worldly wise. I can only presume it refers to the "private rooms for gentlemen" – those hired out by publicans to accommodate their more amorous clientele.'

'Oh!' While wishing the floor would swallow me up, I noticed the other man again, the one who'd tried to kiss Cissy before, and, partly to change the subject and partly from sheer curiosity, I pointed down and brazenly asked, 'Well, as *you* are so very well informed, perhaps you might tell me who that is – that gentleman, standing there on his own?'

His answer was curt. 'I presume you know of Samuels', the department store in Kensington?'

Everyone knew about Samuels', London's most

exclusive emporium, and when I nodded my friend carried on, 'That gentleman is the owner, Nathaniel Samuels . . . and going by all the rumours I've heard, I don't think *he* suffers from Leybourne's complaint.'

'He was speaking with Mrs Stanhope before.' I decided to make no mention of Cissy being related to me, thinking that way I might hope to learn more.

'I suspect he has long admired *her* voice.'

'Really? Do you happen to know him then?'

I looked back to see his eyes harden. The tone of his voice became guarded. 'He and I share a passing acquaintance, though he's not aware I'm here tonight. You might say we—'

I should have let him go on, instead of butting in again. 'He looks very sophisticated. There's something . . . something charismatic about him.'

'So I'm often told. Many women find Nathaniel Samuels to be an attractive man. Even now, even those as young as you.'

'But that didn't appear to be the case when I saw him with Cicely Stanhope.'

'Appearances can be deceptive and—' He suddenly stopped and grabbed my hand. 'You're bleeding. You must have been cut on that glass.'

Very matter-of-fact, I said, 'Oh, so I am.' And though it was only the tiniest cut, the slightest little trickle of red, I silently blessed that broken glass, because that's how I came to be sitting down, and that handsome young man so close at my side, dabbing my wound with his handkerchief.

'Please . . .' I protested, feeling I should, if only for the sake of decorum. 'It's no matter. I hadn't noticed at all.'

But I noticed his body, pressed close to mine and how, all at once, the atmosphere changed, and while staring back into his eyes I could have sworn that we'd met before – the same sensation from earlier on, when I'd first seen that Mr Samuels. And perhaps that was why I didn't object when he did something quite audacious, lifting my injured hand to his mouth, his lips gently brushing against the flesh where beads of red were oozing up, each one like a sparkling ruby. It seemed such an intimate, personal act. I felt myself trapped in his sensual spell – until the magic was broken, when I heard the soft creak of footsteps on boards and saw a moving shadowy shape and the balcony doors slowly swinging closed.

Hurriedly standing, I dragged my hand free, and I knew that if not for that sudden distraction I might very well have been overwhelmed, lost in my yearning response to his touch; the sweet, ringing rush that was filling my ears; the sliding of heat in my belly. It thrilled me. It frightened me too. And that's why I had to run away, and only once did I chance to look back, to see that handkerchief still in his hands. White silk stained with little spots of red.

Going downstairs, I met the boy who'd been filling the dressing room bath before. He told me that Cissy was waiting inside, wanting to take me home. And when we were back in Tredegar Square, once I'd undressed and climbed into my bed, I lay there for hours, shivering with the cold, my breaths a freezing gauze on the air as I pressed the flesh of my hand to my mouth and tasted the metallic tang of the blood – just as the stranger had done before.

34

And I hadn't thought to ask his name. And he hadn't asked for mine.

And who had looked in at the balcony door, and what had they seen, and would they tell? Mama must never know.

3

Were it not for the shadows clustered around, he would have stood out; too conspicuous, the tall man in silk topper and long overcoat, who sucked his cigar in the chill night air. The tip glowed, a small circle of red in the gloom, and a curling silver trail of smoke escaped from the silver-whiskered lips of Nathaniel Samuels.

He stood alone in Wellclose Square, on a corner in front of the mission church, the gardens of which, at such an hour, were more usually inhabited by the thieves and drunken dockers and whores who spilled out from the doors of Wilton's Hall. But that night he was pestered by nothing more than some rustling dead leaves in the gutter, got up by a bitter swirling wind to skitter around his ankles. He watched them a while and then threw his cigar down into the bushes, afterwards plunging hands into pockets as shoulders hunched forward and hooded eyes narrowed, straining to see through the dense night air, obscured yet more by his freezing breaths.

At the far end of Graces Alley he made out the bulk of three or four cabs, hoping to pick up the dribs and drabs of guests now departing the theatre's doors, emerging on the pavement and then melting away like ghosts, drowned in a shimmering sea of fog. He hoped to see Cicely Stanhope amongst them, the ghost who had haunted him for years. He hoped she might chance to be alone.

Arriving at Wilton's that evening he'd been unusually nervous while waiting for the show to start; the show for which he was a sleeping investor, having colluded with Wilton and Collins to bring Mrs Stanhope back onto the stage. A condition of his involvement was that she remain in ignorance, but the symmetry pleased Nathaniel, with John Wilton having provided the venue for Cissy's very first solo performance. Though why lower the tone of the evening by inviting that clown George Leybourne!

Beneath the brim of his hat, Nathaniel's brow lowered and creased in a frown, and, partly to warm his numbing feet and partly from exasperation, he stamped down hard on the pavement flags. Where the brittle ice cracked and splintered it looked like a spider's web.

Collins was more to be trusted than Wilton. Collins was one of Cissy's oldest friends and he'd always shared Nathaniel's hope that she might one day return to the stage. And if, as this evening had surely proved, she was ready at last to resume her career, then might she not also be of a mind to take up other roles from her previous life?

A weary sigh escaped his lips. The affair had ended badly. For that he had only himself to blame. But, seeing her again, and hardly changed . . .

Collins had been angry after the show, considering Nathaniel's behaviour too blatant – to have placed himself in the very front row, knowing full well she might see him there. And she had. And she had been affected, her voice trembling, a momentary pause. But wasn't that what Nathaniel had wanted? And whatever else that Collins advised, when the show had finally come to an end – and God knew it felt like for ever – he had been determined to stay. What if Cissy had pushed him away? He'd never expected anything else. But he'd sensed something more when her eyes met his. And that was enough. That was what mattered, to know she still cared, and—

'Mister . . . Mister.' A high piping voice fractured his thoughts, followed by muffled pattering steps as a small boy came darting out from the alley, skidding to a halt at Nathaniel's side. Wide eyes looked up through clouds of white breath as the child went on with some urgency, 'I asked, like you said. Gaffer told me to tell you she's on 'er way. Look! That's 'er, coming out right now.'

Resting his hand on the boy's narrow shoulder, Nathaniel vaguely registered how thin and worn his clothes, how sharp the jutting bones beneath. But his focus was fixed on Wilton's, and the slanting light that spilled through its doors, like dribbles of copper across the iced cobbles.

'She's not alone,' Nathaniel murmured, his voice so low it was almost a growl.

'That'll be Mrs Riley, along with Bill Wright. Bill said that other one's 'er niece.'

'Her niece?' Nathaniel had not expected that. Age must have mellowed Maud Turner's views, though he very much doubted she'd been there too. Could the sainted one ever sink so low as to enter the walls of a music hall? No – Collins would have warned him. But then, Collins hadn't mentioned the girl. Could that explain Cissy's reaction, her stark refusal even to talk, perhaps fearing her sister would hear of his presence?

The boy interrupted his musings again. 'Phoebe, they call 'er. You would've seen 'er yourself, sir . . . one of them shepherdesses, prancing about on the stage . . . the one with the long black hair. Though why she and that Mrs Stanhope are deemed so important as we 'ad to carry them buckets upstairs, boiling up as much water as there's in the Thames, and all so as they could take a bath . . . Who wants a bath when the weather's like this, freezing the balls off brass monkeys!'

'I didn't notice,' Nathaniel murmured. And now, glancing down again, seeing a narrow grinning face full of such hope and expectancy, he lifted a hand to ruffle the curls which clung damp and greasy against the boy's skull. And from there he reached into his pocket again, producing a large silver coin, the sight of which caused the child's eyes to grow rounder, first doubting, then smiling his disbelief, hardly able to stammer out the words, 'Th-thank you, sir. I never hoped for so much as that!'

'You should never stop hoping.' Nathaniel smiled wryly, watching the boy run off again, watching a cab set off from the hall, both enveloped then lost in the drifts of fog.

4

One day, a week later, I woke very early. Bare feet padded over bare boards. At the window I drew back the fringed edge of curtain. My fingers stroked over the freezing pane, tingling at the burn of ice flowers on glass, and I looked at that little cut on my hand and wondered if any scar would remain, or if it would simply fade away, taking with it the restless yearnings I felt whenever I thought of Wilton's.

Outside was a silvery dream world. Grey-furred branches of bushes and trees glistened with light from the street lamps. All around, on four sides of the gardens, set back on pavements and guarded by railings, many basements exuded their own pale gleam. I heard the milk cart clattering past; saw churns rimmed with creamy circles of white, and I thought of the wreath delivered last night, that was left in front of the door in our hall, that was waiting to go to the cemetery. Because it was 20th November. It was the day of The Ritual, and that year, for the very first time, Mama would not be coming along.

The doctor assured us she was on the mend, but that winter's influenza had been the most virulent outbreak in years, and Mama was still coughing and feverish; yet another cause of my sleepless nights and the dark bruising circles under my eyes.

Luckily, Cissy and I had stayed well, except for that slight sore throat of mine, and the fact that my aunt had seemed very low since the night she performed at the music hall. Even when the bouquets of flowers arrived, and the cards of congratulations, nothing could win back her smile. She didn't sing one note all week, and the house was as silent and grim as a morgue, with Cissy insisting that any noise might disturb Mama's rest and recovery. But Mama had made no complaints before, when Mr Collins was playing the piano, with Cissy rehearsing to play Galatea.

The quiet was disconcerting to me which, I suppose, made the prospect of that year's Ritual more appealing than it would normally be. It was an excuse to get out of the house, and to do what we'd done every single year since I was only five years old: the year when my Grand-father Stanhope died.

My only memory of the man was being dandled on his knee, inhaling his sour and yeasty breath as my fingers stretched up to touch wiry white whiskers growing from ear to jowl, as his rheumy eyes stared down at mine, holding the faintest flicker of . . . what . . . was it sadness, resentment, perhaps disappointment? I had no words to describe it then. But now – now I think I understand.

Anyway, on each anniversary we'd go and visit Bow cemetery, laying a wreath for him and the wife who'd passed on long before with a newly born son. Cissy had no recollection of that, being hardly more than a babe herself, but Mama had been fourteen at the time, and she sometimes still wept when she stood at that grave.

From the cemetery, we'd go down to the docks where the family once owned a warehouse, stocking saddlery for horses and all manner of other leather goods, most of which were shipped out to India, with Grandfather being commissioned to supply the Bombay Cavalry – and a lucrative contract that must have been. But, after the death of his wife and son, the business had been neglected, going into a slow decline, very much like the man himself, much like the state of his warehouse now; a derelict carcass of rotting joists, mazes of stairs that led into thin air. Mama despaired that those parts of the docks were no more than a warren for cut-throats and thieves, which was why we took pains to avoid them. But we still went along to the Dolphin Bar, as Grandfather Stanhope had done every day, until that fateful November night when he died with a tankard of ale in his hand.

I never minded visiting there, but it seemed contradictory of Mama. *Maud's Hypocritical Ritual*, that's what I used to think, never ceasing to wonder at how she was happy to enter that particular bar, and in one of the roughest parts of town, when she would spend the rest of the year handing out Mr Brown's Temperance tracts, calling for all public houses to close.

Well, they could all stay open that day because, as I said, Mama was too ill to go anywhere, and, hearing her groaning, with no maid yet in, I went down to the kitchen to make some tea, then carried a tray back up to her room. But I didn't wake Cissy. Cissy always slept late.

I found Mama swaddled in shawls – so many I wondered that she could move. She might be an exhibit from the British Museum, something from those Egyptian rooms and, surrounded by samplers of religious verses and lurid paintings of Christ on the cross – not to mention that print of my father's grim face – she presented a very sorry sight. It was made even worse by the fact of her tears, mingling with what drooled thick and green from her nose, and having lost so much weight through her illness Mama's new and narrower features created a blurrier version of Cissy – Cissy's flesh melting down into waxy folds. I didn't want to think about that – my beautiful Cissy ravaged by time. Instead, I tried to cheer Mama, even going so far as to make the suggestion that we should delay The Ritual – until she was back on her feet again.

But at that she glared through red-rimmed eyes and wailed at me in a nasally twang, 'Of course you must go. You *have* to go. You must show some respect for your grandfather's name. You're getting as bad as Cissy these days. Next thing, you'll suggest we leave the East End . . . take off and give up the tradition for good.'

To explain what she meant by that, there had been a few times in the past when Cissy had mooted moving up West, suggesting it might be healthier there; the air cleaner, less effluent clogging the gutters, and more of her theatre friends living nearby. But Mama's objection was always the same: 'How can we ever leave Bow? We have to be here, near our parents' grave . . . where Phoebe's father and I were so happy. It's where we belong. We always will.'

I used to suspect that she mentioned that grave as a means of exerting some power over Cissy, some magic to make her live in a place where my aunt really wasn't happy at all. Though why Cissy, a grown woman who'd amassed enough wealth to be perfectly independent by then – well, why she kowtowed to such bullying ways, I couldn't begin to work out.

Later that morning, Cissy and I arrived at the graveyard and walked underneath the arching stone entrance that was carved with Christ's promise of eternity: *I am the Resurrection and the Life.*

I saw no life in that desolate place, except for Cissy who strode on ahead, the wreath clutched tightly against her breast, her booted feet crunching on frosted paths. Even dressed in my warmest black – a thick woollen coat, quilted underskirt, two chemises and two layers of stockings – I still shivered and felt myself chilled to the bone. The wind was so bitter we lowered our heads, and to any observer it must have appeared that we cowered beneath the rimed obelisks, the looming stone angels who might have been swooping down to possess us, spread wings wreathed in the shifting fog. That fog drifted through skeletal trees like ghosts, like fingers of smoke tracing names of the dead, where smog-blackened graves sprouted out of the ground: a giant's monstrous, mouldering teeth.

Another cross. Another stone angel. And, as Cissy crouched down to lay the wreath, her hat's fur trim trembled as if come alive and some loose strands of hair whipped over her face; a face that was lately too pale, though the tip of her nose was burned pink with cold.

I heard a bird screech and glanced around, suddenly sensing we weren't alone. I knew I was being too fanciful but I found myself wishing that Mama was there, no-nonsense Maud who would say some brief words and spill a few tears before bustling us back to the waiting cab. I wished that we could be anywhere else, hating the metallic taste of the smog which caught in my throat and made me cough. And, worse still, while I stared at the grave, I saw the stone angel was weeping. Of course, it was only the icicles melting, frozen tears leaking out from blank marble eyes, dripping across the grey-veined cheeks. And yet, such a morbid vision it made – and I thought about Cissy in Wilton's Hall, and the moment she'd faltered and almost stopped singing, the moment she'd seen that mysterious man.

In the branches I heard a sharp snapping, the black wings of that screeching bird which now flew low above our heads, alighting on top of the angel's head, its big grey beak open as if it was jeering. I think I must have cried out because suddenly Cissy – the real, living Cissy – was standing again, and close at my side, asking, 'Phoebe, what's wrong? Whatever's the matter?'

'Cissy,' I stammered. 'D-do you think Mama's right, th-that the Devil comes seeking his own, that he's walking amongst us every day?'

'Is it that bird? Oh, Phoebe . . . my sweet.' Cissy's lips touched my cheek. 'You look flushed. Are you hot? Are you feeling ill?'

'I haven't been sleeping. I'm tired, that's all.'

'I'm sure we're quite safe here. You don't need to worry, and whatever Maud has to say on the matter, I refuse to believe in Hell. I refuse to believe the Devil exists.'

She didn't seem that convinced to me. She smiled, but she didn't look happy. Inside I was terribly shaken, imagining that weeping angel was some kind of premonition, thinking that crow was Death's harbinger. And all the time I was staring at Cissy, and all the time I was silently thinking: *Your lips felt too cold, like ice, like stone.*

At the end of an alley that led to the docks, we asked the cab driver to pull up and wait. Cissy took my arm as we headed past chop shops and chandlers and smithies, and soon we came to a steep flight of steps where we clung on tight to the splintery rail, where below us dark waters were slapping their hollow laments on stone walls. The wind was brutal and cut like a knife, needling into our faces like wire, and even on such a bitter day, gulls were still screaming and swooping above, or gathering on acres of warehouse roofs, below which windows glinted with amber light. The dim air was spotted with lanterns. Vessels looked almost like phantoms, their rigging all glassy with ice, tall masts piercing through damp mists of cloud.

'Thank goodness the Dolphin's not far.' I was looking forward to finding a fire, my gloved palms thudding together for warmth as we stepped precariously over iced cobbles, past piles of tarred barrels and baskets and crates. High over our heads a piano was swaying, suspended on chains, hoisted up to a ship. Its wood casing creaked. Its strings jangled complaints, above which Cissy started to say, 'Would you mind if we walked a little bit further? There's somewhere I'd like you to see.'

'Cissy,' I moaned. 'It's freezing!'

'Please, Phoebe. It's really not far, and this would mean a great deal to me.'

And, true to her word, before very long she looked back and smiled. 'It's still here, after all of this time!'

I followed, somewhat more cautiously, as Cissy ducked down under nets and tarpaulins, pushing against a narrow door which set off a tinkling bell within. At first, with the light so soupy and dim, it was almost too dark to see a thing. I stubbed my toe on some coils of rope. But any discomfort subsided as fast as my eyes acclimatised to view an Aladdin's cave of delights. Such a strange power that shop seemed to hold with its haphazard tunnel-like aisles, created from sacks of sugar and rice. Faintly lit by paraffin lamps were shelves that were warping beneath glass jars in which biscuits and fruits had turned green with mould. There were cases of candles and tablets of soap nibbled away by vermin. There were wooden barrels of whisky and palm oil, and decorated tins of tea, and gorgeous bolts of coloured silk, the edges embroidered with golden threads, though now sadly frayed and water-stained. I admired some ivory chessmen, and miniature statues of many-limbed gods, every one of them cloaked in a cobweb lace. I lifted a dusty scallop shell, seeing its underside smooth, iridescent, like the slippy rainbowed puddles of black that we'd taken such care to avoid on the wharf. And, as well as the lanterns' oily fumes, I breathed in a pungent cocktail of spices, and peered into boxes with exotic labels of elephants, or tigers, or women who looked like those murals at Wilton's – at which I felt strangely sad and nostalgic, having to blink as I lifted my eyes, as they swam through a chiaroscuro of black shadow and orange flickering light – a light that was dancing on Cissy's face.

'Cissy,' I whispered, 'what is this place?'

'You won't tell Maud, will you? I've always wanted to bring you here . . . to show you where it all began.'

I was going to ask what she could mean, when I heard a strange voice, tremulous, cracked, with the trace of some guttural accent beneath. 'Good morning, ladies. Can I be of assistance?'

An old man shuffled towards us, as ancient as Methu-selah, and although I think he may once have been tall, now his shoulders were stooping, his back very hunched and a long white beard had grown down to his waist. By contrast, his brows were still bristly and black and

47

whatever colour his eyes had been, despite being shaded beneath his hat's brim, I could see they were milky with cataracts.

Cissy took a step towards him, her voice sounding plaintive, almost like a child, when she said, 'Isaac? Do you remember me?'

'Have we met before? Are you the young lady who came in this morning, off to join her husband in India? My assistant will soon be back. He'll bring everything up to your cabin . . . nail down the larger items for safety. He'll even secure that piano of yours. You've no need to hire the ship's carpenter.'

He paused to take some wheezing breaths, leaning forward against the counter top, gnarled fingers pressed down to support his weight. I saw splitting black nails at the end of worn mittens. I saw Cissy removing one of her gloves, and I thought she might place her hand on his, instead of which she reached for a fiddle set down on the other end of the counter. I don't think it could have been played in years, not going by all those layers of grime, and yet Cissy's action seemed reverential, as if that battered old instrument signified some sacred relic. While touching it, she murmured again, 'Isaac?'

Staring back through blind eyes, the old man croaked his recognition. 'Is that you? My little ray of sunshine, come back to light up the darkness . . . come back after all of this time?'

He lifted his arms, filthy fingers reaching to stroke her face. And Cissy didn't mind at all, not seeming the least bit repulsed or afraid. But I was. I couldn't begin to understand how my aunt could bear to be touched like that. I felt something twisting and cold in my gut and started to tug at her sleeve, saying, 'Cissy, I think we should go. I think we should go to the bar.'

'What's that?' The old man's head jerked round, the dead whites of his eyes fused with mine when he asked, 'Cissy, you say? No, no . . .' He sighed. His hands dropped down. 'This is not Cissy. Cissy's only a girl. If you wait, you might see her come in later on. She often calls by when the warehouse shuts up. If you're lucky you may even hear her sing, but . . .' he nodded towards the door, looking furtive and anxious, whispering hoarsely, 'we must watch. We must be careful, in case *he* comes again. This time we must not let him steal her away.'

Cissy was on the brink of tears. 'I'm sorry. I seem to have lost my way. I thought to find someone I used to know, but . . .'

'Oh, there must be no apologies. I'm glad of any disturbance these days. Every time I nod off in here alone I fear I shall wake in the land of the dead. But, until then,' he grinned, 'if there's anything catches your eye, my assistant will very soon be back. Why don't you wait, take some sherry with me . . . perhaps a slice of butter cake?'

Groping around on a shelf behind, he grasped at a sticky-necked bottle and rattled smeared glasses lined up at its side.

'No. Thank you. We really must go. *Shalom.*' Cissy flashed him a final smile, and before he answered *'Aleichem shalom'*, she had already turned her back, was already heading towards the door, and not looking back again, not once, as she walked away with a purposeful step, leading me swiftly along the dock, as if lured by the Dolphin's creaking sign; the slow mournful whine of a siren.

It wasn't very busy that day – a broker, a captain discussing some business, a military man in blue and gold who was reading and ticking through lists of supplies. Standing at the bar were some sailors, most looking woozy with grog. Some dour-faced dockers had lecherous eyes. We ignored them and walked across sloping boards, towards the table that Mama reserved, which was set with the usual tankard of ale, placed in front of the usual empty chair – as if my grandfather's spirit was there, awaiting our arrival. A draught blew through cracks in the small latticed windows, and despite the fire's glow cast on brown panelled walls we huddled in miserable silence. My hands wrapped around a chipped mug of coffee as I blew at the rising plume of steam, grateful that something at least was hot. Our pies were lukewarm, tasting stale and dry, though Cissy ate nothing, only gulped at her wine – and then ordered more. She kept starting to speak then breaking off, finally uttering the words, 'He doesn't remember me. I should have gone back there long before.'

'That old man? Was he a friend of your father's? I don't think he could see a thing. A wonder he does any business at all, what with that shop so neglected and dirty. Do you think he really has an assistant?'

Cissy didn't seem to hear my words but kept on staring into thin air. 'He used to say that I was like starlight. He said I lit up his dreary world. At least he took some notice of me – more than my father ever did.'

She pushed the tankard of ale aside, the one representing my grandfather's place, and frothing brown liquid spilled over the table, dripping down onto the floor. Voices around us became subdued, ears straining to listen as Cissy went on, 'Whatever was good in my father's life was gambled away, or drowned in his beer. This so-called Ritual of Maud's, it's all her twisted idea of a penance, all for the sake of a drunkard's life. A ruined old man . . . a ruined reputation.'

'Oh, I always thought . . .' But I didn't know what to think any more, to see Cissy trembling like that, her cheeks burning red as fire. And then when she suddenly stood, when her chair legs screeched across the boards, I was feeling very conspicuous. I was muttering, 'Cissy, please, won't you sit down?'

Doing as I asked, she leaned in towards me, her voice a little quieter. 'It's a penance because Maud Turner believed what those Hallelujahs used to say . . . that any woman who worked on the stage was as low as the vilest prostitute. But I say she's committed crimes of her own, with her greed and her scheming, her selfish behaviour, all that she's gone on to gain in the process . . . what she would *never* have had without me.'

Though used to the sisters' bickering, I was shocked at such blunt animosity. The silence hung heavy between us, during which Cissy was lost in her thoughts, lifting a finger to draw little circles through puddles of beer on the table top. And, while watching that, I finally said, 'It is a shame, the way Mama dislikes the theatre, always being judgemental about it.'

'Oh, it's much more than that. I would hardly even know where to begin. It stems back to the time when our mother first died, when Maud had to care for a two-year-old child, when our father neglected the living, preferring his drunken dreams of the dead. Our home was soon lost to his gambling debts, as was the warehouse in the end – though Maud kept the business running for years. She always was clever with numbers, sitting behind those big glass partitions, scribbling in ledgers, keeping accounts while I used to sit on the floor at her feet, working through all the readers she bought. But when she was busy with customers, sometimes I used to slip out on my own, and then I'd visit Isaac's shop.' She sniffed. Her eyes were brimming with tears. 'I can't believe he's forgotten me.'

'He must be terribly old. Isaac in the Bible was one hundred and eighty. I don't think that man could have been much less.'

'Yes . . .' she gave a wistful smile, 'I suppose he always did seem old, even all those years ago. He used to play the violin. We used to sing together.'

'That old man used to sing with the opera?!'

'No,' she laughed, 'only in the shop . . .' And then she became more thoughtful, 'Until someone came in and heard me one day, becoming my patron, taking me away.'

'Taking you away? Where to?'

'He found me a tutor, in Holborn.'

'Weren't you afraid . . . to go so far?'

'I was glad to escape. Only Isaac had any time for me then. Our father was stupefied most days by noon, and Maud was increasingly taken up with following that Hallelujah crowd, with courting her blessed Mr Turner.'

'My father?' Whenever Cissy spoke his name, I heard the resentment in her voice. Perhaps that had always clouded my view and encouraged my own antipathy. But I'd never known her so bitter before.

'He used to come down to the docks, to save all the whores who were hanging about. I think that was always his Heaven on earth. It's how he and Maud first happened to meet, when he mistook her for a prostitute, pushing a Bible into her hands . . . some leaflet about the next mission meeting. And Maud was so taken with him, she went.'

'Mama always says that my father was kind, a good and generous friend to you both.'

Cissy stared down at the backs of her hands as if she might find some answer there. 'She thought him a saint. I thought him a fool . . . always riding around on that bicycle, with boxes of leaflets strapped onto the sides and all of his banners flying behind. They tried to get me to join their choir, to offer the gift of my voice to the Lord, but I hated those meetings in draughty, damp halls, and marching around in that uniform.'

'I always hated wearing it too. But the Hallelujahs do a great deal of good.'

'Those members with selfless intentions. The rest of them do more harm.'

I was dumbstruck to hear my aunt so harsh, only able to listen as she carried on: 'When I was first hired for the opera chorus, William and Maud tried to stop me, insisting I come back home. They wrote to me continually, warning of vice on the West End's streets, saying they feared for my mortal soul.' She paused and swallowed hard. 'I saw more danger lurking round here.'

'So . . .' My head buzzed. What was I to think, when Cissy spoke so of my father? 'So, who did you live with instead of them? Was it that patron you mentioned before?'

'No. I used to lodge with my singing coach, everything above board and respectable. My patron must have paid, but I didn't see him again for years, though whenever I sang in public I looked for his face in the audience, and I always used to wish . . .'

She didn't go on. When she lifted her glass, I noticed

her hand was shaking. Dark drops of liquid spilled over her dress. Her face looked as pale as a porcelain doll, splintering with cracks when she started to cry. I thought it must have been the wine – downing three measures in so little time and her voice coming slurred when she spoke again. 'I'm sorry, Phoebe. I don't mean to upset you. I have such a headache. I don't seem to know what I'm saying today.'

Now, looking back, I think Cissy knew perfectly well what she said.

Then, I reached over and touched her arm, coaxing her gently. 'Come on, Cissy. You don't look very well. Let's go now. Let's go back home.'

5

Cissy went straight upstairs to her room, still complaining of having a headache, and Mama, who seemed a little improved, dragged herself out from her blanket cocoon to offer her sister some medicine. Before shuffling back to her own warm bed, Mama asked me how the day had been. I said much the same as usual.

That evening I ate alone, sitting in the little back parlour, a tray on my lap, a book in my hand, a chair dragged up close to the fireside. The servants had left the house hours before and everything was quiet and still, so much so that, at only nine o'clock, I decided to go to bed as well.

When I looked in on Mama I saw she was sleeping, snoring away with her mouth gaping open, the lace edge of her nightcap slipped over her face. Pushing it back, I kissed her cheek, inhaling sour odours of menthol and sweat, stale sheets that were badly in need of a wash.

Going on up to the floor above I found Cissy sleeping too, but with the air in her room so cold, I went to place some more coals in the grate, crouching to watch as ashy white embers smouldered with little spots of red – making me think of those ruby stains on a piece of white silk in Wilton's Hall.

Standing again, flames were leaping to chase me, to send yellow gleams flashing over the mirror, glinting over

the sides of a silver box beneath which was a folded paper
– and I was just about to pry when I heard a low groan
and looked up again, and surveying the room's reflection
I noticed that Cissy had opened her eyes.

'Cissy, I'm sorry. I didn't mean to wake you.' I turned
and went over and kissed her brow, which seemed oddly
clammy and feverish when compared with the room's
chill temperature. 'Do you think you should take some
medicine? Do you want me to send for the doctor?'

'No.' She reached for my hand, her grip hot and firm.
'I'd like you to stay here with me for a while, until I go
back to sleep again.'

Needing no further encouragement, I kicked off my
slippers and lifted the quilt, climbing in at the end of
Cissy's bed and there, with my back pressed against the
brass bars, with my arms wrapped round knees drawn
up to my breast, I looked at my aunt again. Her hair was
spread loose on the pillow, her eyes were wide open,
glistening and dark, and so lovely she was, so fragile that
night, and I honestly thought she'd never so much
resembled that girl in the painting, in the Millais that
hung in our hall. And with that in mind, I suddenly
asked, 'Cissy, why did you give up the stage? Why have
you only come back to it now? And why did you never
marry . . . always living with Mama and me? Did you
never fall in love?'

'I did love someone . . . once.'

That was my chance. At last I could ask. 'Was it that
man from Wilton's?'

'Yes. I was only thirteen when we met. Now, it seems
like a lifetime ago.' Cissy paused and gazed up at the
ceiling where firelight was dancing over the mouldings,

all the elegant plaster flowers and shells. 'I never wanted anyone else.'

'How did you come to meet him?'

'In the shop at the docks . . . where I took you today. Isaac had gone off with a customer, delivering supplies. He left me watching over the counter. I was arranging some tins of tobacco. I was singing to myself. If the doorbell rang I didn't hear, only sensed someone there when a shadow fell over the floor at my feet, when two hands had been placed either side of my waist.' She closed her eyes, carrying on, 'I still remember that moment, how fast my heart pounded, the panic I felt as, slowly, slowly, he twisted me round. I thought it was one of the dockers, always grabbing and calling obscenities. But I saw a gold watch chain, a silk brocade waistcoat, and I smelled, not grime and oil and sweat, but a perfume . . . dense and exotic. Such a glamour there was about him. I felt myself almost intoxicated as I looked at his face, his black eyes, his black hair. I felt his breath, warm and moist on my lips, and I wanted his kiss, like nothing I'd ever wanted before. But . . .' Her eyes opened. She stared at me. 'He didn't kiss me. Not then, anyway. He laughed, and he lifted me up in his arms, and then set me down on the counter top. When he spoke he became very serious, saying I was an angel who squandered her beauty and voice in the darkness, saying I was something precious and rare, a talent that should be nurtured and shared. He said he would change my life. And he did. After that day everything changed. Nothing was ever the same again.'

6

Everything changed when Cissy died. Nothing was ever the same again.

It came as a terrible shock. Already gone ten o'clock in the morning on the day that followed The Ritual, and the first we knew was the crash of a tray, and then a loud scream from Amy, the maid, and then the fast thud of Amy's feet as she thundered her way back down the stairs.

Mama and I were both in the kitchen, much cosier there than the dining room, and though still not out of her dressing gown, Mama was eating a third slice of toast, her appetite returned at last. Unaware of the butter smeared over her chin, she was chatting with Cook, going over new menus and making up lists of what ought to be ordered for Christmas Day when, after we'd been to church in the morning, when Mama had been out in the afternoon doing her charity mission work, we always had dinner with Cissy's friends, and there would be presents and games, and Mr Collins would play the piano, with everyone singing along.

But that year Mama's lists were discarded, faced with the far more onerous task of arranging her sister's funeral. Christmas morning, we still went to church, and then laid another wreath on the grave which by then had been newly turned, and where Cissy's name had been newly inscribed, carved underneath the stone angel's gaze: *Cissy. Beloved Daughter, Sister and Aunt.* And, arriving back at the house that day, we had no presents, no tree, no games, and though Mr Collins and Old Riley came round and shared our turkey meal, it really was very desultory, everyone mourning the ghost at the feast.

During the funeral service, I was sure I'd be sick or faint. I looked down at my feet and the kneeler there, embroidered all over with daisies and roses, and the ornate swirling letters that read: *Nearer my God to Thee.*

I hoped Cissy was nearer to God than me. I'd never felt so abandoned, alone. When I opened my mouth to sing the hymns, nothing came out, the words stuck in my throat. Mama held my hand so hard that it hurt, just as she'd done when we found Cissy dead, when I had done nothing but scream and shout, tearing my hand away from hers and slapping hard at Cissy's cheeks before frantically searching the room for a mirror and then holding that mirror up close to her lips as I prayed for some vestige of misting breath to spread over the surface and cloud the glass. But the mirror stayed clear. It refused to lie.

A snivelling Amy was sent for the doctor. I climbed onto the bed and lay next to my aunt, inhaling the perfume she always wore, that was lingering still on her cooling skin. A mixture of rose petals, cedar and jasmine. Penhaligon's Hammam Bouquet it was called – a strange sort of fragrance; quite masculine, musky and sensual.

I liked it, but Mama did not. She used to sniff and screw up her nose, indicating the view more often voiced that: 'a scent based on smells from a Turkish bath was redolent of nothing but decadence, and those who frequented such places were worse than the sultans who kept shameful harems, ungodly men doing ungodly things while floating in water or wreathed in steam – as hot as the breath of Satan's lust'.

I watched as Mama stared down at the hearth. No heat rising up from that cold, dead ash. I watched as she fiddled around on the mantel, lifting the silver box – the one that I'd noticed there last night. She left the room for a moment or two, but soon enough she was back, reciting a prayer at the end of the bed, though her incantation came to an end when she gasped and stooped down to pick up what had fallen to the floor, what she'd handed to Cissy the night before – that bottle of Roberts' Restorative, and still half-full of the viscous brown liquid the doctor had recommended for Mama, for easing those symptoms of her influenza; for aiding her sleep at night.

With Mama then very much awake, while her free hand grasped onto the bed's brass rail, she muttered as if to herself, 'I told her. I know I did. No more than two or three drops. Didn't she read the label? The directions are clearly laid out on the back. Surely, she wouldn't do this to me now?'

Mama looked at me, distraught and pale. 'Phoebe, get up. Go and get dressed. Quickly . . . before the doctor arrives. You know what this means. You know what she's done. You must not breathe a word to a living soul.'

Well, whatever the cause of Cissy's death – the certificate cited a fever, a sudden congestion of the lungs which led to a failure of the heart – and whatever events occurred after that, there has never been any doubt in my mind that Mama loved Cissy, very much. You see, and I know this is hard to believe, but when I woke the next morning, having spent the whole night in Mama's bed, lying for hours in a torture of grief, and both of us crying till tears ran dry – when I heard Mama's waking groan, when I turned on my side to kiss her cheek, I saw that the hair spilling over the pillow had turned from brown to white. My mother looked like an old woman.

At least on the day of the funeral we needed only to wear what stood for our normal attire, no boiling up clothes in a vat of black dye when black spilled from every cupboard and drawer. And when I made my way downstairs, passing the Millais that hung on the wall, I tried to forget what was still upstairs. I didn't want to see Cissy like that, already in darkness, bedroom shutters all closed, just as the lid of her casket would be when she was laid to her final rest.

Mama was standing by the front door, wringing her hands, complaining the undertakers were late. She glanced back at me. She started to nag. 'Phoebe, look at the state of your hems! They're covered in mud. Go back upstairs . . . get changed, right away!'

'Oh!' I looked down. 'It must have been from our day at the docks. But really, who's going to notice, Mama? Won't everyone's skirts be the same when they've all traipsed around in the cemetery?' And at that I suddenly lost control, shouting: 'What do I care for a few spots of mud? I'd wear rags . . . I'd walk naked down Mile End Road, if I thought that would bring Aunt Cissy back.'

Mama was shocked, snapping back at me, 'We may very well be reduced to rags. And a great deal sooner than *you* might think.'

Sharp flakes of snow spiralled round the stone angel. In the plot at its side was a freshly dug hole. I couldn't have said who was standing around. Wrapped up in my grief, I avoided all eyes, most of which avoided mine; perhaps too afraid of the pain they saw, the rawness of grief like an open wound. I only heard the hacking of coughs, the prayers for the dead, then the pattering little claps like applause when the handful of soil that Mama threw down scattered all over the coffin's lid. I saw the white lily fall from my hand, as if it was thrown by someone else. I wanted to shout, 'No! This isn't right. They've made a mistake. We have to wake Cissy and take her back home.'

When Mama took me home – without Cissy – she told me to wait in the music room. I felt like a stranger amongst my aunt's things, gazing anew at the silk Turkey rugs, the crimson silk curtains, the sofas upholstered in plush purple velvets. Her trinkets were scattered on small japanned tables. Tall Chinese jars stood by white marble hearths where fires were already blazing, having been lit since early that morning to make sure of warming the air. But it still felt too cold and my spirits were dismal. That room only echoed with Aunt Cissy's absence.

Mama flitted around officiously, instructing Amy to light the jets while I stood apart in the big square bay, staring out over black iron railings, up over the roofs of the opposite houses where the sky hung low with trails of smoke from the Bryant and May match factory. It was yellow and thick. It smelled sulphurous; much like that fake lightning created at Wilton's, the moment before Polyphemus appeared.

The first guests were some Temperance ladies, friends from Mama's Hallelujah crowd, though they'd never once entered our door before, not when Aunt Cissy was still alive. They positioned themselves next to one of the hearths as if they were guarding the gates of Hell, prepared to do battle with any mourners who proved to be louche or 'theatrical'. There were two maids I didn't know. They must have been hired in especially, wandering round with silver trays, offering cups of tea and cake which were eagerly snatched and then gulped down. You'd think every guest had been starving for weeks. But how could they eat when Cissy was dead? The smell of that food made me nauseous.

Muted conversations grew louder. Voices were buzzing like flies. The room circled round me, a slow dance of manners as, in twos and threes, more strangers arrived. The hands taking mine were alternately clammy, or greasy, or callused, and so many faces I didn't recall, and all from Cissy's past life, I supposed. I watched their mouths open and close, offering trite consolation. But I only wished they'd go away, go and leave me alone, alone with my grief, leave and bring that pointless charade to an end – though I was glad when Old Riley arrived, the first time I'd seen her since Cissy's death.

She hugged me and dabbed a cloth to her eye, not sparkling but drab as old seaweed that day. 'Oh, Phoebe,' she wept dramatically. 'I should never have let her take that bath. It was cold as ice in that dressing room, and with all that influenza around . . . and only hearing the news last night when Mr Collins turned up at the door, having seen the announcement put up in *The Times*. He's tried to let everyone know, of course, but so little time . . . such a terrible shock.'

I stood there speechless, thinking she might cause a few shocks herself, for she looked quite outrageous, her dress a deep turquoise, decorated with what must be upholstery trimmings, and those thick gilt tassels pinned on the front had surely adorned a stage curtain before.

Mama approached us, her mouth gaping open to see such a sight, and Old Riley let out a passionate sob. 'I'm sorry if you're offended, Maud. But what chance did I have to make other arrangements? Anyway, I don't hold with all of this gloom and doom at wakes. I'm sure Cissy would rather we dressed ourselves up, rather we laughed and wished her well than sit around moaning and moping, looking like something dragged out of the workhouse.'

Glancing back at those Hallelujah bonnets, she patted a hand to her own where a black ostrich feather was stuck high above. I honestly feared it might have been pilfered from one of the horses pulling the hearse and, for a moment, I started to laugh. But that didn't last – thinking again about the glass carriage, the ironwork gilded with cherubs and skulls. And now it was empty. No garlands of flowers. No fairy-tale princess sleeping inside, waiting for a prince to kiss her cheek, to bring Cissy back from Death's sleeping spell.

'Mr Wilton has sent his condolences.' Old Riley's sharp tones broke my reverie. 'He's not been at all well himself of late, though of course he would have liked to come, if only he'd had more notice. I have to say, Maud, you might have written. Finding out from the paper like that . . . well, it was, well . . .'

She stopped, her attention diverted then by another carriage drawn up outside, at which she let out a stifled cry, clasping a red-gloved hand to her mouth.

'Whatever is it now?' Mama leaned forward to take a look, impatiently tugging back the drape, but all I could see were more mourners, making their way up the steps. Mama gave a low sort of groan, pushing straight past me to rush from the room and, at the same time, Old Riley grabbed for one of my hands, holding me firm, sobbing again.

So much for the creed of laughing at wakes! I was glad when Bill Wright from Wilton's appeared, pushing a cup of tea in her hands, to which he then surreptitiously added a splash of dark liquid – it might have been rum – poured from a little silver flask conjured from one of his pockets. And with the poison as deftly concealed, he was telling Old Riley to try and hush up before leading her off to an empty chair. She went with little complaint, only stopping along the way for a brief word with Mr Collins, and to peck at the cheek of a younger man who had followed him in through the music room door. I did find myself wondering if he had caused her earlier gasp, for as he came forward and took my hand, offering his condolences, I noticed how good-looking he was. Very dark hair. Blue eyes, like glass. But I couldn't begin to think who he was – though perhaps if he'd taken his trousers off, or if he'd been wearing that yellow wig, or if he'd smiled, or winked at me—

Then Mr Collins was at my side, asking, 'Phoebe, my dear, are you feeling all right?'

Behind those little round spectacle lenses which were glinting with gold from the firelight, his eyes were as red and swollen as mine. Of course, he'd known Cissy for years and years. He must have been feeling her loss very deeply. I only wished he would play the piano – something slow and respectful, something like that lament from *Dido and Aeneas* which Cissy had always loved to sing. Whenever I heard those tragic words, my skin used to shiver; the hairs would stand up on the back of my neck, and no hymn could have been more appropriate than:

Death invades me;
Death is now a welcome guest.
When I am laid in earth,
May my wrongs create
No trouble in thy breast:
Remember me, but ah! forget my fate.

But Mama had been resolute. Except for the wheezing old organ in church, there was to be no music that day. Cissy's piano was draped in black velvet, the same with the mirrors hung over the mantels; the same with the big marble clock. On the day of the death, when she wound that down, it felt like another heart being stopped. But nature abhors a vacuum, and little wonder the ghosts of the past took hold of that silence to creep inside, bringing with them the nets in which we would be trapped.

'Please, Mr Collins,' I tried to smile, 'don't worry about me. I must find Mama. I can't think what made her run off like that.'

He placed a hand on my arm. 'I'm sure she's attending to other guests. Why don't you sit here . . . have something to eat?'

'I don't want to eat!' I pulled my arm free. Had he developed some new special talent, some addition to his music hall act, now able to see straight through brick walls, because how could he know *where* Mama was, or *what* she was doing, or who with?

She was not in the hall. No one was there. No one was anywhere near the front door. But the door leading to the best parlour had been left to stand slightly ajar and, without any fire, with no jets being lit, all I could see were dark shadows within, a faint radiance from the street lamp outside which filtered its way through the heavy drapes. But I heard Mama's voice distinctly enough, and then that of a man – very deep, very tense,

'. . . and not even to see her, to say a goodbye . . . to hear of the funeral only by chance.'

'Why should you presume any right to be told?' Mama was brusque.

'I have *every* right, as *you* well know.'

My hand touched the brass knob and pushed at the door, only a little – an inch or so more – but enough to see Mama beside the hearth, and then a man's arm being swiftly raised, as if about to strike her. And without even thinking I cried his name, 'No . . . Mr Samuels. Stop!'

Someone snatched at my sleeve from behind. Mr Collins was muttering in my ear. 'Phoebe, come back. You shouldn't be here.'

'Phoebe!' Mama's voice was trembling. 'How do you know this man?'

I cringed beneath that furious gaze, Mama glaring at me through the dingy murk. Mr Samuels' black eyes were gleaming and wide, his features still striking despite being drawn, his chin unshaven and bristled with grey, and I noticed his perfume, Hammam Bouquet, the same as the one that Cissy wore. And, while reeling at such an evocative scent, almost thinking my aunt might be there in the room, I tried to give Mama an answer, to untwist my tongue from its stammering knots. 'I . . . I don't know Mr Samuels. But I . . . I did once hear someone mention his name.'

She started to rail, 'Where? When you went to Wilton's that night no doubt! I knew I should never have let you go, mixing with people like this . . . this man . . . no morality . . . no sense of decorum. How dare he think to come here today, insulting my sister's memory?'

Mr Samuels' laughter was thick with contempt, though I noticed how heavy and fast his breaths, and I saw the emotion play over his face as he pushed a hand back through slick grey hair. 'Mrs Turner, it is you have insulted me . . . denied the opportunity to pay your sister my last respects.'

'Respects!' Mama shrieked, and then paused, as if she had alarmed herself, continuing with more restraint, though her fury still simmered beneath the next words. 'You showed very little respect in the past.'

'Maud,' Mr Collins was warning, 'you have other guests in the house. Surely, this is not the time or place.'

Mama's brow was filmed with a glistening sweat and I knew not to argue when she looked like that, swift to obey when her finger jabbed towards the door, when she issued me with the stern command. 'Phoebe, get out of this room. Go with Mr Collins, right now! Mr Samuels and I will speak privately.'

At that, Mr Collins took my arm and walked with me down the length of the hall, but Mama's next words were spoken so quickly and so very loudly that any within twenty feet would have heard. 'Fornicators and Jews are not welcome here. Better you knock on the gates of Hell! You'll find a warmer welcome there. If you hurry, you'll find Cissy waiting for you, grovelling there on her hands and knees, begging for God's forgiveness!'

His reply to such a terrible thing was measured, but equally cold. 'Maud Turner, you seem to forget and, therefore, I will now repeat that I have *every* right to be here today, to enter this house whenever I wish. I will not tolerate this disrespect, this lack of consideration and manners . . . and you, more than most, should seek to repent, to wash out your hypocritical mouth, and perhaps you should also adhere to the truth that *no one* should speak so ill of the dead.'

I heard nothing more after that. The parlour door opened. Mr Samuels stormed out, and the front door was slammed with such a bang, a wonder the stained-glass panes survived. And, while Mr Collins stood gawping, I ran down the hall and reopened the door, standing beneath the covered porch, staring out through the flurries of snow and the thick veils of breath misting over my eyes. I saw Mr Samuels stride over the road to where, at one corner of the square, a carriage was waiting to take him away.

As the horses walked by I still strained to see, and I'm sure he looked out of the window at me and, however melodramatic it sounds, my heart filled with such a strange yearning, wanting to know the man who'd loved Cissy, wanting to run down the steps to the street, to shout out for Mr Samuels to wait, to ask him to take me away with him. Of course, I was mad with the grief and Mama soon dragged me back inside and, clearly in no mood to hear explanations, she said I could join her, entertaining the guests, or else go upstairs to my room to repent.

Upstairs in my room the fire had burned down. The curtains were closed and I lay there in the darkness, empty and cold. I had to jam a fist to my mouth to stop all the whining sobs, but silent tears still ran down from my eyes, soaking through my hair, then the pillow below as I listened to muted sounds; the voices that floated up through the floors, still buzzing like flies swarming over the dead – the dead who'd committed their mortal sins.

Because Mr Samuels and Cissy had been lovers. Because Mama voiced such horrible things, saying Cissy was now at the gates of Hell.

Is that what she really believed? Is that what she'd thought when she'd watched Cissy's coffin lowered down into that hole, when she'd thrown in her handful of frozen, black soil, mumbling all of her pious Amens? Had she really been damning her sister's soul?

7

As the carriage set off through Tredegar Square, Nathaniel Samuels stared at the window. With a lamp lit within and the darkness outside, at first he saw nothing but his reflection. He barely recognised himself, that twisted expression of sorrow and rage, and reaching up to douse the flame he wondered how in less than two weeks his every hope for a future was crushed, thrown down to the gutter and ground into dust.

Dust to dust. Dust as bitter and dry as the tongue in his mouth. Dust as crumbling and arid as the heart of that bitch of a woman, Maud Turner. It was only thanks to the note Collins sent that Nathaniel had chanced to hear the news. He knew he wouldn't be welcome, and what did he care for religious cant? But he'd still made the journey to Bow cemetery, concealing himself behind some trees to watch Cissy's coffin go into the ground. And the flowers—

Since his visit to Wilton's he'd sent Cissy flowers each morning, each time with a cryptic message attached so that she would know they'd come from him. But what good had they done? All those roses and lilies and hothouse blooms he might just have saved for her funeral.

Blinking away the hot sting of his tears, he sat back and looked out at the black night air, laced with its patterns of falling snow. White flakes drifted down like confetti to catch in the long dark hair of the girl who was standing beneath a porch. She could almost have been on a stage, backlit in gold from the hallway behind. Then she was gone. The door was closed. But Nathaniel briefly saw into a room where the jets were shining brightly, where huddles of mourners gathered like crows to peck at the sorry remains of the dead – of his Cissy.

Grief squeezed at his heart like an iron band. He slumped forward and buried his face in his hands, letting out a long groan as balled fists pressed to eyes. He thought of a day he'd once spent at the docks, when he'd heard a child singing some Klezmer. It had been an incongruous choice of song for a voice as perfect and as sweet as hers:

> My home in Morgan Street
> Ver ich hob voynen git
> Ich hob mine eygen shtip
> Nor es schmacked fun fershtinnkener fish
> Dort shtayt a maidel, mit a kladel
> Untshrart 'Zecks a penny bagel!'

He'd thought, What songbird is locked in this cage, hidden away in the darkness, singing of bagels and stinking fish? He'd placed his hands upon her waist, turned her around, and looked down at the face of an angel. He'd lifted her up; in his arms she'd weighed nothing, as light as a feather, and when setting her down on the counter top he'd been so tempted to taste her lips, to taste much more – but then came the interruption, a voice calling out from the door behind.

'I know you, Nathan Samuels! You've not changed so very much. What do you want, coming back here after all of these years? Didn't you take enough before, thieving from the hand that fed you?'

Nathaniel had turned back with a smile, his arms held out in greeting. His response had been lightly spoken: 'Isaac . . . I've come to repay your loan. I think you'll be pleased with the profits returned on your, shall we say, less than willing investment.'

'I take nothing from you, or your ill-gotten gains. I no longer need that barrow you stole – and who knows what else you pilfered? But remember, God sees us wherever we are. He knows our sins, in darkness or light. So don't think to look on that child. She's not something else for you to steal, to try and turn a profit on.'

'I never expected to find such a light hidden under your bushels.'

'You may mock me.' The old man pressed a hand to his breast. 'But for me the light is not hidden. It is here, in my heart. For me, that is more than enough.'

'For me,' Nathaniel touched a hand to his brow, 'it is here, in my head.' His finger moved down towards his eyes. 'It is here, where I see. And I see a rare jewel, something too precious to hide in here . . . something that will shine far more brightly elsewhere.'

'Pah!' Isaac spat. A thick strand of mucus gleamed on the filthy floor at his feet. 'You mean something for you to tarnish and spoil! She belongs here. Perhaps you should also recall where you come from . . . the orphan who went to the Ragged School, who begged in the Jewish Shelter! What charity do you give in return, ignoring your own, pretending to be what you never were?'

Nathaniel had shrugged, though inside he'd been stung, and then he'd addressed the child again. With one brow slightly raised in question, he'd asked, 'What do you want? You don't have to spend your whole life in this place. Would you like to come away with me?'

With me . . . Nathaniel sighed, relaxing back into the carriage seat as the pain in his breast began to ease. When he closed his eyes he could still see Cissy's cautious smile. He remembered how easy it had been to play the benefactor – meeting her father, arranging for her schooling and lodging elsewhere – though keeping away from her afterwards, that was the hardest part. Cissy was only a child, and he knew he could never have trusted himself. And he'd given his promise to Isaac.

She was eighteen when it started, already singing in Paris by then, in the starring role in *La Sonnambula*. Later, much later, after the show, after the parties and dancing were done, he'd asked if he could go back to her room. In the cab, they'd both been nervous, sitting close, side by side but not touching. He remembered black cobbles where gas-lit reflections turned water to gold, and how humid the air, though there were no clouds, only a midnight sky full of stars. He remembered the sense of astonishment that he, Nathaniel Samuels, could feel such poetic romance in his soul, almost trembling when she'd touched his hand, when she'd lifted her face to his and said, 'I'm so glad you came. That's the only thing that matters to me. I'm only ever singing for you. I remember how everything began. I've never wanted anyone else.'

In the hotel, he'd stood in silence and watched as Cissy unpinned her hair, as her silk chemise slipped down to the floor. And then he'd fastened his gift at her throat. A silver locket: a single white stone in its filigree casing. Its weight lay between the cleft of her breasts where his fingers had stroked before tracing on downwards to girdle her waist, to linger over the swell of her hips, as he'd done all those years before – the first time he'd heard her, singing in darkness.

And, afterwards, when she lay sleeping, he'd kissed her closed eyelids where the skin was so fine that tiny blue tracings of veins could be seen. He'd twisted long strands of her hair through his fingers, inhaling its sweet floral fragrance. He'd dreaded the time when she woke again, when he knew he would have to tell her the truth – to confess he was already married and that Cissy could never be more than his mistress, their relationship always kept hidden, in darkness.

What if that wasn't enough? What if she turned away from him? What if she sang for somebody else? How could he contemplate giving her up? His love was too selfish and jealous for that.

It still was. As horse hooves and wheels splashed through slush and ice, the carriage turned onto the Mile End Road, back towards the cemetery.

8

The evening of Cissy's funeral, when I left the other guests below and went to lie upstairs in my room, I thought I'd been sleeping no more than an hour. Coming to with such a throb in my head, I felt dizzy, disorientated, blinking my eyes at the hazy light, and as my focus began to clear I saw Mama at the end of the bed, and I found myself wondering why it should be that Mama was in her nightgown.

'What time is it, Mama? Have they all gone?'

She looked peeved. 'Of course they've all gone. It's eight o'clock in the morning! Mrs Riley came up before she left – going off to carouse in some bar, no doubt. But as you were already sleeping she thought it was best not to wake you . . . not after such an upsetting day.'

Struggling to sit, I caught a brief glimpse of myself in the mirror: my hair like a bird's nest, half up and half down, my face very pale, eyes swollen and red . . . and quickly drawn back to Mama's again when she spat out the question, 'How did you know that man?'

'Do . . . do you mean Mr Samuels?' I had to be careful. I had to think clearly – make no mention of having first seen him while standing on a stage. 'I told you. I saw him at Wilton's. He must have been in the audience. I think Cissy spoke with him after the show. I wasn't introduced at all, but I did hear someone mention his name . . . saying he was the owner of Samuels' store.'

I felt myself blush to remember the rest. *I don't think he suffers from Leybourne's complaint.*

Mama's lips were pursing together, forming tight little creases of spite. 'Well, everyone knows *who* he is . . . *what* he owns . . . but how he had the nerve, turning up here at the house like that!'

With my thoughts still befuddled, I took a deep breath and asked, 'Mama, why do you dislike him so much?'

'I believe . . .' She paused, her words coming harsher and stronger again. 'I believe that your aunt loved him very much. In return he brought her nothing but ruin. That man has the charm of Satan. It's all a wicked mask. But, Cissy is gone. He won't bother us now. After all, he has nothing to do with our lives. Nothing whatsoever. Do you understand?'

'Yes, Mama.' Such passion was frightening, but I knew it was best to appease her, simply to let her go on with her rant, to wait for the rage to blow itself out.

'Good.' She stepped back, her stance more relaxed. 'From now on, we shall never speak his name. From now on, we shall manage quite well on our own, with no interference from Nathaniel Samuels.'

I thought that was an odd thing to say, seeing as he never had interfered. In Cissy's life, perhaps. But not ours.

9

By the following spring it was perfectly clear we could not manage at all. The upkeep of such a large house was expensive and, night after night, Mama sat in her study totting up figures, surrounded by piles of lists and receipts. But, whatever her calculations, the shops that had given us credit before refused when the bills went unpaid for so long, and what savings we had were dwindling fast, all made worse by some legal issue, something to do with Cissy's will – or rather, the lack of it.

Mama presumed herself sole heir but was then refused access to Cissy's accounts, and even when the solicitor wrote, when both of us had to sign various forms which Mama then took to the bank manager, she still came home in the blackest of moods, looking daggers for days on end.

The first casualty was the gardener, and then it was Amy's turn. We were so sorry to say goodbye, sadder still when the cook gave her notice too, leaving us with no alternative but to take up domestic chores ourselves, though I can't say I felt much enthusiasm, soon finding my fingers red and raw from all of the scrubbing and washing and beating. But for Mama it was a new 'mission', a new Bible found on the pantry shelf in the form of a mildewed old copy of Mrs Beeton's *Book of Household Management*. And, rather than going so much to church, banging her Army tambourines, she took to marching me round the house, preaching aloud from those foxed, yellow pages: 'Cleanliness is next to Godliness, vital to health and prosperity. Frugality and economy are very rare virtues indeed.'

I began to imagine a halo of virtue must surely be shining out of my head, seeping through blisters and cracks in my hands. I was never so glad of the coming spring, with less need to lug scuttles up and down stairs, to be sweeping out ashes and blacking grates. To think of poor Amy, doing that every day, and never once making any complaint! My respite was only those times when Old Riley and Mr Collins came round, but even though the black velvet was lifted, and sometimes he played the piano again, none of us ever attempted to sing.

One April evening we sat in the kitchen, the dining room rarely used any more – it saved on the fetching and carrying. I'd cooked a beef stew, and it smelled good enough, many complimentary noises made, but that scrag end of meat was fatty and tough, and the gravy was greasy with floury lumps, and somehow I'd added much too much salt.

The little we managed to swallow was washed down with several gallons of tea, and when my third cup had been drained, Old Riley made a grab for the handle, tipping the cup upside down in the saucer, her eye squinting hard at the mound of mashed leaves before lifting up to the ceiling to chant, 'I see a new road . . . a dark man crossing over the ocean. I see a bright future of reincarnation. But first, there are sad times ahead . . . and a rose that is not a rose.'

As I may have mentioned before, Old Riley was keen

on that sort of thing, but Mama was distinctly unimpressed. All at once she was standing, face flushed as red as a beetroot, and before sweeping out of the room in a huff, she stopped to look back from the door to pronounce, 'Mrs Riley, you know I cannot abide such superstition and devilry. Those who meddle are sinful deceivers, no better than charlatans. Kindly desist, or leave this house. Leave it and *never* return again!'

Faithful as her shadow, Mr Collins chased after Mama, and meanwhile Old Riley said sorry to me, explaining she'd fallen into a trance and had never intended to cause offence. With that she followed the others upstairs, hoping to make her peace with Mama, but I stayed in the kitchen to clear up the plates, first pulling a rack of damp sheets to the range, to be aired there for pressing next morning. When that was done, when I turned back to look at the mess on the table, the debris left by that horrible meal, I felt too downhearted to stay, deciding my chores could wait.

I found everyone in the music room – and it seemed that the tiff was over and done, the two ladies sitting side by side, and Old Riley patting at Mama's hand. Mr Collins lifted the piano lid and started to play some pretty tune, and I stood at the open back window, looking out through the dusk to see trees in new bud, though the garden smelled dank and mildewy. The lawn was badly in need of a cut, full of yellowy straggling weeds, and the shrubs such a tangle of wilderness you could hardly begin to see the back gate.

Mama hunched over her sewing, now and then pushing back some strands of white hair, or the little black ribbons that hung from her cap, dangling in front of her eyes. She was altering one of her dresses for me and, when she stood up, holding that worn bit of crepe to my back, I started to plead – for what must have been the hundredth time – 'Mama, must I always wear black? I was looking through Mrs Beeton's book, and she wrote several chapters on fashion, and with regard to a young woman's dress, her advice is very specific indeed. She says that' – and I had this memorised for such a moment of revolt – ' "its colour harmonise with her complexion, and its size and pattern with her figure, that its tint allow of its being worn with the other garments she possesses".'

Mama had the edge on that latter point, black always matching with black very well, but thinking that mauve was for mourning too, I stated with great authority, 'Mrs Beeton would dress me quite differently.'

Old Riley chirped up, taking my side. 'I'll have a look through my workroom at home . . . something with a bit more colour and sparkle, something a girl of seventeen years might actually find herself wanting to wear.'

At that, Mama burst into tears, the dress dropped in a heap to the floor, and while she clutched a hand to her breast her face turned a very strange colour indeed – very almost the tone that I'd had in mind.

'It's been barely six months! Can we not mourn Cissy, not even a year, without resorting to vanity? Oh,' she gasped, falling down to the sofa again, 'I'm dying myself! I can hardly breathe.'

'Mr Collins! Quick!' Old Riley squealed, 'Maud's taking a turn over here!' And while she rummaged in her bag, searching around for some smelling salts, Mr Collins made for the drinks cabinet, and though surely used to its contents by then from all of those evenings with Cissy, he fumbled about for what seemed like hours before bringing out the brandy decanter, splashing a great deal of it into a glass. Soon that was pressed to Mama's lips, and – being for medicinal use – she swallowed it down, without any complaint.

Old Riley watched and licked her lips. 'It'll be that stew. It was terrible salty. I must say I feel somewhat parched myself.'

Mr Collins took the hint, going in search of more glasses and, meanwhile, Mama, who seemed much revived, her cheeks a healthier shade of pink, continued with her snivelling. 'I fear the colour of clothes is the least of our worries right now. We may well come to lose the roof over our heads.'

'This house is very large.' I was used to such hysterics of late, not appreciating how dire things were; only pressing on with my selfish intentions. 'Really, it's much bigger than we need. Couldn't we move somewhere smaller instead, live on the money we make from the sale . . . perhaps even hire in Amy again?'

'If only we could.' Mama heaved a great sigh. 'But we don't own this house. We have nothing to sell, and now the bank has threatened eviction. Next thing, they'll be sending the bailiffs round. How shall I ever bear the shame?'

At first no one said a word, all stunned to hear such dramatic news. And while Old Riley made comforting noises, none of them based in the English language, Mr Collins – perhaps also impelled by some less than altruistic thought – said, 'Why don't you let out some of the rooms, take in a few boarders, some actors or singers? You shouldn't have any trouble, what with all the halls around.'

'It's out of the question!' I thought Mama's response very rude, considering the professions of our guests. 'Not *that* type of person, though don't imagine such an idea hasn't already occurred to me. I've been racking my brain for months on end, ever since . . .'

She paused. We all knew she was thinking of Cissy. 'Anyway,' she went on, more officious again, 'I wrote to enquire, but the bank will insist I'd be breaking the terms of any lease, and if we can't settle all of the debts they'll see us thrown out by the end of next month.'

'Next month?' Old Riley's one eye stretched wide. 'Why did you even write to ask? How would they ever have known if you took in a couple of lodgers?'

'Well, I think that some of the neighbours might notice, seeing so many more comings and goings, and at all times of the day and night. And, there might be anyone under our roof. We might be defiled while we slept in our beds – even worse! Don't tell me you've forgotten that murderer . . . the one who used to live on the square?'

'A murderer?' I'd never heard of any such thing.

'Oh,' Mama retorted, 'you were too young. We kept it all from you. We didn't want you being upset. It was that Henry Wainwright, lived at number forty, used to invite all sorts in through his doors, carrying on with dancers and shop girls . . . until he beat one to death with a hammer.'

Old Riley added with relish, 'I heard he shot her in the head. Cut her up into little pieces, he did! Parcelled her up like dog meat and disposed of more bits every time he went out. He would have got clean away with it too, but for that constable, noticed the stench and the blood seeping out from the canvas roll that Wainwright was holding under his arm.'

'He was hanged,' Mr Collins broke in. 'And that was

the end of the matter. The chances of that occurring again are probably one in a million.'

'Still,' Mama persisted, 'it goes to show. You have to be careful with strangers. You never know who's coming in through the door.'

'Well,' I was thinking aloud, 'we might look for some occupation ourselves, try and pay off the bank that way?' And, with a small frisson of growing excitement, I boldly suggested, 'I could help Old Riley, with sewing and working backstage as a dresser.'

Old Riley smiled sadly. 'Oh, dearie, I don't think Maud would like that, do you? And I really don't mean to be rude, but you're not the best with a needle and thread. To tell you the truth, I don't get much work any more myself. All those years with Cissy when she was busy, but now . . . well, it's the end of an era.' She leaned forward, a hand on my knee as if to ensure no hard feelings. 'If I could, you know I'd take you both in. But I'm up to my armpits with lodgers right now. Mind you, when I'm shot of this latest rabble . . . well, then there might be a chance. But you'd have to be prepared for a squeeze. I shall be setting the parlour aside, kitting everything out for my new enterprise.' She tapped her nose confidentially. 'It's something Mr Collins and I have devised to bring in a few coppers ourselves. I was having a bit of practice downstairs when I started to read those leaves of yours. But,' she glanced quickly back at Mama, 'best I say nothing about that now. We all know it's not Maud's sort of thing.'

By then, very restless and worried, I went to the front of the house, staring out of the big bay window, looking up at a sky streamed with yellow smoke. I mused, 'Amy always said there's work to be had at Bryant and May's.'

'So why was she working here instead?' Mama shouted, her voice coming hard and shrill. 'And have you considered the phossy jaw? Cook said her sister lost her teeth. It ate the whole bone away in the end – and all for less than ten shillings a week. Have you seen the state of those factory girls, all those short fringes and feathers they wear, lining up outside the Paragon? We all know about *that* music hall, all that dancing the "cancan", and no end of screeching and drunken behaviour!'

'Maud Turner, perhaps you should calm down, stop your own screeching and mind your manners!' Old Riley touched a hand to her own short fringe which was fashionably curling and recently dyed a bright berry red, above which a long pink feather was fixed – taking colour and sparkle to the extreme. 'We don't all want to look like tatty old relics, something the cat dragged in.'

'I tell you, Mrs Riley,' Mama bristled and got to her feet again, swaying a little while answering back, 'some of those girls make the roughest dock workers look like the purest angels in Heaven.'

For a while, the two women glared at each other, but I wasn't unduly concerned, trying to think of something else, something of which Mama might approve, and suddenly spouting my new idea. 'I've read a lot of books, and Cissy taught me a little French. Perhaps I could work as a governess.'

'A governess!' Mama barely left space to draw any breath, pointing a wavering finger at me. 'What does a governess earn but a pittance, leaving her family, dependent on others, and usually miles away from home. I hear of some treated abominably, and the prettiest ones too often disgraced . . . some of them ending up on the streets.'

There was a slight lull while she gathered herself, while Mr Collins refilled her glass, and then filled three more – brandy for himself and Old Riley, a little port wine for me – though hardly much more than a thimbleful. Without Cissy, supplies had not been replaced, and perhaps that shortage was just as well. Mama was tipsy, gabbling by then and bringing up my father's name, saying that when he worked with the poor, he could never have thought to imagine the day when his wife and child would be destitute too. 'To think' – she was like a banshee – 'to think it should come to this, dependent on charity, even the workhouse!'

With all the tears streaming down her face we thought it best to put her to bed, the three of us helping to drag her upstairs, though by the Millais she struggled to stop, pressing her nose very close to the frame, mumbling, 'Cissy . . . dearest Cissy, forgive me. What choice do I have left?'

'Come now, Maud.' Mr Collins looked pensive before hauling again on her arm, half-carrying her up the rest of the stairs and, while I opened her bedroom door, he stumbled past with a groan of relief, practically flinging her down on the mattress. I loosened the buttons fixed high at her neck, while Old Riley drew up the counterpane, and that's how we left her, snoring away. But at least she had a smile on her face, as if every worry had melted away.

Downstairs again, Old Riley shut up the window. Mr Collins disappeared to the kitchen, a little while later coming back up with a steaming cup of hot chocolate for me. 'Here you are, Phoebe . . . shall I add a splash of that brandy too, something to help with the shock of Maud's news?'

And then they made to leave, me waiting to slide the door's heavy bolts, to turn the key and fix the chain while Old Riley dallied about in the porch, turning to hug me, kissing my cheek, and Mr Collins took my hand, very earnest when he said, 'Don't worry, Phoebe. I'm sure he won't see you thrown out on the streets. I'm sure everything will work out in the end.'

Later, while sipping that chocolate in bed – but not very much, not liking the taste – I was wondering who *he* might happen to be. Perhaps it was Mr Samuels, but then hadn't Mama expressly said that he had nothing to do with our lives. I could only presume that Mr Collins must have referred to the bank manager. Then I wondered if Mr Collins himself might be thinking of doing the very thing of which Old Riley once hinted, requesting Mama's hand. A marriage, in the current circumstances, would prove to be a solution of sorts – until came the horrible hot spreading thought, *What if he is thinking of marrying me?* I was all too aware of his lingering glances, how the eyes behind his spectacle lenses often filled with affection and misty regret.

But, as it turned out, that was one dilemma about which I had no occasion to worry.

I woke in the night, very suddenly. I heard Mama in the room next door, still snoring, still lost in her brandy-glass dreams. Listening to the house's creaks and groans, all seemed unusually amplified, and while tossing and turning, I started to worry – *had Mr Collins remembered to lock the kitchen door?*

After that, I simply could not rest, convinced of someone else in the house, imagining every settling board to be a stranger's tread on the stairs. I was thinking of rapists and murderers, of being cut up into pieces, packed into parcels and fed to the dogs, and when I could stand it no longer, I forced myself to be brave, deciding I might as well die standing up as trembling under the sheets.

Out on the landing, inch by slow inch, I peered round the side of a long brocade drape, on down to the hall below where potted palms cast their feathery shadows, where the front door's stained glass was a blurring of colour as watery light from the street trickled in. I stopped beside *The Somnambulist* – the young woman who looked so very like Cissy, who on that night might also be me, dressed in a white gown, with my hair unbound – and drawing close, as Mama had done, I whispered, 'Why did she ask your forgiveness?'

Cissy made me no answer, but from somewhere else in the house there came such a crashing clanging sound, followed on fast by a rattling thud, and holding my breath, my heart beating fast, I didn't know whether to scream and shout, whether to go and defy the intruder, or simply to run outside to the street. But that would mean leaving Mama alone, and what if it took too long to escape, fiddling with all those locks and chains, the assailant having ample time to creep up on me, to strike from behind?

My limbs turned to jelly. With both hands grasping onto the banisters, I slowly slid down to sit on a stair. And then, as if things weren't bad enough, I heard a horrible howling sound – and that's when I felt very foolish, almost wanting to laugh out loud. Because I knew that sound so well. It was the cat, the one from next door, coming into our house every day that past week, every time the back door was left open, and always hungry and mewing for food or scratching around in the rubbish for scraps.

Enough moonlight shone in through the side-passage windows, illuminating each narrow step as I made my descent to the basement floor, where I soon found that mangy creature brazenly licking cold stew from the bowls, having jumped up onto the table, knocking the big copper pot to the floor – where a gloopy puddle of uneaten sauce was now a dark stain on the flags beneath.

Outside, in the garden, a gusting wind shivered through branches of trees. Long tendrils of ivy whipped hard at the window. The door swung on its hinges, then the same slamming thud I'd heard before. The cat arched its back. Its hackles rose up, but soon enough it relaxed again, resuming its purring and licking. Meanwhile, from behind that rack of damp sheets, the range made soft shushings, coals shifting and hissing, almost a whispering lullaby, and with my toes chilled against the cold stone I thought of the warmth of my bed again.

But first, hoping not to be bitten or scratched, I opened the door and flung the cat out, watching it run through the garden's black shadows, after which I made sure to do the thing that Mr Collins clearly had not – firmly shutting the door and drawing the bolts, turning the big iron key in the lock. And, being so tired, my thoughts slow and blurry, it didn't occur until the next morning that if I'd heard the door slamming before while I was sitting upstairs in the hall, then how had it opened again on its own? How had it come to be standing ajar by the time I arrived on the basement floor?

10

Stretching my arms back over the pillow I felt very lazy and languorous. For the first time in months I smiled to see sunlight creep in through the drapes, to hear the birds singing, the clatter of iron hooves in the street – everything normal, everything reassuring, everything going on as before. When shifting my head I caught the faint odour of Hammam Bouquet, for a moment forgetting that Cissy was dead, but my mind was only playing new tricks, still being too full of last night's dreams.

Coming back up from the basement, I'd felt very thirsty, drinking down what was left of my chocolate, wincing at the dregs – very brandyish. But I soon felt a melting heat in my veins and as my breathing grew deeper and slower, I thought of the ocean, a hushing of waves ebbing and flowing against the shore. And through that I heard a beautiful voice, a song that I couldn't quite make out, and I felt something cold stroke over my cheek, and I opened my eyes to see four steep sides of dank black soil, and above them the flickering light of a candle cutting a circle of gold through the air, and within that halo the face of a man, two black eyes staring down; a mouth speaking a name. But, no matter how hard I tried, my lips wouldn't open to form a reply, to say: 'No, I'm not Cissy . . . I'm Phoebe.'

*

'Phoebe. Phoebe . . . quickly! Wake up!'

Mama's shouting disturbed me. Feeling dizzy, I threw off the blankets and ran from the room, dragging my nightshift down over my thighs and, just as I had the night before, stopped to look down from the landing, to where Mama glared up from the bottom stair. She still hadn't changed out of yesterday's clothes, her skirts all rumpled, her sleeves stained with white, which looked very much like trails of snot. She might be some mad woman from an asylum, white hair hanging loose over sleep-creased jowls, her mouth gawping open, one arm pointing up – so accusingly.

Oh no . . . It must be the mess in the kitchen. 'Mama, I'm sorry. I overslept. I'll get dressed straight away. I'll clear everything up, and—'

'It's gone!' she shrieked. 'It's been stolen. Why didn't you lock the house?'

I thought about the kitchen again. What I saw was the end of the hall; every bolt, every chain of the door undone. But how could that be? Unless . . .

'Mama, have you been outside?'

'No! It's the Millais! Oh, dear God, it's gone.'

She hadn't been pointing at me at all but to an empty space on the wall, a darker rectangular shape where no light had reached to fade the paint. My head filled with panic. My blood gushed and sucked like the sea in my ears, like the sea at the base of those treacherous rocks, above which the sleeping girl had walked. But no one was walking there any more, because someone had stolen our painting away.

For the next few weeks Mama insisted that we kept all the windows shuttered and locked, every room in the house secured on the hall side. Any strangers who called were turned away, no matter what business they might be on, and Mama would shout from a window upstairs. 'You'll have to write . . . introduce yourself in a letter. You'll have to provide us with references.'

Perhaps she'd gone mad. I'm sure that's what everyone else must have thought, and sometimes I feared I'd go mad myself, buried away in that semi-gloom, forced to use candles for every small task with Mama refusing to light any jets, saying, 'Gas costs money. The candles are free. We've got boxes piled up on the pantry shelves.'

I took to staying up in my room, drawing the drapes wide open, raising the sashes while looking down over Tredegar Square, where spring was already transforming the gardens, where children played within the black railings, their uniformed governess sitting on a bench. She looked quite respectable to me; she didn't look ruined, or miserable.

But by then all concerns of employment were gone. By then, I had found my means of escape, a way out of my dreary, depressing existence in a world grown too dark without Cissy, worn down by my mama's constant bad temper; stifled by her clinging affection.

11

On the day of the theft, mid-afternoon and quite out of the blue, Mr Collins arrived at the house, and Mama was soon regaling our news.

'Oh, Mr Collins, can you imagine, waking to find the Millais gone? Phoebe and I walked to Bow police station . . . no cab because, as you know, these days we are forced to economise. But we sat there for hours, for most of the morning, crushed next to stinking drunkards and low life. And there I was, being so naive as to think that when they heard our plight – two defenceless women, living alone, a thief creeping round in the dead of night – those officers might come and investigate. But they only inferred I was drunk as well. They implied I was making the whole thing up, saying that sort of scam goes on all of the time! They said they had more pressing matters to deal with . . . two prostitutes murdered in Limehouse last night, and then,' at this point she glared at me, 'they said bolts and chains don't break free on their own. They said someone inside must have opened them up!'

A few hours before, when we first arrived home, having trudged our grim way back from Bow police station, I was insisting yet again that I'd got up and locked the kitchen door; that the front was secured when our guests had left. Still, Mama's disbelief blasted over my face, and reeking strongly of brandy it was, which those constables had not failed to observe. 'Why are you lying? Shut up, Phoebe, will you! I have a headache. I need to lie down. All of this worry and stress going on. I am reaching the end of my tether.'

Mama retired to the little back parlour, where she sat and sipped from a glass of water, in which a dose of Brain Salt was fizzing – something to settle her stomach and nerves.

Leaving her there, going down to the kitchen, I groaned at the sight of the dirty plates, the pots on the table, the puddle of stew congealed on the floor. And, leaving that morning in such a rush, we hadn't thought to make up the range, which meant the kettle would take ages to boil, that the irons would never be hot enough for pressing those sheets – those sheets!

What had been hidden in darkness was all too apparent during the day. The linen was still draped over the rack but where the white hems pooled on the floor they were covered in muddy footprints, yet more trailing across the flags by the door. Taking a cautious step forward, I kicked out and the wooden horse collapsed, a well-padded clump as it hit the floor, and though there was no one hiding behind, I still felt the pricking rush of my fear to think that, last night, I'd been standing right there, and the thief may well have been watching me, obscured behind those tenting sheets. And what of my dream – a man's face looking down while I lay defenceless, dreaming in bed, thinking myself in Cissy's grave? Had that been real? Had that been 'him'?

I decided not to tell Mama, not wanting to cause her more distress, not with her being at the end of that tether. And then, while I scrubbed at the stains on those sheets, obliterating the evidence, there came a trilling ring at the door.

Rejuvenated by her fizz, Mama had recovered sufficiently to invite Mr Collins in for some tea. I went back down to the kitchen, and while waiting for the kettle to boil, I set out the tray very daintily, using the best silver spoons and pot; even rubbing the tarnish up with a cloth. But when I rattled my way upstairs, rather than appreciating my efforts, Mama looked pained, demanding to know, 'Where have you been hiding that pot away? A wonder it wasn't stolen too!' And then, very earnestly, she turned to Mr Collins and asked, 'Do you happen to know of anyone who might take some good silver off our hands? I'm sure we can manage without it. Would it fetch very much, do you think?'

Before Mr Collins could make a reply, I broke in – I suppose rather peevishly – 'Mama, why don't you set up a stall, right in the middle of Tredegar Square? Or have you considered the Whitechapel Market?'

'You may mock, but our best and last chance has been lost. I hoped for so much from the sale of that painting.'

'You were going to sell *The Somnambulist*? But it was a copy. What would it be worth . . . apart from sentimental value to us?'

She lowered her face in her hands, peering up through the gaps in her fingers, mumbling, 'Phoebe . . . it wasn't a copy.' Those same fingers lowered, twisting round in her lap – a habit that Cissy also had, or used to, when she was still alive.

'It is, it *was* worth thousands of pounds. Mr Millais is so very famous these days. We always said it was a replica in case anyone thought to steal it, which,' Mama slowly shook her head, 'is precisely what has happened now. I should never have held that wake in the house, all those dubious lowlifes roaming around.'

I tried to remain controlled. 'You should have told the police the truth. They may have shown more interest.'

'It was given to Cissy . . . it was a gift. But we have no receipt to show, nothing to prove its provenance.'

Mr Collins coughed, addressing me. 'I fear I may have been at fault, somehow contributing to this event. A few weeks ago, when Maud first mentioned selling the painting, I suggested making enquiries with dealers, only reputable ones, of course, alerting them to the fact that it may be available. I wonder now,' he looked down at the floor, 'if those dealers were all to be trusted.'

'Mr Collins,' Mama reached for his hand, 'you shall not be taken to task over this. You have been the truest of friends. What would we have done without your support?'

She buried her face again, that time in the folds of a napkin, and whether it was the sugary tea or an upsurge of anger I cannot say, but she suddenly threw the cloth to one side, standing up to announce with great fervour, 'Mr Collins, would you come out with me, this very afternoon? We shall visit each one of these dealers in turn. The law may have spurned me, but I shall become detective myself. I shall look in their eyes and if they seem decent . . . well, I shall tell them that it has been stolen and should the painting come into their hands, at least they will know where to find me.'

Mr Collins was hesitant. 'Whatever you wish, Maud. But may I suggest you don't raise your hopes. Really, the artist is very well known. Any thief will already have buyers in mind . . . no doubt has already delivered the goods.'

'Nevertheless, we must try.' Newly energised by

thoughts of her quest, Mama strode out of the room, running upstairs to change into fresh clothes and, hopefully, to freshen her breath.

Meanwhile, Mr Collins turned to me. 'Phoebe, will you be coming along?'

'I'd rather stay here. I hardly slept a wink all night. I'm sure I heard someone moving around. But I haven't mentioned that to Mama.'

'Poor child, all this upset and shock.' Straggly, grey brows drew close in concern. 'Really, I do blame myself. I hate to see you upset.' And then, like Mama, he sprang from his chair – as much as a mature, slightly plump man can do. 'While we're waiting for Maud, shall we check through the house, set your mind at rest that everything's safe?'

Starting with the basement, we worked our way up, searching through every store room and passage, leaving no stone unturned – except for Mama's study which, even before the burglary, she always kept locked when not working inside, always possessive of her private domain.

I followed him right to the top of the house where he even drew the ladder down, gingerly climbing and poking his nose into the dusty attic trap. And, it wasn't that I was ungrateful, but I took the strangest notion that his actions were all a charade; something to humour an anxious child: like a father who crouches down on the floor to prove that no monster lurks under the bed and yet, by his action, prolongs the deceit.

One thing that resulted from our inspection, and how strange that I only noticed then, were all of those items that *had* disappeared: the trinkets and precious ornaments, the things that Mama always cleaned herself. Where was the gold bowl from the front parlour mantel?

Where were the small marble busts of composers, gone from the cabinet by the piano? Naturally, I assumed they'd been stolen too, but when Mama came back downstairs, when I had to inform her of more bad news, while tying hat ribbons and pinching her cheeks, she blithely admitted to selling them off.

How long has this been going on?

While Mr Collins pronounced the house safe, Mama rushed to the end of the hall, taking a key from the ring on her belt and opening up her study door. She soon re-emerged, waving a large brown envelope. 'I've found it, Mr Collins . . . the directory of dealers you brought round before. We can work our way through them one at a time. Come along.' She beckoned impatiently. 'We must make haste or the day will be lost. But with God on our side we shall meet with success. He's never let me down before! And, Phoebe,' she gave me a serious look, 'you look rather tired. Perhaps you should go back to bed for a rest. But do make sure to lock up behind us, and if anyone calls, whoever it is, you must promise me not to answer the door.'

Back in the parlour, I cleared all the tea things onto the tray, but when I stepped out to the hallway again, about to descend the kitchen stairs, I was suddenly nagged by something 'not right', breathing out a long *ah* when I saw what it was. Mama's study door was still open.

Crouching down, I placed the tray on the floor. I knew it was wrong, but still entered that room, confident that she would be absent for hours and even if she did come back, she couldn't possibly catch me there because, as instructed, I'd locked up the door, using every bolt and every chain.

It was terribly dark in that room, with the shutters all

closed and the curtains all drawn, but light enough spilling in from the hall to see that a tinder box lay in the grate. My fumbling fingers soon struck a flame and then twisted the gas burner's lever. It had grown very stiff from lack of use, and I had to jump clear of the hissing blast. But it soon settled down, and beneath its soft illumination I saw the desk's roll-top half-raised, and beneath that were several papers and ledgers, bottles of ink and blotters and pens, and all such a mess, as if Mama had swept her hands through the lot, scrabbling for that list of dealers.

I sat in her cherished mahogany chair – brought from the docks when the warehouse was shut. It rucked up the rug as I shuffled yet closer; apprehensive at this chance to learn the true extent of our penury. Lifting a ledger, flicking through pages of numbers and lists, I saw row upon row in Mama's neat hand. But those figures meant nothing to me, nor did the bills and receipts, meticulously dated, secured with brass clips or rolled into india-rubber bands. The light caught upon some large letters, their gilt glinting out from a creased piece of paper that looked as if it had been screwed up, only then to be pressed quite flat again. And, though much of the writing was damaged or smeared, a great deal was perfectly legible:

Hyde Park Gate, South Kensington, London
7th April, 1882

To Maud Turner
  My solicitors inform me that you have corresponded with them, detailing the somewhat delicate matter regarding your (here I could not decipher some words). *I have* (the paper too damaged again) *which may have swayed your judgement in the past, causing you to* (and

here again) *fully understand and, therefore, with regard to the affection in which I once held your late sister, I make the following proposition as a means of going some small way in assisting your present difficulties.*

My wife, Lydia Samuels, has long considered the prospect of taking a companion. I am prepared to propose a meeting, referencing a certain Miss Phoebe Turner as one of a respectable family with whom I have previously shared a long-standing business acquaintance.

Believe me when I say that such an interview would be a mere formality, and one in which you may rest assured of my absolute integrity. But I close with a word of counsel. In all of my business dealings, even those of a charitable nature, there is an understanding that discretion is mutually upheld.

I remain, respectfully,
Nathaniel Samuels

When I finished reading that letter, I felt frightened but also excited. The role of a lady's companion was something I'd never imagined. But if Mama had written to Mr Samuels offering details of our plight, then why hadn't she mentioned the matter to me? Or had she hoped for some other reply, something that might keep me closer to home? Or was it because she thought *me* indiscreet, for if I were to take the position he offered then clearly his wife must know nothing of Cissy – the actual nature of our connection?

And yet, surely, this had to be a chance, and the best of our limited options. As things stood, what hopes did we have elsewhere?

12

Mama arrived home looking grey with exhaustion. She seemed not to notice the tray on the floor, stepping right past it to enter the parlour where she started to light some candles. Mr Collins rummaged around in a bag from which he fetched out three squashed meat pies – and a brand new bottle of port. He then disappeared to the music room, coming back with three glasses, pouring three measures; forgetting all earlier remorse for Mama's intoxication last night. And once again, to my surprise, she forgot all about her Temperance Pledge, swallowing deeply, closing her eyes, shaking her head as she started to moan, 'Oh, if only we still had that painting to sell. Without it our future could hardly be bleaker. Not one of those dealers showed any interest.'

I sighed with disappointment. *Had she really expected anything else?*

Mr Collins sat in a chair by the hearth, and as he began to eat his pie the sound of his slobbering mastication was irritating beyond all measure, causing my stomach to heave, for on top of that rich gravy smell both he and Mama gave off such an odour of sour perspiration, blending with that other malodorous perfume of hems dragged through filth on the streets.

Slouched in her chair, Mama's fingers were cupping the bowl of her glass. I pulled up a stool to sit at her feet, taking a tentative sip of mine. But the port was too strong, too sweet by far, so I set the glass down in the grate and stared at the thick ruby liquid, and from there to the flocked crimson walls where shadows were shifting in front of my eyes, where red and gilt patterns were glistening – like the swirling gold ink that had formed the words, *Nathaniel Samuels . . . Hyde Park Gate*.

Oh, I had to confess, or I might explode, rising from the stool and leaving the room, very soon coming back with his letter. But if by such an action I'd expected to ease Mama's distress, I could hardly have been more mistaken.

At first she did nothing but blink, her neck craning forward, eyes squinting to focus on what I held, an expression of mild curiosity turning to one of alarm as she grabbed at the page and screeched at me, 'When did you find this? How long have you had it?'

'Only this afternoon, when you left your study door open. I saw it on your desk. Forgive me, Mama. I know it was wrong but I think . . . don't *you* think, this might be for the best? A chance of employment, a chance to—'

'You devious child! What will it be next? Am I violated on every side, even by those who are closest to me?'

'Mama, please—'

I felt hot and ashamed, my pathetic words drowned by her shouted rage. 'I asked for his help in good faith. This proposal is his petty revenge for not being told of the funeral.' She thrust the letter up close to my face. 'These are the words of a wicked, manipulative man . . . one whose sole intention is to spite me, to destroy everything I have left. Oh, I never thought to see such a day, first losing the painting, now faced with this.'

The letter was dropped to the floor, though Mr Collins soon picked it up, and pushing his spectacles back up his nose, his eyes darted swiftly over the page. Mama watched him, her own wide and staring, and looking as demented as when she first told me the painting was gone. Meanwhile, my world seemed to shift on its axis, something so subtle I couldn't quite name it. That little back parlour became too constricting, the burden of guilt on my shoulders too heavy, and somehow I felt – I don't know – as if I'd been exposed in the act of committing the most heinous crime. There was a terrible silence punctuated by no more than the sputtering fizz of those candles, and the patter of rain on the window outside and, over it all, Mama's shuddering breaths.

How I wished I had never gone into her study; never thought to look at her desk. But when I'd first read Mr Samuels' letter my mind had been nothing but a whirl. I'd switched off the gas and closed the door, tripping over the tray on the floor outside, hearing the tinkling smash of a cup, looking back at the trickle of milk on the tiles. But I didn't care, only running upstairs, only hesitating where yesterday the Millais had still been hanging. Its theft was a tightening pain in my breast, like losing a little of Cissy again, but perhaps that oblong of darker wall might hold some secret, might now be a window through which I could climb, to enter a totally different world.

In my bedroom I drew back the curtains. A fading light drizzled over the page as I read Mr Samuels' letter again. Setting it down on the window sill, I stared at the lowering skies. Soon the lamplighter would be doing his rounds, but for now everything was in shadow and murk, and whereas in daylight I'd been less concerned, I found myself fearing another intruder, flinching at every echoing step, every rustling leaf in the bushes and trees. I pressed my cheek against the glass where a draught was blowing up through the gaps. The air was chill, smelled metallic, and turning back to survey my room I felt such a loneliness in my heart; such a terrible yearning for Cissy. I missed her so much. I wanted her back.

After lighting a candle I went upstairs to the second floor where, only a little time before, Mr Collins had opened Cissy's door. Now when I tried to turn the key, it was fastened so stiffly I almost gave up, but then came the dull, clicking sound of release, along with the stench of stagnant air, dense with familiar odours; the fading aroma of Hammam Bouquet. A thin bloom of grey covered carpets and boards, the cushions and quilts that were left on the bed, the wardrobe doors that I opened up, plunging my arms deep inside, holding the fabrics close to my face, shutting my eyes as I made the wish that Cissy's ghost might materialise, filling those folds, making them warm. *Oh, Cissy. What shall I do? Once, you went away from Mama. Once, you had a life of your own. Why shouldn't I do the same?*

I turned to the dust-blurry mirror, holding a cream satin gown to my breast, my fingers caressing minute trailing flowers that were stitched in the palest of pinks and greens. I imagined that gown to be flowing around as I danced in the arms of a handsome man, perhaps in Paris – or even Vienna. But then everything turned a silvery white when a bright spear of lightning streaked through the sky, followed at once by a great crashing clap. The boards were vibrating under my feet. The window frame rattled and, in that one moment, it seemed that my glassy reflection was Cissy's. As I gasped and stepped back, the silk slid from my hands, its hush mingling with tinkling bottles and jars, all neatly lined up on the dresser top, and that sound drew my eye to what was behind them – Cissy's black velvet jewellery box.

I wondered if Mama had rummaged in there, plundering her sister's treasures to pawn. I thought of a locket that Cissy once showed me and, very slowly raising the lid, found myself smiling with relief to see the glint of its silver chain. With that object removed and concealed in my pocket, I closed the lid again and then stooped down to collect the gown, taking it with me to lie on the bed where I pressed the cool satin against my cheek. And as feathery quilts moulded soft to my body, I thought about Cissy lying there, when she was still and cold and dead. But I wasn't afraid. Cissy would never hurt me in life. Why should she seek to harm me now?

I'm not sure how long I slept, suddenly jolted awake by the bell, the hammering knocker and then Mama's voice, very shrill as she called through the letter box, 'Phoebe. Are you there? Come and let us in.'

I stood up too quickly. My forehead was clammy. I felt slightly sick, and while trying to hang Cissy's dress on a hanger it kept slipping off again – which was how I happened upon her old scrapbook, hidden away on a shelf at the back. Thinking to return for that later on, I left the cream silk in a heap on the floor, closed up the closet, snatched up my candle, and twisted the key in the lock.

A very short time afterwards, when I had confronted Mama with The Letter, and when her initial outburst was done, with tears in my eyes I apologised and tried to discuss it more rationally. 'I'm sorry, Mama, but don't you think Mr Samuels offers me this post out of his regard for Cissy? Because we are her relations. Because he wishes to help.'

I looked at Mr Collins, the offending item still in his hands, thinking he might have some words of advice – only hearing Mama's stern reprimand, 'You stupid girl! You speak of his regard, when that man took my sister away from me, from all that was decent and Christian. She waited on his every whim, every lying promise he ever made. How could I know you'd be safe in his house?'

Mr Collins broke in to protest, small crumbs of pastry spat into his beard. 'Maud, really! This offer seems genuine enough.'

'But how can I bear it? A strange act of kindness, taking a child away from her mother! And for what purpose? Have you not wondered that? Why should I be rewarded like this . . . no husband, my sister dead, and now threatened with being thrown out on the streets!'

She was weeping again, and I knelt at her side with my head in her lap, at a loss as to how to console her. 'Mama, I never intended to hurt you. We'll forget all about it. We'll manage somehow. I'm sure I can find some other work.'

While I spoke, Mr Collins set down the paper and sipped at his port. When making to stand, his half-eaten pastry fell into the grate but he didn't seem to notice that, only coughed and cleared his throat to recite, as if his words were not spontaneous but something he'd previously memorised, 'So many young ladies of Phoebe's age have already left home, either for marriage or seeking employment. Maud, may I suggest you sleep on this matter and, tomorrow, perhaps, you'll reply to that letter and agree to an interview with Mrs Samuels. And only when you have had a chance to ascertain the true character of the lady involved . . . the terms and conditions she offers . . . only then need any decision be made. I have heard she is of a most generous nature, a most—'

'And since when did *you* come to have such an intimate knowledge of that household of infidels?'

Mr Collins flinched at Mama's response, and taking a small step back, his heel squashed down into his pastry and his elbow bumped hard on the cast iron hearth, which only seemed to drive him on. 'Mrs Samuels does not work in the theatre, and neither is she of Jewish extraction . . . if that is what you mean to imply!' By then, he was losing all patience, his usually mild manner turned fierce and indignant. 'I held Cissy's friendship in the highest regard. I was proud that she often confided in me. I know she cared deeply for Mr Samuels, and it is my firm belief that this man you portray as the Devil incarnate once felt much the same about her. I make no claim to know every detail about their private situation, or what occurred to cause their rift . . . but surely *none* of us should judge.'

That stark confrontation silenced Mama, if only for a moment or two, after which she stood up, and with trembling breaths she bade her old friend a calm goodnight. And, once he'd been ushered out of the parlour, once she'd dragged his hat and coat from the stand, thrusting both items into his arms, Mr Collins made his way through the door which Mama then slammed very firmly behind.

But then, like two bickering lovers keen to make up

after having a tiff, by the following afternoon he was back. And, with their differences resolved, beneath Mr Collins' watchful eye, Mama sat down with a pen in her hand and made a reply to that letter.

13

The houses in Hyde Park Gate, of which there were only five or six, were all very large and set apart as they bordered a quiet secluded road. It actually led to no others, but looped around circular gardens so that any carriage driving in need only follow that crescent round to find itself at the approach again. Down at the end nearest Kensington Road and viewed behind tall iron railings, Mr Samuels' house was stuccoed white, all classical columns and balconied windows, and only the shortest of walks away were the big metal gates into Kensington Gardens, and beyond them wide walkways, lush borders of flowers, everything smelling new and green. No cloying sweet burn from the sugar refineries. No sulphurous cloud from Bryant and May's to form a thick pall over his part of town.

During our journey Mama looked dour, but I was goggle-eyed at the passing sights. I'd seen Westminster, and Buckingham Palace before, but not the new Kensington museums – great Gothic structures like sprawling cathedrals – and no less impressed when we passed the vast frontage of Samuels' emporium, seeing those red and gilt shop signs, and the red and gilt flags that flew above, and enormous plate glass windows with hundreds of miniature blazing jets that shimmered like water, like rippling gold, all over the precious wares displayed. I thought to ask Mama if we'd ever been. I felt such a strong sense of déjà vu. But her head was bowed as if in prayer, her eyes firmly closed, intent on mumbling some biblical quote. The one about rich men and camels and needles.

When the Samuels' front door was opened up we were faced by a butler whose thin yellow hair had been plastered down flat to a bulbous head. Unblinking eyes gazed out at a point vaguely over our shoulders. A hooked finger lifted to beckon us in. Our feet echoed loud on the marble tiles and, while Mama and I were left there to wait, I stared up in awe at a staircase that split into two as it reached the first floor. At first I thought I saw a face, looking down from the landing that circled above, but it was only a trick of the light, the shadows flickering around. No one spied on me from *that* balcony, not as I'd once done in Wilton's Hall; an occasion of which I'd not thought in months. Too painful to think about Cissy that night, and how lovely she'd looked on that stage, and that glimmer of love briefly offered to me by the stranger whose name I'd never known.

Where Wilton's had those exotic murals, the Samuels' house had a tall arching window set at the very top of the stairs. It looked like something you'd find in a church – a Garden of Eden with flowers and birds, with lovely colours shafting down to spread and dilute on the floor at our feet. I thought Mama might approve of that; less so the pictures that covered the walls: mythical settings where scantily clad maidens cowered from dragons, or posed as drowned corpses in flower-strewn streams. There were some wonderful landscapes, viewed as if through a watery lens – muted splashings of sheer liquid colour at which Mama tutted, grumbling under her breath that the artist had needed spectacles. She told me to sit down at her side on a settle. She told me to try and stay still or else risk completely dislodging my bustle, by which time the butler returned to announce, 'Mrs Samuels will see you now.'

Ushered into a room at the back of the house, the sunshine was blinding at first. My eyes made out a blurred silhouette, a tall slender woman standing in front of a pair of open garden doors. She drew nearer. I saw she was dressed in white, with small beads of pearls stitched high at her throat, and her hair, very fair, was streaked lightly with grey which glinted like silver when caught by the light. Long racemes of wisteria were hanging behind, a mauve curtain that dripped from gnarled branches, and as I breathed in that powdery scent, for a moment the long whippy tendrils of green looked like snakes uncoiling and stretching towards me.

Beyond them, I saw a stone terrace, a square of perfectly manicured lawn edged with box hedging, and straight gravel walkways leading on into a dark arching tunnel. Compared to our own neglected back garden, this was a miniature paradise, this woman its guardian angel, though I have to confess to a slight disappointment when I realised that she was alone, with no Mr Samuels to greet us that day which, I supposed, was for the best, with Mama holding such disdain for the man.

As usual I was dressed in black. As usual I felt very dowdy and drab; my skirts grown too short in the hem, too tight in the bodice, the velvet too hot for such a mild day. A wonder Mama did not faint with the heat, wearing so many layers of crepe, a fringed woollen shawl and felt winter hat, and though fanning a hand in front of her face, nothing reduced the puce of her cheeks over which the sweat dribbled down from her brow.

Mrs Samuels looked cool, smelled of lavender. When I dared to glance at her face, I realised that she and Mama were probably of a similar age, that behind a thick layer of powder, her skin was slightly lined, and what appeared a pale pallor at first could not conceal spots of red at the cheeks – not so unlike the tubercular bloom that I'd seen on the faces of dirty old men who sat and begged on the Mile End Road.

'May I offer you some tea?' She addressed Mama in a low, husky voice, motioning towards a round table where we were to sit on the silk-covered chairs, where a breeze hushed in through the garden doors, where the lace panels swelled then blew out again.

Mrs Samuels stared intently at me and, despite being shadowed and heavy beneath, her blue eyes were glistening like diamonds when she turned to speak with Mama. 'My husband is otherwise occupied though no doubt he preferred us to meet alone. He finds these domestic matters too trivial by far.'

'Trivial?' Mama tilted her chin, as if she was set for a sparring match. 'I presumed we were here to discuss my daughter's role in your household. If that is considered a trivial matter, then—'

'Mrs Turner, forgive me. I have a habit of speaking too plainly. But then, I imagine you are also a woman who prefers to adhere to clarity' – she paused, one of her brows slightly arched – 'for the truth to be exposed?'

Mama did not reply, if anything looked a little cowed, and Mrs Samuels was lost in her thoughts, a long finger stroking the rim of her cup, though, when I lifted my tea to my lips, the tinkle of china betrayed my nerves, drawing her attention again. While gazing at me, she asked Mama, 'Mrs Turner, as Phoebe is your only daughter, will you not find it too lonely without her? It is my understanding that you are a widow.'

Mama nodded. 'It is very hard. If it were not for necessity . . .'

'Ah, yes. My husband did explain the delicacy of your circumstance. How your families were once well known to each other, how he sees this opportunity as a way to ease both our burdens. But then, this position is all of his making, a companion for me being something to ease his own conscience . . . while he remains here in town, while I spend my time in the country. I wonder,' she looked at me, 'would you not find that too dull? How would you begin to amuse yourself? Do you play any instruments or perhaps . . . sing? Of course, there is Bodlington church.' A slight frown before she carried on, 'I *think* they have a choir.'

At the mention of singing I felt sick inside. Did Mrs Samuels know about Cissy? I glanced back at Mama to seek some direction, but Mama only avoided my eye, and left unaided I stammered an answer. 'I . . . I do play the piano, though not very well. I can sing, but only passably. I really don't possess any talent. But I read a great deal, and I like to sketch.'

'These interests may be sufficient. But would you feel comfortable with me? I am old enough to be your mother.'

Again I hesitated, deciding that whatever I said Mrs Samuels was going to send us away, that she had not taken to me at all. 'I don't really know anyone my own age. I've never minded that before . . .' I trailed off, aware of how odd that must sound. But I'd never felt lonely. I'd never felt bored – at least, not when Cissy was still in the house.

Mrs Samuels looked quizzical, then smiled, as if all reservations had floated away. 'I like you, Miss Turner. Perhaps we should see how we get on. But, for now, I suggest you go back home and think carefully on this proposal. You will be leaving all that you know, and Herefordshire could not be more different to London.'

She glanced out at the garden before going on, 'A mother has need of a daughter. Sons are different, only ever on loan, too soon taking up their own lives and concerns. Our daughters are our truest friends. They never really leave.'

Mama stiffened and turned very pale. Those words must have cut her deeply, because if I accepted this offer then she was the one who would be alone. And, while pondering that, feeling very glum, I heard Mrs Samuels question me.

'How old are you, Miss Turner?'

'I was seventeen, this past February.'

'February . . .'

She broke off. From out in the hall came the dull beat of footsteps, and then a closing door, and during the silence that followed her fingers plucked the tablecloth's lace until, all at once, she stood, and then made to leave the room, only once turning back to say, 'Well, Phoebe Turner, my husband may be right. Perhaps you will do me some good after all.'

The next morning I stood at Cissy's piano, picking out a few random notes and worrying so about leaving Mama. Steeling my courage, I went down to the kitchen and there she was waiting, already up, the table laid with the best china service, some opened post lying next to her plate. Tensing myself for more recriminations, I lifted one of the envelopes. The frank was strange and I ventured to ask, 'What's this, Mama? Who is it from?'

It was snatched from my hand and stuffed into her pocket, and Mama was blushing when she replied, 'That is no concern of yours. It's from an old friend in America who has recently heard of Cissy's death. But look, Phoebe!' She pointed to another letter, her chest puffing out like a smug black hen. 'Mr Samuels has also written today, sending his terms of employment. I would never have swayed you, of course, you know that, but he quite understands my dilemma. He says you are free to come back and visit at least once a quarter, and in return, as long as you live with the Samuels, this house is secured for me, all expenses waived in lieu of your wages. But then, you won't need any money. You'll have everything you need . . . and Mrs Samuels has added a note, requesting we send on your measurements. She must be providing a uniform.'

'Then you really don't mind if I go, after all?' It was hard to take in such a change of heart; another example of Mama's convenient hypocrisy as, blind to my own consternation, she said, 'Whatever misgivings I may have had with regard to Nathaniel Samuels, his wife is all that Mr Collins suggested . . . a most benevolent woman.'

Very benevolent indeed! How many companions were employed on such terms? Surely it wasn't normal. Where my own mood had been eager before, now I was filled with nothing but doubt. But too late because by the end of the week, before I had even started to pack, Mama – her spirits much revived – had already employed a new gardener and instructed the nearest agency to find her a maid and a cook, and it seemed that the chance of reclaiming her life was all that it took to surrender mine, to let that frayed end of rope drop to the floor. I could almost think that with Cissy gone, there was no reason to fight any more, no reason to go on with the game, that tug of war they used to play, the war Mr Samuels had won.

14

The shop had already been closed up when Nathaniel Samuels shook hands with his guests and wished them good evening. Walking as far as the office door, where the corridor was all shadow and murk, he lingered to watch his assistant escort the two gentlemen away. Turning back, he stared hard at the ornate glass with the swirling gilt letters that formed his name, behind them the polished panelled walls, the bookshelves and desks and cabinets, the tall palms each side of double doors that separated this formal frontage from his private rooms.

There, the negotiations had reached their conclusion – but what a tedious afternoon, hours and hours spent with the textiles curators who'd come from the Victoria and Albert Museum, their institution keen to acquire some of Samuels' antique embroideries. The arrangement would be a lucrative one; and no harm to the shop's reputation. There had been a time when his heart might rejoice to secure such prestigious connections, but Nathaniel found it hard to care, his mind fixed on other, more personal transactions.

With slow, heavy steps he returned to his desk. He sat and stared at the exquisite fabrics still strewn across tables and chairs. Who could fail to admire such treasures, some of which were centuries old? Patterned block-prints with threads of gold, tiny mirrors and pearls and glittering jewels which trapped and reflected the fading light. Set against dark mahogany walls, the depth of their colour and texture was stunning. The last shipment had been remarkable. His son had done well in India, better than Nathaniel had expected, proving to have a discerning eye for the buying of art and antiquities.

But then, last week, the letter arrived to say that Joseph would soon be home, having recently become engaged to be married. Nathaniel knew the girl's name, was already acquainted with her father, though he doubted Lord Faulkener would approve or allow such a union to proceed – unless things had already proceeded too far. The two men had long-standing business connections; the store buying in large quantities of the cottons and silks produced by Faulkener's Bombay factories. But, as far as trading a daughter went, Nathaniel suspected the price of that stock would not descend to the offer of a bridegroom whose veins ran rich with the blood of a Jew.

Hadn't Lydia's father been the same? Nathaniel would wait until Joseph was back, to assess the degree of Lord Faulkener's offence before telling his wife the news. No reason to cause her distress when such prejudice might only reopen old scars, though, for himself, Nathaniel was now inured to the festering hypocrisy at the heart of the British Establishment – at the centre of which he once yearned to belong.

Not any longer. What was it that Isaac used to say? *A wolf might lose his hair, but he does not lose his nature.* A wolf would always be an outsider, a creature to be reviled and feared. But what was Nathaniel's nature now? He hardly knew himself – only that since the arrangements were made for Phoebe Turner to leave her home and live with his wife in Herefordshire, he'd felt such a sense of shame.

It was a sordid game he'd played, and the speed of concession surprised him, both on the part of his wife and on that of Maud Turner. He'd expected a lengthier siege, but the way Lydia had acquiesced when he suggested she take a companion, and then to accept the girl like that, with no questions asked, and all civilised smiles when, after the interview was done, she'd turned up unexpectedly at the shop to inform him of her decision.

How ironic that after all of his scheming Nathaniel had come to suspect his wife, uncertain of what her motives might be. She'd made some veiled reference to Cissy's death – but did that mean she knew of the family connection? Still, if she knew, if she took the girl on and chose to pretend things were otherwise, well, wasn't pretence his wife's forte?

Why should he deny his affections? If he couldn't have Cissy, he'd take the girl, whatever the cost might happen to be. And as it turned out that price was no more than that of a house he already owned. He'd expected Maud Turner to fight tooth and claw. He'd been convinced she would call his bluff, standing firm by her pride and principles, vacating her home in Tredegar Square to knock on the doors of the workhouse instead. That would have pleased him most – to leave her to rot and beg on the streets while he offered her daughter salvation. What sweet revenge that would have been for the grief that woman once brought to him. But this time he would keep his purchase close. This time he knew all the bitch's tricks. A case of once bitten, twice shy.

When Maud brought Phoebe along to Hyde Park Gate he'd looked down to the hall from the landing above, at which point he could do nothing more than wait, because everyone's fates lay in Lydia's hands, whatever decision she made that day.

His eyes had been drawn to the girl. Even though she'd lost weight since the funeral and was dressed in ugly black garb, it couldn't disguise her beauty. She'd looked so appealing down there, with her face bathed in colours of light from the window, feet fidgeting, shuffling over the floor. Her features reflected so little of Maud's, so much more of Cissy's when she was that age. Thinking of that, he'd almost stepped forward out of the shadows—

When the butler called them through to his wife, Nathaniel managed to gather himself, to walk down the stairs and leave the house. Hearing no more than a clumping thud as the front door closed behind, he'd stepped through the open garden gate and stood absolutely still on the pavement, as if he'd forgotten who he was, as if he no longer knew where he belonged. There was his carriage, the driver sitting erect on his box, four matched bays groomed and glossed to perfection. The sunlight was blinding. It glanced off the harness. It sparkled on lacquer, subdued by the darker gloom within. That gloom was not waiting for him, but the visitors soon to return to Bow.

Walking to the shop through the park that day, Nathaniel's mind eventually cleared. Perhaps he had not lost all passion, the desire to live and love again. Yet, even if everything went to plan and Lydia chose to employ the girl, he would have to be patient and wait, until Phoebe had settled in her new life – well away from scandal and prying eyes.

Nathaniel turned to the door, his reverie interrupted by the sense of being watched. Abruptly, he told his assistant to leave. He would deal with the textile samples himself, folding them, locking them up for safe keeping. Time enough in the morning to arrange for the paperwork and delivery.

When sure of being alone again, he reached forward and lifted the nearest shawl, running the cloth through his fingers, its texture as fluid as water. He was thinking how well it might look upon Cissy, when suddenly jolted back to the present, as if physically struck by the pain of his loss, of his memory's cruel aberration. His vision blurred. The shawl slipped, whispering through his fingers, a small silky pool on the floor.

PART TWO

Wretched lovers! Fate has passed
This sad decree: no joy shall last.

(From Handel's *Acis and Galatea*)

15

10th May, 1882

Dearest Mama,

    I hope all is well in Tredegar Square. I am safely arrived here at Dinwood Court, though the journey took over ten hours, the train much delayed by a tree fallen down on the tracks in a storm. Consequently, I reached the house very late, only to find Mrs Samuels out, having been called back to London on some urgent matter of business. I have no idea as to what it could be.

    Not that I am alone. There are several members of staff around, but they leave me to do more or less as I please. I have spent many hours exploring the house, and in truth it is more like a castle. It even has crenellations and towers, and so many winding passages. I have found myself lost more than once. I am almost afraid to touch anything, such fine ornaments and furnishings there are, except for the hallway and corridors which remain as they would have been centuries past, really very grim, with dark panelled walls and worn stone floors and blackened old portraits staring down.

    There is a music room — very grand. But now, as I write, I am sitting in the library. I like it here best of all and due to the constant rain outside it is where I am spending most of my time, playing patience, reading books and magazines, and newspapers delivered most every day.

My own room is at the back of the house, overlooking a courtyard garden, and behind that are great swathes of woodland. The countryside here is best described as resembling Mr Constable's paintings, all very rural and picturesque, and not a trace of smog in the air. But it is very isolated, and that is the hardest thing. Sometimes, when the wind blows in the right direction, I do hear the train running past in the distance, but mostly there is nothing but quiet, just birds singing, just fields, just sheep and trees. I might be Eve in the Garden of Eden. But, Mama, please do not be alarmed. There is no Adam residing here, unless you count the gardeners who potter around in the pouring rain and, from what I have seen of them so far, not one could be much less than ninety years.

For now, that is my news. I shall keep this letter and hope to add more when Mrs Samuels returns to the house. In the meantime, I am often thinking of you and send you my fondest affection,

Your own loving child,

Phoebe Turner

PS. Could you send me Old Riley's address? The details she gave me got wet in the rain and the ink is all run and unreadable.

A strange and isolated time. What I didn't tell Mama – what I didn't write on that pristine white paper, *Dinwood Court* embossed in gold at the top – was quite how alone and discarded I felt, as if I'd been banished to Limbo Land, where every day was exactly the same, where I seemed to be walking through water, where I thought I should drown in a daze of homesickness – though mostly it was Cissy I missed. And Cissy would never be seen again, wherever I happened to live.

Those first mornings, when it was so dull and wet, I spent most of my time in the library, peering at glass-fronted cabinets – collections with faded copperplate labels and dates going back over centuries. There were rows of shells and ammonites, and other strange fossilised conical stones. There were gleaming, armoured beetles, and butterflies speared on glistening pins; their fragile wings of such gorgeous hues. But those glass fronts were dusty, sometimes even cracked, and the contents were littered with dried husks of dead flies, soiled with black spots of their faeces.

Sometimes I took sheets of that headed paper and used it to make inky sketches, trying to capture the gardens outside. At others I looked through magazines, or pulled down books from mahogany shelves and read them for hours until it was dark, when the library grew less welcoming. If the temperature had not been so mild, I might have asked for a fire to be lit to bring some life to the big stone hearth. But instead, as dusk fell, I stared listlessly out through the windows, watching the low and slanting light as I tried to imagine how it would be with sunshine flooding into the house, taking on quite a different complexion. As it was, if not for the thrash of rain, my new world was as silent and grey as the grave – and that world sucked me in, every day growing yet more lethargic.

In Bow, there had always been some sort of noise: Cissy singing, the clatter of horse hooves and wheels in the street, the roistering shouts from the public house that stood on the corner of Coburn Road. Mama used to say it was a good thing that the square's garden gates were locked up at dusk, keeping those sinful drunkards out. But then, she slept in a room at the back, and there were some nights when I peeked through the curtains and watched as those men clambered over the railings. And some mornings I saw them still there, groaning, or lolling unconscious on grass, surrounded by bottles and broken glass.

In Herefordshire, I began to fear that perhaps I'd been drunk and insensible, far too willing to enter a different world, to leave Mama's prison in Tredegar Square, only to find myself trapped in another.

I'd never travelled by train before. It was frightening. It was exciting. Sitting alone in a first-class compartment, staring out through the smuts and fiery sparks that blew from the engine's funnel, I saw the backs of tall tenement buildings, broken windows from which washing lines were suspended, and most of them draped with shabby rags. But there was one shift, so white, so fine, it didn't look real. It looked like a fluttering ghost to me.

We passed stretches of ugly industrial landscape, ramshackle tin shelters and endless successions of telegraph poles, until – so much sooner than I had expected – there were fields, with cows and sheep and pigs, and a farmer urging on a horse, his plough cutting furrows in rich red soil.

The further we went, the more anxious I felt, with no notion of what to be frightened about, and no mental picture of where I was heading except for a hazy mist of 'not knowing'. But, lulled by the rhythmic rock of the carriage, soon I was yawning and must have dozed off. I dreamed about Mrs Samuels, who was smiling and beckoning to me – though when the train screeched to a juddering halt, I came to with a gasp, blinking my eyes to see driving diagonal streaks of rain lashing down over the windows outside. And when I looked up through the dimming light, I saw a peaked cap, two bloodshot eyes, two flabby jowls like loose slabs of meat that wobbled about when the guard proclaimed abruptly, 'We've stopped! I've come to light the gas. There's a tree got blown down on the line. We'll be stuck 'ere a while till they move it.'

'Oh.' I stood up, looking out at the steep grassy sidings, the shingled tracks all puddled and bleak, and no sign of a platform anywhere. I asked with a growing note of alarm, 'Do you happen to know what time we'll arrive? Are we very far away?'

'That depends where you're heading to, miss, and how long it takes to get going again.'

'Dinwood. Dinwood Court. I'm being met at the station at six.'

'Well, we're almost there now . . . though only the good Lord knows what time he intends us arriving. Still, don't you be moithered. You're perfectly safe, though the last time such an event occurred we were stuck on the tracks for the rest of the night . . . had passengers kipping down on the benches, snuggling up together for warmth.' He chuckled − a foul whiff of onion breath. 'They should have got out and walked instead. Shanks's pony would have been faster than the Great Western was that day.'

I sat down, feeling nervous at what might come next, determined that no one should 'snuggle' with me as I thought back to Mama's warning: 'Never let your bags out of sight, and never speak to any strange men. A young woman travelling alone may lure undesired attention.'

Well, I didn't know about any strange men, but I

didn't much like that guard, and while he fiddled around with the gas I picked up the *London Illustrated*, which a previous passenger had left. I held it high to cover my face, but I couldn't concentrate to read, only able to glance at the pictures instead, and advertisements for *Wright's Coal Tar Soap*, or *Floriline for the teeth and breath* had never seemed so alluring – what with that guard's breath wafting around. I was much relieved when the gas flickered up, when he left and closed the door behind. But several hours were to pass before the train moved on again, before the guard was back to warn, 'Next stop's Hereford. After that's Dinwood . . . a short way down the line. Once we come out of the tunnel, you're there.'

The carriage lights dipped, the noise of the engine grew horribly loud and my ears became blocked, as if stuffed up with rags – a *pop pop popping* whenever I swallowed. I feared we might be buried alive, rushing headlong into the darkness like that, and I thought of Old Riley at Paddington station, kissing me hard on both cheeks as she pressed a paper into my hand on which she had written her address. She'd been tutting at Mama's threats of strange men. She'd said, 'Maud Turner, whatever next! You'll have this poor child believing she's about to set off for Hell.'

Well, I began to think I was, with the train's whistle screaming like Beelzebub, and delving a hand deep into my pocket, I clutched at Old Riley's address as if it might be a talisman, to give me luck, to keep me safe. My free hand was groping forward to rest on the handle of my trunk. Mr Collins had dragged that onto the train, stumbling and puffing, pushing Old Riley aside as he murmured some words of advice to me – which was when the shrill whistle blasted, announcing the train was set to depart, and Mama was left with no more than a moment to give me her trembling hug, though she seemed unwilling to look in my eye, or perhaps she didn't want me to see whatever emotion lay behind hers.

As the engine chugged off I drew down the window and leaned out as far as I possibly dared, waving at Mama still there on the platform, seeing her lift a hand to an eye, and it might have been to brush off a tear, or perhaps it was only to rub at some grit because, after that, when she turned to face Mr Collins whose hand was supporting her arm, her expression seemed more like relief than regret, as if my leaving was setting her free. It's hard to describe how I felt – like an object no longer of use, like a parcel packed up in string and brown paper, dispatched without a second thought. And later, within that dark tunnel, one thing was crystal clear. Nothing was certain any more. No one could know what the future held, when people as young as Cissy died, when cherished things could be stolen or sold. And, where I had once been her valued possession, now Mama seemed more concerned with a uniformed maid to scrub the steps and polish the brass on the door.

The last I saw of Mama that day, she was dwarfed beneath Paddington station's vast arching structure of iron and glass, then lost in the billowing clouds of steam through which the diminishing criss-crossing tracks looked to me like winding lengths of rope, as tangled and muddled as my thoughts when I tried to recall Mr Collins' words – 'You know, this is all for the best, my dear. And you mustn't think badly of Maud. Everyone prospers from such an arrangement.'

If there had been time, I might have remarked on how *he* appeared to be prospering, attired in new suits and red waistcoats, his straggly beard trimmed and oiled. And during those last weeks before my departure I'd started to have wicked thoughts, fretting that his transformation had been all too coincidental, coming so soon on the theft of our Millais – for hadn't he left the kitchen door open, after practically drowning my mother in brandy, then offering more to me; something in that chocolate to help me rest?

But Old Riley had laughed when I broached my suspicions. She said I was being too fanciful. She said that I should take it from her – Eddie Collins was gaining deserved success, making his mark in the halls at last. She said I should be happy and wish him luck. She said I wasn't the only one about to embark on a brand new life.

16

My new life began at the end of that tunnel. The train slowed to a shuddering halt. The guard reappeared to give me a hand which, it transpired, involved no more than flinging my trunk down the steps, where it splashed into puddles which drenched my skirts. But then, I was soon to be soaked from above, the rain streaming down through the weave of my hat. Half choked from the engine's sooty steam, I lifted a hand to wipe my eyes, blinking hard as I watched the train depart, its carriages trailing into the gloom; a swaying necklace of blurring gold.

I could hardly have felt more miserable. There I was half-blind and abandoned in some godforsaken place which amounted to two narrow platforms and a rickety bridge in between. A creaking sign said DINWOOD and, below that, the hands of a big round clock were pointing to after eleven o'clock. I knocked at the ticket office door, which was locked, with no sign of any life. The door beside that bore a nameplate – THE DINWOOD CIDER COMPANY – and behind barred windows were barrels and bottles, and some other slinking shapes which I feared could only be vermin. Pushing through a creaking gate at the side I saw nothing but piles of logs and slag. I shouted 'hello' but my voice was drowned out in the beat of the rain. Much dejected, I went back to sit on my trunk, wondering what to do for the best – which is when I saw the light of a lantern, the thin silhouette of an arm reaching out, impossibly long, with a hook at the end, and having read all those sensational stories where young women were lost to cruel fates on dark nights, I became quite convinced that this was some lunatic monster set on a blood-crazed, murdering spree. But when I opened my mouth to scream, a deep burring voice was asking me, 'Is it Miss Turner . . . Miss Turner come for Dinwood Court?'

Raising a hand to my brow, shielding my eyes from the rain once more, I saw no monster, only an old man in a drooping straw hat with a fringe of white hair plastered wet to his brow. His chin was hoary with stubble. His cheeks were threaded purple with veins, but his eyes were a clear and sparkling brown, looking friendly enough as I nervously said, 'Yes . . . that's me. Who are you?'

'Tom Meldicott, been sent to collect you, miss. Brought this here umbrella along, though there's little point by the looks of you now. We might as well cover up a drowned rat!'

Seeing what he was holding, I felt very foolish, and was startled again when he yelled, 'Jim, get yourself around here and give me a hand with this luggage before the whole lot gets washed down the tracks.' And then, more gently, taking my arm, he said, 'Come along, miss. You'll have to excuse us, not having the carriage, but Jim's fixed up a bit of tarpaulin.'

A bit late for that, wet through to the skin I found myself in a rattling trap, a draughty, flapping roof on top, and with both hands gripping the greasy side I tried not to slip on the splintery bench while continually listing towards the boy Jim. His appearance, being skinny and short, had already belied his strength, for he easily carried my trunk from the platform, slinging it into the back of the cart, and now he glanced sideways through darting eyes, enquiring in a reedy voice, 'You some sort of relative, then?'

From his place at the front, in the driver's seat, Mr Meldicott craned his neck to say, 'Miss Turner, you'll 'ave to excuse our Jim. He's not best blessed with manners. He should button his mouth and leave you in peace.'

Jim scowled grudgingly and slumped low in a sulk. I took off my hat and rubbed my eyes, looking ahead where the road glowed beneath Mr Meldicott's lantern, where there were no pavements, only verges of grass, muddy ditches and hedges with white flowers gleaming. The air smelled damp and mushroomy. A few windows radiated light. Now and then a curious face stared out. I supposed visitors must be rare events, particularly those arriving so late, and on such inhospitable nights.

Mr Meldicott whistled some popular tune, something that Cissy once used to sing, though I couldn't remember the name. His accompaniment was the clop of the hooves, the squeaking splashing of big wooden wheels, the drip, drip, dripping from branches above where trees on either side of the road formed a dark arching tunnel high over our heads. From time to time he stopped, clicked his tongue, soothing the horse when it whinnied or shied, skitting at shadows that danced ahead.

I shivered and yawned with exhaustion, finally letting my eyes droop closed, only stirring when Jim pushed my head from his shoulder, when he jumped from the cart to close up some gates which, being of iron, very heavy and large, made the most horrible clanking sound. And now, wide awake from that raucous alarm, as we drove on past expanses of lawns, nothing prevented my view of the house – a central square tower above an arched entrance, castellated walls running either side, and so many windows, I couldn't count, and each one unlit and unwelcoming. But as the moon's face broke through fast-scudding clouds I saw something else that quite took my breath, the thing that was lying behind that house, spreading upwards and outwards for several miles: the dense, sloping woodlands that glistened like silver. Being quite overawed, and sounding far more like Old Riley than me, I exclaimed, 'Strike a light! What a wonder. I've never seen so many trees in my life.'

The boy answered back with a grin. 'Ain't you never seen woods before? The train would have travelled beneath the whole lot.'

'Oh.' I hardly knew what to say. It was all beyond what I'd expected, even after that grand house in Hyde Park Gate. 'Mr Samuels must be a very rich man.'

'Ain't his to own!' Mr Meldicott's answer was blunt. 'Everything you see here belongs to his wife.'

As he spoke, the trap rattled under an arch, coming to a halt in a cobbled yard where, from the high stone walls around, several gargoyles were staring down on us – monstrous menacing features most of them had, with wide-open mouths that still spewed with trickling twists of rain, draining from gutters and roofs above.

This time, Mr Meldicott dealt with my trunk. But before running off, and who knew where to, Jim pulled on the bell of a studded oak door; like something you'd see in a dungeon. Above that, a scroll had been engraved with the year of 1452, and I thought that the house must be terribly ancient, and I feared I might be about to enter some grimly Gothic world resembling Mr Walpole's *Castle of Otranto*.

With my feet planted once again on firm ground, I asked Mr Meldicott timidly, 'Do you think Mrs Samuels will still be awake? She must be wondering what happened to me.'

'I shouldn't imagine she's that much concerned,' the old man answered through a snort. 'Not unless you're expected up London way.'

'She's in London?'

Had he heard the dismay in my voice? He answered more sympathetically. 'Well, I reckon it came as a shock to her too, to be called back up there again, so soon. She took the carriage, early this morning, what with the trains all being delayed. I can't say that she was very much pleased.'

17

When I woke, I didn't know where I was. I saw yellow walls, Chinese flowers and birds; a far prettier sight than those gargoyles outside, or the big draughty hall with its long shadowed bars thrown down from stone balustrades above.

The previous night, with very little ceremony, I had been led up some wide stone stairs where several frayed tapestries hung on the walls, mostly depicting woodland scenes where foxes were being chased by hounds, where deer seemed almost to be alive, leaping through the wavering light of the candle held high by a yawning maid.

When we reached the first floor the maid turned left, trudging on down a long passageway where the candle hissed and smoked, where the floorboards were whining under our feet, repeated by Mr Meldicott's moans as he struggled behind with my trunk. Finally, the maid opened a door. Mr Meldicott's burden thumped down to the floor and, when I assured them both that I wanted no help with unpacking my things, and had no desire to eat or drink, they wished me goodnight and left me alone, with only a fluttering light on the stand to give any warmth or company. But, being exhausted and desperate for sleep, I longed for no more than to strip off my clothes and to change into something dry and warm –

which was when I discovered my trunk had been leaking, every item of clothing within it wet through.

Determined not to cry, shivering and miserable, I stripped naked and crept beneath cold starched sheets, hugging myself into a ball. When the candle eventually died, I'd never known a world so black, where even with the shutters left open, the sky was so big and dense with cloud, any light from the moon completely obscured. I bit every fingernail down to the quick as my eyes darted round through the murk of that room, my heart thumping hard at strange noises outside, the mournful hootings and shrieks and howls; everything alien, animal. But as the hours of night passed by, as the rain resumed then eased again, its thin hissing afforded a comforting sound and I almost believed it might be the street lamp outside my room in Tredegar Square. And when the misty fingers of dawn began to edge their way into the room, my eyes closed. I sank into a dreamless sleep.

A knock at the door. A maid came in. A different one from the night before. Not that I'd taken much notice then. This one wore a blue dress and a starched white cap. Some fair curls stuck out at the side. She had big brown eyes which were very round. She looked to be about thirty years old.

Addressing the bed in the same earthy brogue as Mr Meldicott before, she said, 'Morning, miss, I've brought you some . . .'

Breaking off in confusion, she peered round the room, finding me already up and standing in the window bay, still quite naked but for the sheet dragged around.

I'd been staring down at a formal walled garden where three of the surrounding walls were actually wings of the house itself, and at the far end was a hedge, within which an arch led through to some lawns, and then another boundary wall, very much lower, grown over with ivy. Beyond that there were the meadows, and then the rising escarpment of woodlands; a natural expanse of such vivid green, even more stunning in morning light. I felt as if I'd been cast in its spell, until something different caught my eye: the fountain set under my window, a lovely stone nymph surrounded by shells; though there was no song escaping her lips, only the incessant trickle of water. It put me in mind of Cissy, and how she would never sing again, and how poignant and raw was the grief of her loss, still able to twist like a knife in my breast.

The maid brought some welcome distraction, even if she did blush and turn away, still clutching onto her breakfast tray as I snatched some of yesterday's clothes from the floor, a twisted damp muddle of black and white. Struggling to pull a shift over my head, I eventually managed to cover my shame and announced, 'You can look. I'm decent again.'

'I'm sorry, miss . . .' she glanced over her shoulder, 'I came up before and you didn't stir. But now, with it being gone ten o'clock, we assumed you'd be hungry and . . .'

'Gone ten o'clock! Is it really that late? It's so quiet here, so different to where I . . .' I was going to say where I belong.

With her tray now set down on a table, the maid looked a little cheerier, asking, 'Do you like your room? Mrs Samuels had it done out in a rush . . . new paint, new paper, new everything. Sent her own tradesmen from London, she did.'

It was very opulent. I looked at the bed in which I'd

slept, where pretty wooden barley-twist posts had been draped in a fabric the colour of corn. Against one wall was a white marble hearth ornamented with flowers and grapes and leaves. Silk cushions were spread on a window seat and, in the opposite bay, a dressing table had been placed. Even on mornings as dreary as that, when surrounded by those yellow walls you might sit there and think yourself bathed in gold.

But, before I could give any answer, the maid was wittering on, 'Well of course, you'll have come from their London house. I dare say it's all very splendid there.' And then she gave me a sideways look. 'Perhaps you've some news of Joseph for us?'

'I'm sorry. I have come from London, but . . .' I had no clue who this Joseph could be and simply explained the state of my dress. 'I'm afraid my clothes . . . everything in my trunk got soaked in the storm last night.'

She sniffed. 'It does smell a bit dank. I'll take your things down to the laundry, get everything washed and pressed.'

'Will that take very long? It's just that I've nothing else to wear.'

She looked surprised. 'Didn't that girl explain last night? There's a wardrobe next door, full of new things, everything you could possibly need. I unpacked all the boxes myself . . . everything sent from Samuels'.'

Mute as a shadow, I followed behind as she opened up another door. I hadn't even noticed it there, painted with the same oriental designs as those that covered the bedroom walls. A narrow corridor behind led the way to a bathroom – a room that I desperately needed to use – and opposite that a dressing room, with a tall chest of drawers and a mirrored armoire in which, when its doors had been opened up, I saw rows and rows of hanging gowns, shelves full of shoes and boots and gloves and under-garments and stockings and lace – even hats and shawls and fans. It was almost like standing inside a shop, inhaling the lovely sweet smell of new cloth. It was all I could do not to laugh out loud, to rush forward and search through those treasures at once. Instead of which I meekly said, 'Mrs Samuels is . . . she is very kind. I thought to be wearing a uniform. But there doesn't appear to be anything black. I'm not sure what Mama would . . .'

My voice broke off, and even though the day was mild, with me being dressed in that clinging damp shift, I found myself cold and shivering.

'Black!' the maid exclaimed in shock. 'Are you in mourning then? Only, Mrs Samuels won't have black in the house . . . except for the gentlemen of course.'

'I was wearing black when I met her before. She made no mention about it then.'

The maid gave me a long hard look, and I felt yet more unnerved when she said, 'We expected someone a bit older than you . . . more of the spinsterish type. Not that she's had a companion before.'

'When do you think she's coming back?'

'I really don't know. But she left you a letter. It's there, next door, on the breakfast tray.'

A little while later, having sipped some cold tea and eaten cold toast, having brushed all the buttery crumbs from my hands, I opened Mrs Samuels' letter. It was really no more than a few scribbled lines in which she apologised for her absence, saying she hoped to return very shortly and, in the meantime, I must be sure to treat Dinwood Court as if it were my own.

Setting the page back down on the tray, I watched as the maid pulled the clothes from my trunk. Only when she'd gone again did I think of the box that I'd packed in the base, in which had been placed all my personal effects, including Aunt Cissy's scrapbook – and what a relief it was to find that tin perfectly watertight; everything in it undamaged and dry.

There was the little brass frame that Mama pressed into my hands as I packed, the one from her wedding day. I barely knew the woman there, smiling, fresh-faced, her eyes filled with light – though my father, for all his youth, looked no less stern and daunting to me than he did in that picture she kept by her bed. And, with only the slightest twinge of guilt, I opened a drawer in the dressing table and hid that picture away at the back. Mama need never know.

From a velvet pouch, I drew out Cissy's silver locket. Even though the day was dull, its light caught the diamond set in the front, causing the facets to glisten and flash as I opened the filigree casing and looked at the strands of hair inside.

Cissy's coil, a deep golden brown, was entwined with another, its colour jet black. I assumed that must have once belonged on the head of Mr Samuels, which was why I'd never worn it before, not wishing to cause Mama offence, with her so averse to all jewellery, except for her mourning brooches and rings.

But, on that first morning in Dinwood Court, as soon as I fastened the clasp at my neck and felt the locket's cool weight at my breast, I decided to wear it every day.

And that would be how I remembered my aunt – no longer dressing in dreary black gowns.

That way I might please Mrs Samuels. And that way I might please myself.

18

That first week, the days were as dingy as night, with bruising dark clouds eclipsing the light and the air so oppressive, humid and damp. Everywhere were the sounds of water – the sucking and glugging of drainpipes and gutters, the tapping of branches and leaves against windows. It was almost as if someone sought to come in. But it was not Mrs Samuels. Mrs Samuels had not returned.

That first morning, I dressed in a pale grey silk, plain enough for Mama to approve, though I wasn't so sure about what was beneath, the silk undergarments that slipped over flesh, soft and cool and sensual.

Taking Mrs Samuels at her word, I found my way down to the entrance hall where I turned in slow circles, looking up at a ceiling where stone vaults were bossed with acanthus flowers. All over the walls were cracked blackened portraits: everything ancient, dark and austere. Corridors led to the left and right, along which I was tempted to walk and explore – if not for the distraction of cooking smells, the muted chatter of voices and laughter which lured me towards a baize service door.

Soon I was looking into a kitchen, and everything built on such a grand scale as if designed with a giant in mind. One dresser covered an entire wall. The range was as big as a carriage, and though it was really too early for lunch, an enormous scrubbed table was piled high with what looked like a banquet to me. Steaming jugs of gravy. Roast chickens and chops. Baskets filled with great hunks of bread; and quite a crowd sitting around it all – though not Mr Meldicott or the boy Jim. The men, all seated at the end nearest to me, were dressed in scruffy working clothes, though I wondered how anyone managed to work after eating so much at that time of the day but, of course – I didn't realise then – they would have been up and about since dawn. Next to them were some maids in blue. A few more, further up, were dressed in grey and, at the top of the table, presiding over them all was a much older woman who wore a white apron who, I presumed, must be the cook. She looked to be an ogre to me with her heavy lined brow and wiry hair, and every eye in that room followed hers when she chanced to stare my way, and every mouth in that room fell open, a gaping silence falling round, broken only by cutlery rattling on plates, and then the scraping back of chairs as every man stood and bowed his head. I imagine I must have looked mortified, which caused some amusement to one of the maids who suddenly started sniggering – at which the cook clouted her head with a spoon.

But worse was to come when she spoke to me. 'Is this our Miss Turner? Of course, you're most welcome, but . . .' She paused, her expression so fixed and stern that I felt not the slightest bit welcome at all; a supposition only confirmed when she then continued with, 'We weren't expecting you down in the kitchens. We assumed you'd be taking your meals in the house. About seven is when Mrs Samuels likes dinner. Lunch is generally at one. Of course, while she's away, if you have any other preferences then perhaps you'll let us know.'

I wished the floor would swallow me up. All the cooks I'd ever known at home liked nothing better than to have a good natter, sharing some cake and a pot of tea. Clearly things were different here, and knowing I no more belonged in that realm than a cuckoo's egg in a robin's nest, I shuffled my way back into the passage, mumbling my apologies, 'I'm sorry. I didn't mean to disturb you, I . . .'

'Meg . . .' Cook nudged the arm of a maid in blue. When she spoke her command was as much for me, a threat that I should learn my place, not cross the boundaries of that feudal world. 'Miss Turner has lost her way. Go and show her around the house.'

The maid, the same one who'd brought breakfast before, was looking regretfully down at her plate. But then she shrugged and grinned at me, and I could have blessed her for that sweet glance, so relieved when she led me back to the hall, where she turned and brightly said, 'Well, where shall we start? There's a music room, and a library . . . if you like books you'll find yourself plenty in there. The village is quite a way to walk, but pleasant enough when the weather allows. And, Miss Turner,' she paused, 'don't you go getting upset over Cook. She likes to queen it over us, but she's nowhere as fierce as she seems to be.'

'I'm glad to hear that.' I tried to smile.

How I wished the real queen was back.

19

A few days later, and one as dull and wet as the rest, I stayed in the library, reading a novel. Curled up in a big brown leather chair, I inhaled the smells of tobacco and leather and the faintest trace of something else; something so comforting and familiar. It might almost be Hammam Bouquet. Lulled by that and the patter of rain as it beat against glass, and the burbling coos of a pigeon from somewhere high up in the chimney stacks, I must have fallen asleep.

It was dark when I woke, and with such a start, to feel someone shaking at my arm. Meg's voice was full of concern when she cried, 'Miss Turner! I've been frantic with worry. I thought you'd gone and run back up to London.'

Yawning, looking around in confusion, I felt irritable and was tempted to ask, 'And how might I do that, without any money, without any means of travelling there?'

Instead I said sorry and went to my room where she asked if I'd like to take a bath. No gas had been piped up to the first floor, but the bedrooms were plumbed for hot water and heat, though when I'd tried turning the taps before they'd made some alarming banging sounds. Still, Meg was not unduly concerned when all of that rattling started again, explaining to me about air in the system, and after some spluttering burps and stops, and the first emissions the colour of rust, clear streams of white water came gushing out.

While Meg bustled round in the bedroom next door, arranging my things, drawing down sheets, I sat in a deep zinc tub, watching steam mist over marble and mirrors, feeling hot water lap at my flesh, above which foam bubbles were glistening, like the diamond set in my locket which lay on a table next to the bath. Alongside that were tablets of soaps and several bottles of perfumed oil – all with a Samuels' label on the front – and, feeling very spoiled and indulgent, I lifted one up, removing the stopper, breathing the delicate fragrance of rose. After smoothing that over my arms and face I sank down under the water again and, closing my eyes, for the first time in weeks my thoughts strayed back to Wilton's Hall. Holding a hand to my mouth – a hand no longer red and rough from working as Mama's char at home – I smiled as I licked at that scarred inch of flesh, trying to picture a young man's face, making a wish that he might appear, to kiss my lips, to caress my breasts, to stroke where my fingers were stroking then.

What a foolish fancy that turned out to be. I should have thought more about Mama, and all of her warnings of fleshy seductions. But, for then, I savoured the moment, plunging my head under water, my hair wreathing round like a mermaid, and—

What was that sound, that wailing? It pierced through my rippling, muffled world. Raising my head, streams of water ran down through my hair, through my eyes, and then as I heard it again, such an eerie, high whining note it was, you might almost think it the scream of a child. With my heart beating fast, I stepped out of the bath and snatched up a towel and ran to the bedroom where the cry was coming from under the window. Quite breathless by then, I started to ask, 'Meg, what was that? That—'

'Don't you worry, miss. It's only a fox, probably crying out for its mate. Sometimes they climb over the walls, get into the gardens . . . get after the chickens. The gardeners would kill them if they could, only Mrs Samuels won't have it. Plain refuses to have any fox destroyed. But then, she does have some very queer ways.'

I pulled back the shutters to see slivers of light caught on thin drifts of rain, illuminating the fountain below. I saw no fox, or perhaps the creature did not care for that spotlight upon its performance, because after that there was no sound – only a sudden dull thump behind, and when I turned back to the room again Meg was crouching on the floor. She held Cissy's scrapbook in her arms. She looked up, her face bleached in the candlelight, wavering shadows distorting her features which appeared oddly sheepish and guilty to me. And when standing again, when setting the book on the table, she said, 'I'm sorry . . . it got knocked to the floor. It fell open. I couldn't help seeing.'

'Oh, that's all right. I don't mind.' I sat down in front of the mirror where two dark eyes stared back through wet hair – hair that was gleaming, as black as jet. I looked down at my arms, still sheened in oil, repelling the water that dripped from my head; like teardrops they shimmered against the white skin. And perhaps I was shameless, no longer minding if Meg saw my body, but then she'd seen enough before, when she'd helped me to dress, and earlier, when I'd stripped for the bath. Now, she brought a towel to place round my shoulders, but she kept her eyes lowered, avoiding mine, and when she began to comb out my hair, her fingers were rough, snagging on knots.

'Ow . . . that hurts,' I complained, and then, 'Meg . . . I'm sorry. You look tired tonight. Why don't you go on to bed? I can manage perfectly well myself.'

'Before I go, Miss Phoebe, may I ask you something about your book?'

Before I could answer, she'd opened the cover, flicking through some of the pages inside and settling on a newspaper cutting where, at its side, Aunt Cissy had written, *July 1871. Maurel. Don Giovanni.*

In the fading picture, Cissy was wearing an evening gown, and kissing her hand was Victor Maurel, the famous French baritone. He was dressed in stage costume, with tight hose and breeches, and in his free hand was a large plumed hat. He had laughing eyes and an easy smile, and I'd often heard Old Riley pronounce how dashing and charming and handsome he was, and how Cissy must have been mad to refuse that time when he went down on bended knee, proposing, professing his undying love.

'Who is she?' Meg asked. 'She is beautiful.'

'My aunt. Yes, she is. She was. I . . .' I had to steel myself to be strong, swallowing hard at the stone of grief that was always too quick to rise up in my throat. 'She's dead.'

'I'm sorry. Is she the one you've been mourning? Was she an actress then?'

'No. A singer. She must have been Maurel's guest that night. She was always being invited out, to parties and shows, and things like that.'

'And him, the man standing behind?' Meg's finger was pointing to someone else, someone I'd not even noticed before, barely visible at the edge of the frame. When I'd seen him in Wilton's, and then at our house, his hair had been grey, no longer black, but this was the very same saturnine face, the same intense, defiant eyes, and I whispered without even thinking, 'That's Mr Samuels!'

'Have you known them long then . . . the Samuels?'

Such prying suspicion was making me anxious. Mr Samuels had demanded discretion . . . and how to explain without also confessing that Cissy and he had been lovers? I liked Meg well enough. But how did I know that she could be trusted, that there would be no speculation or gossip? I took a deep breath, answering in a manner I hoped was convincing. 'No. But, Mr Samuels is known to support the opera. I can only suppose that's why he was there . . . that he somehow knew Cissy professionally.'

'It must be very glamorous, being part of a theatrical family. I love all the songs from the halls myself.'

'Oh, my mama is extremely religious. She doesn't approve of the theatre at all. It's not the same since Cissy . . .'

I couldn't go on, and Meg murmured, 'I'm sorry. I don't mean to upset you. I should never have looked at your private things.'

And with that she left, and I went on to bed but found it impossible to sleep, lying there with eyes open, staring into the darkness, listening to the ceaseless patter of rain which hissed in my ear like a whispering prayer, and every word of that prayer the same – *Cissy, Cissy, Cissy.*

I had to have faith. I had to grasp onto some understanding as to why I'd been sent to such a strange place, and why a week had already elapsed, and still Mrs

Samuels had not returned. Had she forgotten about my existence, or was this some test; some sort of game?

As another dawn crept in through gaps in the shutters, I could see that the light was different that day – clearer and sharper, less dismal. When I got up and went to look out, the garden's black puddles were splintered with silver, reflecting the rays of a rising sun. And it seemed to me that something *had* changed – had broken – both out there, and inside the house.

20

Rock, thy hollow womb disclose!
The bubbling fountain, lo! It flows:
Through the plains he joys to rove,
Murm'ring still his gentle love.

(From Handel's *Acis and Galatea*)

My skirts brushed against the damp grasses. Directly ahead trees were steaming with moisture almost as if they were living and breathing. I hesitated, and all Nature's sounds seemed to hesitate too, as if those woods sensed my arrival, the stranger about to enter their dawn realm of dappled green gloom.

The hallway that morning had been just as shadowed. The main door was locked, no key to be found. But when I heard some sounds of life, the clinkings of china and clangings of pans, I made my way back to the kitchens again.

Feeling very nervous, I peered inside, seeing the heads of grey-uniformed maids hanging low over bowls of grey porridge. The stern, grey-haired cook was stirring a pot. Mr Meldicott was there at her side, in a sagging old chair pulled up close to the range – and at least *he* had a welcoming smile, his deeply lined face looking somehow absurd beneath such a boyish thatch of white hair.

'Well, well, if it's not our Miss Turner . . . our little

drowned rat. Does she always rise this early then? I thought you fancy London types liked to sleep in a bit later than this.'

'Like Burlington Bertie, I rise at ten thirty!' Happy to see him, I quoted the song and then carried on with, 'Actually, I don't often sleep late. I was hoping to go for a walk outside, seeing the weather's dry for a change.'

'I'd say we're in for a beautiful day. Where were you thinking of heading then?'

'I thought I'd go up to the woods. Is there a way out, through the back of the house?'

Cook scraped her pot to one side, her hands wiping roughly down over her apron, her eyes narrowed, her voice as gruff as before – though I sensed a note of caution there. 'I'm not so sure about that.' She glanced down at Mr Meldicott. 'Don't reckon Mrs Samuels would be any too pleased.'

'Oh, woman, don't take on so foolish. Miss Turner's not a child. We can't tie her up like a bird in a cage. She managed to get here alone on the train. I'm quite sure she's able to go for a stroll.'

'Well.' Cook gave me another long look. 'You give a good shout if there's others about. You keep to the paths, and you watch out for poachers working those woods.'

A high voice piped up, 'No poachers out there in broad daylight! Why don't I show Miss Turner the way?'

I hadn't noticed Jim before, sitting cross-legged on the floor, his back resting against Mr Meldicott's chair as he chewed away on a slice of toast.

'Steady up, young Master Meldicott,' the older man was laughing. 'Miss Turner's not for the likes of you. You may take her as far as the field, but no more. I need you back in the stable yard.'

Mr Meldicott then grinned up at me. 'Off you go then. Looks like you could do with a bit of fresh air . . . put some colour into those cheeks. And you might as well make the most of your freedom. Who's to say when her ladyship's set to return?'

I followed Jim through a scullery, and into another walled garden – this one laid out with vegetable plots, haphazard arrangements of sheds and glasshouses, and chickens cooped up in long wire runs – protected from foxes allowed to roam freely. Fruit trees were espaliered against the brick walls. An old iron gate opened up to more lawns where cedars cast looming black shadows on green. Rose gardens were bordered by tall laurel hedges, and erected along one wall of the house was an orangery; all sparkling windows and stone castellations. As we were wandering past, for want of some conversation I asked Jim how old he might happen to be, very surprised to hear the reply, 'Near 'nough fourteen as makes little difference.'

'Fourteen?' I'd assumed him to be nine or ten, what with being so small, all elbows and knees, and hardly a spare ounce of flesh on his bones. I think my reaction upset him. After that he became tight-lipped, until we arrived at another hedge, where a gap had been set with a swinging gate – the point where the gardens turned into pasture, the meadows which led to the edge of the woods.

'You know what this is?'

'Well now, let me think . . . could it possibly be a wooden gate?'

'A wooden gate . . . and a kissing gate.' He dallied a while, one boot scuffing at grass, but if young Master Meldicott hoped for a toll he was soon to be disappointed, for I started to laugh. 'You've got some cheek. I think you should hurry up and get back. I wouldn't want you to be late for work.'

He smirked and lifted a skinny arm, pointing back towards the woods. 'You head up through those trees and you might find the Look Out. If you make a wish there it always comes true.'

'Have you made one then?'

He looked very solemn. 'Yes. It was my wish to fly.'

'And how are you going to manage that?' I didn't mean to laugh again.

'You come over to Ludlow with Pa and me. We go to the races there. We see horses that run as fast as the wind. I mean to be a jockey.' He nodded and gave another smirk. 'Do you like to go riding, miss? We've a nice little mare to suit you . . . steady like.'

'I've never ridden a horse in my life. I think I should be quite petrified!'

Jim shrugged his shoulders and rolled his eyes, looking as if he thought me mad. 'That's what's wrong with you fancy London types.'

I didn't look very fancy that day. I was wearing my old black gown, and what did I care if it caught and tore on brambles or any sharp tips of twigs? My fingers scraped over the rough bark of trees as I gazed up into the canopy where branches were woven so tightly together, where shafts of gold light filled the gaps in the green, where the wood was creaking as leaves weighed low, still heavy and dripping with jewels of rain. There was a stream – a waterfall – that splashed over boulders furred velvet with moss, and I stood in that verdant, magical place and almost believed it was welcoming me, that the birds in the branches were singing my name, the prettiest: *fee bee, fee bee.*

But then I recalled Galatea's song: 'Hush ye pretty warbling quire! Your thrilling strains awake my pains.' The pain of my loss never slept for long.

I walked on through those trees for well over an hour, up stony tracks, steep and slippy with mud. But being unused to such exercise, my legs were soon aching, my chest heaving so hard that I needed to stop and rest a while. I sat on the ground in a clearing where wheel furrows scarred the grass around, leading on down to a roadside verge where sawn logs and trunks had been stacked into piles. Two wood pigeons flew overhead, and while watching them disappear into green a sudden vibration ran up through the ground, followed by the rumbling sound of wheels. The flash of black lacquer, the clanging of iron, and four handsome grey horses went cantering by. A coachman called 'whoa' as he pulled on his reins before the sudden descent of the hill and I glimpsed some passengers sitting inside and, from her place nearest the window, recognised Mrs Samuels.

She was back. I was out. I must look such a mess. Slipping and skittering down the path, I took a wrong turning and somehow got lost, and then my foot snagged on a straggling root and I stumbled against some low railings, falling flat on my face on a slab of stone. Momentarily dazed, I managed to struggle up to my feet and, not daring to risk any more delay, hurried on back through the meadows and gardens, back through the kitchens and then the baize door and there in the hallway – cr*ash!* – I collided with something else solid and hard.

Looking down, I saw puddles of water, broken fragments of blue and white china, and Meg's voice was all shock and sharp irritation. 'Miss Phoebe! What on earth are you doing? Your dress, it's all torn. It's covered in mud. Mrs Samuels is back. She's been asking for you . . . and now there's this mess to clear up as well.'

'Oh, I'm sorry. I'm sorry!' Still gasping for breath, it was all I could do to apologise while Meg muttered on about finding a cloth, gathering up several shards of vase before rushing away to the kitchens.

Left alone, unsure of what to do, as I stooped down to pick up the lilac and roses, the stems broken, the flower heads battered and bruised, I saw a strange vision of myself in an old silvered mirror hung over a console – a dishevelled creature, her hair tangled with grasses, a dark stain of mud streaking over one cheek. Standing again, I heard a door slam, the stamp of more footsteps across the flags, and before I could even think to move I found myself face to face with a man – and it seemed like for ever we stared at each other, my brain's slow whirrings surely as loud as the tock of the long-case clock on the stairs, its ponderous beat tapping out my thoughts: *How can he be here? He doesn't belong. He should be in London, in Wilton's Hall.*

My heart gave a lurch when he took a step nearer, a quizzical look on his face when he asked, 'Is it you . . . little shepherdess?'

As if in a dream, as if paralysed, I let him touch a hand to my head where he picked out a few strands of ivy. When one of his fingers brushed over my cheek I saw something glistening, and it might have been the gold of his hair – even paler when seen in the light of day, without the dark sheen of Macassar oil. Or it could have been his wedding band. *Had he been wearing a ring before?*

Still clutching those broken flowers in my arms I felt

like the parody of a bride: a bride dressed in black rather than white, my hair with its garland of mangled green. Before any more could be said, Meg reappeared through the service door, a quick grin and a blush as she curtseyed low, as if greeting the king of England. 'Good morning, Mr Samuels. We hadn't expected to see you down here . . . not so soon after the wedding as this.'

She stopped to look back as another man followed – very neatly made, of average height, with mousy thin hair parted straight in the middle, a little white growing in at the temples. His face was lean, his cheeks sallow and smooth – except for the left which was marred with a puckering line of scars, above which his brown eyes were serious, intent on assessing me. Thin lips were moistened and slick as he licked them. When he spoke, his voice was surprisingly mellow, tinged with a soft lilting accent, which Meg later told me was Welsh.

'Surely, *this* is not our Miss Turner?'

'Yes, sir.' Meg bobbed, and then gave me one of her sideways looks, mumbling, 'This is Mr Stephens . . . Mrs Samuels' butler.'

Whoever he was, the younger man chose to ignore him; at best an arrogant glance of contempt. Meanwhile, the butler surveyed the floor, and I heard the cryptic tone in his voice. 'We must get this confusion cleared up. Miss Turner, perhaps you'd go to your room and change into more appropriate clothes?'

Somehow his words were like balm to my ears, soothing the tense atmosphere in that hall. I followed Meg upstairs, forgetting those flowers still held in my arms, stopping on the half landing to look back down, to see grey eyes still following me, only now they were narrowed, clouded and hard. And there, at his side, the butler still stood; still being ignored by the younger man.

'Well, who'd have thought it?' The bedroom door had hardly closed when Meg folded her arms and pursed her lips, whistling out a long note of surprise. 'Fancy, Joseph getting married like that? They kept that one quiet. No one guessed Mrs Samuels had gone back to London to see her son wed!'

I sat down on the edge of the bed. All I wanted to do was scream, instead of which I snapped at Meg, very rude as I ordered her to shut up. All I could think was: *His name is Joseph Samuels. He is Nathaniel Samuels' son. He is already married to somebody else.* I heard myself pleading, 'Meg, are you sure?'

She pulled at my muddy boots and, clearly blind to my distress, offered her tart reply, 'As far as I know, there's only one son the Samuels have. So yes, I am sure . . . not that he's brought his wife today, and we're longing to know what she looks like.'

Her voice became softer as fingers lifted to tease more ivy and grass from my hair. 'How did you come to be in such a state? Get up now and let me unfasten your dress.'

As the black cotton fell to my feet, I thought it looked like a filthy rag. But where old rags could be thrown away, my sorrow was locked in some cruel tricking place where fate sought to mock me, to tease and torment me, to pierce through my heart like a splinter of ice.

I offered my dull explanation. 'I fell, while running back down through the woods. I hit my head on a stone . . . only,' I paused, 'I think it must have been a grave. There was a withered bouquet of flowers. There was a name . . .'

'Esther.'

'Yes, that's what it said. Who was Esther? Why is she buried out there?'

'She was Joseph's sister . . . some years older than him when she died. I believe there was an accident, though it happened long before my time, and all very much hushed up. They say Mrs Samuels took a strange notion, having her daughter buried out there, though she had to get special permission and it caused quite a stir when the vicar objected. He and Mrs Samuels fell out over that. I don't think she's ever set foot in church since.'

'Where is Mrs Samuels now? She must be expecting me.'

Meg crouched on the floor to pick up the flowers that I'd thrown down, peering back up at me when she said, 'There's no rush. Mr Stephens says she's gone to her room . . . resting after the journey. I'm sure he'll send word when she wants you. And, Miss Phoebe,' Meg sounded anxious, 'best to say nothing about Esther's grave. Not unless Mrs Samuels mentions it first.'

21

Sometimes your mind keeps on turning, going over the same thing again and again. It's like scratching an itch, even when the skin breaks and begins to bleed, and you know you should leave it alone. But you can't.

I thought about Joseph all that day. I stayed in my room and fretted for hours – what to wear, what to say when I saw him again. But when Meg came up with some tea and cake she told me he'd already gone back to London, driven down to the station to catch the train, and less than an hour after we'd met.

Alone again, I lay on the bed, pounding a fist at the pillow, burying my face in the blankets' folds, trying to smother the sound of my sobs. He hadn't even said a goodbye! But then, why should he? What was I but his mother's companion, a mere employee of the family? What had we shared but the briefest flirtation? And how cruel, that he was the Samuels' son, that while I'd been dreaming of Wilton's Hall and what had occurred on that balcony, he'd been planning a marriage to somebody else – not giving his silly shepherdess so much as a second thought.

Around seven o'clock in the evening – by which time I had recovered enough to act with some semblance of dignity – Meg came back to say Mrs Samuels was waiting, that she'd asked for me to join her at dinner.

I dressed and followed Meg downstairs, soon left alone in a large square room; one which, until then, had remained locked up. Dark boards were spread with Aubusson rugs. Giltwood chairs were upholstered in watery silks; the same fabric lining three of the walls, and all hung with Sèvres porcelain plates and paintings in large ornate gilt frames. A fourth wall was completely open, a marble pillar on either side. Marble steps led the way to the orangery. I wandered on into that palace of glass, along the tiled pathways, past palms and ferns, inhaling such lovely perfumes: the sweetness of jasmine, the dense creaminess of gardenia. But when passing some lilies I thought about Cissy, the garland we'd placed on top of her coffin, the single white stem thrown into the grave, and I felt such a rushing of sorrow again, for a moment unable to swallow or breathe. But the spasm soon passed and at last I moved on, catching a different perfume then – that of lavender.

Suddenly, I was distracted, feeling a fluttering draught on my cheek, the lightest snapping brush of wings – soft as the breath of a lover. Spinning round, I saw a blurring of brown flying towards open terrace doors, through which a cool evening breeze blew in – through which that little bird blew out. I watched as it dipped across the lawns, soaring up as it headed towards the woods: the darkening mass below purple skies.

Someone spoke and broke the spell in which I'd found myself enthralled. 'They say it's a bad omen, a bird coming into the house like that. They say it's a portent of death. But it's flown away now . . . so I think we may hope for a little reprieve.'

Mrs Samuels was sitting at a table. She looked very handsome, dressed in red silk, her gown's neckline high and frothy with lace. That white lace contrasted starkly with the dark rouge that stained her lips, the red bleeding out into splintering lines.

Come, Phoebe.' She beckoned for me to go nearer, and I thought of my dream on the train. 'Won't you sit down? I hope you've been well enough cared for . . . beginning to feel at home. Tell me, what have you done with yourself while I've been away?'

'I've been reading, and sketching a little. This morning I went for a walk in the woods.'

'Ah, yes. Stephens did mention that.' She leaned forward and picked up a small brass bell and, summoned at once by its tinkling, the butler appeared through another side door, followed by a maid who was wheeling a trolley; some rattling, silver-domed dishes on top. While the maid set about arranging the table, the butler lit candles in tall glass sticks. It was almost as if they were setting a stage and, all the while, even when they placed linen cloths in our laps, or served the food up onto our plates, Mrs Samuels ignored them and spoke only to me.

'I like to dine here. I like the view.'

'It is very pleasant.' I tried to smile back, wondering how to put any food in my mouth; still nauseous after that morning's encounter.

'I must apologise for my absence. I was called back to town for a wedding . . . my son's as it happens, and most unexpected. Ah well . . .' She twirled a hand through the air, a fork poised between gilt-edged plate and red lips. 'At least he set some time aside, accompanying me on the journey back here. I had hoped he would stay, if only one night. All too soon he'll be leaving for India again.' She glanced away and sighed. 'I blame his father . . . for sending him there in the first place. And Joseph only too glad to go, and now even wanting to make it his home. That's where he met *her* . . . his wife.'

Consumed with a masochistic desire to learn something more of Joseph's wife, I asked, 'Does she meet with your approval?'

Mrs Samuels' frank answer was shocking to me. 'Oh, Caroline is pretty enough. A little redhead, the sort that has most men's tongues hanging out, panting like dogs round a bitch on heat, but by no means as young or as virginal as she likes everyone to think. I would say that her greatest asset by far is the fact that her father has shared interests with my husband, both involved in the import of cloth, both ruthless men with a greed for expansion. Personally, I find it all rather vulgar. I wonder how covetous men can be . . . and why enough is never enough.'

She dabbed a corner of cloth to her lips, the white linen tinged with the scarlet stain, above which her smile was brittle, lending a severe look of pinched disappointment. 'Do you know, there was even a time when my husband had hopes of expanding his trade, founding another shop in New York? I ask you . . . what would we have seen of him then?'

'I know nothing about Mr Samuels' business . . . that is, apart from the London store.'

'Really?' Her gaze was interrogating, almost as if she suspected I lied. 'Then perhaps I should enlighten you. He's the son of Jewish immigrants. His mother died when he was born. His father . . . well, who knows what he did to survive. He passed on when his son was still very young and for years Nathan begged around the docks. He found work in a provisions store, after which he set up his own barrow, hawking ribbons and lace on the Mile End Road . . . eventually leasing a Bloomsbury shop in the streets they call "New Jerusalem". But he wasn't satisfied with that. By night he read, educating himself, though the wisest thing he ever did was to see an opening arise; when Prince Albert set up the Great Exhibition. Nathan requested a loan from my father, the banker, Lord Cavendish. He took a shop very near to Hyde Park where thousands of visitors passed each day, buying themselves refreshments, or copies of the most popular exhibits – Chinese and Indian figurines, sculptures and paintings, porcelain tea sets. Nathan set up many foreign connections and managed to do so well, he was able to pay off every debt, and then purchase the present Samuels' site . . . after which he requested my hand.

'My father was moved to refuse. Financial dealings were one thing, but when it came to personal matters, well . . . like so many others, he entertained certain prejudices, more concerned with presenting me at court, bringing me out as a debutante, introducing me to what he considered to be the most suitable candidates. But nothing could stop me. I was very stubborn, and by then I adored Nathan Samuels . . . some thought to the point of madness. But, whatever anyone said at the time, it wasn't my family's money he wanted. He already had quite enough of his own. I suppose . . . I suppose it was the name, and the doors that opened up for him, the respect in which my father was held. But still, I thought we were happy once. I thought he cared for me.'

How painful to me was such intimacy, picturing him with Cissy instead, but when finally daring to look up, expecting a face as sad as the voice, I felt my heart lighten to see Mrs Samuels bestowing the sweetest of smiles on me – even if her next words were stern. 'I believe you met my son . . . before he left Dinwood, this morning?'

'Oh, yes.' I nodded, feeling the hot spreading rise of a blush, looking back at the butler who stood in the doorway, lips thin, and fixed, and grim.

Mrs Samuels leaned forward. Her hand rested on mine, though I noticed that little effort caused her a great deal of discomfort. She gasped, and then a deep intake of breath before changing the subject and making some comment upon my appearance. 'You look very well this evening.'

I looked down at my locket, the pale pink gown. 'Forgive me . . . you must think me rude . . . not yet to have thanked you for all of the clothes.'

Inside, I was wondering why it should matter what I wore, hidden away from the rest of the world, when Joseph had seen me in torn black skirts, my face all streaked with grass and mud.

Mrs Samuels' eyes glittered with light from the candles. Dark pupils were wide, almost filling the blue. 'Seeing you wear them will give me great pleasure. You should not be dressed in mourning. You are very lovely, though I don't think you know it . . . not yet. The best I can do is to warn you. Don't let your beauty become your curse. Take good care where you cast your eye, and beware of those cast back at you. You *do* understand, don't you, Phoebe?'

Why did she talk about curses? I felt uneasy and out of my depth, sensing that under her manners and smiles something darker and calculating might lie. The butler, who'd seen where *my* eye cast that morning, was hovering round us, clearing up plates, pouring more wine into glasses, until Mrs Samuels said dinner was done.

Abruptly, she rose from her seat. Making to follow, I felt slightly dizzy and thrust out a hand, grabbing onto the back of my chair for support.

'Are you all right?' She looked back with concern.

'Yes . . . I'm not really used to wine.'

'An early night may do us both good. But then,' she heaved another sigh, 'I'm told this fatigue must be endured, simply a part of my malaise.'

'I'm sorry. Are you unwell?'

'Don't be sorry,' she snapped, and then closed her eyes. When they opened, the smiling sphinx was back. 'We must simply learn to accept our lot. Having you here may well be my best tonic, better than any doctoring skills. And before we part tonight you must tell me, is there anything *else* you desire, anything that will help to pass your time? I did warn you. It is very quiet here.'

'Is there a post box nearby? I have a letter for Mama. I made some sketches of the house. I was hoping to show her how lovely it is.'

'Stephens? What are we going to do about letters?'

The butler stepped forward, purring his answer. 'If Miss Turner would leave her mail in the hall, on the salver that's placed on the console, I'll ensure any letters get posted on.'

'Thank you,' I said. 'I'll put something there in the morning.'

And then, following Mrs Samuels, I retreated through shadows of wavering green, though on reaching the steps to the drawing room she stopped and stood very still. I noticed the sheen on her brow and, unsure as to whether to offer my arm, wary of causing any offence, I averted my eye and looked back at the table where we had dined, where the butler was already dousing the candles, snuffing each flame between finger and thumb.

And there he remained, so very still he might be some *tableau vivant* in a show. Plumes of white smoke curled over his face. Brown eyes stared up at a large glass dome, around which slow vapours were drifting, circling, languid as ghosts. And through the glass's curving refraction, a bright disc of white was blurred and distorted, looking as if the full moon had a twin — as if it might somehow be splitting in two.

22

For us the zephyr blows,
For us distills the dew,
For us unfolds the rose,
And flow'rs display their hue . . .
(From Handel's *Acis and Galatea*)

The next day, I entered the library and saw a large walnut box. Its surface was inlaid with patterns of gold. A card with my name had been placed at the side. In a state of great anticipation I lifted the lid and was thrilled to see all the brushes and papers, and sticks of black charcoal, and crayons exuding oily odours, and tablets of watercolour paints, even small stoppered bottles in which to hold water.

I made some dreadful messes at first. But within a few days I'd more or less mastered the medium. Inky outlines were tinted with watery hues, mostly depicting the gardens. And almost every evening, after we'd dined in the orangery, Mrs Samuels would ask to see what I'd done, and was always most complimentary. I knew those sketches were pretty enough but they lacked the true essence of any art; as nothing compared to those other works already adorning her drawing room walls.

One that I liked to look at the most was a portrait of Mrs Samuels, created when she was very much younger.

Dressed in blue muslin, her flaxen hair had been plaited and bound in ribbons, imitating the classical Grecian style. She had been very beautiful and radiating the confidence of one who had never yet known any pain – though that sadness was waiting, close alongside, where, in an idealised scene, two children were posed beneath a tree.

Holding a little clay pipe to his lips, Joseph, who must have been seven or eight, looked positively angelic, and so very like his mother. Esther, his sister, clearly much older and in the first bloom of her adolescence, was holding a white china bowl in her lap; the source of those bubbles her brother blew. She put me in mind of her father. The very same intense black eyes. Black ringlets fell to her shoulders. Pink rosebuds and lace edged the neck of her gown. And how poignant to glimpse, growing out of her back, the little white feathers to symbolise that the girl was now dead and residing in Heaven – though those wings were the work of a later hand, the craftsmanship crude, lacking delicacy.

One evening, while standing there absorbed, I suddenly heard Mrs Samuels say, 'Those bubbles depict the fragility of youth, as my daughter's sad fate went on to prove.'

Despite my curiosity – wondering when and how Esther had died – before I was able to make a response Stephens stepped forward, asking his mistress, 'Are you in need of anything?'

He was always watching and listening like that; alert to her every movement and word. But it made me uncomfortable to be so closely scrutinised, as if he was her protector, or guard.

Mrs Samuels looked irritated, waving her butler away,

and once she and I were alone again, she said, 'Phoebe. I was wondering . . . and I hope you don't find this a morbid request, but would you paint my daughter's grave? I'm no longer able to walk so far, but Stephens could show you where it is.'

She sat back and closed her eyes, as if simply the effort of that request had already taken a toll on her strength. But I was glad at the prospect of having some real employment at last, some specific task to fill my day, saying, 'Of course. I know where it is . . . at the edge of the woods. I'll go tomorrow, if the weather still holds.'

'Thank you.' She touched her hand to mine. 'Such a remembrance would mean a great deal. And now, I think I shall retire. I didn't sleep at all well last night. I thought I heard you cry out in your sleep? Are you homesick? Are you unhappy here?'

Could the fox have been calling again? 'I don't *think* it was me, though I do confess that I sometimes miss Bow. If only I'd heard some word from Mama. I suppose . . .' I felt almost embarrassed to ask, 'I suppose that my letters have been sent?'

'I'll ask Stephens. I'm sure they have. And I'm sure that your mother will write . . . in due course.'

The matter was dismissed, and at that very moment Stephens reappeared, offering his arm as she rose from her chair, escorting her out of the room. Watching them go, it was only then I realised how *he* was always at her side, how he was her true companion, not I.

That night, I did hear the fox calling again: high and shrill, other-worldly it seemed. But that was not what woke me. I had already been disturbed by low subdued voices and thudding feet, running up and down the stairs.

Waiting till dawn, when all was calm, I dressed in one of my old black gowns – my London clothes come to very good use for painting or walking about in the grounds, though that morning I'd hardly gone any distance, still wandering over the house's lawns, when I saw something flash at the edge of my eye.

Behind the laurel hedge where the rising sun glinted on dark, waxy leaves, I saw it again, fluttering, white – a nightgown blown high above two naked legs, two blue eyes staring out through pale tangles of hair. She was holding some roses, most of them white, still dewy, the palest green tinge at their edges. But one had petals, a deep velvety red, perfectly matched with the ugly marks that scarred her arms, where the flesh had been torn and scratched by thorns.

When she came closer, I noticed her perfume, though the lavender fragrance was fainter that day. There was something else, sickly sweet, and below it the stench of stale urine and then, when she opened her lips, the breath she exhaled was horribly sour. 'You will take these, won't you? You will keep your promise and go to the grave?'

Before I could answer another voice called, 'Quickly! She's here . . . in the garden.'

This time the flash was of blue – the dress of the maid who served dinner each night, who now ran around from the front of the house, pursued by an elderly, top-hatted man who was holding a battered, brown leather bag, his black coat-tails flapping behind, like a crow.

Mrs Samuels looked bemused. 'Has the doctor been called again? Why are they making all of this fuss?'

'We couldn't find you anywhere, madam.' The maid was flushed and panting. 'Mr Stephens was showing the doctor upstairs when we realised you'd disappeared.'

The doctor stepped forward, also breathless: 'Mrs Samuels, we let a great deal of blood . . . a large dose of medication last night. You really should be resting in bed.'

'But why? I feel so much better. I've not felt so well in years. I've no pain at all and—'

'And we want to make sure that continues. But you have to give yourself time.'

At that, Stephens emerged from the orangery doors, and when he reached Mrs Samuels' side, he spoke in gentle, anxious tones. 'Lydia, please. You must come back to bed.'

I thought it strange that he should address her so intimately. But, as if a mesmerist had snapped his fingers, Mrs Samuels blinked and returned to her senses. Clearly distressed, she stared at each one of us in turn, and then clutched her shift up close to her throat, above which her features fell suddenly slack and a feverish colour flooded her cheeks. The butler bent forward, lifting her effortlessly in his arms, and she acquiesced, no objection at all, lying as limp and as mute as a doll, her face pressing into his shoulder.

As he carried her back to the house, as I watched the other two trailing behind, I thought of consumption again; the delirium that condition could bring. But when had I heard Mrs Samuels cough, or seen bloody spittle on handkerchiefs?

Later that day, I returned to the house. My feet trod the vertical shaftings of light that slanted through hallway windows, forming a ladder across the bare boards to lead me to Mrs Samuels' room.

Inside, all the curtains were shut, not enough

ventilation; a smell of the sick room, of syrup and slops and stale perspiration. I tried to keep my breaths shallow, casting around through the dingy light to see Mrs Samuels propped up on some pillows, and, framed by her bed's ornate gilt posts, with those red damask drapes on either side, the effect was almost theatrical. With only a sheet to cover her form, hip bones and knees jutted sharply beneath and when she moved that sheet fell away, exposing a rusty stain on her gown.

Stephens was there, straight away at her side, drawing the cloth back up again before going to stand at a bureau where he lifted the lid on a medicine chest, where I saw the thin glint of a metal syringe, neat rows of little corked bottles and jars. I thought about Mrs Samuels' arm and how those scratches and puncture marks might not have been caused by thorns alone. I thought about Cissy before she died, and that bottle of Roberts' Restorative. Mama's so-called miraculous cure. The cure that brought nothing but ruin to us.

Mrs Samuels was shaking her head, her eyes peering up like blue beads in bruised hollows. She said, very clearly, 'No, Stephens, not yet. My mind must be clear. I want to talk with Phoebe first.' She lifted a hand, patting the mattress at her side. 'Come, won't you sit . . . show me what you've done?'

Stephens moved aside to let me pass as I offered the paper held in my hands, and she lifted that sketch very close to her face, saying, 'How it has changed, and in a few months, the grass so much longer, the woods come to life.' She exhaled a long sigh. 'I shall cherish this picture. And now, with you here, perhaps Esther will rest. Perhaps she will even stop haunting my dreams.'

I didn't know how to respond. I felt Stephens' hand,

very light on my arm as he murmured, 'Miss Turner, perhaps you should leave.'

He followed me out to the passage, speaking more freely once we were alone, with the door to her bedroom closed behind. 'Mrs Samuels may sometimes say strange things. The medication helps to ease her pain, but her thoughts can tend to wander. She misses her daughter, you see.'

Back in my own room, I stood at the window and stared at the distant woods. Dusk skies above were streaked pewter and pink, and I thought of the grave, the light fading there, the roses all wilted and dead in the heat – red petals turned black, white petals turned grey.

I hadn't minded painting that scene, observing the stone's mossy edges, so prettily capped with its wreathing of leaves, and the simple inscription, no more than a name, unmarred by any maudlin verse. I'd done my best to capture it all, every nuance and tone, all the textures around, every blade of grass and tendril of ivy that twined through the rusted railings.

And, many hours later, when it was done, I stretched out my arms, staring up through green leaves at a cloudless blue sky as I took off my shoes and stockings and pulled my skirts up to my thighs, stretching out my legs to soak up the sun. My back rested against the hard bark of a tree, though I did find it somewhat unsettling to think that it might be the very same one beneath which a brother and sister had posed for that painting in Mrs Samuels' room. Its twisting, raised roots formed a guard at my feet. My toes curled down through dry grasses and soil and, perhaps, even deeper, those very same roots might now cradle Esther Samuels' bones.

I felt so warm and alive that day, and no scene was further from my mind than that wintry morning in Bow cemetery, when I'd stood at Cissy's side with freezing air icing the breath in our lungs. But then, when I looked back at Esther's grave, I started to shiver. I felt very cold, and my eyes were suddenly blinded with white through which I saw violent splashes of red – like the spots of my blood on a man's handkerchief – like a single red rose on a snow-covered stone.

And it wasn't just sweat that was stinging my eyes. I wept for Aunt Cissy all over again – and I wept for a girl I had never known; who had nothing to do with my life at all.

23

The next morning, I went down to the hallway and stared at the empty salver, biting down on my lip to suppress disappointment because, yet again, there was no letter waiting for me.

Hearing some movements behind, I turned to see Stephens, looking far from his usual immaculate self. His suit was creased, his voice weary and hoarse. 'Is there anything for Mrs Samuels? I missed the postman's arrival and . . .'

'No. There's nothing. Nothing at all. Is Mrs Samuels better? Should I go and sit with her a while?'

His answer was curtly dismissive. 'No. She has an appointment this morning. Her solicitor is coming from Hereford.'

'Then perhaps I'll walk into the village. Is it very far?'

'A mile or so. Would you like me to have the carriage brought round?'

'I'm happy to walk.'

'Then Meg should come too. We don't want you to go and get lost now, do we? Mrs Samuels would never forgive me for that.'

Brown eyes locked with mine. I felt distinctly uneasy. I sensed he was going to say something more. But he turned and walked away, and when his heel squeaked across the stone floor it sounded like the squeal of a rat.

An old iron gate gave a grudging groan as Meg and I left the house's grounds. We headed through fields of brown and white cows, towards the tower of Bodlington church which rose like a beacon to guide our path. Booted feet trudged over the grasses, the ground still soft from weeks of rain. Our shadows fell long in wavering shapes, our heads distorted by wide straw hats. Meg had insisted we wear them. Mid-morning and the sun was already scorching, beating down hot on our backs.

The last stile we climbed led us into the churchyard, though really it was more like a meadow, simple head-stones amongst the long grasses, here and there clumps of yellow buttercups, and thinking of Esther's lonely grave, I asked, 'Do the Samuels have a plot?'

'The Cavendish grave is right over there.' Meg pointed towards the church door where, in the shade of a yew, was something more befitting the grandeur I'd known in Bow cemetery. An elaborate tomb with a lion's clawed feet, and a great weathered basalt urn on top – but very neglected, and the grass all around it untended and weedy. When I made to go closer and look, Meg grabbed at my arm. 'Come on, Miss Phoebe. Who wants to loiter around with the dead?'

At the end of a lane we came to the village – something of a disappointment to me, being as quiet as the graveyard before. There was an inn, a grocer's shop, and then no more than a long straight road, bordered now and then by a new brick house – though most were quite ancient, black and white timbered, all sloping angles and low thatched roofs. The only sign of any life was that of an old woman who dozed on a roadside bench and, as we drew nearer, Meg started to murmur, 'Miss Everett used to work at the house.' And then she was shouting, 'Morning, Miss Everett. We've not seen you around for some time.'

Despite such hot weather, the old lady was wearing several shawls. A slack, vein-slugged hand gripped onto the handle of an umbrella. A fraying black bonnet perched on top of her head, looking almost like a lid, its tatty silk flowers fluttering about when she struggled to stand, cocking a hand to one ear as she asked, 'Who's that? What's that you . . .'

She never did finish her question. Watery eyes were filled with confusion, and then the umbrella dropped from her hand as, with both her arms flung wide, she tottered towards us. I'm not really sure how long I was held in such a surprisingly vice-like grip but when the old woman stepped back, she lifted her hands to the sky to chant, 'Praise be to the Lord! He's let you come back. He's let you walk amongst us again. Oh my poor child, what you suffered! God bless you, Esther. God bless you, my dear.'

Meg picked up the fallen umbrella, pressing it into Miss Everett's hands, explaining very loud and slow, 'This isn't Esther. This is Phoebe . . . Miss Turner. I think you should go back home. This weather has sent you delirious.'

Without more ado, the sniffling old woman obeyed Meg's command, lowering her head and shuffling off, her umbrella used as a walking stick, tip-tapping along the stony path, and as we stood there watching her go I felt on the brink of tears myself, until Meg took my hand and said, 'Cheer up, Miss Phoebe, don't be so glum. I'd say you made Miss Everett's day!'

But I noticed a tremor in her voice, the same in my

own when I replied, 'What do you mean? She thought I was one of the walking dead. How do you think that makes me feel? Do I really look that much like Esther?'

'Oh, I doubt Miss Everett would know herself – that is, if she glanced in the mirror these days.'

'What did she do, when she worked at the house?'

'It was well before my time. She was the children's nursemaid. They say she was heartbroken when Esther died, that it played on her mind something terrible. Both she and Mrs Samuels got obsessed with that table-knocking game, having mediums brought down from London . . . a whole procession by all accounts, until Mr Samuels got wind of it. And then the nonsense was stopped, and Miss Everett was sacked, since when she's not been right at all.'

We went back by a different route, traipsing in silence along grassy verges, strolling through hedged tunnels of shade. Several times, I tried to summon my courage to ask what had actually caused Esther's death, but – and I really can't say why – I found something holding me back, the prospect of knowing somehow too daunting.

We came to a fast-flowing river where I took very little persuading to follow when Meg shuffled down a steep bank, to stand underneath a bridge's arch, where the dark stone was cool and slimed with green, a welcome shade from the blazing sun. I reached down to pick up some bleached, white wood. It felt warm and hard, like fossilised bone. I cupped a flat pebble between my palms, throwing it into the water. *Plish*. The surface shivered as if alive, and ripples spread out into circles.

Meg said she wanted to go for a paddle, sitting down, pulling off her stockings and boots, hoisting her skirts and petticoats high, and the giggles and splashing sounds she made were accompanied by the songs of the birds and the zither of insects and, very soon, I was paddling too – heeding her warning to stay near the banks as I limped on sharp stones, as I gasped at the cold, as my toes burrowed deep into gluey silt. I stared down, entranced by the tiny black fish that darted through quicksilver flashes of light. I heard wooden wheels rumbling over our heads, and a few strands of hay drifted down to the water, fine wisps of gold in an eddy of air – and it seemed as if time was standing still until, in the distance, the church bell rang out, only the once; one chiming reminder that we should be getting back to the house.

The rest of the way I walked in bare feet, my toes hot and blistered and much relieved when we finally rounded a bend and saw Dinwood Court's tall iron gates. But those barriers put me in mind of a gaol, and I thought of the sadness confined in that house – of Miss Everett, of Mrs Samuels, both women still mourning a girl in the woods.

When Meg left me, I stood alone in the hall. Observed by all of its ancient cracked portraits, I took off my hat and bent forward, peering into the console's dim mirror – and there, I saw Phoebe Turner, not Esther, and the sun had freckled Phoebe's cheeks, and I wondered what Mama might say about that, almost able to hear her tut-tutting. What if she knew I went round like a 'heathen', walking unchaperoned in the woods, splashing around in rivers? She'd ask me what sinful passions might lead from all of my new-found decadent ways. She'd surely insist I went back home.

While contemplating such an event, I heard a dull creaking sound behind and was startled to see a dark shape in the shadows, about to let out a cry of alarm when . . .

'I'm sorry.' Stephens' lips twitched in a narrow smile, as if my uneasiness pleased him. 'Did I frighten you? Meg said you were back. I wanted to give you these letters. They arrived while you were out. The postman sends his apologies. He didn't recognise your name, what with the address being smeared by the rain. It was only today when a second one came that the mystery was solved.'

24

Back upstairs in my room, I lay on the bed and tore open Mama's first letter. But to tell you the truth, as I started to read I feared that she'd been at the brandy again. And I wondered if I could ever return to the house that we'd shared in Tredegar Square, for it sounded as if she was making plans to turn it into a mission hall, filling each room with the drunk and the homeless. Not that she said anything so specific. My assumptions were all based on what was implied; what had been written between the lines.

Tredegar Square

June 13th, 1882

My dearest daughter, Phoebe,

I hope you will not think me heartless for taking so long to write. But, I swore to Mrs Samuels that some weeks should elapse before sending word, and though it is hard we must allow you the time to settle, to grow used to what will be your new life.

Last night, I went into your bedroom and prayed by the empty bed. I tried to imagine you sleeping elsewhere and accept that this fate must be endured. If I'd known what would happen when you were born, but only God knows what our futures will hold, and all we can do is trust in Him and look for His guidance and do what is Right.

Your letter did bring me some peace of mind, and though I know that pride is a sin, I intend on showing your sketches to everyone who comes in through the door. They shine such a light upon your new world, as God is shining His mercies on mine.

I see now, it was when we let down our guard that evil came creeping into the house, and yet I confess to my own secret shame, being drunk as I was when the Millais was stolen. I have come to sincerely believe that theft was God's way of punishing me, of bringing me back into His flock, to be held once again in His loving arms.

Catherine Brown, our dear leader's wife, has been very kind, assuring that we are all tempted at times, all saved through hard work and commitment to Christ, a firm adherence to follow _His_ _Path_. And having tasted the demon drink and come close to destitution myself, faced with the prospect of that dreadful plight endured by so many on London's streets, I have started to work with the fallen again, helping those other ignorant souls still merrily dancing to Satan's tune. I go out with the Army most every day, administering the three 'S's, which as you well know are _Soup_, _Soap_ and _Salvation_. Perhaps I shall do even more in time.

Mrs Riley and Mr Collins still make the occasional visit to Bow. But nothing as frequently as before, and I fear Mr Collins has been disappointed, having long nurtured certain 'expectations'. As to Mrs Riley, she prys into all of my private affairs, jealous of the time I spend with the Browns. Catherine says that I should show patience and turn the other cheek. But I think Mrs Riley and I shall have to go our separate ways. She always was

Cissy's friend more than mine. Really, we have nothing in common at all.

Mr Collins is a far more sensitive soul. When he stood at my side in Paddington station, while we waved you off on that train, he assured me that it was all for the best. I can only pray that he was right.

Believe me,
Your most loving Mama,
Maud Turner

The second letter, the one where the ink was all run, which by rights should have reached me some days before, had not been written by Mama at all. How foolish I was in daring to hope that it might come from Joseph Samuels. Old Riley, the author, would surely have laughed. She would say there were plenty more fish in the sea. She would tell me to go out and cast a few nets. If only I hadn't already been caught!

But still, I was heartened to read her news.

6 Paradise Mews, Stepney Green
Wednesday, 1st June

Dearest Phoebe,

How lovely it was when I saw your letter and the pictures you sent, that last time I popped round to visit with Maud. Dinwood Court looks to be a beautiful place and I hope you are happy enough down there, though I know it must seem very strange at first.

We were all of us sad, having to wave you off on that train. It made me feel quite nostalgic, thinking back to those years gone by, those wonderful times when Cissy and I were touring around from place to place. But the theatre's not the same these days, filled with too many old codgers like me, too many dear ones who've gone by the way. And what's happened at Wilton's you wouldn't believe, with everything taking a turn for the worse since poor Mr Wilton went and passed on. You never would credit the rabble and lowlife frequenting that hall these days. When I think back to all his hard work, all the years of commitment put into that place!

Georgie Leybourne was topping the bill last night, and half of the audience prostitutes, caterwauling down from the balcony. Not that he minds any of that. He wouldn't know if he stood on the stage at Wilton's, the Paragon, or the Alhambra, as long as he's got some fizz in his hand, and a woman to warm his bed of a night. But there's talk of the drinks being plied these days, of souls going missing, then found in the Thames, their pockets all picked and a knife in their backs. And now there's a rumour going around that the Hallelujahs will get it closed down, converting it into a mission hall, serving up soup to the down and outs. Well, good luck to them, that's all I can say! They'll only end up with the same old crowd that pays good money now to go in through the doors.

Anyway, enough of all that. It's too depressing to think about, and I've looked at the clock and realised that I promised to go round and visit with Maud. I shall write again a bit later on.

Well, Phoebe, what a surprise! I came home to lie down to get over the shock.

Your mother's come out of her mourning! What do you think about that? If I didn't know better, I'd say there was something suspicious about it, perhaps even a male of the species involved.

She was wearing a flowery gown, and turned very red to see me at the door. But what an improvement it was on that Hallelujah uniform, which could not be any drabber, and the way they go round with those banners and cans – well, as you know, they rattle my nerves. But then, I suppose, if it makes Maud happy, taking her mind off the missing of you, then that's something we should be grateful for. But it's Catherine Brown this and Mr Brown that, and no hope for Mr Collins round there – though there was a time when I supposed that he and Maud might even wed.

Not that he's too disappointed, not now that he has other things on his mind. He and a friend have set themselves up, composing, and putting together an act. They've already got several bookings – the Victoria in Hoxton next week! What a coup! Didn't I tell you before, about that twinkle in Eddie's eye!

And me, I'm giving them both a hand, and they're giving me one in return, helping to build up my own little trade – and a very nice earner it is as well. 'Madame Riley's Phantasmagorical Wonders!' That's what it says in the advertisements, and in all the very best spiritualist journals. If only I'd started years ago. Of course, it's all my eye and Aunt Betty, and don't breathe a word about it to Maud. She'll be bringing those Browns round to pray at the door, frightening all of the clients away.

In fact, I'm expecting some visitors now and shall have to draw these lines to a close, but I'll make sure to post them, first thing in the morning – even though Maud said I wasn't to write, not for another month at least, claiming that's what Mrs Samuels insisted. But I clocked the address at the top of your letter – could hardly have missed all that glittering gold! And I noticed you asked for my address. So now, here you are, you shall have it again.

Mr Collins sends his very best wishes. We both think it's important that you should have word, and know that we're here and thinking of you. And we hope that you might write back very soon, for we do like to hear how our Phoebe goes on.

God bless you my dear,
From your most affectionate friend,
Mrs Riley

PS – I've made a few trips to the cemetery, leaving some flowers on Cissy's grave. I thought you might like to know about that.

25

Stephens was coming up the stairs. I was going down – still limping and sore from my blisters, not planning on very much walking that day. He carried a vase of roses – the palest shell pink they were, giving off a sweet, peppery fragrance. I presumed them for Mrs Samuels, and when I asked after her health, he said, 'Perhaps you'd like to take these to her room. She's feeling a little better today.'

Though it was again very warm, while placing those roses down on the table beside Mrs Samuels' bed, I saw, as if through another's eyes, my little sketch of Esther's grave, and it gave me quite a shivering turn. What do they call that prickling thing? A goose walking over your grave? Meeting with Miss Everett had unnerved me, more than I realised.

Poor Mrs Samuels looked very frail, propped up amongst piles of pillows again. But at least on that day the drapes were drawn back, the shutters and windows all opened wide, the room smelling fresh and clean. I heard the lazy buzz of a fly, now and then silenced when hitting the glass, above which Mrs Samuels murmured, 'Phoebe? Phoebe, is that you?'

'Mr Stephens sent up these roses.'

'What a lovely perfume they have.' She shifted towards the edge of the bed and reached out a hand to take one of the stems, but her grip was too weak, the rose dropped to the floor – and I really didn't mean to pry, but while picking it up I couldn't help but notice what lay behind a tapestry screen that had now been erected close by. It was a narrow divan, and at first I presumed her maid must use that, on hand for her mistress during the night. But since when did a maid own what lay on that pillow – a white collar, a waistcoat, a plain grey tie – the same as those Mr Stephens wore? My thoughts were racing. I was truly shocked at such a peculiar arrangement and, standing again, passing the rose back into her hand, I suddenly asked, 'Mrs Samuels, does your husband ever visit here? Does he ever come to Dinwood Court?'

'My husband . . . come to Dinwood Court?' She repeated my words, her voice bitter and taut. 'Very rarely.'

'Does he know how ill you've been?'

'No. I've cried wolf before. I've played far too many games in the past. And now, contrary as it seems, I'd rather he wasn't told.'

I wondered if she was playing with me. But then, Mrs Samuels seemed trapped in a spell in which she was ageing before my eyes, when only a short time before she'd been elegant and dignified. Now, the bones of her skull were too prominent beneath such a crepey, papery skin, and a thin trail of spittle drooled over her chin. Did she know? I supposed she must, for she dropped the rose to the floor again and lifted a hand to wipe over her mouth, and then crooked a finger to beckon me near. I thought she was going to tell me some secret. Her breath on my cheek was like butterfly wings, her usual lavender perfume suffused once again with that of decay.

She only asked for assistance, to get up and walk to a window – one overlooking the courtyard below. And there she lay upon a chaise, and while shadows and sunlight caressed her face, she asked me to read from a poetry book. But she lacked concentration to listen, continually interrupting the lines, saying how pretty the sound of the fountain, or how sweet the bird that perched on the sill.

Only, no bird was perched on that sill.

It must have been the medicine, for easing her pain, for aiding her rest – though I came to discover on certain occasions that the tincture had quite the reverse effect because sometimes Mrs Samuels did not sleep. Sometimes, at night, she left her room. Sometimes, she visited mine.

26

I woke from the deepest sleep. But then, with my feet all healed again, I'd taken to going back to the woods, lugging my sketch book, pencils and paints, walking for hours and hours each day, each evening exhausted when coming back home.

Late afternoon, the day before, I'd followed the trickling path of a stream – reminded again of Handel's operetta, with its 'purling streams and bubbling fountains' – until I could go no further, my way blocked by a sheer wall of stone. It must have been all of twenty feet high, very craggy and damp where the water gushed out from a crevice low down, around which sprouted little pink flowers and ferns.

Veering off to the right, I climbed a steep bank, rising through black and green shadows to see far below me a hollow, a pool as placid and smooth as a mirror. I presumed this oasis had once been a quarry, seeing deep ridges hewn into the stone and, on the opposite ridge, the gnarled roots of several dead trees – though only the stumps now remained above to form nature's own crenellations.

Wondering what such a castle might guard, I put down my bag and hitched up my skirts and, with my hands soon sore and grazed from clinging to thorny bramble growth, I descended into that hollow, skirted my way around the pool and then scaled the wall of the precipice ledge. Panting with exhilaration, I clung onto some of those roots for dear life, as the wind snapped and gusted hard around, whipping loose strands of hair against my cheeks through which I stared down at the fields below – fields that looked like patchwork quilts, criss-crossed with hedging and copses of trees, and the sinuous bend of the river, and narrow grey roads, and the rooftops of houses, and, far in the distance, hazy hills and, behind them, the rays of the setting sun, a radiant red wheel of shafting light.

I knew I must be at Jim's Look Out. I'd found it, and all on my own. I felt like a goddess who looked down from the heavens, my spirit elated and, for that one moment, I almost believed that if I had the courage to step off the edge, I might even be able to fly away. I might fly anywhere I wished and be free – if only I knew where to go.

It was almost dark when I knocked on Mrs Samuels' door, hoping to tell her what I'd seen, and to show her the latest sketches I'd made. But Stephens came out to the corridor, closing the door behind to tell me the doctor was visiting, that I should come back in the morning.

Meg brought a tray of cold cuts to my room. We ate them together, and when she'd gone, I lay a long time in the big zinc bath. When the plug was pulled, as the water gurgled into the drain, I imagined myself in a cold metal coffin.

I was not in the brightest of spirits that night, filled with such longing to hear Cissy laughing, to see her face poking around the door.

In bed, I drew up my knees and looked at the candle

and, when its flame died, stared out through the unshuttered window instead to see a full moon that was haloed in gold. Old Riley would call that a moon made for lovers, and perhaps there were lovers out there in the woods where treetops shone silver, as if crusted in snow. I don't know how long I gazed at that scene but I must have drifted off to sleep, until something disturbed my slumber, though not so much that I opened my eyes, only vaguely aware of a light tread of footsteps outside in the hall, and then the rattling sound of a knob, then the soft whine of opening hinges. It seemed that the sheets were lifted up, and the mattress sank down as another warm body crept in at my side. But I wasn't afraid, it was only a dream, and my dream was of Cissy, her arms curled around me, pulling me close as her lips brushed my cheek, and I never wanted that dream to end, to have to remember that Cissy had gone – though I did think it strange when my dream Cissy whispered, 'Don't be frightened. Mama is with you. Mama will keep you warm.'

What was that knocking? I surfaced to consciousness, dragging my head from beneath the sheets, seeing Meg come in with a breakfast tray. Shaking the cobwebs of sleep away, I got up and went to the window seat. From there, I watched her rolling back blankets, smoothing the creases out of the linen, her arms working a strong steady rhythm. In between tearing off mouthfuls of toast I was telling her about my dream, how lucid and real it had seemed when, all at once, Meg's arms were stilled. She leaned forward and lifted something from the pillow, and when she came nearer I saw what she held – some long fair hairs, a few of them grey.

The slice of toast dropped from my hand. Had I slept in the arms of a memory, or had Mrs Samuels been in my bed? I said nothing, only able to watch as Meg flicked those hairs straight out of the window. When she turned back she started to laugh. 'I must be moulting, about to turn bald . . . keep finding my hairs all over the place.'

But no matter how hard I looked, I never did see the grey in Meg's hair.

The following night I had more vivid dreams. I was standing in thick clumps of bracken, my face bathed in the moon's milky glow. I heard something rustling near to my feet and looked down to see parting fronds of fern through which a fox was creeping, dragging one bloody leg behind as, slowly, it limped towards Esther's grave. And there it lay on the mossed grey stone. It buried its snout in its brush, and slept.

I woke with the sheets tented over my head, the world seen through a tiny spyhole of light, and while my fugged mind began to clear, once the covers were pushed away, for a moment I thought myself to be back at home in Tredegar Square, staring blankly at yellow walls, at the drapes which were hanging from barley-twist posts – posts shaped like those in Wilton's Hall. I smelled something familiar, a lavender perfume, my heart thudding fast while inspecting the pillow, and I did find some hairs, but all straight and dark. Every one of those hairs was mine.

Soon after that, Meg came in, and very cheery she was that day, teasing me for my idleness. 'Wake up, you lazybones. Are you going to languish in bed all— oh, what's that?'

As I followed her gaze, only then did I see what was lying across the end of the bed, and despite the warm light flooding into the room, the promise of yet another fine day, my world seemed to darken and grow very cold as I stammered, 'D-did you put that there?'

'No!' Meg picked the garment up, shaking out yards of shimmering pink, a voluminous hem swagged with rosebuds of silk, the puffed sleeves and neckline ruched with lace. She stared down at that gown, and then up at me. 'It's very old-fashioned.' She sniffed at the bodice. 'It smells like mothballs . . . like lavender too.'

I felt my throat tighten. I managed to say, 'It's the dress from that portrait downstairs . . . the one with Esther and Joseph.'

And then I noticed something else, reaching forward to snatch up a little white card, beginning to read its message out loud: *My dearest – for your brother's visit* . . .

There was more, but I couldn't go on. Meanwhile, Meg looked distinctly whey-faced, her chin puckered in dimples as if she might cry. 'Do you think Mrs Samuels brought it in?'

'I don't know. What shall I do?' My voice was very small.

Meg answered by throwing the dress back down. 'Stay right there. I won't be long.'

When she'd gone, I did move a little, but only enough to touch the dress, drawing the satin folds into my lap, staring down as pale pink became spotted with red, stained with the wetness of my tears.

And that was how Stephens found me, when Meg brought him into the room, when I looked up to see his pained grimace as he lifted that little note from the bed.

When he'd read it, he looked like a man who might break, the wires of emotion pulled too tight, deepening every line in his face. And though the scars on his cheek remained pale, the flesh all around them was livid.

Meg was the first to speak. 'She might have been in before. We found some hairs in Miss Phoebe's bed. I thought they were mine, but, now . . .'

'She'd be mortified if she knew what she'd done.' He spoke very quietly, as if to himself. 'It's the illness, the medicine affecting her mind.'

He pressed a hand to the marks on his face, and then to his brow where a vein was distended, pulsing fast at the temple. 'I would have known if she'd left her bed. I would have known if . . .' Those last words were more question than statement, but he was soon assertive again. 'Miss Turner, in future, I think it would be best if you kept your door locked up at night.'

'Was this Esther's room?' The question had only then occurred.

'No. The children's rooms were in a suite situated above Mrs Samuels' wing. But that floor has been closed for years . . . ever since the death.'

With that, he slipped the note into his pocket, and gathered the dress in his arms. What he did with them afterwards, I never knew. But a single silk rose fell from the hem and, for some reason, I kept it. I still have it to this very day.

Back then, with it clutched in my hand, I said, 'I don't think Mrs Samuels means any harm, but perhaps I should leave here and return to London. It seems that my presence is causing distress.'

'Please, won't you wait?' He sounded alarmed. 'We have guests arriving tomorrow . . . Joseph and his wife will be paying a visit before they travel to India. A telegram came, only yesterday. I know Mrs Samuels would be upset if she lost you, on top of . . . of everything else. She has become,' he looked down at the gown clutched in his arms, 'she is very fond of you.'

When I gave a brief nod, his stance relaxed – a visible lifting of tension.

Outside, a breeze rustled through leaves in the garden. It sounded like a sigh of relief.

Mrs Samuels was either a wonderful actress, or else she was truly unaware of what had gone on the previous night.

When I went in to see her that morning, trying to act as if nothing had happened, I couldn't help thinking how tired she looked, almost as wan as a corpse. And yet it was *she* who fretted for me, asking, 'Phoebe, my dear, you look drawn. Have you had trouble sleeping? It must be this heat. Such oppressive weather.'

I looked at the vase of roses, still standing beside the bed where all the pink petals were wilting to brown. I thought of the rosebuds on Esther's gown and how those made of silk would never die. And when Mrs Samuels took my hand, I tried not to think of her in my bed, and I wondered if she was tormenting me, teasing her prey like a cat with a mouse. But, I could see no deceit in her eyes, and I really don't know what she looked for in mine.

Was it Phoebe, or was it Esther?

I kept thinking about that little card, and what she'd inscribed in faint, spidery words – what I already knew as a prayer for the dead:

God our Father,
Your power brings us to birth,
Your providence guides our lives . . .
Lord, those who die still live in Your presence,
Their lives change but do not end.

27

If anything, the weather was hotter. It seemed that all the rain in the sky had poured down that very first week I arrived, and what had been blue skies were now harsh and white as the sun glared on fields where grasses were parched – but not in the gardens where hosepipes were sprinkled on borders and lawns, where all was an idyll of peace and perfection, an oasis, an Eden, a heaven on earth.

In the kitchen, the world was a little more hellish with Cook's verbal outrage hard to ignore as she screeched and cursed at the scullery maids who were polishing silver and washing the china, or whipping up bowls of batters and cream. Mr Meldicott was plucking some pheasants. Watching him work, I felt repulsed and yet also fascinated, drawn by the beauty and sheen of those feathers; the brown speckles, the lustrous blue-green. I was thinking Old Riley would love some of those, but when I stepped forward, about to reach down, I heard a low growl, saw curled lips, yellow fangs . . . though that raw aggression soon turned to a whine when Mr Meldicott grabbed at the neck of a terrier sitting between his feet.

'Don't you go near this little bastard,' he warned. 'Might look sweet enough, but Harry's a ratter . . . and don't much mind who he happens to bite.'

Cook scolded. 'He should be kept in the stables. You

shouldn't go bringing him into the house. It's not like we've got any rats inside.'

'Except for the human sort . . .' Mr Meldicott's reply trailed off as Mr Stephens entered the room, and I suddenly wondered if that little dog might have caused the butler's facial scars. Stephens certainly glowered to see the dog there, and Mr Meldicott looked guilty enough, changing the subject when asking me, 'Are you off on your perambulation, Miss Turner? I reckon this weather's soon due to break . . . that this is the calm before the storm.'

'Well, so long as it lasts for tonight,' Stephens answered in my place, prodding a finger at some tarts left to cool on a marble slab. 'Mrs Samuels is hoping to dine outside.'

'It *might*.' Mr Meldicott gave a sage nod. 'But I wouldn't go laying any bets. Round by the stables there's ants been a-swarming, spiders all leaving their webs. You seen them cows lying down in the grass over by Bodlington way? Always a sure sign of rain, is that.'

Mr Stephens' brow lowered. His lips formed a scowl. 'I prefer to read the barometer – the mercury is more scientific than listening to old wives' tales.'

But, as it turned out, the old wives were right. Rain was on its way.

I got lost in the woods that day. I kept thinking about that dress in my room, and almost in tears by the time I returned, when I saw Meg running over the lawns, frantically waving and crying out, 'Oh, Miss Phoebe . . . there you are! Mrs Samuels was asking. Mr Meldicott's already set off for the station, collecting those visitors coming by train.'

As she wittered on about me being late, with so little time to get washed and changed, I wasn't really listening, only fretting at seeing Joseph again, and wondering if Mrs Samuels would even be well enough to dine. While glancing up at her windows, I saw a face staring back down, then a bright ray of sunlight flashed over the panes, and though my eyes closed for only a moment, when I looked back the face was gone.

Upstairs, in my room, I heard the faint crunching of wheels on the drive, the echoing beat of steps on the stairs, soon fading to somewhere else in the house. Some-one was laughing below in the courtyard, a pretty, un-familiar voice, and when I peered out of the window, I guessed it belonged to Joseph's wife.

'It's beautiful!' she was calling. 'I love it. Why didn't you bring me before?'

She looked like some slight, mischievous child, spin-ning around with her arms held wide; auburn hair gleam-ing and bright in the fiery rays of a low late sun. Joseph was walking towards her, no time for me to take a step back before he looked up, grey eyes narrowed to slits, his beautiful features too soon eclipsed and replaced by the shocked expression of Meg reflected in small diamonds of glass. As she drew even closer behind me, she chided, 'Miss Phoebe! Come away from that window. What if anyone happens to see you like that, in nothing more than your chemise?'

It was almost a mirror of that day when Joseph had been in the hallway below, when I left him there to ascend the stairs, when I'd been wearing a ruined black gown, hold-ing a ruined bouquet in my arms. The clock tocked the same steady beat, counting my steps like a metronome, but this time I dressed in silver and white, and drifted alone through the empty hall, and on to another part of the house where I heard some familiar piano notes.

My hand pushed against the music room door where the air was prematurely dark, the walls being shaded a dark forest green, though in each panelled section a gilt roundel was painted, glimmering, bright as a star. In such sombre splendour a Steinway grand was standing upon a Turkey rug. Several chairs were set around its fringed borders, as if an invisible audience listened.

Did I think myself invisible too? Did I really imagine the silver-haired man at the instrument had failed to notice my cautious approach? He looked up through the shadows. I stood very still, circled in ghosts of vibrating bass notes, over which a deep voice announced my name. 'Phoebe?'

'Mr Samuels. I hadn't realised . . . I hadn't thought to see you here. I'm sorry. I didn't mean to intrude. I wondered who was playing, that's all. I should go. Mrs Samuels will be waiting.'

He rose from the stool and, walking towards me, he offered a hand. As if his reflection I offered mine back, not knowing what to do for the best, what might be the proper etiquette. All at once, the room grew darker, the door swinging silently back on its hinges, closing us off from the rest of the house. He drew nearer. I felt breathless and frightened to be alone with the very man who had so influenced Cissy's life, whose actions dictated my own since her death. Up until then he might not have existed; a name rarely spoken, someone in the distance. But Mr Samuels was real enough and his eyes drew me back to Wilton's again, seeing the flash of the chandelier crystals, the tiny sparks glittering in his black pupils and something too knowing about his expression. He seemed to know *me*, to look into my soul. I felt as if I'd been possessed – much as I sometimes did with his wife: like a fly stuck fast in a spider's web.

With barely a whisper of air in between us, he lifted his hands, placing a palm either side of my face, his thumbs tracing slowly over each cheek, and from there they trailed down to the base of my neck where his fingers then stroked the links of my chain and I could have sworn that, just like the woods on that very first morning of my approach, even the shadows were holding their breath, trembling, as they waited to hear me say, 'It was Cissy's.'

'Yes, I know.' He lifted the locket. I lowered my eyes, seeing his fingers working the clasp, holding it open in his hand as he stared at what lay in the oval of glass, and then when the locket was shut – *snap* – it was like an end, a full stop as he let it fall back against my breast.

Stepping away, he reached for the door, but before it was fully open, he asked, 'Are you happy here? You must let me know if my wife makes too many demands on your time. And Phoebe,' he paused, 'you must not be afraid to tell me the truth. I would never consider that indiscreet.'

'Mrs Samuels has been very kind to me. But, I wonder, do you . . .'

How to find the right words? How to tell him how ill his wife had been? But then, he was here. He could see for himself. But what of the dress she'd left on my bed? How could I ever mention that without also causing him distress, because Esther had been his daughter too. So all that I said was, 'It is beautiful here . . . though I do sometimes find myself missing Bow.'

'Do you? We all cling to what we know the best. Perhaps that's why Lydia loves Dinwood, and why I prefer the crowds . . . all the noise and the filth of London's streets.' He gave a wry smile. 'Perhaps my soul is simply too black to be happy somewhere as lovely as this.'

Pressing his hand to the small of my back he steered me out to the passage, where the library's open door ahead was the light at the end of a tunnel, and as we drew closer, like moths to a flame, I answered, 'I know what you mean. I found Dinwood much too quiet at first, hardly able to sleep for missing the noise. But,' the force of my passion surprised me, 'now, whenever I'm out in the woods, I feel as if my soul comes alive. It's like having my very own secret world. I never felt such a thing before.'

His fingers tensed. He stopped and turned, and I could have bitten off my tongue – those woods being home to his daughter's grave. But he only touched Cissy's locket again, and while staring at that he quietly said, 'You know . . . every heart holds its secrets.'

A riddle. I did not understand, though when Mr Samuels looked into my eyes, when he smiled at me, I felt – oh, I don't know – somehow unique, and special, and safe. But I had seen Cissy push him away. Mrs Samuels had warned of men and their curses. Mrs Samuels had said, 'Take good care where you cast your eye, and beware of those cast back at you.'

And that's when I began to fear that something corrupt had tainted my soul, for what else could account for this affinity, these shameful dark things taking seed in my heart, to feel an affection for two different men; the one a father, the other a son?

28

When the girl came into the music room, Nathaniel looked up. He felt his gut twist. He'd known she would be in the house. He'd known the others were out in the garden and that she was yet to come downstairs, that she might chance to hear him playing the piano; not very well, but that melody had been a particular favourite of Cissy's. Phoebe might know it too. She might find her curiosity stirred.

When he'd stood in that other darkened room, in the house in Tredegar Square, on the evening of Cissy's funeral, Nathaniel had seethed with frustration and anger. That was when his resolve had been born, to exact his revenge on Maud Turner, the woman who'd damned her own sister to Hell.

He'd given her a taste of Hell. He was the devil who'd howled at her door, who'd starved the witch out, who'd broken her will. But now, seeing what he'd stolen, his victory tasted bitter. The girl looked tired, timid and sad, and he wondered if he'd been wrong after all, to uproot her from everything she'd known. Whatever revenge had been in his heart, nothing could bring back what was lost. Phoebe wasn't Cissy, and could she forgive him, even if she knew the truth? Would she ever be able to understand?

When he'd opened the locket she wore at her throat,

he'd thought back to a cold day, one February. It was less than a week after Esther's death. It was when he and Cissy had planned to elope, to make a new life in America. He'd written to her, to try and explain, though she'd surely seen all the headlines by then.

Tragedy Strikes Emporium King
Samuels' New York Expansion on Hold

How could he leave now that Esther was dead? How could he could think to abandon his son with Lydia taking leave of her senses; one moment blaming herself, the next screaming and shouting her rage at the boy, constantly begging her husband to stay? The doctors suggested, tactfully, that Nathaniel address his conscience, or else prepare for the consequences; the risk of another life being lost – to the asylum, if not some worse fate.

And so the arrangements were made. Unmade.

And so Nathaniel arrived at the bedside where Cissy was lying, looking ill and exhausted. What an act they both put on, she struggling to say she was sorry, he standing there rigid and businesslike, voicing those formal assurances that she would never go without. She nodded. But she wouldn't look in his eyes. She only stared down at what lay in her arms.

The child's hair was darker than Cissy's. A tiny, puckering mouth blew out little bubbles of milky white spittle, and when he stepped closer, brushing a finger over her lips, wiping the glistening moisture away, she nuzzled against it, trying to suck, and black, black eyes gazed up at his, as if they knew him already. There was a moment he could have sworn that those eyes belonged in another face. But, of course, it was only a trick of the light. It was only his grief – because Esther was dead.

Cissy had gasped when he drew the knife from his pocket, the blade's metal like mercury, melting, amorphous – his vision distorted by tears. He felt the trembling weight of her hand as she tried to grab at the handle, and then the dull clang as the knife hit the floor.

Kneeling down to retrieve it, Nathaniel tried to explain that he'd never intended any harm. He held out his palm and showed her the proof – only a strand of the baby's hair. He reached up to touch Cissy's locket and said, 'Will you twist it with mine? Will you keep it there?'

The tears then falling from Cissy's eyes were dripping over the child's brow, as if she was somehow being baptised, and Nathaniel asked, 'Does she have a name?'

As if on cue, another voice answered. No knock on the door announcing her entrance. 'My sister has chosen Phoebe. The child will be called Phoebe Turner.'

Maud Turner stood in the open door, backlit in a halo of wintery light – an aura of self-righteous, smug satisfaction. Nathaniel looked back at Cissy, shaking his head, asking, 'Why . . . why call her Turner?'

Cissy's sister came further into the room, and walked to the opposite side of the bed where she lifted the baby from Cissy's arms – which was when she'd sneered her victory. 'Phoebe will be raised as my own. She will have a decent married mother. She will have a decent legitimate father. And now, Mr Samuels, I think you should leave. My sister is upset. She has suffered a great deal. She needs to rest. She needs to repent . . . and receiving gentleman callers like this, well, it is hardly appropriate. We must all think of our reputations.'

Maud Turner had hated him right from the start, and now she would steal his daughter's name. Her husband would usurp his place. Nathaniel stared back at her, fuming. He had to think of what was best – best for Cissy, best for the child – the child now rocked in her new mother's arms, her tiny mouth opening wide in a yawn.

Cissy stared down at her empty arms, and when she looked up at Nathaniel again, he noticed how swollen and bloodshot her eyes which were welling new tears as she started to sob, 'Tell me . . . tell me, Nathan. What choice do I have? She says we must start as we mean to go on.'

Nathaniel Samuels shook his head. He was defeated. There was no choice. There was only one winner in this little game, this fight over a life that should never have been; the price he and Cissy would have to pay.

Call it ransom or karma, call it revenge. In the end, it came down to the very same thing: a lifetime of loss and regret.

29

Oh the pleasure of the plains!
Happy nymphs and happy swains,
Harmless, merry, free and gay,
Dance and sport the hours away.
(From Handel's *Acis and Galatea*)

'But are there any wild creatures? Any ghosts or horned satyrs who'd seek to dishonour and ravish me? Those woods look so dark and threatening.'

We'd heard the yelping bark of a fox and Caroline Samuels, her honeyed tongue loosened by wine, dramatically clutched at her husband's arm as she answered her brother, Mr Peter Faulkener, who despite the late hour – being well past eleven – had suggested a walk in the woods.

Mr Samuels' sardonic expression was veiled by thick drifts of cigar smoke and when he finally deigned to speak no effort was made to conceal his contempt. 'Personally, I shall retire to my bed, having had my fill of excitement tonight. But, I dare say Mr Faulkener may be feeling the need for some exercise.'

Mr Faulkener, as his fleshy cheeks and wide girth would suggest, had been slurping his way through every dish served – and Cook had excelled herself that night, in quantity, if not quality. There were three different soups, terrines and roast fowl. There were cheeses, fruit compotes and strawberry tarts, all washed down with several bottles of wine. To watch him eat was compulsive, a ghastly entertainment, a continual question of *will he really lift that last fork to his mouth? Could he possibly swallow another glass?* And the answer was yes, every time. And *still* he was not ready for bed, his tongue licking over greasy slack lips as he turned to his sister and drawled, 'I'm sure it's quite safe. We're not in India now, my dear. No tigers or snakes in Herefordshire!'

Though the air was still muggy and warm, lanterns that dangled from branches above were beginning to sway in small gusts of breeze. Mrs Samuels shivered, lifting a hand, beckoning to Stephens who, when not overseeing the waiting staff, remained very close to her chair all night. He now drew it back as she made to rise, but when she stumbled forward, falling against the table, it was her husband who offered assistance.

Once recovered, she bade everyone goodnight, and supported on Mr Samuels' arm she left us by way of an arch in the hedge where she paused to look back, offering Mr Faulkener her barbed riposte. 'I think you should know, there are vipers that live in those woods, and their bite can be fatal as any cobra. But I dare say they'll leave you alone . . . far more likely to meet with those satyrs or ghosts.'

Was she speaking the truth? If she was, then why had I never been warned about snakes, when I walked in those woods almost every day?

Mr Samuels looked exasperated. Joseph Samuels glared his sullen reproach. But then, he'd been glaring for most of the night – at Stephens – at his father – at me. To be honest, his behaviour was spiteful and fractious. I hardly knew the same charming young man who had almost seduced me in Wilton's Hall.

When Mr Samuels first led me out through the library's garden doors, we came upon his wife at once. Mrs Samuels was sitting beneath a loggia, a black lace parasol held in her hands and looking almost like a frail paper cut-out, with the vine's leaves creating a jagged frame through which she stared at the garden's back wall, in which a wooden door had been opened, exposing the meadows and woodlands beyond.

Another frame. Another view. If my sight had been keen enough, I could have seen Esther's grave. The trees were so dark they might be in mourning, but above them the sky was a riot of colour, low stretches of cloud, melting like brushstrokes of blurred orange and gold. I feared Mr Meldicott's prophesied storm, it being so hot, the air heavy and dense. But Mrs Samuels seemed unaffected – as usual wearing a high-necked gown, the cloth a thick satin, the colour dark crimson, more suited to winter than summer months.

When she reached for my hand, her own was limp. The palm was damp and sticky to the touch, and I prayed she was well and would not mistake me for Esther, or ask why I'd not worn her daughter's gown.

Stephens waited a little way off by the doors. Did he notice how rigid her stance and how, every now and then, she flinched? His concentration was focused elsewhere, intent on the couple who stood at the fountain; the bride clinging onto her husband's hand, as if she feared he might run away. Glancing at them, I felt sick to the pit of my stomach when hearing Mr Samuels say, 'Phoebe, you must be introduced to my son . . . and to his new wife, Caroline.'

As he took my arm and led me on, I heard the first rumbles of thunder, looking up at a flight of startled birds, wings beating a snapping tattoo on the air as they circled low over the roofs of the house. No one else seemed to notice. Joseph looked serene. But I didn't know then that he wore a mask, the inner turmoil he might conceal, or how like his mother he really was – so unlike the father who prowled at my side, who seemed too constrained by that garden's formal structured lines. I thought Mr Samuels would be better suited to walk in the woods, a wilder, more natural setting. But when he inclined his head, lifting, then kissing Caroline's hand, he was once again all mannered poise – and I have to confess to some small pricking needle of jealousy, to see those pink frills, pink cheeks, pink lips; and how very finely made she was, with her creamy skin and her red hair coiled in emerald bands that drew out the glistening green of her eyes.

With some pathetic notion of triumph I noticed her nose had been burned by the sun, flaking and slightly red at the tip – as red as Cissy's once had been when burned by the cold in a cemetery. But I pushed that thought to the back of my mind, and as far as Caroline Samuels went, well, that little chink in her armour only served to enhance the appeal, and when she extended a hand to me, her voice was as clear and sweet as a bell. 'You must be Phoebe Turner. Mrs Samuels showed us some of your work . . . those sketches you left in the library. Would you paint me with Joseph, in front of this fountain? It would make the most charming remembrance, don't you think?'

I tried to smile back, thinking I would cut off my hand rather than paint such a scene as that and, meanwhile, she giggled and stood up on tiptoes, a little bird straining to peck Joseph's cheek where rouged lips left behind the faintest brand. Below that, much nearer his mouth, I noticed a cut where his razor must have slipped when he shaved; I felt such an urge to reach out and touch it, and I had to avert my eyes, aware of him staring back at me. Or was I only imagining that, being so tense and self-conscious, wishing the ground would swallow me up when he offered no hand of welcome, and only dismissive when he said, 'Miss Turner and I have already met.'

'Oh, when?' A slight knit in Caroline's brow. A brief flash of discomposure though, in the blink of an eye, it was gone.

'After the wedding, when I escorted Mother back here from London.'

'You didn't tell me! I should have worried about you more . . . all the temptations the country might bring.'

Joseph ignored his wife's teasing, addressing his father instead, though surely his words were designed for me. 'I'd assumed that this evening was to be a private, family affair. Does Miss Turner fall into that category? Should we ask Stephens to be guest of honour?'

As Joseph glanced back at the butler, his grey eyes were shining with malice. His snide implication was perfectly clear. Servants had no right to mix with their betters. Stunned at such venom, my eyes pricking with tears, I contemplated feigning some illness, some excuse to allow me to go back upstairs. But then a hand came to rest on my arm, very light, very warm against the bare skin. I turned to see Mrs Samuels, and even beneath her parasol's shade her blue eyes were shining, unnaturally bright as she fixed her son with a steady gaze.

'As my companion, and in *my* own home, Miss Turner is welcome to dine with us. She has shared more time with me these past weeks than my son has done in several years . . . but then, *he* has been too busy, much like my husband, pursuing his own amusements in town, rushing headlong into foolish commitments, with no thought of advice from those older and wiser.'

Joseph said nothing, only looked bored, as if this complaint was too regular. But his wife's pretty feathers had clearly been ruffled, her chin thrust out defiantly – and then someone called from the library doors.

At first sight he put me in mind of a toad: a waddling walk, a paunchy round belly, his curling hair of a carroty hue, and very much coarser than Caroline's. On top of his head was a little bald patch, beneath which his green eyes were darting and greedy, and I felt my flesh crawl when they rested on me, thinking his grin like a monkey's – a rictus smile framed by gingery bristles, a moustache that looked like a wire brush. And, while he was still a little way off, I turned back to Caroline and asked, 'Is this your father?'

'Oh, gracious,' she laughed, 'Peter's my twin.' And what she said next made me come to suspect that Mrs Samuels may not be alone in her disapproval of this match. 'My parents were sadly unable to come. My father was indisposed for the wedding, hardly able to get out of bed for the gout. It was Peter who gave me away. Mama found it all a terrible strain!'

When Peter Faulkener approached, apologising for his lateness, Mrs Samuels gave him an icy glare. 'Well, if we are all here, at last, I think we should go and sit down to eat.'

She led the way to an arch in the hedge, going through to the lawns on the other side where a canopied table had been set up, and several servants standing behind it – even Jim Meldicott, looking po-faced, togged up like some miniature butler.

Once we had all been seated, Caroline began to complain. 'It's almost as hot as India, and what *are* these little black midges?'

'Thunderbugs.' Mr Samuels was dour. 'They usually swarm before a storm. Later on, the bats will be swooping to eat them.'

'Bats!' she squealed. 'Bats carry rabies in India.'

India, it seemed, was her favourite topic, starting with how she and Joseph first met, less than six months before – which, I realised, would have been after I'd met him at Wilton's. 'How ironic it was,' she began (and I thought, with a silent pang of remorse), 'that my parents despaired of me marrying here, sending me off to Bombay instead . . . hoping Peter might find me an officer there. But, no one appealed, until I met Joseph, who was travelling there, and practically my next-door neighbour in London, and our fathers conducting business together . . . and yet we'd never been introduced!'

She spoke of their Paris honeymoon, a visit to Versailles, of which these gardens reminded her – and then of their night at the opera. 'The Theatre Imperial was glorious! Why, we should have singing later on. Peter plays the piano tolerably well, at least, when he's sober enough.'

Her attention then turned to me. 'Do you play or sing, Miss Turner? Do you like to go to the opera?'

I tried to gather my thoughts, to think of the best response, and with darkness encroaching all around I hoped that no one would notice my blush. But there were oil lanterns hanging from branches which threw yellow beams across the white cloth, the swags of white roses and jasmine, the candelabra and epergnes, the glittering crystal glass – and me, as I finally made an answer. 'I have been to Wilton's. It's in the East End. It's really very small, but my . . .'

Peter Faulkener let out a loud guffaw. 'My dear, that's not an opera house! That's a common-or-garden music hall, and not one with the best reputation these days!'

Mortified, I stared down at my lap, at the scar on my hand that was quickly concealed in the tablecloth's folds as I tried not to think about that night, at which the two Samuels men had been present.

Meanwhile, Mr Faulkener went on, 'Caro and Joseph will be travelling to India ahead of me. I wonder, Miss Turner, if you should find yourself lonely in London, perhaps I might improve your education . . . escort you to Covent Garden one night. We could go dancing. Do you like to dance?' His greasy smile was lascivious. 'I love to see the young ladies gliding around a room, the rose rising up in a maiden's cheek. Even so, compared with the Indians, we Brits really are too prudish by far.'

Again, I thought about Wilton's – those murals I'd seen on the balcony wall, how alluring and decadent they'd seemed, how Joseph Samuels had been sitting below, his lips pressed against my bleeding hand. I suddenly found myself blurting out, 'I imagine India is very exotic, though I've never been myself. But my grandfather once owned a saddlery warehouse, supplying the Bombay Cavalry . . .'

I stopped in mid-flow, aware of Joseph's glacial stare, though the silence was very soon filled by his wife who turned to Mrs Samuels and asked, 'Have you ever been to India? I presume you must, what with Samuels' importing so many goods.'

'No,' Mrs Samuels responded. 'I am too old now for such an ordeal, and when younger I really had no need to go gallivanting halfway round the globe, touting myself on the marriage stakes.'

'Mother, please!' Joseph snapped. But Caroline continued to smile, extracting revenge more through actions than words, lifting a strawberry up to her lips, the wet tip of her tongue licking over the fruit, at the melting chocolate in which it was dipped.

Mama would have said how outrageous it was, to see a young woman behaving like that. But then, the heat, not to say the wine, was contributing to the languorous mood – despite all those insects circling round, lured by the flames of candles and lamps. If that Peter Faulkener had been a fly I would gladly have squashed him flat, especially when he resumed his talk, making *his* play at 'the market' again.

'Miss Turner, if you came to India I should be delighted to show you around. I was once a cavalry man myself, though now retired from military life. I manage the family's factories, producing cottons and silks, a great deal of it being sent back to England . . . the very best sold in Samuels'. But,' he became more reflective, 'much like its heathen gods, India presents two faces. One can be violent and cruel, the other all seduction and charm . . . very much like yourself, if I might be so bold.'

I looked down, quite abashed at his forwardness, staring again at my gown, at the intricate trails of silver threads. At last, I managed an answer. 'Thank you for the compliment, but I fear you are mistaken . . . as my friend Mrs Riley might say, it is the fine feathers that make the fine bird.'

Caroline laughed. 'Who is this Mrs Riley?'

'Oh, she's an old friend of the family, a theatrical dresser, and quite mad for the fashions. Sometimes she even does palm reading too.'

Straight away, I remembered what Meg had said about Mrs Samuels and the spiritualists, and how much her husband had disapproved, but too late because Caroline eagerly joined, 'How fascinating! Mama went to a séance last year . . . when the College for Psychical Research was formed, and only down the road from our house. She was entirely convinced. The gentleman medium spun round in circles and then levitated, right up to the ceiling, banging his head on the chandelier! Does your friend ever do that sort of thing?'

Joseph snorted his contempt. 'That business is full of charlatans, nothing but tricks of shadow and light. Now that I come to think of it' – he looked directly at me – 'perhaps my mother's companion is something of a charlatan too. I could swear that I once saw *her* engaged in quite another profession. Could it have been the theatre? Could it have been in Wilton's . . . or was there another Miss Turner who trod the boards as a shepherdess?'

Growing dizzy and flustered I thought I should faint, but there was an anger rising inside as I took a deep breath and gathered myself, looking straight back into Joseph's eyes. 'Yes. You may *once* have seen me there, my first and last appearance on stage, and not an occasion of which I am proud. I prefer to forget all about that night.'

'How did you come to be involved?' He seemed intent on making me squirm.

I did my best to speak evenly. 'The connection was my aunt. She was a singer, though now . . .' All at once the air seemed too thick to breathe, and through the corner of my eye I noticed Mr Samuels; one hand gripping onto his cigar, the other clasping the stem of his glass as I concluded, 'Now . . . she is dead.'

Around me each sound was amplified. The trickle of liquid splashed against glass, the tinkle of cutlery scraping on china. And when I looked up again, Joseph was no longer staring at me but facing his father when he asked, 'And this aunt was Cicely Stanhope?'

His mother broke in. 'We should leave this subject. Miss Turner is clearly upset at the recent loss of her relative.'

Mrs Samuels' breathing was laboured. Her face had turned very white. She motioned to Stephens who gave a brief nod and then disappeared, very soon coming back with a glass in his hand, its contents concealed by a napkin wrapped round, though that cloth was to slip when she started to drink, exposing clear water swirling with brown; surely some form of opiate.

A sudden silence fell over the table. It was Peter Faulkener who showed some tact, also raising his glass to make the toast, 'To Joseph and Caroline! A safe journey to India. A long and happy life!'

'We should all make a wish,' Caroline replied. 'I think everyone here should close their eyes and hope for what-ever they most desire.'

'And then,' added Peter, 'we should each confess our wishes in turn. That is,' he gave me a drooling glance, 'if they are decent enough to be shared!'

'Oh, Peter!' his sister sighed. 'Won't you leave Miss Turner alone? My wish, for what it is worth, would be for you to go to bed. And now,' she turned to her father-in-law, flirtatiously resting a hand on his arm, 'it is your turn, Mr Samuels. What is it that *you* most desire?'

His arm was drawn away, subtle and slow and deliberate. 'I don't believe in wishes. I believe in making things happen . . . that is, if you want them enough.'

I was thinking about the music room. I was wondering, *does Mr Samuels want me?* when Mrs Samuels broke in again with, 'Phoebe, do you have a wish, or would you, like me, rather not indulge in these silly games?'

Perhaps it was the wine I'd been drinking that gave me the courage to say, 'I once made a wish at the Look Out . . . a place I found up in the woods. Jim Meldicott told me about it. He said any wish made there comes true.'

'Who is this Jim Meldicott? Is he your beau?' Caroline's eyes grew wider.

'Oh, no!' I laughed, quickly looking around in the hope that I hadn't offended Jim. 'No, he's one of the staff in the house. He was here, a little earlier on . . . the young man serving up the wine.'

'You mean that scrawny, pimply youth?' She yawned, all interest gone. 'Oh well, at least tell if your wish came true.'

'I think . . .' Peter steepled his hands, double chin and red whiskers resting on top. 'I think Miss Turner should take us to this place . . . lead us out on an expedition.'

'But the woods will be much too dark, and . . .'

And that's when we heard the fox calling, putting a stop to my protest, when Caroline spoke about satyrs and ghosts, when Mrs Samuels decided to leave, and

Mr Samuels stubbed out his cigar, rising to take his wife's arm, to steady her after she'd stumbled. While he escorted her back to the house, Stephens followed at a small distance.

Joseph stared after and then he jeered, 'Look at him, crawling after my mother. He might be some pandering dog.'

His wife looked confused. 'Joseph. It's unlike you to be so rude. You said he rarely comes here. You said your father . . .'

'Not my father! Stephens, her butler . . . though they might as well call *him* Lord Dinwood. He likes to think he owns the place!'

She replied, 'Oh, stop being so irritable.' And then she was coaxing, 'Please, Joseph. Won't you come for this walk in the woods? Let's find this Look Out . . . let's all make our wishes and watch the dawn rise. We'll have plenty of time for sleeping, soon cooped up on the ship for days on end. Anyway, you *must* come. You must come and protect me. What if we happen to see any snakes? You know how pathetic Peter can be.'

Joseph apologised to his wife. 'I'm sorry. We'll go, if that's what you want, though I'm quite sure we won't be troubled by snakes, and *if* there are any ghosts in those woods, it's only my mother can see them.'

A sudden wind caused the lanterns to swing, and criss-crossing lights flashed across linen cloth, the white billowing out like the sails of a ship.

Peter looked up. 'We'll take these lamps.' He plucked two glowing fruits from a branch.

Meanwhile, Joseph turned to me, suddenly far more solicitous. 'Miss Turner, could you show us the way? I think I went there when I was a boy. But it's so long ago, I'm really not sure I remember.'

I thought he looked sad. I thought of his sister, and how he might want to avoid the grave. Is that why I agreed to go?

30

Wretched lovers quit your dream!
Behold the monster Polypheme!
See what ample strides he takes!
The mountain nods, the forest shakes . . .
Hark, how the thund'ring giant roars!
(From Handel's *Acis and Galatea*)

None of us noticed the first drops of rain, shielded as we were by the tree canopy, a natural umbrella of densely grown leaf, beneath which came the sound of the waterfall; its bubbling splash so much louder at night.

When I led the way from the gardens – through the arch in the hedge, through the arch of the door, then an old iron gate to the meadow, where we skirted a path at its edge – it felt as if we explored a new land, so alien without the sun, only the lanterns' low swinging beams and, now and then, when exposed by the clouds, the moon crowned our heads in silver, as if we'd been dusted in ice.

Processing through long grasses, we looked like some monochrome vision; the men in black trousers and open white shirts, and Caroline's gown as pale as my own. A rising wind snatched at long folds of silk – much like Peter Faulkener's fingers which continually pawed and grabbed at my arm, as he slurred his endearments into my ear; such foolish things as, 'The moon must be shining for you, little Phoebe.'

Why he called me little, I really don't know, being a good head taller than him.

'Our little goddess of light,' he droned on, 'skin white as the moon, hair black as the night, her form as slender as the birch.'

At that, he laughed and threw out an arm. 'You've inspired me to poetic thoughts. I shall write them all down. You shall be my muse! I shall make you the queen of my harem. I shall dress you in emeralds and rubies and pearls, reclining all day on silk cushions and throws.'

I returned what I hoped was a withering glance, thinking him a ridiculous, drunken oaf. One of Old Riley's sayings sprang into my mind: 'You're all leering eyes, false words and flat feet!' Those flat feet waddled on at my side until we arrived at the waterfall, its frothing a gold effervescence at night. And, when a great flash of lightning masked every face with white, when thunder growled low in the distance, Mr Faulkener's mood began to change.

'What if we're struck by lightning?' he whined. 'Don't they say the worst thing to do in a storm is to stand anywhere near a tree? Here, there are trees everywhere!'

I wondered what else he'd expected, and Joseph ignored him, now striding ahead, leading us into the densest parts, where tall trunks of firs were like bars of a cage, where we might have been trapped in a dungeon, not even a glimpse of the heavens above and only dried pine needles crunching below. Something rustled and crashed through the thicket ahead – the white bobbing tails of some deer, a stag's eyes reflecting the lanterns' beams, its horns spread like great forking branches. I held my breath, as if locked in its spell, as if seeing some ancient forest god. But Caroline, far more anxious than awed, said, 'Joseph, I'm frightened. I think Peter's right. I think we ought to go back to the house.'

'Those deer are far more frightened of you, and the thunder's still miles away from here,' Joseph answered, then carried on walking, and as we trudged after we came to a place where the tree growth was sparser, deciduous again, where the rain appeared much heavier, spitting off bark, battering through leaves, bouncing like little stones at our feet.

'Wait here,' Joseph shouted, running ahead. 'I remember . . . a place we can shelter.'

All I saw was the flickering trace of his lamp, a diminishing firefly doused in black, and behind me Caroline called out for Peter, who'd fallen a long way behind, a panting troll gasping for breath, heaving his way up the muddy path, where he suddenly dropped down on all fours, crashing around through nettles and scrub.

His sister cried out, 'Oh no . . . he's sick!'

I was far more concerned when his lantern rolled over, relieved that it didn't snuff out. And then he was standing, snatching it up, stumbling towards us and, to my disgust, he threw himself forward to give me a kiss. Pushing him off, it was all I could do not to retch, for as flabby dribbling lips sought mine there was such an assault of noxious breath; a horrible stink of vomit and wine. I thanked my lucky stars when his sister gave him a walloping slap, and it was a good thing that I was a spirited girl, having seen a few tussles down Mile End Road, and having experienced one of my own, I was nowhere as shocked as I might have been. But let us say that whatever snakes Mrs Samuels may have been speaking about, right then what hung limp from that gentleman's fly was far more alarming than any mute creatures that slid through the grass at our feet.

Caroline saw his exposed manhood and shrieked, 'Peter! Cover yourself. You make me ashamed! How can you behave so abominably? Apologise to Miss Turner, at once.'

Her brother wiped the rain from his eyes, as testy as a petulant child, 'Darned stupid idea to come when there's clearly no sport to be had. I'm wet. I'm tired. I want my bed.'

She snatched at his arm, imploring me, 'What if he passes out up here? We'll have to go with him, make sure he's not lost . . . before this storm gets any worse.'

'We can't go and leave Joseph. How will he know—'

But before my objection was done, there came another lightning crack. More fat drops of water splashed down through the leaves, at which Peter began descending the path, his sister still clutching onto his arm. They looked like an overgrown Hansel and Gretel, and Gretel called over her shoulder at me, 'Will you wait and tell Joseph where we are? You'll soon be able to catch up with us.'

Another lantern's light faded away and now, unable to see a thing, I felt abandoned, turning round in small circles, feet tripping on tree roots and ivy. I stumbled into some bushes, and shaking sticky wet leaves from my hands, I thought of a story I'd recently read where a nymph was turned into a tree, with roots growing out of her toes and feet, with bark scaling over her flesh and face, her arms turned to branches, her fingers to twigs. Meanwhile, the storm was directly above with zigzagging flashes of searing blue light and, through the violent crashes and booms, I was sobbing and calling hysterically, 'Joseph! Where are you? I'm frightened. I'm lost.'

A disembodied voice called back, 'Quickly. Up here. I've found it.'

Chasing his lantern's dipping beam, I half ran, half slipped my way up the track until faced with that same solid wall of rock that I'd found when I came to the Look Out before. But instead of taking the path to the right, Joseph's arm was pointing left. 'Behind that boulder. Go in, where it's dry. You take the lantern. I'll find the others.'

Through a lull in the thunder, I answered, 'It's only me. They've already left . . . already gone back to the house.'

Half blinded, my eyes full of water, I had to crouch down to enter the cave while Joseph crawled on ahead, holding his lantern well in front, pushing through dank, dusty curtains of green. When they fell back, brushing over my face, I tried not to think about spiders and beetles and other creeping, slithering things.

Once inside I sat on a ledge, stretching forward and wringing out twists of torn cloth that were sodden and clinging and cold to my flesh. But all thoughts of discomfort were soon eclipsed when my vision cleared, when I saw what was lying around and behind us, where twining stems of ivy wound around alien cone-like shapes – like icicles – only sculpted from stone, and some of them reaching right down to the floor. Gilded in the lantern's glow, they looked like columns of molten gold, like those barley-twist pillars in Wilton's Hall. And I heard the sweetest tinkling sounds as water oozed in through small holes in the rock, trickling down over tapering tips;

dripping into the puddles beneath. But every one of those chimes was a warning, and I should have listened more carefully. I should have been less beguiled.

'What are those shapes?' My words were hushed, but still echoing faintly around us. 'I saw some in the library cases, but they looked dead. Here, they almost seem alive. This place feels sacred, like being in a church. How did you ever know it was here?'

'They're stalactites.' His voice was dull. 'Esther, my sister, she once brought me here. But I never saw it at night . . . not like this.'

'It's beautiful. And we must be right under the Look Out, but . . .' It was suddenly quiet outside. I drew back some strands of ivy and, peering out at the darkness, said, 'The rain has stopped. We should go back down.'

'Yes, we should. But first . . .' his hand grasped my arm, pulling me round to face him, 'don't you owe me some explanation, the reason you're here at all? I must say the guise of my mother's companion is rather ingenious. Only my father could have construed something as perverse as that.'

'Perverse? I don't know what you mean. Let go of my arm. You're hurting me!'

Relaxing his grip a little, he said, 'Well, let's start with Wilton's. I'd say you were far more intrigued with him than you ever were with me at the time. Is that why you rushed away . . . to go off in search of my father?'

'No!' My voice faltered. 'Is that what you thought?' I paused and looked down, avoiding his eye. 'I admit, I was curious. There was . . . there *is* some glamour about him. Cissy, my aunt, she had it too.'

'He seemed to think so.'

'He may have done once, but that was a very long time

ago. I don't think they'd seen each other for years, not until that night at Wilton's, and soon after that she died, and then my family's circumstances changed. Your father came to know of our plight, and then he was kind enough to write, suggesting the post of your mother's companion. But I swear, since receiving that letter, I have not seen him . . . not until tonight.'

I thought of the music room earlier on, and how to any observer that meeting may not have seemed innocent. Meanwhile, Joseph's taunting went on, 'There were always rumours . . . about him and your aunt, even when I was still at school. That's why I went to Wilton's that night . . . to see what all the fuss was about. And, yes, I could see why he might have desired her, why he now might want you in her place.'

'But, you're wrong!'

'Am I? When you stood at your window this evening I saw someone else in the room behind. And how coincidental that both of you should arrive in the garden arm in arm! Do you not wonder why it is that my mother hides away down here, if not to escape all the scandals and insults affecting her reputation in London? And now he dangles you under her nose. You should be careful, a little less brazen.'

'Why won't you believe me? He is *not* my lover. That was Meg in my room. You saw the maid!' Too loud, my voice rang back all around us, too obvious the emotion it held. 'I've longed for no one . . . for no one but you, ever since we met at Wilton's. I had no idea who you were at the time. Now I find you are married to somebody else.'

Cringing at my candid confession, I tried to forget how he'd once held my hand, and how he was touching that same hand again, lifting it close to his lips, so close I

232

could feel his hot breath on my skin as he kissed what remained of the little scar.

Pulling back, I was pleading, 'Don't do that. We have to go. They'll be wondering where we are. They'll think—'

'You disappeared. You ran off. I didn't even know your name, and then I was travelling in India. I met Caro, and now . . .'

'And now, it's too late.' I couldn't bear it, struggling not to cry.

In response, he rested a hand on my shoulder and buried his face in my hair, and what happened next, I did try to resist, to push him away, as Cissy had done with his father before. But, God forgive me, I didn't, only wanting more when his lips touched mine, when his hand slid beneath the damp silk of my bodice as I gasped and arched my body against him. My eyes were open, gazing at the thick growths of ivy which blew inwards, like ghosts that were trying to enter, but never coming far enough to save me from that craving desire. As Joseph reached for the back of my neck, grasping my hair, holding me still, I saw our two shadows dance over rock walls, a flickering magic-lantern show where those stalactites wavered, like flames. And when he asked, 'Do you want me to stop?' I thought of the forked tongue of Satan, his guile hissing hot and wet in my ear – or was that the rush of the waterfall – or was that the sound of feet walking on bracken, sucking and splashing through mud outside?

I froze. I whispered, 'Someone's there.' Pushing down skirts, I was panicking. 'Can't you hear? What if they've seen the light of the lantern? We have to go back. This is wrong.'

Joseph pandered to my fears, crawling towards the mouth of the cave, looking out, giving his blunt assurance, 'It's no one. It's nothing.'

And then he was back, kneeling before me, fumbling with his trousers, his actions more urgent, determined to finish what was begun. He was gripping my chin, too hard, forcing my eyes to look into his own, to see his dark pupils dilated and glassy, shot through with gold slivers of light from the lamp. I thought that expression too brutal, too angry. For some reason, I thought about Cissy at Wilton's – her eyes glistening, reflecting the glare of the limelights below, and how those eyes were now dead and dull, never destined to open or shine again – except when lit with the fires of Hell, which was where Mama insisted she'd gone, to be punished for all eternity for the mortal sin of adulterous love. And I was committing that very same act.

There was no decorum, no holding back. I should have tried harder to break from his grasp. We may not have gone to the Look Out that night, but we were still poised on some precipice edge as he twisted me round, and then pushed me down to kneel on all fours, my cheek being grazed against the rough stone as I heard fabric tear, as he dragged my skirts higher, as I felt the press of his hands on my buttocks, gasping with the pain and the shock as he rammed himself into the heat of me, as he plunged both our souls to damnation. And what was worse? That aggressive, cruel thrusting that seemed to last an eternity, or the way his hand clamped over my mouth, hardly able to breathe as he muffled my sobs, or how, when I tried to look back, to look at Joseph's face, I saw it was turned away from me, looking back to the entrance of the cave, and such a horrible, grinning expression as if he performed for an audience there, as if I was no more than a lump of meat – as if I was no one, as if I was nothing.

When he was done, with his eyes closed and panting for breath, he stayed there a while, curling over my body, locked like a dog with a bitch. When withdrawing he made no effort to help me, only sat at my side on the cold hard ledge, lifting my skirts to wipe himself down, the cloth that was already ruined with mud now smeared with our mingled mucus and blood. The air was too warm, too thick with the musky odour of sex and when I got up, when his seed trickled from me, that slow sticky fluid made me feel filthy.

I left him there, adjusting his trousers and dragged myself out from that womb of stone to stand on the path and stare down at the house. I was shaking with shame, feeling much too exposed as I looked at the mass of dripping trees, above which the whole world appeared to be blessed by a moon auraed silver in cloudless black skies, and around that moon were a million stars – and I thought every one was a prying eye that watched as Joseph followed me out, as he came close behind and placed both his hands on my shoulders, and asked, 'You never did tell me. What was your wish at the Look Out?'

'It was my wish to be free.' I spoke without even glancing back.

I thought, *But not every wish comes true. How will I ever be free of you, and what you have done to me?*

By the time we walked back through the arched garden gate, I felt like a drained automaton, her mechanism about to run down, her insides aching, stinging and sore

– and further dismayed to see Caroline, waiting for us at the library doors.

Her damp hair was brushed out, hanging loose at her shoulders. She was wearing a fine embroidered wrap and without the constraints of corsetry, the swell of her belly and breasts appeared far more rounded than I had expected. And surely there were tears in her eyes when she ran towards her husband and cried, 'Joseph, you're back. I've been worried . . . Peter practically woke the whole house, shouting and banging around, even trying to drag a maid into bed. I wish he'd never come.'

'Well, I dare say *he's* sated and sleeping now.' Her husband's tone was cold and severe.

'I'm sorry.' Caroline looked down. As if only then aware of my presence she raised her eyes in a sullen stare. 'What were you doing, up there for so long? Why didn't you come back sooner?'

My turn to look down, struggling for words, praying she saw no guilt in my eyes, and if she had noticed that blood on my gown, in the dark, she might only think it mud.

Joseph spoke for me, still curt and dismissive. 'We got lost in the woods. We should never have gone there. We should all forget that this night ever happened.'

31

How could I forget? Back in my room, sore and exhausted, I stripped off wet clothes and went to the bathroom and washed away the sticky mess that was already drying between my thighs. I thought: *Is this love? Is this what all the fuss is about?*

Afterwards, I lay on the bed, cradling a pillow, staring out through the window where shutters and curtains were open still, where the moon was a giant unblinking eye. My own eyes closed, only disturbed by the dawn's dull light along with the scratching of birds in the eaves, and perhaps something else; a faint creaking of boards in the hallway outside. I held my breath. *Have I forgotten to lock the door? Is Mrs Samuels lurking out there?* But when I got up to look, the corridor was empty and with much relief I went to the window, to close up the curtains against the day, wanting only to crawl back into bed, to hide in a dark oblivion.

Such plans were forgotten when I saw the man walking out through the misted meadows, heading towards the woods. He stopped to look back, staring up at the house. Thinking he might have seen me there, thinking he might want me to follow, I hurriedly dressed in an old black gown and crept downstairs and stood in the hall where my eyes searched through murky webbings of light to see that the clock said a quarter past four.

Outside, in the gardens, I might be the only creature on earth, the first to view that sun's glittering haze; a halo that crested the tops of trees. But I wasn't alone. I already knew that, though I'm not even sure Joseph heard my approach, kneeling there, motionless at the grave where one of his hands gripped the top of the stone, one finger tracing over the letters that carved out his sister's name. He didn't look back when my feet snapped on twigs. He didn't look up when some water dripped down from the branches above us, darkening his hair and the back of his shirt – the same shirt he'd worn when we parted, still clinging and damp and creased.

When he finally did turn back I knew that I wasn't wanted there, about to leave and go back to the house when something impelled me to speak, to ask, 'What happened to your sister . . . to Esther?'

He looked at the stone again, his voice hoarse and low when he answered.

'It was one winter. She was fourteen. I was eight. We'd come back after spending Christmas in London, but Esther had wanted to stay. She kept crying and screaming at Mother, saying how much she hated it here, how she wanted to be with Father.'

'Did you?'

'I hardly knew him. He was so rarely here. Stephens was more of a father to me.' He stopped for a moment before going on, 'I woke in the middle of the night. It was quiet, the air strangely muffled and cold. I got up and went through to Esther's room. The sheets were still warm, but no one was there. I don't know what made me look out of the window, but that's when I saw how in just a few hours the whole world had changed, all covered in snow, tinged with a luminous blue from the sky. And

Esther was walking out through the meadow, making her way towards the woods. I didn't know she was still asleep. When she stopped to look back at the window like that, I thought that she'd seen me . . . I thought she might want me to follow.'

I thought the same thing when I saw you this morning.

'I pulled on some clothes, creeping past the nurse-maid's door . . . though there wasn't much fear of her waking. Esther always said she stole wine from the cellars, was snoring and dead to the world most nights. Everyone else was sleeping too. All of the rooms below were in darkness, but the door in the hallway was open wide. I know now, I should have shouted. I should have gone back to wake Mother, but when I saw Esther's prints in the snow, all I wanted to do was run after her. It felt so exciting. It . . .'

He looked back at me, his eyes moist, almost pleading. 'By the time I caught up, she was already here, and I knew straight away that something was wrong. She wore nothing more than a nightgown. When I reached for her hand, it felt like ice. But she didn't seem to notice, leaning close and whispering in my ear, "Ssh, Joseph. Be quiet. Don't move . . . can you see it? Can you see the fox?"

'She kept saying it, over and over again. "Look, Joseph. Look at the fox." But her finger was pointing into thin air. Nothing was there . . . except in her dream.'

'Like this.' As I spoke, I lifted an arm. My fingers were tingling with cold, and when I glanced back, I could have sworn that I saw something russet slinking away, concealed within the bracken leaves. My breaths were white in the darkness. But how could that be? It was warm. It was summer. The morning was growing brighter each moment.

Joseph seemed unaware of any atmospheric change – *if* there was anything to see beyond my fertile imagining. He looked back at the stone, his head bowed when he said, 'She left me. She walked on into the woods. I heard a loud crack, like the snap of a branch. She only screamed once . . . but her mouth was still open long after. She kept looking around as if she had no idea where she was, and all I could do was watch as the snow at her feet began to melt, an inky red-black . . . the colour of blood in that strange blue light. And then she collapsed. She was moaning. She kept staring up at me, saying, "Joseph, tell Mama. Tell Mama I'm hurt." '

Filled with a sense of profound desolation I began to step backwards, only stopping when my spine hit the trunk of a tree. But I still heard the fast panting breaths and I still saw the sharp white flakes of snow, a cobalt blue sky, a child's face looking down, his eyes stung red by his tears, by the cold. A steamed rush of breath streamed out from his lips and I could no longer see a thing. It was like being trapped in a London smog, the air clinging and ashy and sulphurous, and somewhere beyond it a voice kept on calling, calling my name, high and shrill. 'Get up, Esther. Please . . . you have to get up. It's too cold. You have to come back to the house.'

The next thing I knew was a tugging sensation, a hand on my arm, and the tones of those pleas metamorphosing, stretching through time, become slower and deeper and, when the fog lifted, when my eyes had refocused, I saw a man's face, his drained cheeks stubbled gold, his lips parting to mouth the urgent words, 'Phoebe. Get up. Get up . . . what's wrong?'

Joseph told me I'd fainted. He walked with me most of the way to the house, and when we arrived at the kissing gate I was hopeful there might be some crumb of affection. But there were no more kisses for me – perhaps a brief moment when his eyes softened, when a finger was lifted to brush a stray strand of hair from my face – before my heart sank, when he left me there, too wary of being seen by the servants, of eyes that might watch, of tongues that might start to wag with their lies; though I would discover soon enough that the cruellest of lying tongues was his.

I did as he told me. I loitered a while in the gardens, and then, seeing some gardeners emerge from a shed, quickly stole back through the kitchens again. But nobody took any notice of me, all used to my early wanderings.

Once back in my room I bathed, and scrubbed at the stains on last night's gown – as if that would wash my sins away. Some time after that Meg came upstairs and, being the font of all knowledge that day, told me that breakfast was formally served with everyone down in the dining room, after which Joseph and Caroline would be heading back up to London again, to stay a few nights with her parents in town, before setting sail for India – and a good job that Peter Faulkener was off, having spent the whole night with ringing his bell, fair terrorising one of the maids.

By the time I went down to join them no one was left in the dining room. Barely touched were the big silver dishes of kedgeree, porridge and eggs, enough toast and preserves to keep a small army going for weeks. Perhaps Cook had assumed that the guests would be marching to London on foot. There were certainly heavy lumbering steps, the sounds of bags being bumped down the stairs.

Going to stand at a window overlooking the entrance yard, I saw two carriages waiting there, the horses impatient and stamping, chewing on jangling bits. Jim and Mr Meldicott were loading some luggage in one of the boxes. Joseph was watching, a small way off, and though cleanly shaven and changed by then, he looked as weary and sour as before. At his side, Caroline was as fresh as a daisy – a vision in green and gold. She was light as the air. She was lovely. *Why would he look at me?*

I knew I should go and say a goodbye, especially when Mrs Samuels emerged, with Peter Faulkener shuffling behind, a hand pressed dramatically to his brow. Very dishevelled he was, and every bit as ugly as the gargoyles that gloated down from the walls – and how happy I was to see *him* leave; never needing to look on that face again. But Joseph . . . despite what he'd done, I felt a yearning in my heart, such a sorrow for what he'd once seen as a child.

Going to stand in the hallway, I lurked at the open door, watching Mrs Samuels embrace her son, deigning to peck each of Caroline's cheeks. Peter Faulkener was climbing some carriage steps, calling back, 'Au revoir, Mrs Samuels, and do remember, I'm staying in town. If you and Miss Turner should happen to visit, only send me your card and I shall come knocking.'

'Oh, Peter . . . be quiet!' His sister grimaced with exasperation. 'Why not make yourself useful for once. You could go and fetch my shawl. I left it in the orangery.'

'I'll get it,' I called 'usefully' from the door, more selfishly hoping to save myself from her brother's unwanted attentions again.

Soon enough I found the shawl, draped over the back of a wicker chair. It was very beautiful, the red silk worked through with little glass mirrors that sparkled like jewels when they caught the light. While admiring such an effect, I sensed something moving behind, and then came the sound of a man's deep voice.

'Ah, that's where you're hiding. Meg told me you'd come downstairs. I was hoping to find you before we left.'

I couldn't help but return his smile, so open and affectionate, and holding out the shawl in my hands, I offered my explanation, 'I was fetching this for Caroline. Isn't it lovely! It looks oriental.'

'It was Joseph's wedding gift to his wife . . . something he found in India.'

'Oh.' Hard to hide my dismay, my hands dropping, the silk hanging limp in front. 'Well, I really should take it. They're waiting to leave.'

'I'll come with you. I wanted to talk . . . about last night.'

He sounded too serious. With a hammering heart, I lowered my face as Mr Samuels walked at my side, over the floor's mosaic tiles, through the leafy tunnels of green, up the white marble steps to the drawing room, and all the while I was dreading whatever he might next say – because what if he'd followed us up to the cave? What if I'd really heard something outside? What if he'd been there and seen—

'I'm sorry.' His smile was rueful. 'Few evenings could be as tedious. Few guests as boorish as that Peter Faulkener.'

Such was my relief, I actually laughed. 'Well, I tend to agree, though I haven't met that many men to compare.'

'I'm sure you must feel the same about Joseph.'

I said nothing. What could I answer to that? I was grateful for Mr Samuels' concern, and I know it might sound peculiar, but I didn't find it the least bit strange when he stopped and touched a hand to my face, as he'd done in the music room before, as Joseph had done at the kissing gate. But this time there was a kiss for me. First the tickling prickle of his moustache, and then the soft brush of his lips on my cheek, and his voice a low murmuring in my ear, 'Goodbye . . . sweet Phoebe. I'll come back and see you again.'

Only that. Nothing more, and then he was gone, steps already fading across the hall flags as I hugged the red silk of the shawl to my breast until, recalling my mission, about to follow him out, I found my way barred by another man who quickly stepped in through the open door, pulling it closed behind him.

'You have my wife's shawl.' Joseph spoke in neutral tones.

'Yes. Here it is. I was on my way. I was—'

'You were delayed with my father. I didn't want to disturb you. I waited outside, as any other gentleman would when faced with such indiscretions.'

'There was no indiscretion. He was only saying goodbye.'

'To his "sweet Phoebe"? That's a fonder goodbye than most men would bestow on a servant. Does he know you were with me in that cave? Didn't he miss you warming his bed? You must think me a fool. You must think me blind, not to see what's been going on in this house . . . and you, clearly no more than a whore! I know what you're doing here, hoping to steal everything that your precious aunt failed to gain. Well, I warn you, Miss Turner, while there's breath in my lungs, I would rather see Dinwood razed to the ground than see *you* take my mother's place. I would rather see my father dead than—'

Stepping away in alarm, I tripped on the edge of a rug, falling hard against a wall. 'Stop saying these things.' My protest was sobbed. 'It is you who have wronged and abused *my* trust. I was a virgin until last night . . . and . . .' A horrible thought then entered my mind, 'What will I do if there is a child?'

He laughed. 'How could you know it was mine? Let my father claim any bastard of yours. But don't imagine you'll be unique. I've heard he has others hidden away.'

As I looked at Joseph's twisted expression it felt as if something inside me had started to shrivel and die. And yet I still pleaded, forgetting all pride. 'Please, Joseph, don't do this. Don't say these things. You don't understand, you—'

All at once, he recoiled. A strange sort of choking sound in his throat as, looking right past me, he stared at the portrait hung at my side, the one where two children posed in the woods. And then before grabbing the shawl from my hands, he leaned forward and brought his lips to my ear, and such trembling hostility when he whispered, 'You say that *I* don't understand. But now, I'm beginning to wonder . . . are *you* the blindest fool of all?'

And yes, I was blind, and I was a fool, having no idea as to what he implied, and despite the blank gaze in his eyes, when he lowered his mouth to mine I truly expected something else, entirely unprepared for the shock – when Joseph Samuels spat in my face.

Running out of the room and up the stairs, I flung myself down by a window ledge, hiding in dusty curtain folds, desperately trying to comprehend how Joseph could say such terrible things, comparing me with prostitutes, with those fallen women who blackened their souls, who fornicated their way to Hell.

How I wished my mama was there to give Joseph Samuels a piece of her mind, to bring out her whip against lechery and lash at his wicked, sordid thoughts. But then, she might use it on me instead, because she would know that I had sinned, and now I was just as 'worldly wise' as any one of those theatre girls who played the PRFG game.

And what was the point of thinking of Mama, when Mama was so very far away, when the only whips being cracked that day were the ones flicking over the horses' backs as two carriages set off down the drive, rolling out through the open iron gates?

32

The following day, I was travelling too, sitting in a railway carriage, lulled by the artificial shade where all of the blinds had been drawn down. But there was no hiding from Joseph's words. With every rattle and chug of the engine I heard them repeated, again and again. *And you, clearly no more than a whore!*

The train seemed too public a method of transport, considering Mrs Samuels' health. But Stephens insisted it was the best option, the smoothest and fastest route by far. He sat at my side and stared straight ahead, very businesslike in his dark grey suit, a black bowler hat atop his head, and holding a leather bag in his lap, in which were his mistress's personal effects. She lay on the opposite banquette, gently rocked by the train's swaying motion, a pillow supporting her head as she slept.

The trip had come as a surprise, and only announced the previous day when a few hours after the guests had departed Stephens was knocking on my door, requesting I go to his mistress's room.

I wished my eyes weren't so red and sore, fearing Mrs Samuels might think to ask why. But I need not have worried. She was far too distracted with thoughts of her own, hardly even glancing up from her chaise when she made the announcement, 'Phoebe, you'll need to pack some things. I have decided to travel to London . . . to see Joseph off from the docks after all. We'll be leaving tomorrow afternoon.'

At once dreading the prospect of such an excursion, I asked, 'Are you sure? Are you well enough?'

But my show of concern only caused irritation. 'You sound like that meddling doctor. Nothing will dissuade me. My son is sailing for India, and I should be there to say goodbye. I may never chance to see him again.'

Back in my room, Meg helped me to pack the few things I might need, the plan being to return in three or four days. All the while she was chattering on, 'The doctor's been in this morning. I heard him with Mr Stephens. Very against all this he is. Says he won't be held responsible. But still,' she folded her arms, 'Mr Stephens says she's made up her mind, and there's nothing to do to change it.

'And, what about you, Miss Phoebe?' Her tone became softer, less certain. 'Are you still thinking about going home, leaving us . . . leaving Dinwood for good?'

I didn't give any answer because, really, I didn't know. And the following day when we left for the station, when I wound down the carriage window, looking back out and waving at Meg, I felt strangely bereft as I stared on up at the battlement walls, and beyond to the dark spreading swathes of the woods, where I sensed something calling to me, as if it wanted me to stay, as if it might yet have some secrets to tell.

33

It was well after nine in the evening when we entered the house at Hyde Park Gate. I wondered if Mr Samuels was home. If he was, he did not come to greet us.

Mr Turnbull, the London butler, was professional enough not to show his surprise at our late, unexpected arrival. Perhaps a slight creasing of the brow, and the faintest red tinge rising up from his collar, on up to where his yellow hair was still glossed and flat and immaculate, as if it were made of brass, as if he'd been buffing it up with a cloth.

While Stephens carried the bags upstairs, Turnbull led us through some double doors, past tall blue and white china vases that were filled with tall stems of delphinium, on into a room where the watery walls reflected those mauve and purple hues, here and there puddled slightly brighter where bathed in the thin hissing light of jets.

When a maid came in with refreshments, Mrs Samuels turned to the butler and asked, 'Is my husband at home this evening?'

Turnbull's back stiffened. 'No, madam. We presumed he was still in the country, with you.'

'Oh . . . yes.' She sounded defeated and when the servants left us alone she sighed and then settled back into her chair, looking too small, looking lost and confused. Her skin was the colour of ashes. Her breaths were rasping and much too fast. When she sipped at some tea, blue eyes stared above the cup's rim at me. When it lowered, she spoke confidentially, as if we were gossiping friends.

'You know, I used to wait in here . . . during those last months, before Joseph was born. Sometimes, I'd stay up until dawn, until the staff started moving around. He used to tell me he'd been at his club. But I knew he was lying. I knew it had started.'

My head buzzed with panic. What did she mean? Was she speaking of Cissy? Such a relief when Stephens appeared, a small bow for his mistress before he announced, 'The bedrooms have been prepared.'

With that she stood up and followed him out, leaving me there with my own cup of tea, wondering what to do with myself – until a maid returned to enquire if I might be hungry. But despite a gnawing cramp in my belly I was much too anxious and tired to eat, thinking only to do as my mistress before and asking to go on up to my room.

Stephens was there, in the window bay, struggling to open some wide curving sashes that reached all the way to the floor. One suddenly eased, lifting up with a *swoosh*, allowing a welcome breeze to rush in, after which I was left alone again. Through the light of a candle on a stand I found myself staring at plain white walls, at the large white bowl filled with water to wash, at the chairs upholstered in creamy white velvets, and white damask curtains, and silky white carpets patterned with twining tendrils and roses. On one side of the hearth was a small escritoire, on the other a large brass bed. Its crisp sheets had been turned down. A nightshift was laid on a pillow.

An hour or so later, unable to sleep, I got up and ducked beneath the sash to stand on a narrow balcony. Staring out through the darkness, I breathed in the garden's sweet night stocks and jasmine, looking beyond to see silhouettes of trees that were growing in the park. But compared with Dinwood such a pastoral scene seemed too contrived, more like a painted theatrical backdrop. The sound effects were poignant enough, being so peculiar to London – bells tolling, doors banging, stable men laughing, iron-clad hooves clopping over the cobbles. I thought any one of those cabs or traps might ferry me back to Bow again, through the endless, shimmering, gas-lit streets, beneath all the roofs strung with telegraph wires, past shop fronts and grand palace theatres, the steeples and towers of churches, and then straight on down the Mile End Road, and back to our house in Tredegar Square.

Mama was probably sleeping by then. Could she sense me near and feel how, that night, we would both be lying beneath the same sky – a sky that was filled with glistening stars, every one so clear and bright that if I could stretch my arms high enough I might even be able to touch them.

Could Joseph Samuels see them too, the last English stars before sailing away; the same stars that would guide him across the sea? He was the star I had touched and should not. He was the light that had burned me. Hot tears stung my eyes and ran over my cheeks, and I wished the next morning would never come, because how could I face seeing him at the docks, having to smile and wave goodbye, when we'd already parted so horribly?

When I woke the next morning, when a maid knocked at dawn, she found me half in and half out of the bed, doubled up with the pains of my monthly curse. She left and came back shortly after, bringing some rags and medicine, and a sympathetic smile when she said, 'I've told Mr Stephens you're indisposed. He says you're to stay right here and rest. No need for you to go out today.'

'But Mrs Samuels . . . she can hardly go to the docks alone.'

'There'll be Joseph, along with the Faulkeners. And Mr Samuels got in late last night. So naturally he'll be with her. And then there's Mr Stephens . . . nowhere she goes without *him* in tow.' She smiled and raised a knowing brow. 'There's some of us think that a very rum way to go on; that to all intents and purposes, she might as well have two husbands!'

Deep down, I knew she was right. It was a strange way to carry on. But I said nothing, not caring to gossip, and only when she'd gone again did I gingerly pick up her medicine bottle, hurriedly swallowing down a few drops – almost gagging at the sickly taste. I hated the colour, a brown almost black, I tried not to think of that bottle of 'Roberts', the one that led to Cissy's death. But the tincture quickly worked its charm, soothing my cramps, and so very well that soon I was able to doze again, until woken by a slamming door.

With a groan, I crawled down from the mattress edge and wandered on out to the corridor, where I felt strangely light and invisible, as if red walls were sucking me into their shadows. My fingers drew back a window's lace panel, looking down at the street below where thin drifts of fog floated past like ghosts, where Mr Samuels was dressed in pale grey, looking to me like some silvery god as he helped his wife into the carriage. Stephens was the last to climb in, for as that gossipy maid had said, Mrs Samuels went nowhere without him in tow.

While watching the carriage head off down the road

my vision became as confused as my thoughts, as dense as the curling fog that embroidered itself around trees on the pavement, in which I saw faces of angels and demons, threaded fingers of smoke that crept in through the glass, on into my mind, and all I could think of was Cissy, and that last day we'd spent at the docks, and I knew I could never have gone there again – with or without Joseph Samuels.

Later, when my thoughts were clearer, there came a sharp knock at the bedroom door. It sounded too loud, like a hammering crash. The same with the jangling voice of the maid who was soon at my side, nudging my arm, asking, 'Miss Turner, are you awake? Mr and Mrs Samuels are home.'

My throat was parched, my voice was hoarse. 'They're back?'

'It's already past noon. Mrs Samuels appears to be most upset. She's gone to her bed. Mr Stephens says she must not be disturbed. But . . .' she gave me a knowing look, 'Mr Samuels is out in the garden. *He* says you'd be welcome to join him.'

I trod the hall's black and white tiles, heading for the square of yellow light which led to the garden terrace beyond. The fog had lifted long ago. I walked from the house into dry warm air, over the smooth hard paving stones, the springy softness of the lawns, and then along the gravel path which wound its way through the wisteria tunnel to where, at its end, Mr Samuels was sitting. One arm was draped on the back of the bench and, though seeming to be engrossed in his paper, he glanced up at my cautious crunching approach and smiled, 'Phoebe . . . would you care for some coffee?'

When he lifted the silver pot from the table, I saw my reflection, cheeks marbled red, eyes stretching wide, looking like those of a frightened child. I noticed the black silty dregs in his cup and I thought of Old Riley and wondered what fanciful tale she'd concoct if those grounds were tipped into his saucer right now.

I accepted the cup he offered but, with there being only one bench, I found myself reluctant to sit; not after that maid's snide insinuations. What if he did have immoral designs as Joseph so wickedly implied? Well, I was not so innocent now. I knew the things that men could do and, steeling myself, glancing back at the house, my voice shaking and weak from the medicine, I said, 'I'd rather stand . . . if you don't mind. I fear our relationship may be misconstrued. Others believe . . . I think Joseph believed that my place in this household may not be entirely appropriate.'

Mr Samuels tensed. 'Then my son is misguided.' Each word was pronounced in a deep slow voice. For a moment his features were clouded with green, as shadows of leaves tinged his hair and moustache. His dark eyes were narrowed, the pupils contracting to tiny white pinpoints of light.

'Did he ask where I was this morning?' My tongue was too loose, and I wished that I'd held it, at once realising how desperate that sounded.

'No.' His brow furrowed. 'Though that clown, Peter Faulkener, was most disappointed, even asking permission to call on you here.' He looked up with the faintest twitch of a smile. 'Don't look so shocked. I left him in no doubt about his attentions, on this or any other day . . .

254

though being as thick-skinned as that gentleman is, he still spent the rest of the morning petitioning my wife.'

'I hope Mrs Samuels is well. A maid told me how upset she was.'

'To see Joseph off like that was hard. To lose sight of a child . . . it's . . .'

He broke off and, meanwhile, I thought of Mama, and how I'd last seen her at Paddington station. Unconsciously touching a hand to my locket, I started to babble, 'I think it must be very hard. My mama must also be missing me. I should like to go and see her today, that is, if it would be convenient. But I have no money, no means of travel. I would happily walk, but I'm not even sure of finding the way, and . . .'

'Phoebe . . . I'm sorry.' He was leaning towards me. 'I didn't think. That was selfish of me. Go now if you like. I'll arrange for the carriage to be brought round.'

All at once, in that coffee pot's gleaming reflection I might be Mr Carroll's Cheshire cat, a grinning face backlit by green leaves and branches. But then I saw Mr Samuels' dark eyes which were narrowed again, and I heard the slight catch in his voice when he said, 'Only, you will promise to come back? I wouldn't want you to disappear.'

It would have been hard to disappear, with Mama not even being at home, and little chance of me running away when chaperoned by one of the Samuels' maids – and the one at the door in Tredegar Square refusing to let me set foot in the place. I could have sworn her cheeks were rouged, very surprised that Mama allowed that, and as to her manner, to call it brash would surely have been a compliment.

'They've shipped off to one of them church mission meetings . . . gone slumming to round up some more lost souls. Come back tonight or tomorra instead and you might 'ave a bit more luck.'

'But I'm Phoebe . . . Mrs Turner's daughter. I think . . . if you don't mind, I'll come in and wait.'

'You must *think* me as green as cabbage water! I don't know you from Adam. I don't know nothing about any daughter. You might be some thief, scheming to trick me with ploys and deceits. You might be any Tom, Dick or 'arry trying to get in through the door.' At which point the door was shut in my face.

Sitting in the carriage again, not really knowing what else to do, I was feeling very downhearted. I was thinking of finding a flower stall and going to visit Cissy's grave. But I had no money, and the prim little maid who sat at my side was protesting, 'Miss Turner . . . it took us an age to get here. What if the traffic's as bad going back? Mr Samuels might need the carriage himself.'

Doubly thwarted, as we drove up the Mile End Road I tried to breathe deeply, to hold back the tears. I could always come back the following day, and Mama and I could walk to the grave. Or, perhaps, later on, when she got home, when she knew that I'd called, she might come and visit with me instead.

While the carriage was heading through Stepney Green, I started to rack my brains. *Doesn't Old Riley live nearby?* But my head was still fuzzed from the tincture I'd taken. I couldn't think clearly any more. And then, around about Whitechapel, when we had to pull up in a jam, the maid seemed set on a fit of hysterics, fiddling with her bonnet ties, pressing a handkerchief up to her nose, snivelling and moaning away at me, 'Is it very far? Can we get out and walk?'

She wound down the window, yelling for the driver to hurry along. The cool draught that rushed in was welcome at first, but not the ripe stench that followed – what I'd always been used to breathing before, and then hardly even noticing the stale odours of sewage and soot, rotting vegetables and fried onions. At the side of the street, fancy flash costers were whistling through fingers, or else pursing their lips to blow us some kisses, offering gifts of apples and eggs. All around, other drivers were cursing and swearing, our own shouting back for the maid to be quiet, and I couldn't repeat the words he used. Everything seemed too boisterous, too loud. I found myself wishing for Dinwood Court – the stillness, the cleanness, the smell of fresh air.

'Won't you close up that window!' I was sharp with the maid. 'And no, we can't walk. We've hardly gone any distance at all.'

Muttering objections under her breath, something about an afternoon off, she grudgingly did as I asked, sitting back in her seat, her arms stiffly crossed, one foot tap-tapping upon the floor – almost like the ticking of a clock. Meanwhile, with every second that passed, I grew more indignant, wishing I'd been bolder and ignored Mama's maid, wishing I'd forced my way into the house. On top of that growing annoyance, my belly was aching. I needed to wash. Sweat trickled and tickled down my back, between my breasts, under my arms, and pressing a hand against my brow, trying to ease a throbbing pain, I started to speak, as if to myself –

'The house looked different. There was dust all over

the ornaments. Mama was never neglectful like that. There was . . .' I stopped short, only thinking the rest.

There was a man's hat on the stand, a pair of men's shoes at the base of the stairs. They must have been Mr Collins'. But why would he take them off, and if they were his, and if he was inside, then surely he would have heard my voice, and surely he would have come to the door and told that maid to let me in. Perhaps he'd gone out with Mama. Hadn't the maid expressly said, 'they'? But how could he go anywhere without shoes, and why would he leave his hat on the stand – and since when did Mr Collins go out saving any lost souls?

With those thoughts spinning round in my mind, with that wretched journey taking hours, we might as well have got out and walked. When Mr Turnbull opened the door, Mr Stephens appeared on the landing above, coming downstairs to inform me that the Samuels expected to see me at dinner – that dinner was served at seven o'clock – that now it was almost half past six.

His face was oddly blotchy and red. But being so full of my own concerns, I thought very little of his, only running upstairs to my room, to wash off the East End's grime and sweat. But not the day's disappointment – that clung on, stubbornly, like a leech.

'. . . India is so far away. I fear I shall never see Joseph again.'

Lydia Samuels concluded her speech, and then stared back down at her untouched plate, and I suddenly saw how much thinner she was, hollow-eyed and unnaturally wan, with misery etched all over her face. Or were those lines simply more visible owing to the fact that, for once, she'd left off her layers of powder and paint?

I felt distinctly uncomfortable to be part of that tableau

of jaundiced lives, with the three of us seated around a large table, surrounded by walls of vivid green, with black japanned consoles and giltwood chairs and where, though barely dusk outside, many candles were casting a mellow light.

No mellow emotions in that room, though Mr Samuels was tactful enough to ask the servants to leave before turning to make a reply to his wife. 'You should be more discreet. Of course you'll see Joseph again. But you can't hope to keep your son in chains.'

'You could have asked him to stay.' Mrs Samuels dabbed a cloth to her eye.

'To do what?' His tone was exasperated. 'You've always complained of his idling ways, and what has Joseph ever done but seek to distance himself from me, from what I am, from what I've made? In India, he has employment, sourcing articles for the shop. And when Lord Faulkener's objections relax, with his connections in the House, his belief in free trade and expansion . . . why the business can only profit more.'

Mrs Samuels was abrupt. 'Oh yes . . . I was forgetting. It is always about the business, the profit!'

Her husband banged a fist on the table, raising his voice in reply. 'Believe what you will! But you're right about not seeing Joseph again. You'll surely have starved yourself to death! Lydia . . . please,' he reached for her hand, 'you must at least make an effort to eat.'

I heard his concern. I heard his frustration. I wondered when he had stopped loving her, and if it really was Cissy's fault. My aunt and Mrs Samuels could not have been more different – like day and night, like fire and ice, like Heaven and—

Mama's cruel words came to haunt me again,

imagining Cissy at the gates of Hell. Mrs Samuels looked like an angel that night, with her white moiré gown, her pale glittering eyes, and something ethereal about her – until she took a deep breath, and her chest rattled faintly, a high wheezing sound, followed by the sharp exhalation of words. 'I could eat for a week, for a month. *Nothing* would make any difference.'

Mr Samuels glowered. His knife scraped on his plate. When he set down his glass, wine splashed on the cloth – like drops of red on virgin snow.

My nose filled with mingling aromas. Mrs Samuels' cloying lavender perfume, the sweet berry fumes of the wine, and the faintest taint of something else which made me cringe, to think such a stench may be coming from me. But the beef was very rare, the plates swimming in little puddles of blood and, like Mrs Samuels, I did no more than prod at my food, pushing aside congealed sauce and meat, exposing the china on which they lay – the delicate blue and white design. *A crooked fence. Two little birds flying over. Two lovers sailing away in a boat.*

I thought of the docks, an image bleached of colour and light. I'd only been there in winter. It must be different in summer months, with the sky like a great bowl of blue above, gulls screeching and tilting, and sails unfurled, and little flags fluttering under the masts and, below them, Joseph Samuels, standing on a deck, his grey eyes squinting back over the waves, seeing all London lost in a haze, the ship's wake a glittering trail of foam. A trail I would never follow.

I was so glad when the final course ended, thinking to go to bed. But Mrs Samuels was the first to retire, wishing me a goodnight, leaning forward and grazing my cheek with her dry cracked lips.

She did not kiss her husband.

When he and I were alone, when the staff had been dismissed again, Mr Samuels lifted his glass to drink, his black gaze above it intense, scrutinising, until he finally said, 'Lydia was concerned, when I told her where you'd gone. Like me, she began to grow anxious . . . to fear you may not be coming back.'

'Mama was out. But I should like to try again . . . perhaps in the morning. That is, if we're not travelling back to Dinwood.'

His answer was dour and to the point. 'I have no idea of Lydia's plans. I presume she'll stay on for a few more days.'

Again, I was unable to sleep. Again, I went out to the balcony, staring up at the clear dark skies, feeling very weary and low as I fretted at Joseph's loathing for me. And there was the fact that I'd missed Mama, and that she'd made no effort to visit with me – not even so much as to send a note.

What if that maid hadn't mentioned my visit? She hadn't seemed very reliable and, with that in mind, I went inside and opened a drawer in the escritoire, soon finding some paper, a pen and some ink with which I composed a few brief lines. I told Mama that I was unhappy, asking if I could go back home, and even if that was not allowed, well, at least she would know of my presence in town.

With that done, with the envelope sealed, I decided to take it down to the hall, wondering if there was a salver, like the one in Dinwood Court, hoping my letter might be picked up, to find Mama with the earliest post.

The hall was in darkness and hazed with cigar smoke

that spilled through an open door below, coiling on up to the galleried landing, drifting over the risers like spirit snakes. Descending towards them, I stopped at the sound of a groan. I felt sure Mr Samuels was smoking below, but dare I go any further, disturbing the man who – I could now see through that open door – was sitting in front of a desk, and held in his hand was a pen, and scattered all over the rug at his feet were discarded and torn sheets of paper. Perhaps he was also writing a letter. I should not invade his privacy. And what if any servants appeared? What would they think at such a late hour, to find us alone, and me in no decent state of dress? And what if he wanted to know what I held, and who *I* had been writing to? I no longer knew what to do for the best. Bad enough to lose Joseph but, on top of that, to think of a life where I never saw Mr Samuels again.

I heard a clock strike – twelve chimes in all. I know because I started to count as I turned to ascend the stairs once more, that letter for Mama screwed up in my hand, my eyes fixed ahead on the big stained-glass window, where moonlight was suddenly shafting in through the panes of that Garden of Eden. But at night, and when wreathed in tobacco smoke, its translucent flowers and trees and birds were lacking in colour, were dingy and dull, as if all of God's blessings had been withdrawn.

34

For over an hour Nathaniel remained in the dining room where he thought, and he drank, and he smoked alone. One by one, the candles died. At last, when the dark green walls looked black, he went through to his study and poured out some whisky.

He wanted – he needed – to write to his son. But how to explain, how to tell the truth? Was it better to let the lies go on?

They'd started when Joseph was still a child. As a father, Nathaniel should have cared more. He should have tried harder when Esther died and Lydia insisted the boy live in Dinwood, faced every day with the tragedy in which he'd been forced to play a part. Nathaniel had been selfish, grieving for more than one daughter's loss, and too engrossed in his own affairs to think to take the boy away.

Had Joseph discovered who Phoebe was? What else could explain his son's recent behaviour? And what had he witnessed at Wilton's, where he must have followed to spy on his father? It was surely enough to make him suspect the reason for Phoebe's place in the house. But to taunt her so cruelly – and then, at the docks that morning, to have shunned his own father so publicly. What Lydia said at dinner was true. Joseph was lost – to them both.

Was his wife lost too? Nathaniel had been shocked to see her at Dinwood, more than surprised when she'd travelled to London. She'd looked ghastly at dinner that evening, eating nothing, her breathing laboured. And so rarely did she smile any more, except when she looked at Phoebe. Was that natural? Was it right? He should have thought more. He'd been obsessed with his own situation, seeing only one end – his revenge on Maud Turner. And now that was done, what was he going to do with the girl? What was he—

What was that sound in the hall?

He'd left the study door open, with it being so late and everyone else gone on to bed. Looking up at a mirror set on the wall, he watched the vision unfolding there: a pale hand sliding over the banister rail, two bare feet descending the stairs, and caught in that light, dark and misted with smoke, she could have been Cissy. She—

Had Phoebe heard his groan? She stopped, seemed to listen – perhaps she could see him. Perhaps she would come on down to the study. If she did, then she'd see the proof of his guilt. The cabinet doors were open. He could get up and shut them. He still had time. But why not let fate decide?

A clock whirred as springs and coils tightened, tensing, preparing to strike, counting down to the moment when he would be judged.

But that night Nathaniel was granted a reprieve because as each doleful chime rang out, Phoebe turned and walked back up the stairs.

35

The last chime rang out as the bedroom door closed. There were none the following morning when servants moved mutely through every room, stopping the hands of every clock – because during the night Death had walked through the house.

After tearing my letter into shreds I climbed into bed and, with only a slight hesitation, reached for that morning's medicine bottle, thinking – *one drop, one little brown drop, a taste as bitter and dark as my thoughts. One drop to help me sleep.*

Sleep came fast. I dreamed of the nymph, Galatea, now forever lost beneath the waves, while Joseph was sailing above them and the sea's silver foam sprayed over his face – but soft – like a kiss, like a blessing. I thought I heard the cry of the fox. It was only the distant bark of a dog and then – what was that? – something shuffling, scratching?

My pulse began racing. My skin was cold but running with sweat. I held my breath, burying my head down under the covers, trying to block out the whimpering sounds from whatever was there, outside in the hall. Only when it was quiet again, after fumbling to light the stub, did I get up and make my way to the door where my fingers curled slowly around the brass knob, willing cold metal to infuse me with courage, wincing at the click of the latch's release.

The corridor was empty – or so I thought, until a slight movement caught my eye. Much further down, near the top of the stairs, I saw Mrs Samuels, her shift floating behind as she walked, the muslin cloth billowing out like wings. I think she must have heard my gasp, for she stopped, and turned, and, as she came slowly processing towards me her face was quite blank, blue eyes staring, not seeing. Her hair was a wisping halo of gold and how strange it was that when she drew close, so close that our breaths might mingle, the hairs prickled up on the back of my neck as those small clouds of vapour froze on the air, strung thick with glistening pearls of ice. And although Mrs Samuels was facing me, I clearly saw the back of her head in a mirror that hung on the opposite wall. And there I also saw myself, the girl who looked out from an open door, her face starkly lit in the candle's flame – a face that was made of shadow and light – a girl with black hair, white skin, black eyes.

Only *she* wasn't *me*.

Where my mouth was open, the source of a pitiful moaning sound, hers was closed, with the faintest trace of a smile. I knew that I'd seen that expression before, in a painting that hung in Dinwood Court, and I already knew the reply when I asked, 'Who are you?'

'Esther,' said the girl in the mirror.

'Mama,' said the woman who stood in the hall, who looked at my feet and called plaintively, 'Oh . . . my love, you're still hurt. You're still bleeding.'

She took a step forward. I took a step back, glancing down to see a slight stain on my shift; surely a leaking of blood from my courses. But it must have been an illusion,

266

that other thing I saw, when a shadow cast over the crimson walls drew my eyes straight back to the looking glass and there, in that reflection, a glistening dark wetness continued to spread, the white hems of Esther's nightgown now soaked with a dripping red – a colour that mingled through flowers in the carpet, the weave blooming and blurring before my eyes.

Another step back. Esther did not move, and through the fast gasps of my trembling breaths I heard Mrs Samuels speaking again, her words slow and rhythmic, mechanical. 'Don't run away, Esther. Please, let me hold you. Let me keep you warm.'

As she sought to embrace me, her hand snagged a ribbon come loose at the neckline of her gown. The lace of the collar was dragged to one side, dislodging a bloodied dressing of gauze, exposing the withered flesh of her breast; an affliction that caused such a shock of remembrance, bringing back those words Old Riley pronounced when reading my leaves in Tredegar Square: *I see a rose that is not a rose.*

The growth had the look of raw liver; a purplish red, with moist puckering petals that blossomed around the pale bud of a nipple. And beneath the lavender perfume that Mrs Samuels always wore, that rose exuded an odour – a distinctive stench of rot.

Fighting to quell my panic and tears, I made a desperate, choking plea. 'Please wake up, Mrs Samuels. Wake up. I'm not Esther. I'm Phoebe . . . I'm Phoebe.'

She blinked and looked round. She was conscious again but dismayed and confused, as she'd been in the garden at Dinwood before, asking, 'Phoebe? Where am I? What's happening?'

I left her there. I ran downstairs to find Mr Samuels still

in his study, slumped in a chair, his head lolling forward onto his chest, his long legs stretched out, ungainly in front. Immediately disturbed by my presence, he shifted and groaned, then pushed back the hair fallen over his brow. For a while, his eyes stared blankly at mine. His lips formed a word, and I'm sure it was Cissy. But then he was standing, pushing right past me to close up the doors of a big japanned cupboard, and having done that he turned to grunt, 'Phoebe, whatever is it? What's wrong?'

My voice was quite clear and unnaturally calm. 'It's Mrs Samuels. You have to come. She's upstairs in my room. She's not well at all.'

Turnbull was woken and sent for the doctor, but it was hours before anyone came. I sat on a chair pulled up close to her bed. On the nightstand I noticed the sketch I'd once made – the one she'd requested of Esther's grave. Mrs Samuels had brought it with her, all the way from Dinwood Court.

Someone had alerted Stephens. A motionless and expressionless guard, he took up his post inside the door, and who could know what he was thinking about. Like me, he heard her rasping breaths, and the dull beat of feet marching over the floor as Mr Samuels paced the room, pushing back shirt sleeves, rubbing a finger around the unfastened neck of his collar, and all the while pleading with his wife. 'How long have you suffered with this? Why didn't you tell me before? We could have consulted with other physicians. I swear that quack of yours in the country is not fit to—'

'He's done all he can,' she broke in. 'I saw the specialists long ago. There is no cure for this disease . . . this punishment is the badge of my shame.'

'What shame?' He sat on the end of the bed, leaning forward and holding his head in his hands.

'Oh, Nathan,' she whispered. 'I was the cause of Esther's death.'

His head jerked back. 'You don't know what you're saying. It was that fox snare, an accident. You were nowhere near those woods. You—'

'You don't understand.' Mrs Samuels paused, twisting around to look at me; the bleakest of smiles on her lips, but still addressing her husband. 'When we got back to Dinwood that day, she found out that you planned on leaving me.'

'Lydia. Not now.' Mr Samuels hushed her, the very next moment demanding to know, '*How?* How could you . . . how could Esther have possibly known?'

Looking back at her husband again, the strength of her answer surprised me. 'There was an anonymous letter, penned by a so-called well-wishing friend . . . and when Esther found that in my room every one of those wicked wishes came true. The spite in that ink damned us all in the end. *That* was how Esther discovered the truth.'

Gasping now, she glanced over at Stephens before continuing, 'Without having seen that, she'd still be here. Reading that filth, about you, about . . . well, she wasn't a child any more. She understood every single word. But for her to blame *me*, for Esther to say those terrible things . . .'

Mrs Samuels was racked by a choking spasm but when it was over, despite her distress, pressing a hand against her breast, somehow she managed to carry on. 'I said things that a mother should never say . . . that you didn't want her, that she should forget you. I never imagined she'd go outside. We'd found her sleepwalking before,

269

when she'd been frightened, when she was upset, but never to leave the house like that. I'd taken a draught to help me rest, and when Joseph came back to wake me, crying and asking for help, I couldn't think clearly, I couldn't make sense of what he was saying, only furious to see him so cold and wet, only angry with Esther for taking him out to the woods like that. I couldn't think how to calm the child. I gave him some of my laudanum, and soon he lay still in my arms, both of us sleeping till morning . . . when Miss Everett came knocking to tell me that Esther had disappeared. She woke Stephens. He and some others went out to search. It didn't take long to find her . . . to follow her prints through the snow, though by then . . . by then, it was too late.'

'You can't blame yourself.' Mr Samuels persisted. 'The inquest said—'

'The inquest was wrong!' She struggled to rise on her pillow. 'That injury didn't kill her. Esther lay there and froze to death while I seethed in my bed, while I burned with the fire of my jealousy, to think that she cared more for you than me, to think that you . . . Oh, Nathan,' she looked into his eyes, her own streaming with tears, 'may God forgive me for what I did. When I knew she was dead, my soul rejoiced, because then I knew you wouldn't leave. And now,' she was panting, her voice thin and strained, 'now I must pay for such wickedness.'

'Joseph must never know about this.' Mr Samuels was adamant.

His wife tried to lift her head again, an action that cost her great effort. 'You *must* tell him. I don't care if he hates me.' And then, as if filled with new vigour, she shouted, 'Why should he bear any guilt, blaming himself, thinking that if he'd stayed at her side or gone to find help from somebody else . . . But he was so young,' she was weeping again, 'he was only a child. When they laid her body on the bed, he cried all day for a fire to be lit. He wanted to hold her, to make her warm. He wanted his sister to wake again. He couldn't begin to understand.'

She fell back on the pillows, fighting for breath. She didn't say another word, only watched as thin rays of the morning sun began to shine in through the lace at the window. And it did look very beautiful; a trellis of silvery light on red walls, and I thought of those visions I'd had in the woods, all the red and the white and the snow and the cold, somehow sensing that Esther was trying to speak. But whatever Lydia Samuels confessed, I might as well have been blind and deaf; still unable to see my own part in all this.

When the doctor arrived, he shook his head. He examined her breast and took her pulse, muttering on about her heart. He gave an injection and, soon after that, her brow was unlined, all signs of anguish smoothed away. Sleeping like that, in Morpheus' arms, she did look very peaceful – her hair spread over the pillow, her breathing still shallow, but regular. And all the time she was holding my hand, and I wondered if she thought me Esther again.

When she gave a long sigh, and then breathed no more, when the sheet was drawn up to cover her face, while the doctor asked questions and jotted down notes, I could still see her last metamorphosis – that death mask, that final portrait. I thought all of life was illusion; a sketch, a work in progress. The end, the only reality, was no more than an empty withered shell. But if that was so, then what about Cissy? Cissy had still been healthy and strong, and even her corpse had been beautiful. Cissy had never done anything wrong, except to love a married man.

I jumped at the touch of a hand on my arm. Mr Samuels said we should leave the room. But Stephens remained at his post on the door, as still as a statue, though not quite made of stone because there were tears spilling from his brown eyes.

As we passed, Mr Samuels spoke low in his ear. I wasn't able to hear what he said, but when the door was closed behind, he left his wife and her butler alone, just as he'd done so often before.

36

Somehow I was able to think clearly enough to throw some belongings into a bag and, wearing pale grey, the closest to mourning I'd brought along, my feet crossed the trails of red flowers on the floor where, in the clear streams of morning's light, I saw no sinister stains of blood. But I still let out a sigh of relief when the bedroom door swung closed behind and, with that bag clutched tight to my breast as if it might offer protection, I automatically lowered my eyes, avoiding the mirror fixed on the hall wall as I went on downstairs to wait in the room where Lydia Samuels and I first met.

A bell rang. I heard Turnbull invite someone in. I went to look out, to see who it was; still thinking that Mama might chance to arrive.

It wasn't her. Mr Samuels was shaking hands with a grim-faced, obsequious man who wore a black tailcoat and black silk hat, and I knew it must be an undertaker: another one of those scavenging beetles who'd taken Aunt Cissy away in a box, in a carriage of gilded cherubs and skulls.

In the backdrop for *Acis and Galatea* there had been cherubs too and it suddenly struck me that ever since Wilton's, the first time I saw Mr Samuels' face, my life had been cursed with sadness and death. That's why, when he turned to glance back at me, I could only look away, thinking of Lydia Samuels' warnings, unable to face the shame, to know it had been his affair with my aunt that had caused his family such grief, that had – however indirectly – led to his daughter's death.

I went to sit down near the closed garden doors and started to tremble violently, my hands gripping hard at the table edge as the air spun around me, a vortex which fractured then split into shards; little rainbows of glistening, glassy light. And when some of the servants came near my side, when they started to murmur – *Are you all right? Won't you go back upstairs and lie down for a while? Won't you drink this sweet tea? Won't you take this laudanum for the shock?* – what I heard was not kindness, but sneering doubt. What I heard was – *Who is she? Why is she here? What right does she have to be in this house? What is he going to do with her now?*

I ignored them and stared at the garden. Out there life went on as before. A blackbird pecked worms from damp grasses. Sleepy bees buzzed over the lavender bushes – that perfume forever now Lydia Samuels. But there was no dripping wisteria. All those purple buds had long wilted away, though the leaves formed an emerald curtain still, whippy tendrils of green curling over the window; and when my eyes closed at the glare of the sun I could still see those coiling serpent shapes, as black as death, as black as the sin of adultery.

Someone came in with a letter, setting it next to a fresh cup of tea, taking the old cup of tea away. My fingers fumbled with the envelope, eventually able to open it up, to read Mama's words through misting eyes, the words that she'd written the evening before:

My dearest Phoebe,

We have arrived home, and very late, and only to hear that we missed your call. But the maid has assured me that you will return, and very sorry she is for her error. I can only blame myself, instilling such caution into these girls — especially after the Millais theft.

But Phoebe, my dear, I have such news! We have been blessed with a Great Expectation — the chance to begin again. They say all <u>Good</u> <u>Things</u> come to those who wait and now I know how true those words and, suffice to say, when we next meet, that very same truth shall be told unto you!

Make haste and come home as soon as you can.

From Maud Turner,

Your affectionate and devoted Mother

While worrying over that letter, that 'we' that Mama used, the conundrum of what her news could be, I heard the front door give a shuddering bang, a sound much too loud, disrespectful it was.

Getting up from my seat to look out again, that time I saw Mr Samuels alone, standing quite still at the foot of the stairs. His red-rimmed eyes stared up at the window above, which suffused his face in its patterns of light, and I thought he looked like an anguished saint, lost in an intimate moment of prayer.

Breaking through the silence, I started to speak, muttering something about being aware that my role in his household no longer existed, and that I should now return to Bow.

In response he looked down at the bag at my feet and merely gave a distracted nod, and told me the carriage was waiting outside. Was it so very contrary of me, to find myself wishing he'd ask me to stay, wanting to press my face to his chest, to breathe in the stale smoky scent of cigars, and that other perfume – Hammam Bouquet – so comforting, so familiar?

'Mr Samuels . . .' I hesitated. Should I mention that vision of Esther last night, or would he simply think me mad? 'Do you believe in ghosts?'

Dark eyes were locked with mine. 'I believe that we can be haunted . . . by sorrow, by love, by the wrongs that we've done. I'm not sure if that's quite the same thing as a ghost.'

I should have asked him then – if he was still haunted by Cissy. I think if I had then he might have confessed the things that his wife had tried to tell that, deep down, I must have already known, there in the darkness of my soul, in a place where the truth was safely locked.

But that was the morning I thought it best to throw away the key, and I said nothing more, only picked up my bag and made for the door – looking back, too late, as he turned away, as Mr Samuels ascended the stairs.

37

When he heard the door closing, Nathaniel stopped to look back from the stairs. Was it too late, or might Phoebe return, as Esther had done that time before, when she ran up behind him and grabbed at his jacket, and wrapped her arms around his waist, and pleaded, 'Papa, please . . . don't send me away. Won't you let me stay here with you this time?'

This time – this time, things might be different. This time, Nathaniel might make amends. Then, he'd held Esther's hands in his. He'd kissed her cheek and tried to smile. 'You know I'll come and visit. I'll come back and see you as soon as I can. But I'm going to be travelling on business. I'll be out of the country for several months, and your mother would miss you . . . and what about Joseph? What would he do without his big sister?'

'But, Joseph's so young. He's different to me. I'm you. He's Mama. And next year he's going away to school. What am I going to do? It's like being buried alive down there. I hate Dinwood, Papa. I'm lonely and bored. I miss you so much, and—'

'Esther, your mother is waiting.' Stephens appeared at the open door.

Nathaniel's daughter grew stiff in his arms. When she started to cry he cupped her chin and wiped at damp cheeks with his fingertips. But all he could think of was

Cissy, and the other child now in his life. He asked Esther to try and be patient. He promised that he would write. He promised that things would be different soon.

And they were. Because somebody else had already written, and that letter was waiting in Dinwood Court, and the next time Nathaniel saw her – and so much sooner than he had expected – Esther, his beautiful girl, was dead.

Thinking of that, with trembling breaths, his eyes blinking hard to hold back tears, Nathaniel continued to climb the stairs. The undertakers would soon return and then they would carry Lydia off, taking the box through the very same door through which Esther had passed on that final day, through which Phoebe had passed that morning – gone back to the woman he'd come to hate, and now with more venom than ever before because, when Lydia spoke of a letter, an anonymous letter that Esther had found, he'd instinctively known the source of attack, the cunning, wicked, deceitful means by which Maud Turner reclaimed her prize – his lover, his daughter, both stolen as ransom.

He could still strike back and ruin the bitch – but that would mean telling Phoebe the truth, and how much more harm would such actions cause? The girl had already suffered enough. God knows what she'd gone through in Dinwood Court. She was his daughter, not a possession, not a pawn with which to fight his war. The kindest thing was to give her up.

He had to think about Lydia, a consideration too long denied. He must think about how and where his wife might have wished to be buried. It was something they'd never spoken about. He would have to ask Stephens. Stephens would know.

PART THREE

There's a star shining brightly above.
And now that I've seen it my heart has been lost.

(From 'Phoebe' by Collins & MacKenna)

38

A row of small houses was terraced together, all of them fronted by a walled alley. While opening up the gate of the last my skirts snagged on the thorns of a mildewy rose, but something else was tugging behind, and spinning around I felt such relief to see only a nervous-looking boy, wide-eyed as he whispered dramatically, 'She's got one of them circles going on . . . a couple of posh old women today. You'll have to wait your turn. Mrs Riley don't want no disturbance.'

'Who are you?' My voice was shrill and aggressive, as if it belonged to somebody else.

'I lives next door but one. She pays me a penny to guard the door.'

'Well, you're not guarding me!'

Tearing my skirts from the tangles of rose and pushing that scrawny urchin aside, I made my way to the window bay and pressed my hands against the glass to stare in through a gap in the closed-up drapes. There, the light of a single white candle illuminated what might very well be a scene from some Arabian tale, where dark blue walls were stuck with glass stars, more dangling down from the ceiling above, in the centre of which a brass lantern was hung, ornately punched with tiny holes, through which diffused a misting smoke. From a hook at its end a tent was suspended, some sort of contraption made of black netting and, combined with the murky swirling fug, the vision within it was blurred and dim. But then, my eyes were not at their best, being exhausted from too little sleep, from the hours I'd spent trailing around through the streets.

Was it only that morning I'd sat in a carriage, my life with the Samuels left behind, no idea that before the day was out my life with Mama would be over as well – that as far as Maud Turner was concerned I might as well have ceased to exist?

The cause was her 'Great Expectation', descending the stairs in Tredegar Square at the very same moment when that new maid finally consented to usher me in. Mama's letter could not have begun to prepare me for such a surprise as that, for it seemed that my mind was unravelling, leaving one nightmare behind only to find myself dreaming another. A flash of stark recognition and I knew that man's face at once – the glowering brow and stern dark eyes that had glared out from Mama's bedside for years. Side whiskers, a lighter shade than I'd thought, were now joined by a thick and grizzled beard, and the hair on his head was streaked with white, but there was no doubting this was my dead father. My mama's faded sepia image was manifested as a fully formed man who was living and breathing there on the half landing, who gazed down at me as if from a pulpit, William Turner paused at the very spot from which Cissy's face had once stared out, before *The Somnambulist* disappeared.

It was all too much. Mrs Samuels was only that morning dead and now the dead were walking again and, for a moment, I honestly thought that Mama had changed her allegiances, taking up with the spiritualists after all and invoking some 'other powers' to bring back those souls passed through Death's Iron Door. I grew dizzy, unable to focus, as if the whole world had been plunged under water, where Mama was swimming along at my side, and dressed in dark blue – not the flowery gown Old Riley had seen, and then mentioned in her letter to me. But, it was still a shock, all my life only ever knowing this woman when dressed in black, in her widow's weeds.

Mama took a very firm hold on my arm and led me through to the music room, and there she insisted I rest on a sofa, sitting down at my side while fussing and fretting, 'Phoebe, my dear, you look so strange. You must tell us what's happened. Have you been ill?'

Even in such a state of confusion I saw that Mama looked very well – a little plumper, a glow in her cheeks, and her eyes more alive than I'd seen them in years. But how could she ask me what was wrong? Had she not seen him, that ghost on the stairs?

My voice, when it came, was breathless. 'Mrs Samuels . . . she died. I can never go back. And now, out there . . . out there in the hall, when, when I—'

'She's dead!' Was Mama smiling? She certainly sounded more pleased than shocked. 'Then the Good Lord has spared you and answered our prayers, guiding you back to the righteous flock, to share in His higher purpose once more.'

I wondered, could she have understood, to be so unmoved by another's death? But I never did get to ask, for when I looked at Mama again her face was glazed in pure adoration, smiling back at what loomed in the open door, and that spectre all too substantial and real. He was draped in a long black coat; a full black cravat knotted at his throat – a style of dress not quite fashionable, but carried off with a certain aplomb. One might even think him a 'theatrical type'.

I must have cried out, though Mama soon sought to allay my distress, stating proudly, 'Phoebe . . . this is your father. Of course, it must be a surprise, seeing him here in the house like this. I felt the same . . . that first time he wrote. But now you shall have a good man to respect, to look up to and—'

Her speech came to a halt when the maid bustled in, such a knowing smirk pasted over her face and no mention of what had gone on yesterday, still not a word of apology! The tray in her hands was set down with a thump, causing china to rattle, and little crumbs to be flung out in every direction. And while watching that, while looking around, I noticed how shabby the room had become – new stains on the cushions and carpets, smeared fingerprints over the windows and mirrors. *What would Mrs Beeton have said!*

Mama said, 'I know . . . I know what you're thinking. But Mr Turner has shown me the light. We must be patient and train Sophy up, the same with the other girls downstairs. This way of life is so new to them . . . useful employment and self-respect. How else can they enter our privileged world and how else can they hope to change, unless we their betters give them a chance? Isn't that what our own Mr Gladstone has been striving so hard to achieve?'

'You mean she's . . .' Were my ears deceiving me? Was Mama living with prostitutes?

'Yes,' she stammered, becoming somewhat flustered and pink, almost as pink as the circles of powder dabbed on Miss Sophy's dimpled cheeks. 'Yes, well she was, but she's not any more. Sophy's a decent girl these days. We have great hopes, don't we, my dear?' With a simpering grin, she looked up at William Turner again, at which point his silence was broken.

His voice was much higher than I had expected, reedy, the slightest American twang, and not without a certain power of oration. 'Sophy will be joining my church, returning with us to America. I am only back to atone for my sin, to reclaim the wife I abandoned before.'

He stepped closer to Mama, and she looked up at him with – what? Was it pride, or desire? Afterwards, when I came to forgive her, I hoped Mr Turner responded in kind, that he gave her no cause for unhappiness. But it was hard, always thinking of when that maid left the room, when she squeezed past him, much too close, and the way his hand brushed against her breast, lingering there a little too long.

I don't think Mama noticed. If she did, she preferred to be blind. But what a strange trinity it made when only the three of us remained – my mother, and me, and my father – the man who now stepped into the room, drawing a Bible from one of his pockets, his lips kissing the gilt cross embossed on its cover and then, while holding it close to his heart, he stared a long time at Mama, before sitting down on my other side – me squashed like the filling between the Lord's bread.

With his Bible set on a table, he took both of my hands in his, at which I felt nauseous and thought I should faint for, despite his immaculate attire, there was such an unpleasant odour about him, something sweaty and yeasty as if he'd not washed. Was I unnatural to be so repulsed by the touch of my very own father, to snatch my fingers away like that?

His lips remained curled in a rigid smile. But I did not

smile back. I felt tainted, distinctly uneasy and, looking away, avoiding those fierce and burning eyes, I noticed the boxes by Cissy's piano – some sealed up with string but others still open, and all of them brim-full of leaflets and books.

Mama followed my gaze, and so light were her words that she might be discussing the weather. 'Those are our missionary pamphlets and Bibles. I was wondering about the piano, shipping that off to America too. But Mrs Brown needs a new instrument, so—'

'You're leaving this house!' I looked at Mama in disbelief. 'You're leaving Bow! You're giving Cissy's piano away? What about Mr Collins? Perhaps he might like it. What about me? This is my home. I don't want to go to America to live with a man I don't even know.'

Mama's cheeks flushed even redder and her brow was sheened with sweat – that predictable sign of her imminent rage. 'How dare you speak to me like that? You are still a minor . . . no choice but to obey your parents, as the law of the land and as God commands, thou shalt honour thy father and mother!'

My answer was low, almost a sob. 'Does Mr Collins know about this? Is this the reason you threw him off?'

Clearly irritated by my persisting in bringing up Mr Collins' name, Mama looked anxious, glancing on past me to where Mr Turner was silent and grim, listening intently to every word.

'You know very well.' She bristled. 'Mr Collins was always Cissy's friend. I can hardly be blamed if his feelings developed. I certainly never encouraged it. I can't think where he ever got such ideas.'

'But he thought you a widow. As did we all! Old Riley suspected that something was up, but I—'

'What do you mean? Has Mrs Riley been writing to you with her gossip? I expressly forbade it. That woman can't bear to see joy in my life. What's more, she is dabbling in blasphemous acts . . . tapping at tables, invoking the Devil.'

'You seem glad of the fortune she told in *your* favour. This dark man . . .' I stood up and pointed towards him, 'this traveller come from over the sea! At least Mrs Riley does not lie. She does not say that people are dead when they're not!'

Mama seemed to shrink at the weight of my insults, but then quickly gathered herself again, sitting up straight, tilting her chin. 'What Mrs Riley said that day, well, I must confess, I have come to believe *that* particular message was sent from the Lord Himself. But as to—'

'Enough!' Mr Turner stood up, his looks withering and his voice very loud. 'All soothsayers speak with forked tongues. The reason I came back to England again was because the Lord Jesus drew my eye to the copy of an old English newspaper. It was there I read about Cicely's death, at which I rejoiced and gave thanks to God, because that was the sign that your poor martyred mother was spared from her sin and released from her bondage, ready to share in my future once more.'

'I don't understand. You didn't die. You left Mama alone with a child, only returning all these years later . . . and only then because Cissy was dead?'

I turned back to Mama. 'Are you sure that this man is your husband? He's been gone for nearly twenty years. He might be some swindler, come to defraud you, and—'

'What nonsense is this?' Mama was standing, wringing her hands. 'I know my own husband, for Heaven's sake! Mr Turner has travelled all of this way, hoping for me to share in his life, in his church, in America . . . where he works to redeem fallen women. The work for which *you* should show some respect.'

'I don't respect him. I don't even know him. I don't want to go to America, to live in a house full of prostitutes. Cissy said that was his Heaven on earth, to spend all his time with the whores at the docks. Well, that doesn't sound much like Heaven to me!'

I had said too much. Mama was clutching a hand to her breast, gathering strength for her next tirade. 'Cissy had no right to say such things. She should have lain down and kissed this man's feet. You don't know how we suffered, what it did to our marriage when I chose to stay here, in England with you. I gave William up. I gave up this *good* man, for the sake of *your* reputations . . . for that monster, Nathaniel Samuels. He's nothing, he's no one, an Antichrist Jew. I used to see *him* when he was a boy, begging and thieving around the docks. And what good works did *he* ever do? He only dragged my sister down, disgracing her, making her into his whore, deceiving her with his decadent shine. Oh yes, he had all the glamour of Satan, but she would never listen to me. And you, you're no different . . . as wilful as Cissy. I should have known better. I should have been stricter. She turned your head with those trips to the theatre, reading those wicked, sensational novels.'

The biggest sensation was yet to come, but for then I was fuming to hear Cissy's name so cruelly denounced, screaming back at the top of my voice, 'I loved Cissy. Cissy made me happy. I want what we had before Cissy died. How can you think to leave me now, to go off and live with this . . . this man?'

Mama brought her face very close to mine. 'You were

happy enough to go off and leave me, to start a new life with the Samuels. What were they if not strangers to you? And how willingly you contrived it all, prying through my things, stealing that letter, forcing my hand at every turn.'

I started to weep. 'You were happy enough to send me off, exchanging me in return for this house, more than satisfied with the price they paid.'

'Which continued as long as you lived in *his* house, which means the arrangement is ended now . . . which means we are back where we were before, about to lose the roof over our heads. Well, I don't have to care about that any more. I won't be enslaved by Nathaniel Samuels and all of his devious blackmailing plots.'

'No one will be enslaved by that man!' William Turner raised his arms in the air. He looked like some vengeful Old Testament prophet. 'We will leave this house of ill-gotten gains. And you . . .' he was glaring hard at me, 'you are free to go back to the Sinner, to go back where you belong. I should never have listened to Maud. Why should I let you into our lives? The Lord knows I tried hard enough before, when you were first born, when . . .'

He broke off, his fists clenched and white at his sides, and I flinched at a face so ugly and twisted, through which came the venting of vicious spleen, so sharp that it cut through my heart like a knife. 'No more of these lies! You should know the truth . . . how we saw that Jew's face when we looked at yours . . . how we saw Cissy's sin shining out through your eyes.'

A sudden silence. I felt my face crumple. I asked, 'Mama, what is he saying? Mama?'

I reached out my arms, wanting to hold her, wanting her to hold me. I couldn't begin to take it in, to comprehend those evil words – not that Mr Turner left me in doubt, lunging forward and grabbing my wrist, wrenching my arm as he dragged me around, his fingernails digging into my flesh, his voice low and hissing when he said, 'The truth is this . . . like mother, like daughter. The truth is bad blood will always out. Maud Turner was never your mother, and she has protected *you* long enough.'

'No, William. Don't do it like this.' Mama spoke, but much too late.

'Why not?' he growled back. 'This ungrateful bitch needs to know who has wronged her, and who has not. She should know who has sinned, and who has not.'

What sin had I done to inspire such hate – the same as when Joseph spat in my face? I knew, as Cissy had known before, that to live with this man would destroy my soul. This zealot caused Cissy to run away, to chase her Pied Piper – Nathaniel Samuels.

Nathaniel Samuels. If he was my father, then . . .

I gasped. My eyes closed. It was almost like trying to look at the sun, a thing too big, too bright to see, a truth that could only blind me.

Meanwhile, William Turner was ranting on, 'Maud's right. You're no different to *her*. Look at you, strutting around like some hussy, baring your arms and breasts like that. You might be some common prostitute!'

I opened my eyes to see that his were fixed on the scooping neck of my gown where Cissy's precious locket hung, and I saw all too clearly *his* violent lust, the pent-up passion, the jealous rage, and with bitter defiance I made my reply, 'Would you like me better if that was the case? Cissy knew what you were . . . and I know it too.'

He let my wrist drop, but before I could move his fist struck my face, sending me reeling across the room where my head knocked against the stone mantel. I think Mama screamed, but it could have been me. Somehow, I managed to right myself, though the room was still spinning around in small circles, and then lurching forwards, with both hands pressed hard to the mirror's glass, where one of my paintings of Dinwood Court was propped behind an ornament, I looked past that and saw Mr Turner's reflection glaring straight back. I thought of his picture by Mama's bed and how I had always hated that, and how as a child I would stand at this mirror, touching my fingers against the glass, praying to see nothing of him in me. As my breaths misted over my features, I would wait to see if they changed, if different hands might melt into mine, dragging me in through the looking glass, into the imaginary world where I once believed my father lived, the world of death and shadows and ghosts.

But my father had never been a ghost. And all those years when Maud was pretending that she was my mother, the whole house was no more than her fraudulent theatre, with dust swept under carpets, with paper stuck over the cracks in the walls, where the glue of deceit was only then beginning to come unstuck.

Looking back at my face in the glass I watched a trickling line of sweat running down from my brow and over my cheek. I saw Mr Turner's face sheened the same. But there any similarity ended. That man had no claim on my life. I had no part to play in his. Standing up straight, mustering all of my dignity, I turned to Mama and asked, 'Will you still go away with him?'

She nodded. She whispered her answer, 'Yes.'

What more was there for me to say? I walked past her and out of the room. I walked down the hall and opened the door. For a moment, I didn't know what to do. The

Samuels' carriage had long since gone, and while dithering there beneath the porch I heard heavy footsteps approaching behind, and then Mama calling for William Turner to hurry and fetch me back inside. And that's when I practically flew down the steps and ran for my life through Tredegar Square.

I don't remember finding my way to the cemetery. I don't know how long I knelt at the grave, sobbing as I tore daisies up from the grass, ripping tiny petals and stems to shreds. What need did I have for daisy chains now, or those silly prayers I used to make, when Cissy – the one I loved the best – had been my mother all along? And she'd tried to tell me that last day at the docks. And, she'd tried to tell me that last night in her room, when she'd called me her Sweet Phoebe – when she spoke of Nathaniel Samuels. It struck me again, like a lightning bolt, *Nathaniel Samuels is my father. Joseph Samuels is my brother.*

It started to rain, a thin, dirty drizzle, through which I stared up at thickening clouds, begging for God to give me some sign, to tell me my soul had not been damned, that He spared those who sinned in ignorance. But then, I was guilty of more than one crime. And reliving those scenes in the cave in the woods, remembering what Joseph and I had done, I knew I was doomed, and I was convinced that what Mr Turner had said was right – my shame must be shining straight out through my eyes – the dark eyes of the Jew that Mama despised.

I wondered how often one heart could be broken before it stopped feeling at all. I think, for a while, I must have gone mad, digging down into the earth with bare hands, smearing black soil on my face, on my breasts and the silver locket hanging there, thinking that way to cover myself, to cover the brand of incestuous sin, the mark left when Joseph spat in my face.

When I finally came to my senses again, I was shivering, dazed and soaking wet. I didn't know what to do, where to go – but I suddenly heard Cissy's whispering voice. It might just have been the wind in the trees – but since when did those leaves know Old Riley's address? – *6 Paradise Mews, Stepney Green*.

I ran through the empty cemetery, beneath the stone arch with its scroll that read *I am the Resurrection and the Life*. Well, plenty of life on the Mile End Road, the most direct route to Stepney Green which would normally take me less than an hour. But fearing the Turners out looking for me, I ventured instead through side streets and alleys and tenement squares, and all the time I whispered those words, repeating them like a mantra or prayer, over and over and over again – *Paradise Mews – Paradise Mews*.

I did get some very peculiar looks. But Old Riley's address seemed a secret enchantment that helped to keep me safe, and luckily it was broad daylight, and Providence chose to be kind, though my feet were rubbed as raw as my nerves, having to dodge to avoid leering eyes that fixed on the good silver chain at my neck, that noted the good silk cloth of my gown – even if it was covered in grass stains and mud, the hems soaked with horse piss and shit from the streets. But any who snatched or got too close received the vilest of curses back – words that I'd learned all those years ago when rattling a Hallelujah can, which had, after all, set me in good stead, proving to be a salvation of sorts.

39

Peering in through her dusty front window, as my eyes adjusted to the gloom, I made out Old Riley well enough. She was holding hands with two elderly women; the three of them sitting within her string tent, in front of a table scattered with cards, in the centre of which was a crystal ball. I heard a piano; faint jangling notes in a minor key, though I saw no instrument in view, only a curtain partitioning off the far end of the room – and one corner of that being drawn aside, through which a young man was emerging.

His slender torso was wound in white. His face gleamed with some luminous silvery paint, and on top of his golden curls a crown of laurel leaves was set. In one hand he was holding a scroll, just like an ancient Athenian orator, magicked straight out of a history book, and I might not have heard his oracle but I'm sure everyone in that room heard me, my fists banging hard against the glass, and calling out Old Riley's name. At such a disturbance her circle was broken, a commotion of hands held to breasts and mouths, and the next thing I knew the front door opened up, the Greek vision having a grab at my arm. But my flesh was so muddy and wet with the rain he found me as slippery as an eel, squirming free, running past him and into the hall, ducking beneath a black velvet drape, on into that room of shadowy blue.

A sweet smoke caught the back of my throat. I had to gasp to catch my breath as Old Riley stepped out through a flap in her web, looking anxious and murmuring, 'Phoebe . . . Phoebe dearie, whatever's the matter?'

'Did you know, all along?' I was raving by then. 'Did you know Mrs Samuels is dead . . . that I am betrayed, not what I thought? They should have put me in that grave. I should have been buried at Cissy's side.'

One of the strangers was moaning, 'Madame Riley, what spirit is this?'

Old Riley glanced back at her visitors and muttered some words of assurance, though soon drowned out as I ranted on, 'I've been back to the house. I've seen Mama. And now she's with him . . . with the walking dead.'

The second old lady, whose stiff grey curls were trembling over her forehead, whose thin lips were twitching, began to wail, 'Does she come to warn us of death? What can the spirit wraith mean?'

It was quite a performance Old Riley gave when she finally managed an answer, chanting away in a sing-song voice. 'Do not fear. The phantasm means us no harm. Our little séance has drawn this lost soul, invoking her vital energies. But we must not look too long on her light. Such a vivid manifestation will feed on our own corporeal essence. Close your eyes, my dears. Quickly now, bow your heads and pray for deliverance. I shall invoke Demosthenes . . . my spirit guide . . . my exorcist.' She took a deep breath and then called out, 'Demosthenes. Come again to my side.' Raising an arm, she pointed at me, and as her guide glided into the room, Old Riley sighed, 'Ah, he returns. Lo, the spirit is fading.'

Before I could turn or make a complaint, one of his hands pressed over my mouth, and as I was bundled out to the hall, as we passed through that door's velvet curtain again, its softness was like a balm on my cheek, and the very last thing that I recall was the sudden sensation of falling – looking up at the face of an angel.

I woke in an old iron bed, in a room with the walls very close around, and all of them covered with paisley throws, or signed photographs of theatrical acts, or colourful prints of angels and saints. Velvet flowers and ribbons were looped around bedposts. A mirrored wardrobe door hung ajar, the garments inside spilling out at the edge.

In a chair by the hearth Old Riley was sitting. 'Look at you.' She smiled sadly. 'When I saw you outside the window like that, your face all streaked with muck and tears, you looked like a corpse dug up from the grave. Mind you,' she gave a low chuckle, 'I dare say that's done no harm to my trade, not when those old biddies start spreading the word. Nearly wet themselves with the fright, they did, weeping and making the sign of the cross, but . . .' she frowned, her hand reaching for mine, 'whatever caused you to turn up like that? I had no idea you were even in town.'

Struggling to sit, I gabbled an answer. 'Mrs Samuels wanted to see her son off, before he travelled to India. But she's been very ill, and today she died, and then I found out who I really am!'

Old Riley heaved a great sigh. 'So, Nathaniel Samuels told you then.'

'No . . . not him! It was that Mr Turner, my so-called dead father, living with Mama in Tredegar Square. He told me that Cissy was . . . was . . . he said . . .'

Old Riley leaned nearer, cupping my face in her hands.

'Oh dearie, don't cry. Don't fret like this. The biggest surprise to me was that you never guessed before.'

'How could I guess, when everyone lied? But why? Why did Cissy give me up?'

'She gave everything up, her career, her friends. For years, she more or less hid from the world so as to stay living close to you. And every day it broke her heart, having you think that Maud was your mother when it should never have been that way. When they knew you were coming along, Cissy and your father planned on going away, setting up a new life elsewhere. But events conspired to ruin all that. And the world can be a very cruel place, and what choice did poor Cissy have in the end . . . except to try and protect your name?'

'What name?' I broke free from Old Riley's embrace, burying my face in my hands, my next words no more than muffled sobs. 'I'm a bastard. I'm worse things too. Why should anyone want a sinner like me? Oh, Old Riley.' I looked up and implored, 'What am I going to do?'

She sighed again and shook her head, and I felt such a cold despair in my heart. What must Cissy have felt that day I was born, when Nathaniel Samuels remained with his wife, abandoning her, abandoning me? Poor Mrs Samuels. Poor Cissy. Poor Esther. All three of them dead – all because I existed.

40

I slept again. I woke to hear a man's deep voice. 'Is Ma Riley's new waif and stray awake? No chance of a kiss then, to bring Beauty back to the land of the living?'

As Old Riley had taken my ruined dress, I was hurriedly pulling up the sheets, trying to protect my modesty from the apparition I saw ahead. Well, two apparitions, I suppose. On one side there was my reflection, staring back from the wardrobe's mirrored door, looking more like a mad woman than any beauty, for despite a good rubbing with Old Riley's flannel, my face was still grubby, my eyes were still puffy from all of the weeping. My hair looked as if I'd been dragged through a hedge.

On the other side, in the frame of the door, was a man with a smile cracked over his face. But who he was, I hadn't a clue. He was dressed in an elegant dinner suit and looked to be very nonchalant, with one of his arms propped against the jamb, but the moment he shifted as if to step further into the room, I called out, 'Stay there! I'll scream if you come any nearer.'

'You didn't complain a few hours before, when I carried you up the stairs to bed.'

'That was Demosthenes, or whatever his real name happens to be!'

'Oh, but he's me. I'm him. A miracle what the greasepaint achieves.'

A miracle what nature achieved on its own. As he pushed a hand back through thick dark hair, I couldn't help notice how long were his lashes, and how his eyes were the deepest of blues – almost violet when caught in the dimming light – and still staring intently at me when he said, 'I'm Quin. Quin MacKenna. Actor, singer, and sometime Greek orator . . . spirit guide to the indomitable Madame Riley, who is, I might say, a dab hand with old sheets and a yellow wig. Mind you, if the truth be told, you and I have already met before.'

'I don't think so.' Despite my hostile tone, despite all the day's dreadful sorrow and shock, I found myself being curious, wanting this Quin to go on, to stay wrapped in his sonorous, lilting tones, for there was *something* familiar about him. And then I remembered – the shepherd boy, Acis, on Wilton's stage, with his golden curls, and his cheeky wink, and then at Cissy's funeral, the dark-haired young man who was with Mr Collins – the very same incarnation who was standing before me now. But before I could think of what to say someone else was calling from down below, shouting impatiently up the stairs. 'Come on, Quin. The cab's waiting. We'll miss the turn.'

I knew that voice immediately. 'Mr Collins! What's he doing here?'

'Mr Collins provides the music for Old Riley's psychic performances, playing from "behind the veil" as it were. But the halls are our main occupation these days, and I really must go or we'll be late.'

Turning to leave, still framed in the door, he glanced back over his shoulder and smiled. 'Perhaps you'll come and listen one night. I know Eddie Collins would like that, and I know he'll be pleased to hear you're awake, though, of course, unlike me, he's far too well bred to intrude on a lady in dishabille.'

And with that he was gone, his feet a light pattering down the stairs, a brief shout of goodbye, and then the rattling slam of a door – after which I heard heavier steps trudging up, and saw Old Riley shuffling in, holding a steaming cup in each hand.

'I thought you might be awake by now, hearing that row going on down there. What about something to eat?'

'I'm not hungry.'

'Well, I've made you a cup of tea . . . six spoons of sugar to help with the shock, and a good swig of brandy too.'

'He was up here.'

'Who was? Mr Collins?'

'He told me his name was Quin.'

Old Riley's tongue clicked, her eye raised to the ceiling. She let out a sigh and then, 'Why should I be surprised at that? A right cheeky bugger, he is. Still, they'll be gone for hours now, so we shall be sure of some peace and quiet. I like an early night when they're out, but with the pair of them kipping downstairs I hope you don't mind shipping in with me, until we can get ourselves sorted out.'

How can anything ever be sorted out?

I was grateful for Old Riley's bed. I was glad of her company as well, watching as she pulled the pins from her hair, thinking that all those vibrant red tresses were really quite striking in candlelight. And after a great deal of huffing and puffing, when her corsets had finally been unleashed, I noticed how smooth her abundance of flesh, how Old Riley was nowhere near as *old* as I'd always assumed her to be. But she *was* very large and when she climbed into the bed at my side the mattress springs tilted and twanged in complaint, though in no time at all we were settled, the room warm and cosy in candlelight. After a while, when our cups had been drained, when she asked if I wanted to say anything about what had occurred in Tredegar Square, I shook my head. I said, no, not yet, and she said we had all the time in the world, that I was quite safe in Paradise Mews, that no one and nothing would harm me there – not without climbing over her dead body.

Pressed up against the wall like that I thought they would have a long way to climb. But exhausted, mind fuggy with brandy and sorrow, I gradually settled into the pillows, slipping along the slope of the mattress and into the warmth of Old Riley's arms, where I heard the regular hush of her breaths mixed with the patter of rain on the panes, and the splashing that came from cracked gutters above – a sound like a waterfall in a wood. Somehow that calmed me. I managed to sleep. But such strange dreams I had that night . . .

I'm on the stage at Wilton's Hall. I'm dressed as a shepherdess again, but my arms are held out so stiff in front, and my wrists have been tied with a length of rope, and it stretches high over the audience's heads – right up to the back, to the balcony. I'm straining to look through the limes' white glare, through all of the shadows and steam and murk, and suddenly I see Joseph there, and Joseph is holding the rope's other end. On his one side is Lydia Samuels. On the other is Mr Stephens, all three of them staring down at me, all three of them ghoulish, as if embalmed corpses.

I'm frightened. I don't want to join them up there. I try to resist the pull on the rope, and it takes every ounce of my strength to stand firm. Frantically glancing around the stage,

I see that Cissy is near behind, and Cissy is dressed as the nymph, Galatea, and the giant Polyphemus is holding her arm, and when Cissy struggles his mask falls away, and I see Polyphemus is not a man. I see the face of Maud Turner. Maud Turner looks right past me and smiles, and when I follow the line of her gaze, when I look back at the audience, I see the Hallelujah crowd, a whole army of peaked caps and rosetted bonnets, all waving their Temperance banners and flags, and William Turner is there in the front, his arms raised high, conducting them all as they sing, 'Bless His Name, He Sets Me Free'.

'Who will set me free?' I shout to be heard. I think my head must surely explode from such a cacophony. But then the shepherd boy, Acis, appears, materialising out of thin air to stand between me and the front of the stage and, as he unties those knots at my wrists, the audience claps and shouts 'bravo', and when I look up at the balcony, Joseph and his mother have turned away. They seem to be melting into the air, until only Mr Stephens remains, still staring down at the stage, at me, still holding onto that end of rope—

I suddenly woke with a gasp. I was sweating, my heart thumping fast in my chest and the words of that hymn were still in my head as I sensed something move at the end of the bed. Had Quin MacKenna crept in again? But no, it was no one – only the creak of the wardrobe door, still swinging open a little bit more. Old Riley must have heard it too, stirring and rubbing at her eye, asking, 'What? What's that . . .'

She broke off with a moan when she saw what I saw, what was hooked on the other side of the door, what Cissy had worn on Wilton's stage – that lovely gown of turquoise blue that was seeded all over with shells and pearls, lustrous and gleaming in the candlelight.

'Oh dearie, I'm sorry. I hadn't the heart to pass it on, and that wretched wardrobe won't ever stay shut. I'll get up and close it. I'll—'

'No. Don't do that.' I lay back on the pillow and stared and stared. And when the candle sputtered its last, its fizzing light throwing strange shapes around, I imagined those twists of aquamarine to be moving a little, as if Cissy was living and breathing inside them, and when there was nothing but blackness left, and when I had no more tears to cry, I drifted back into a dreamless sleep – like floating through warm dark waters.

Such a banging there was in the morning. Rolling over, the blankets drawn high to my ears, I couldn't shut out what I knew so well; Maud Turner's voice, very strident and loud, and shouting as if to wake the dead.

'I know you must have her. I've searched high and low. I've even been to Hyde Park Gate. That Nathaniel Samuels was raging like thunder. That poor woman's passing has turned his mind. I won't have him casting the blame on me. He's only brought this on himself. I told him as much. I told him, each man shall reap as he sows. And what if she's come to harm on the streets? How shall I ever forgive myself? Mr Turner will have to go on his own, he'll have to—'

'No, Mama,' I called from the top of the stairs. 'You must go with your husband. That's what you want.'

In the corridor below, Mr Collins was holding the open front door. No cravat or red satin waistcoat that day, only a shirt fastened up all wrong, creased tails hanging over his trouser tops.

Mama was crammed in alongside Old Riley who stood like a dragon before the black velvet, guarding the door to her chamber of stars. Not that Mama was concerned with that, intent only on looking up at me, both hands clutching onto the newel post.

'Phoebe . . .' She spoke in more measured tones. 'We are leaving London tomorrow, sailing from Liverpool early next week. Won't you change your mind and come with us? Mr Turner is not a vengeful man. In time, he'll forgive you, and you'll grow to look upon *him* as a father. You'll see that what happened was never his fault.'

'I don't want his forgiveness. He hates me. I hate him. And you . . . if I hadn't come back to London, if Mrs Samuels hadn't died, would you simply have gone away with him . . . left me in Dinwood . . . no word of goodbye?'

'Would you resent my happiness, when I've prayed so long for this day to come, to be free at last of the infidel's trap? And now, praise be, you are free of him too.'

A slight catch, a slight tremble to my voice, but otherwise it was level enough, the fury rising cold and slow when I thought of William Turner's face, when I thought about calling *him* Father, when I thought of how long I'd called *her* Mama – when Maud Turner was never my mother at all. 'How could you have lied for so long? How could you have sent me away like that . . . not to tell me the truth when Cissy died? Have you any idea of the evil your actions went on to cause?'

'My actions! What about his? What about Nathaniel Samuels?'

She was giving me that Medusa stare, the one that could turn my heart to stone, and nowhere to hide as she bawled up the stairs, 'Look at you, standing there bold as brass, wearing no more than your petticoats. Are you lacking all common decency? Is this the way you choose to live? Well, William saw it, right from the start. Didn't he say . . . bad blood will out!'

I froze. I thought back to a day long ago when I was still a little girl, when we went on a trip to Dorset Road – a notorious den of iniquity, with brothels and gambling dens and bars, and many a fallen soul to save, and many a Hallelujah march. Mama and I had been standing right next to the mission's mobile church. I used to like that. It looked like a gypsy caravan, only rather than being painted with stars and colourful signs of the zodiac it was covered all over with crosses and doves, and slogans that said things like GOD IS LOVE, or BELIEVE IN THE LORD JESUS CHRIST AND YOU WILL BE REDEEMED.

A small group of women squeezed to walk past us, sniggering, swigging from bottles of gin and one of them, very pretty she was, looked over her shoulder and blew me a kiss. When Mama saw that she caught hold of my arm, muttering angrily under her breath, saying they'd sold their souls to the Devil, that those whores were not worth one ounce of redemption – at which I suddenly shouted back, 'Then I don't want to be redeemed. I want to be like that lady. I like her red dress and red lips and red cheeks. I hate wearing this horrible uniform.'

Mama slapped me hard across the face, and then a bushy white beard appeared, a grim face peering out from the back of the wagon. Mr Brown looked like a painting of God, glaring down and pointing a finger at me as he thundered, 'The apple doesn't fall far from the tree. Even those harvested in the Lord's baskets can be rotten right through to the core, their souls eaten away with the black worm of sin.'

Mama went puce, started shaking, just as she was then

in Old Riley's hall, while I thought about Joseph Samuels and felt unable to face her wrath because, after all, Mr Brown had been right. My soul was rotten and black to the core.

I turned away and walked back to the bedroom and lay on the floor and curled into a ball and stared at the triangle of light that gradually widened over the boards where the air was moted with diamonds of dust, and a cool draught rushed in as I felt more than heard the solid thud of a closing door.

Knowing then that Maud Turner had finally gone I was suddenly able to breathe again, watching as more light spilled into the room, and how in its midst there were two naked feet, two black trouser hems and, higher still, a string vest, a darkly stubbled chin.

I guessed Mama's shouting had woken him too, that he'd thrown on some clothes for decency's sake – or perhaps that was how he always slept. Leastways, Quin MacKenna was making a habit of coming upon me unawares, and with Mama's words ringing loud in my ears, thinking I must look like some half-naked hussy, I quickly sat up, shuffling back on my buttocks, one arm hitting hard on the bed's iron frame, where I reached up and grabbed for a blanket, once again hoping to cover my shame though, in truth, it was much too late for that.

He knelt at my side and set an enamelled mug on the floor, and then lifted a corner of the sheet to dab at the wetness on my face. He said, 'Mrs Riley and Eddie have gone on down the lane . . . to make sure of seeing your mother off.'

'She's not my mother.' My voice came ragged with emotion. 'My mother is Cissy. Mrs Stanhope. Galatea. My mother is dead!'

His eyes widened. A brief look of surprise as he let the sheet drop and, standing again, he pulled a white stick from behind his ear and then took a match from a box on the mantel, striking it, lighting his cigarette. A long moment passed while he sucked at its tip, before looking down at me again. 'I'm sorry. Truly I am. Everyone was a little in love with her.'

'Did you . . . did you know Cissy well?'

'Only through Eddie Collins. He hired me into the Wilton's production when their Acis went down with a dose of that flu. But I'm not really one for the opera work' – he gave a wry grin, waving his cigarette through the air – 'too fond of the smoking and beer.'

'You'll ruin your voice.' I tried to smile back.

'So they all say.' He sat on the bed, a small creak of the springs, above which his voice was barely a murmur. 'That night at Wilton's, after the show, I came up to the balcony. I was looking for you.'

The balcony. Don't think about that. Don't think about Joseph Samuels.

'For me? I very much doubt it. I saw *you* in the bar a bit earlier on, spooning there with some other shepherdess. I can't say she looked very much like me. Perhaps there's something wrong with your eyes.'

'There's nothing wrong with my eyes. What's to say that I didn't find you there, spooning away with a beau of your own?'

'He's not my beau!' My denial was sharp. My fingers plucked at the blanket wrapped round, recalling the balcony doors swinging closed, and the shadow of someone retreating behind. I stared down at the floor, avoiding Quin's gaze, my next words much slower, much more resigned. 'He's someone I'll never see again.'

'Don't go letting your coffee grow cold.' Quin changed the subject, for which I was glad. His bare foot gently nudged at the mug on the boards – and, it was shortly after that, while sipping the bitter-sweet liquid, I glanced up as he dragged on his cigarette, seeing the glow of its crimson tip and how, when it dulled to grey, a stream of white smoke wisped out from his lips, past narrowed blue eyes that stared down into mine, on up through the air like the ghost of a kiss as it floated past Galatea's gown.

A strange sort of moment that was.

And then another bang below, more footsteps thumping up the stairs, and when Old Riley walked into the room she didn't seem in the least perturbed to find a man at the end of bed, and me there on the floor, and still only half-dressed. She merely tutted and poked at Quin's arm. 'I told you before . . . you're not to go pestering Phoebe up here. She's not some flighty flibbertigibbet, quick for a fumble round the stage door. Go and make yourself useful downstairs for a change.'

The moment he'd gone she closed the door, turning back to say to me, 'That boy is incorrigible. More or less weaned in the theatre, you see . . . thinks nothing of chatting up girls in their bloomers.'

'How long have you known him?'

'I used to dress his mother.' Old Riley became confidential, her voice much lowered when she said, 'A lovely looking thing she was, part of a novelty dancing act, a bit of singing thrown in at the end. But her main performance was after the shows' – she gave a knowing nod, a finger tapping the side of her nose – '*if* you get my drift. Netted herself a lord in the end, shipped back to Ireland to live like a queen. Always had a thing for the Irish she did, and already married to one before . . . one of the light men at Wilton's he was, and handsome enough, but a brute of a man. I dare say she was glad to get away,' Old Riley sighed, 'though you can never escape your fate. Riches can't buy you everything. Her new friend wanted her, but not little Quin. Emilia left her son behind, and then orphaned him giving birth to the next . . . or so all the rumours went at the time.'

'Quin was brought up by his father?'

'Well, there's the rub. His father took to drowning his sorrows, most nights beating the boy black and blue. A good thing when *he* went and disappeared! We heard he got stabbed in a gambling den. I say good riddance to bad rubbish. Quin was better off without him, and we try to look after our own in the theatre. There's never been a shortage of offers . . . not with Quin's looks, not with his charm.'

She smiled wistfully. 'Hark at me, rambling on like this, when you've already got enough things on your mind. What do you say to a visit with Maud, to kiss and make up before she leaves? She's very upset, you know, torn between you and that William Turner, just as she was all those years before.'

'I can't go back. Not with him still there.' I felt panicked and frightened all over again. 'What if they force me to stay? How can I trust her to tell me the truth when she's had me in mourning for all of my life, for someone who wasn't even dead . . . who wasn't even my father!'

Old Riley shook her head. 'Our very own Lazarus raised from the grave. Believe me, we all thought *him* gone for good. But,' she patted my arm, 'you should try not to judge Maud too harshly.'

'She lied!'

'Yes, she lied. But things aren't always black and white.'

Old Riley sat heavily down in her chair. 'Cissy was like a daughter to Maud. She cared for her sister from a babe, practically bringing her up alone. It was only when Maud met William Turner that she started to have any life of her own . . . not one that would suit us all, I know. But up until then she'd worked every hour God gave, keeping that family business afloat, struggling to put food on the table. Anyway, by the time she wed, Cissy had already gone away . . . and when she came back, and expecting you, the Turners were planning on leaving, heading out to New York on slum missionary work. And that was an irony too, considering what Cissy and Nathaniel had planned to . . . Oh well, you know the rest. Maud stayed here with her sister. William Turner went. And the next thing we knew she told us he'd died . . . succumbed on the ship to a cholera fever, never again to step on dry land.

'I dare say they'd agreed between themselves for him to be thought of as being dead, to make a new life of his own elsewhere, for her to be thought a respectable widow, bringing up her orphaned child . . . living with her unmarried sister in Bow.'

Old Riley clicked her tongue. 'For him to go and turn up like that, out of the blue, like a great ugly genie rubbed out of a bottle. And how Maud could have egged Eddie Collins on, for all of those years, and with him so besotted, and out there right now, escorting her home!

'Still, she asked him to go and collect your bag. She said there was something she wished to pass on . . . some sort of a leaving gift for you.'

41

With my grey dress so damaged, beyond repair, Old Riley rummaged around in her wardrobe and found something for me to wear – though it hardly befitted my dismal mood, that wrap in a lovely emerald green, embroidered with red and white peonies.

For a while, when she'd gone downstairs again, I stood on the landing, staring in through the door of her sewing room where bolts of fabric were stacked against walls, and in pride of place on an iron stand there was Old Riley's sewing machine. The black metal was polished up till it gleamed, japanned all over with gold scrolls and roses and behind it were shelves with boxes and jars, full of threads, feathers, buttons and pins, and cards wound with braiding and tassels and lace.

She'd said I must choose whatever I wanted. She'd promised to run up a brand new gown, and once, I would have loved all that. But now I would happily wear my black. I had no heart left for frivolous things, walking instead to a room at the front which was currently used as a parlour. Here was another riot of colour, the ceiling hanging with more strands of crystals that tinkled like bells when my arm brushed past. Walls and cushions were patterned in vibrant brocades. Gaudy vases were filled with enormous silk flowers, and on a whatnot pushed into a corner, a grinning stuffed monkey sat on its haunches, wearing a monocle and a cravat, a copy of Mr Darwin's book clutched in its wrinkled pink fingers. A good thing Mama had *not* seen that: one more thing to consider as blasphemous.

Looking down through the lace at the window, I saw Old Riley's juvenile guard. He was kicking a stone against a wall; a repetitive *chink, chink, chink* it made. And through that came the sound of more footsteps as Mr Collins walked down the lane, holding my travelling bag in his arms.

I didn't hear him ascend the stairs, but he soon appeared in the parlour door, wheezing, 'My dear girl, that's where you are. How sorry I am for all that's occurred. I've left your bag in the bedroom. But, your mother . . . she asked me to be sure to place this directly into your hands.'

My hands remained stiff and still at my sides. I bit my tongue. I wanted to scream, because Maud was not my mother, because everyone else – Mr Collins, Old Riley, and Cissy too – had spent all those years deceiving me. And what a conspiracy it had been!

Seeing how unresponsive I was, he walked to a table and set some things down: a silver box and an envelope. He said, 'Mrs Riley is making the breakfast. We'll both be downstairs, should you need anything.'

I looked away, remaining tight-lipped, until he left the room again, when curiosity led me to open up the letter, to read the words that were scratched there so untidily over the page, as if Mama – as if Maud Turner – had been writing in desperate haste.

Dearest Phoebe,
    It is hard to know where to begin, so perhaps at your birth would be a good place – and it is *a good place, and it*

was a good thing, and I hoped you would never discover the truth. I never expected Cissy to die, or to see my husband come back again. And now everything has been turned on its head.

When Cissy first took up that decadent life, parading herself around on the stage, it very nearly broke my heart. But later, I saw in her shame and misfortune, a way of bringing her safely home, bringing her back to the Righteous Path. And, where my own marriage had proved to be barren, her unborn child might yet be a blessing, a gift sent from Heaven, for William and me.

But Nathaniel Samuels was selfish. He set up his scheming to try and outwit me, planning on taking Cissy away. When she refused to see reason, what choice did I have but to write to his wife, describing her husband's immoral intentions? How else could I be sure of keeping you with me, of saving your souls from the flames of Hell?

Not that I needed to worry for Righteousness was on my side. The Lord smites and He saves in equal measure. When one life began another one ended. When you were born, the Samuels' legitimate daughter died. The Sinner was forced to remain with his wife and thereafter repent of his evil ways.

Any other man would have been grateful to me, for saving his reputation like that. But he only ever despised the fact that I gave his bastard a decent name! *He* had no care for what *I* might have suffered, how *my* marriage was ruined by taking you on. And William did try. He was willing to claim you as his own, to make a new start when we travelled abroad. But he wouldn't have Cissy come with us, and how could I leave my sister behind, alone as she was, so ill in the months that followed your birth? I think something inside her was broken then. My *sister was never the same again, always blaming herself for that other girl's death – and always resenting my sacrifice.*

Not that anyone ever resented you. You were our angel, the sweetest child. But as the years passed, it pained me to see you so drawn to her. I was always afraid she might tell you the truth, that Nathaniel Samuels might one day come back and try to steal you both away. I guessed he was only biding his time, like a snake in the grass, waiting to strike. I saw all those letters he used to send. Cissy hid them away, but I found them. I burned every one when she died – all full of Satan's lust and guile, and always bemoaning the love he'd lost. Well, thanks to that adulterous man, we all lost more than we gained in the end. We all lost Cissy, the one we loved best, and . . .

There, the ink had been smeared, as if tears had fallen and been wiped off, and the writing was bigger, scrappier too, as if she was shouting out through the page. But the following words were neater, the tone somewhat calmer again.

Mr Collins has promised to pass on this letter. This box and its contents once belonged to Cissy. I hid them away when she died. But now, what secrets are left to conceal? I take strength from what Jesus has told us. 'The Truth shall set you free.' He watches and waits for every lost sheep. He welcomes all sinners back into His fold, never rejoicing so much as when the prodigal lamb returns.

I leave you to ponder on that. And I leave you with this consolation. 'Weeping may endure for a night, but joy cometh in the morning.' I hope one day that you will wake and see that I only did what was Right.

I pray that you will believe me.

Maud Turner, your loving aunt.

'Weeping may endure for a night, but joy cometh in the morning.'

Maud Turner was only lying again. Truth was a tyrant. She liked to keep slaves. What joy could there be for me any more?

A box of lucifers lay on the mantel. When my hands had stopped shaking I managed to strike one and then, crouching down by the hearth, I held that letter to the flame, watching as little blue tongues of fire licked and blazed up into gold. And as the paper blackened and curled, as I felt the heat of its bitter reproach, I wished that Lydia Samuels had done the very same. I wished that her daughter had never seen Maud Turner's version of The Truth.

When that was done, when only charred ashes remained in the grate, I knelt with my palms pressed hard to my ears trying to shut out the scratching of pens, the sound of sharp nibs that were dipped in black bile, dripping with spite and jealousy – until I heard Mr Collins' voice, and looked up to see melancholy eyes, magnified by his spectacle lenses.

'Maud loves you, Phoebe.' He spoke very softly. 'Maud only wants to set you free.'

I stood up to face him. I said very calmly: 'Mr Collins, if you believe that, then I think you must be a fool! I was only ever the bait. I was the means to keep Cissy close. And now Cissy is dead I'm no longer of use. And what's more, where Maud Turner is concerned, *you* should take off those rose-tinted spectacles.'

The child he'd once known didn't mean to be cruel, but she was no longer innocent. Her heart had been poisoned. She'd lost all her sweetness, and everything else she'd ever owned – no longer possessing so much as a name.

42

That wasn't quite true. Cissy's silver box, I still owned that.

I should have had it when she first died, when Maud Turner wickedly stole it away, because of the precious things it contained – precious to me, anyway.

If only I'd lifted the lid before, that night when I went into Cissy's room, when standing in front of the mantel with Cissy's sleeping reflection behind. If only I'd seen what lay inside: a folded birth certificate, a small golden figurine – an eastern goddess that looked foreign, exotic, reminding me of those murals at Wilton's.

I closed the curtains and picked up the statue, holding the cold metal against my breast where Cissy's silver locket hung. Standing very still and bathed in false darkness I listened to sounds coming up from below – the clinking of china, the rushing of taps, and Old Riley speaking, and Quin MacKenna's deep answering tones. There was a piano – surely Mr Collins – playing something mournful and slow. Those curling notes formed a musical cage, rising up through the air, locking me in my grief. I stayed in that room, on that bed, for days. I lost all sense of time and place, refusing to wash or dress, refusing to eat, hardly drinking a thing, only wishing that I was dead as well. My mind kept on swimming in moithering circles, and always returning to the same thing – Cissy and her love for

Nathaniel Samuels, and how that love had created me, and how that love destroyed everything else. And, I wondered if anyone stood at his side at Lydia Samuels' funeral because, surely, she must have been buried by then – and I should have been there to pay my respects.

Sometimes, Mr Collins looked in at the door. Sometimes, I smelled burning cigarettes and, through the floating wisps of smoke Quin MacKenna's blue eyes would be staring down. And once, as I twisted away, turning my face to the wall, I felt the touch of his hand on mine.

Old Riley had the patience of saints, sleeping on the parlour sofa by night, sitting beside me during the days. She chatted away while sewing, or quoted from articles placed in the papers, reporting on all the West End shows and any performers she happened to know, racking her brains to think of things to lure me out of that lethargy.

Now and then a séance was booked downstairs, and then I was left alone again, though not before she'd decked herself up like some pantomime Widow Twankey, with roses and combs sticking out of her hair and a vibrant kimono wrapped over her skirts, and a miniature accordion strapped to one leg, concealed underneath her petticoats.

One time, she gave me a small demonstration, pumping it hard between her thighs, making the most discordant sounds. She told me about the cutlery that Quin had fixed under the table top, where her fingers might pluck at the hidden wires to strum out a tinkling tune on the spoons. With the clients convinced of a musical ghost, Old Riley would babble and sing in strange tongues while Mr Collins – concealed by a drape at the very far end of the darkened room – would play tuneless notes on a hidden piano; the instrument's dampers all muted with felt, which created a very eerie sound. And then came the grand finale, when Madame Riley's spirit guide would materialise – the golden-haired Demosthenes, who was otherwise known as Quin.

I wondered that anyone could have been fooled by such a crude display of tricks, but Old Riley was unrepentant. 'People believe what they want to believe. They see what they want to see. We send them all off with happier hearts, all the better for having a nice little chat with their loved ones from over the other side.'

I thought about Cissy, and where she might be. I asked in a small and cautious voice, 'But, Old Riley, tell me honestly. Have you ever seen a ghost . . . a real one, I mean?'

'Oh, who's to say if they really exist, though I'm of a tendency to assume it's a mystery we'll be pondering until our final hour comes.'

'You made a good enough guess in the past. You knew about Mr Turner, coming from over the sea. And you saw the rose that wasn't a rose . . .'

I couldn't go on. I couldn't explain what I meant by that, thinking of Lydia Samuels, the disease that had bloomed upon her breast with its stinking, mutant petals of flesh. And now she was dead. Dead like Cissy before. Dead like Esther Samuels. And the next time a séance was held in the house, while I listened to twangings and mumblings below, the only thing I knew for sure was that nothing would ever induce me to join in those shady games. I should be too afraid that the rules might change, that my mind might conjure some real apparitions.

Did that make me something unnatural? What was it

Maud Turner used to say? 'Never trust those who call up the dead for such things are abominations to God'?

Was I an abomination? Was the Devil waiting with open arms?

The last time a séance was held in the house, when some peace and quiet had been restored, I let out a long sigh and stared up at the ceiling where cracks in blown plaster appeared to be swirling around in the dusk's dim and pearly light. It was almost like looking through water.

Down below, the piano was playing again, the notes still muffled but far more melodic. And then, Quin Mac-Kenna started to sing, and I recognised the words at once, from the poem, 'To One in Paradise' by Edgar Allan Poe.

To my jaded ears, that song was a prayer, so sweetly nostalgic, invoking a beautiful picture of Cissy when she'd been on the stage at Wilton's. And I thought of another pastoral scene, and that one was of Dinwood Court with its trees and its splashing waterfall, and the cave that I'd once thought to be a shrine . . .

> *Thou wast all that to me, love,*
> *For which my soul did pine –*
> *A green isle in the sea, love,*
> *A fountain and a shrine . . .*
> *And all my days are trances,*
> *And all my nightly dreams*
> *Are where thy grey eye glances,*
> *And where thy footstep gleams –*
> *In what ethereal dances,*
> *By what eternal streams.*

I woke very early, turning onto my side, staring a long time at the little gold goddess that lay on the pillow next to mine. Everywhere was quiet, except for Old Riley's snores which came from the parlour down the hall: the same sound I'd heard many mornings before.

But that day was going to be different. That day, I pushed back the grubby sheets and crawled over the quilts and knelt a long time at the end of the bed. Reaching out to touch Galatea's gown, I held the cloth up close to my face to breathe Cissy's lingering fragrance. I think it was that, and the words Quin had sung, that brought me back to the present again, realising that for too many nights I'd lain with eyes open, drowning in sorrow, lost in grief's wavering watery shadows. But no matter how heavy the stone of my heart, the weight of despair under which I had sunk, it was time to start living again, to rise up from self-pitying misery, or else what was Cissy's sacrifice for?

I lifted the silver box from the mantel and placed the little goddess inside, cocooned in the folds of a blue velvet lining. I rummaged around in the travelling bag brought back for me from Tredegar Square, and with a fresh shift draped over one arm, I crept down the stairs and past the black curtain, along the passage and on through a door where I stepped over flags that were littered with crumbs, sticky and crunchy under my feet. A table was strewn with used matches and fag ends and several drained bottles of beer. Skirting around it, I passed through another door and entered a narrow scullery kitchen, at one end of which was a large tin tub. Draped over a rope hitched up above were towels and items of underwear. Some, trimmed with lace, were formidably large; the rest plainer, decidedly masculine. I peered through those damp and dripping flags to see a mirror on the wall, in need of a dust but clear enough to reflect a pair of bruised dark eyes that stared back from a wasted pallid face, around which black hair hung greasy and lank.

I didn't want to look like that.

Seeing a kettle I filled it up from the tap fixed above the scullery sink. Very cold that water was, but soon warmed on the kitchen range, after which I returned to the sink again, stripped off my shift and picked up a bar of carbolic soap.

It was far from the splendour of Dinwood Court where I'd once been surrounded by marble and mirrors. In Paradise Mews, my locket lay on a rickety table. A soiled petticoat was my washing cloth. But, oh, it felt good to be clean again, my skin and hair all lathered up, everything scrubbed, tingling, new. And when I was done, reaching out for a towel that looked the least grey, rubbing most of the wetness and gooseflesh away, I put on my chain and the clean white shift and wandered back through to the kitchen.

With the kettle set to boil again, while biting the end from a chunk of stale bread, I looked around for a pot and some tea, deciding to make a cup for Old Riley – to give her a nice surprise for a change. But, as it turned out, that brew of mine never did find its way to her lips because, when about to take it upstairs, when I carried that cup along the hall, I heard a low groan and then a deep sigh that came from behind the curtained door.

Drawing an edge of the velvet aside, I thought only to take the quickest peek, looking in through the dingy light where the air smelled as rank as my room upstairs. But *if* Mr Collins was sleeping in there, then I might try to make amends for my rudeness. I might ask if he fancied some tea as well.

Mr Collins wasn't there – at least he was nowhere I

could see. But Quin MacKenna certainly was, sprawled flat out on a mattress set on the floor. Surrounded by those midnight walls and all of the little crystal stars he put me in mind of a fairy tale, only one where the roles had been reversed, where the princess now waited to wake the prince. His face might be blemished with stubble, but sleeping as soundly as that, somehow he looked younger, less polished, more perfect – and I felt a frisson of wanting excitement, and I could have watched him for ever, with the sheet thrown off, with his arms flung out, the dark hair on his chest grown down in a tapering line to his navel, where the flesh of his belly was hard and spare, where the hip bones were jutting, enticing my eye to glance even lower, to—

Had I been so corrupted? Was this how the journey began, with small flames of flickering lust in the belly until your whole body was blackened and charred, your soul being burned in the fires of Hell? I knew I should kneel down and pray for forgiveness, but might I take one more look at his face – a face where the eyes were now open, where the mouth was curled in a knowing smile, Quin MacKenna not seeming the least bit perturbed either by my gaze or his nakedness.

I turned on my heel and ran upstairs, only to find my way barred at the top with Old Riley there on the landing, where I took the full blast of her sleep-stale breath. 'What's going on here? It's not like you to be up and about.'

'I went down to wash. I made you this cup of tea.' I tried to squeeze past her while looking back down to where Quin MacKenna was now at the bottom, having already pulled on some trousers, and calling up in a husky voice, 'Morning, ladies! And what a glorious morning it is, though in truth I was sorry to wake, for I was having the best of dreams . . . with Phoebe standing right here in the door, and the light shining in through her shift from behind. They do say that dreams sometimes come true. What do you think? Have I reason to hope?'

'You cheeky bugger,' Old Riley chided, just as the cup tipped in my hand, amber liquid splashing over the wall.

'Oh, I'm sorry. I'm sorry . . . I've made such a mess.'

She smiled and took the cup from my hand, streaks of old rouge cracking over her cheeks, and she didn't seem very bothered. In fact, she sounded pleased as Punch, as if I'd offered her liquid gold.

'Don't you fret! We'll soon wipe all this mess away. You go and get dressed while I make a fresh pot. And as Mr MacKenna is already up, he can go out and find us some bacon and bread. We'll have us a proper cooked breakfast for once and then maybe a little excursion outside . . . a nice walk in the sun and fresh air.'

43

That little walk led as far as a cab, and then an excursion to Hyde Park Gate where my heart was hammering out of my breast as I stared at the gleam of the black lacquered door. If not for Mr Collins there, his reassuring hand on my arm, I might have run back out to the street, back to the safety and cramped dusty clutter of Old Riley's house in Paradise Mews – instead of which I took a deep breath, knowing that my resolve must be strong, if only for Cissy, to do what she wanted, to pass on her message to Nathaniel Samuels.

We found it before any breakfast was made, while I helped Old Riley with changing the bed, throwing sheets and blankets up in the air which then caught on the side of my silver box, sending it crashing down to the floor. The birth certificate lay in the grate. The little gold goddess rolled under the bed, the length of blue velvet in which she'd been wrapped unravelling all over the boards . . . where some other items fell free from its folds – things I'd not noticed there before.

Puffing from her exertions, Old Riley sat on the bed while I lay down to reach underneath, springs dipping and twanging over my head as my fingers grabbed onto the gold figurine. At its side was a scrolled piece of paper, neatly tied with a length of white ribbon, and when I emerged back into the light, holding it up for Old Riley to see, we both had to strain to read the name that Cissy had written along one edge.

'Well, well . . .' Old Riley was matter of fact. 'Something here for Nathaniel Samuels. Perhaps Mr Collins can give us advice on how best to go about dealing with that.' And then she was pointing down to the floor. 'Oh, Phoebe, look . . . there's something else!'

Beside the leg of the chair another piece of paper lay. It was folded in half, and on the front in clear black ink were the words that I saw with no difficulty, that simply said, *For Phoebe*.

Still kneeling, I picked it up, unfolding the page to see a date. It was November 20th. It was the day of The Ritual. I couldn't bear to read the rest, passing it up to Old Riley's hands, listening to her low and quavering voice:

My Sweet Phoebe,

Once upon a time, when you were very small someone wanted to give me a gift. I wonder if you can remember that day? He asked you to choose, and you found this little gold goddess. And now, if you wish, you may take it back. Take it to a man called Nathaniel Samuels. You will find his name on your birth certificate. And there, you will also find mine.

Phoebe, my dearest, don't be afraid. What you do with this truth is your choice alone. You may wish to ignore it and go on as before, and should that be the case then I deeply regret the pain that such knowledge may bring — both to you, and to Maud, for I know she will only despise me for this. But I can't go on with living her lies, and I won't go on deceiving you.

Nathan will never turn you away. He has so often wanted to see you — he asked again when I saw him at Wilton's. I lied then. I told him that you were at home. I wasn't sure what to do for the best. But since our return from the docks today, my mind has been completely clear. I don't want your spirit and dreams to be crushed, even if my own are lost. I sinned, and I had to give up what I loved. But at least I had you, and you were the light in my darkness, my Phoebe — the name that Isaac once called me when I used to sing in his shop as a child.

Whatever you choose to do, you know that Maud loves you, and so does your father, and perhaps you will come to love him in return, as much as I have always done.

I pray you will find it in your heart to forgive me one day, and to understand.

God bless you, my daughter, Sweet Phoebe,
Cissy

Once upon a time Cissy was alive. Cissy loved me and then, when she died, she left that message for me to find. She was right about Maud being angry, though not bargaining on her still hiding the truth, thwarting her sister's wishes for months while Cissy lay buried and cold in her grave.

Maud Turner's theft kept me in ignorance. Maud Turner's theft stole my innocence and led to the vilest of wrongs. At that moment I could not have hated her more, and I hated Nathaniel Samuels too for damning me with his duplicity. But I wept for Cissy all over again, and I thought I should never get over her loss, and I prayed that she might be in Heaven, and that God might forgive her, as I had done.

*

Mr Samuels – my father – received us in the drawing room. It was almost as if he expected the visit, though we'd sent no letter or word on ahead, already deciding that if he was out we would simply leave Cissy's gift behind.

His greeting was impersonal and rather abrupt, briefly shaking Mr Collins' hand, then dismissing him with a curt, 'Thank you for this. I'll arrange to bring Phoebe back later on.'

Mr Collins said nothing. He nodded, then followed Turnbull out to the hall, and only when the door had been closed did Nathaniel Samuels turn to me.

'You look tired. You look thin. Are they caring for you as they should?'

I tried to smile my assurance. 'Mrs Riley has been very kind, and . . .' I looked down at the silver box in my hands, and against that the red silk cloth of my gown – the one that Old Riley had found in my bag, quickly pressing it up before I came out. It could not have been less appropriate and I felt acutely embarrassed. 'I . . . I should never have gone like that. I should have stayed on for the funeral. And this dress . . . it is disrespectful. But I had no other, I—'

'Phoebe.' He moved forward, extending his hands before they dropped limply down to his sides. 'I care nothing for what you wear. The funeral was a private affair, really no more than a formality. Stephens and I took the ashes to Dinwood. That's what Lydia wanted. Nothing more.'

Silence hung heavy, a spectre between us. I needed to draw on all of my strength to hold back my tears, to say, 'When Cissy died, there was something she wanted you to have. I didn't know until recently, when I . . .' I stopped again, overwhelmed by that spacious room, seeing only the colours of death. The jet muslin draped over the mirrors. The white of my hands as they gripped the box. I kept thinking about a white bedroom upstairs, the white carpet with roses like splashes of blood, Mrs Samuels' white face, and the ghost in the glass – *if* it had been a ghost, and not some hallucination conjured from laudanum dreams.

My hands began shaking. His were the same as they reached out to take the gift. Only then did I notice how loose was his jacket, how sallow and strained the flesh of his face, more deeply etched than it had been before; and his voice so flat and dull when he asked, 'Have you looked inside?'

'Yes. She left me a letter . . . and also my birth certificate.'

'Then you know.'

'I do now.' My tone was accusing. 'It was Mr Turner, my so-called dead father. He was the one who told me the truth . . . who told me *who* and *what* I am.'

The real father baulked. 'Phoebe, forgive me. I wanted to tell you. I didn't know how. When Lydia died, I should have done then, but it didn't . . . well, you seemed set on leaving. You seemed so unhappy. I thought it might be for the best, for you to remain in ignorance, to go back to the life you'd always known, as if . . .'

'As if what? As if nothing had changed!'

'I didn't know William Turner was back, not until Maud came here the next day, to tell me of your disappearance.'

Sitting down on a chair by the window I was finding it hard to breathe. 'Did you not wonder where I'd gone? Did you not fear for my safety too?'

'Of course!' He placed the box on a table, pausing as if

to gather his thoughts. 'I would never risk you coming to harm. I soon discovered that you were safe. Mr Collins who brought you here today . . . he has always been kind enough to let me know how you are going on.'

'You mean Mr Collins is your spy!' I was aghast.

'No.' He was shaking his head. His lips were curved in a rueful smile. 'He was Cissy's friend, from her earliest days in the theatre, and after your birth he agreed to pass letters between us . . . to arrange those few times when we could meet, when Cissy could bring you to visit me. But she always feared being found out and later, when you were older, there was the risk that you might tell Maud. So . . . Mr Collins kept me informed.'

'Did you go on meeting Cissy, alone?'

'Sometimes . . . when we could. Not for very long.'

I thought of that photograph Meg had found, the one of Cissy with Victor Maurel, and the other man who'd been standing behind, the one possessively holding her arm. And, only then, I remembered – 'Cissy's scrapbook! It's still at Dinwood. I *must* have it back. I have nothing else. Only this locket. Only her letter.'

All at once he was kneeling before me, his sweet, musky perfume singing through my senses, his hand gently lifting my chin, forcing my eyes to meet with his.

'Phoebe, don't cry. You shall have it. You shall have whatever you want. If only I could bring back the past. If only things had been different.'

I wanted to tell him I understood. I desperately wanted to hold him, but instead I froze, like a statue – like Cissy in Wilton's Music Hall, when she sat in the dressing room after the show. Maud Turner might claim to have set me free, but I was no less constrained by the truth.

What was I but the usurper; the daughter who lived when the other had died?

When he stood up and moved away, I felt bereft at the gulf, at the whole world now gaping between us. Twisting my hands in my lap, I watched as he lifted the lid of the box, as his fingers closed over the little gold goddess.

I was the first to speak. 'Cissy said I chose it.'

'Yes. I remember.'

'And there is something else . . . a scroll.'

'Yes, I see. I'll look at that later.'

He set the gold ornament back in its box, and then walked to the window, looking over the gardens where plants were all fading, grown jaded and dull, and his voice much the same when at last he said, 'You were six years old. It was one Christmas. Everything was closed up for the holiday. I'd asked Cissy to bring you to me at the shop. But we had so little time . . . before Lydia and Joseph returned from church. Before Maud missed you.'

'It was one Christmas.' My voice echoed his. 'I think . . . yes, I think I remember now. I'd always thought that to be a dream – like a palace, like somewhere a giant might live with enormous halls and balconies, and a stained-glass dome with Venus and Cupid, and all of the perfumes, and all the bright colours, and everything sparkling, silver and gold . . . and those beautiful women who stood still as statues. Of course, they must have been mannequins, but I thought they were locked in a secret enchantment, like the fairy princesses who slept all day and danced all night, until their feet bled and their shoes wore out. I wanted to lift up their dresses and look.'

'Did you?' He glanced back from the window and smiled – such a melancholy, beautiful smile.

I looked away, looked down at my lap, still lost in the

dream that had not been a dream, recalling a man with black eyes and black hair, a man so tall that I'd had to crane my neck right back to be able to see his face, and I'd laughed when he lifted me up in his arms, when he swung me in circles, around and around, and . . .

'And Cissy was laughing.' My voice was like that of one in a trance. 'But then, when it was time to go, she started to cry and you asked me to find her a present, something to cheer her and make her feel better. I remember now . . . what that present was.'

I stared at the goddess and suddenly asked, 'Did you ever love your wife?'

'I like to think that I did. But then I met Cissy, and though she was barely more than a child, it was different. I knew. I always knew. And later, there were opportunities. And then, there were the consequences.'

'Is that what I am, a consequence?'

'No!' His brow furrowed. 'It was never like that. Cissy and I planned on going away, to start again, to live with you. But everything ended when Esther died. *That* was the consequence. Cissy thought . . . she believed Esther's death was her judgement. The Turners had her brainwashed, always preaching of retribution and sin. What blessed Samaritans they were! And I let them do it. I let them have you. If only . . .' His eyes closed. He passed a hand over his brow. 'If only Cissy was still alive. We could have been together at last, we could have . . .'

He broke off once more to contain his emotion, before pleading, 'Phoebe, you must let me make it right. You must come back. Come and live here, with me, in this house. No more of these secrets. No more of this hiding. What do I care for society's views? There's no one to hurt or offend any more.'

'But there is!' Did he hear me, my voice guarded and low? Soon, I grew braver, insisting, 'There's Joseph. How could I ever live here with you, without him also knowing the truth? He already thinks I'm your whore. Others will think the same. What of your reputation, of mine?'

His eyes narrowed. And then, to my horror, he said, 'Then we should travel to India. We'll explain to Joseph, face to face. I should have told him before. I should have avoided these misunderstandings.'

A panic was welling inside me. 'No! You *can't* tell him. I won't let you do that. Joseph will hate me for this. He'll hate you! You can't suddenly start to dictate my whole life. I was happy before . . . before Wilton's, before everything changed. I was there. Did you know? I saw you with Cissy. I saw . . .'

How could I ever tell about Joseph? Yes, things might well have been different once. I might have had a brother to love. But not now. Now, my shame must stay hidden away – and there was only one way to ensure such a thing.

'That night has led on to consequences, things I would rather forget. You must let me go back to Old Riley's house. You must not tell anyone who I am. Please . . .' I was almost weeping again. 'Please, if you care, won't you promise me that? I don't think we should ever meet again.'

His expression was rigid. He reached a hand into his jacket, and I saw the gold arc of his watch chain below, a glittering smile in the afternoon light, and then something else, glinting, metallic, held in the palm of his hand.

'Very well . . . if you're sure that's what you want. This is the key to Tredegar Square. The Turners have gone. The lock has been changed. The house now belongs to you, as it belonged to Cissy before. I'll set up an allowance in your name, an account with reserves for contingencies. If you have any needs or concerns, you know where to find me. I'll always be here . . . waiting, if you should change your mind.'

44

Nathaniel Samuels waited at the far end of Paradise Mews. He lifted a hand to wave goodbye when Phoebe glanced back from Old Riley's door. And then, the door opened. And then, she was gone.

Earlier, when driving to Stepney Green, she'd asked him to take her to Bow, to go and visit Cissy's grave.

He'd last made a trip to the cemetery on the night of Cissy's funeral, when he'd stood in the bitter cold darkness and watched the snow cover a mound of black soil. And now Phoebe, their daughter, was holding his hand, leaning her head on his shoulder. The way her hair fell loose on his arm, it could have been Esther's, as black as jet, as black as his own had been – when he'd still been young – when he thought he held the whole world in his hand.

Phoebe knelt down at the railings' edge. The red of her skirts puddled over the grass as she started to pick some daisies. Deftly, she wove them, making a garland of white, gold and green, and when that frail chain was long enough she used it to crown the angel's head. Watching that offering being made, Nathaniel's mind was suddenly filled with the words of the Jewish prayer for the dead:

'As for man, his days are but grass; as the flower of the field, so he flourishes. For the wind passes over it and it is gone; and the place thereof shall know it no more. But the loving kindness of the Lord is from everlasting to everlasting . . . The Lord gave and the Lord has taken away.'

The Lord would soon take Phoebe away, and how could Nathaniel object? How could he expect her to bear the shame of being his bastard, of being a—

He felt a cold touch on his shoulder. What was that sighing sound? Only the hush of a breeze parting a path through long grasses, as if someone unseen had been walking towards them – or away. And then came a sudden fluttering snap as a bird flew up from some branches above and a tiny white feather floated down, hanging like a whisper of gauze on the air. He reached out and caught it – a gift. Others might call it a curse, with feathers forbidden at Jewish graves, considered vulgar and too ostentatious, when death should be entered in humility. But Cissy had never been a Jew, and since when had Nathaniel Samuels been humble? And since when had he followed old customs and habits, all those superstitions that clung from his past?

Why were they coming back to him now?

Back home – alone again – Nathaniel went through the office dispatch box, all neglected and long-overdue correspondence. Since Lydia's death, he'd avoided the shop. Tomorrow he'd meet with his lawyers again, to sign more papers, to read through the contracts to set himself free. The company was to be publicly floated; he and Joseph retaining nominal roles, continuing to act as directors. Not that his son held any interest. And Nathaniel was weary, he'd lost all ambition. And trouble was brewing.

The riots had started a few weeks before, with the looting of shops in Commercial Road; slogans of hatred daubed on the walls. Nathaniel knew there was worse to come. For some reason, he'd found himself worrying for Isaac. One evening he'd travelled down to the docks, and there his worst fears had been realised.

The store was completely destroyed; nothing left but a burned-out shell, the timbers scorched and greasy with soot, the ground still littered with shards of glass.

Eventually, he'd gathered his wits and entered the door of the Dolphin, hoping to make some enquiries there. But the surly barman would only say that no one knew of Isaac's fate, leaning towards him over the counter, scowling and gruff when he said, 'We don't want no trouble here. We don't know if he's alive or dead.'

A woman came lurching towards him, a cheap bawd who was shouting her drunken bile. 'Get out of here, you stinking Jew! That old man had what was coming to him. We know he stole that baby gone missing . . . the evil old blood-sucking leech. You're all the same. Nothing but infidels, parasites, coming here taking our money and jobs . . . nothing but thieving, murderous scum.'

'It wasn't the first time.' A slurring male voice, its owner removing a thick leather belt, callused hands caressing the slab of the buckle. 'There was that other girl, years ago. Pretty thing she was as well . . . used to sing in his shop, till she went and disappeared.'

Looking around that bar, Nathaniel's blood ran cold, seeing the hatred in every eye. What difference was there between him and Isaac, both transient souls who'd lived their lives belonging nowhere, to nothing, to no one? Isaac might have sat amongst clutter and tat while Nathaniel ruled over his palace of gold, but what had either achieved in the end? Now Isaac was gone. What was left for

Nathaniel Samuels; an ageing Midas whose curse had been to destroy everything he'd ever held dear?

A sudden flashing of light caught his eye – the threatening gleam of a waiting knife. He turned away, turned the other cheek, making his way towards the door. There he stopped and extended both arms, holding onto the frame like their Christ on his cross. Right then, he would willingly give up his life. He silently dared them to do it, to plunge the cold steel deep into his back. But nobody moved, and there was barely a sound to be heard when he lowered his arms and opened the door, and then stood beneath the Dolphin's sign as he took one last glance at Isaac's store.

Retracing his steps along the dock, Nathaniel heard music, someone playing a fiddle on one of the ships. Two or three whores were wandering past. One of them was singing. She was young, hardly more than a child. Her long hair was waving and brown. She stopped when she noticed the way he was staring, coming closer to touch his arm, laughing and twirling and lifting her hems, asking if he'd like to take her home.

He followed her into an alley and fucked her against the wall. It was brutal and squalid. Filling his lungs with the fetid air, the dank odours of salt and oil and sex, he felt himself trapped in the nets of his past, as if time was some filth clinging onto his hair, burrowing down through the skin of his scalp, crawling through his veins like a curse or disease. He would carry the stigma wherever he went. He would never get away.

Several hours later, Nathaniel opened a drawer in his desk, took out a bottle and unscrewed the lid, tipping some little white pills in his palm. Swallowing them down, he closed his eyes, waiting for the dark tearing pain to subside.

Why didn't he die as the doctors warned? It was only a matter of luck or time. But what did they know of what hearts could endure? Hearts could be twisted and squeezed and distorted. Look at Lydia's will – the affidavits he'd had to swear to confirm that his wife had been of sound mind. Had she acted out of some malice, to ensure Joseph knew of his father's crimes, or had she really gone mad in the end, believing that some part of Phoebe was Esther, her own daughter's spirit reborn in another?

Nathaniel reached into his pocket. He was thinking of Cissy with a child in her arms. He was thinking about a dreaming girl, walking out through the night, walking out through the snow, going into the woods to meet her death. With a cry of anguish escaping his lips, he stood, then slumped forward, down to his knees, staring at what was held in his hand – a white ribbon, a rolled piece of paper, the message inside it that Cissy had written.

> *Oh, didst thou know the pains of absent love,*
> *Acis would ne'er from Galatea rove.*

All he could do was groan his response, 'When did Acis become Polyphemus?' His passion and greed had caused Lydia's madness, caused Esther's death, caused Phoebe's life to be stolen away. And Cissy . . . he'd never meant to hurt Cissy.

Eleven years had gone by since that Christmas Day when she and Phoebe came to the shop, when he'd sent Phoebe off to look for a present, when he'd taken Cissy in his arms, kissing her, begging her not to cry. His words then had been so insistent, so certain. 'We have to stop living this lie. Phoebe's still young. Joseph's settled at school. Lydia rarely leaves Dinwood Court. We should be together. We should start again. It's not too late . . .'

She'd smiled sadly. Her finger pressed soft to his lips. Who knew what answer she might have made – but that was the moment the watchman appeared, skulking through shadows, thinking them thieves, his shouted reproach transformed to a nervous, pandering laugh when he saw his employer standing there. And Nathaniel knew that he was condemned, as soon as that fool mouthed his drunken words. 'Sorry, sir . . . didn't expect you today. Thought you'd be tucked up at home with your wife. Another of your special purchases, is it? I'll turn a blind eye again, shall I . . . let you get on with the business in hand?'

The fool had the nerve to hold out his palm as if expecting a bribe or reward. Nathaniel's response was cold with threat, telling that wretch to get out of his sight. But Cissy had frozen in his arms. How could he convince her those women meant nothing when she wouldn't listen, when she pushed him away, calling for Phoebe, insisting they leave. All he could do was stand and look on, impotent, fuming, still feeling the warmth of her lips against his, her lips that were suddenly icy, reproachful, saying she didn't want to go on, that he should consider his wife and son, that Phoebe was growing too old for such games, that it wasn't right to confuse the girl . . . because Maud was her mother, and Maud was a widow, and, as far as the rest of the world was concerned, Phoebe Turner's father was dead.

It was then that the child had come running towards them. His heart missed a beat to see what she held: the little gold goddess from India, Parvarti, the wife of the

Hindoo God Shiva, who legend said brought her nothing but sorrow, because Shiva was faithless and yet he still loved her, desiring Parvarti above every other.

Nathaniel said nothing of that, only stooped down to circle the girl in his arms, to say that he loved her, and she should remember that he would always be her friend, and if she was ever sad or alone she need only bring that gift to him. With every word spoken, he'd stared up at Cissy, never dreaming that it would be so long – that she would be dead before Phoebe returned.

45

After we left the cemetery, when we arrived back in Stepney Green, my father told the coachman to wait while he walked with me to the end of the passage that led to the door of Old Riley's house. He didn't come any further, just said goodbye and kissed my cheek, his own scraping roughly against my skin. He gave me a present, a little white feather. My fingers curled tightly around it, afraid that it might blow away, being so small and downy, as light as the air, as a fairy's wing.

When the door opened up a smell of fried meat and onions blew out. Old Riley led me through to the kitchen, all spruced up and swept and cleaned since that morning. Mr Collins and Quin were there at the table, and I was soon sitting to join them. For the very first time in weeks I found myself to be ravenous, shovelling potato into my mouth, having to pause to swallow it down before I could answer Old Riley's enquiries as to what had gone on with my day.

Most things I kept to myself, hidden away in my heart, and I hardly knew how to broach the rest. But before I could think I found myself gushing, 'Old Riley, you'll never guess! I have the keys to Tredegar Square. My father . . . Mr Samuels . . . he says that the house is mine. We could all live there. There's so much more room. You could do your séances down in the basement, if we don't have any maids living in. And Mr Collins can use Cissy's piano . . . so long as the Hallelujahs don't have it, only,' I felt myself blush, 'Mr Collins, you must not spy on me.'

'Are you sure about this?' Old Riley's lips pursed.

Mr Collins said nothing, only looked thoughtful, and then Quin MacKenna stretched out an arm, reaching right past me to grab at the butter while giving me one of his slow, steady grins, his face lit up like the rising sun.

'And what about me? Am I also invited?'

'Oh, I hadn't thought, I . . .' I felt the warmth of his leg against mine and my head filled with what I'd looked at that morning, having to lower my eyes in shame, quite convinced that Old Riley might then have developed the art of mental divination – for she gave me one of her long hard looks, arching an orange-pencilled brow, stating slowly but firmly, 'Best Quin stays put. He could keep this place on. Not that I've yet seen one penny in rent.'

'Rent?' Quin exclaimed in mock surprise. 'Why, Mrs Riley, there I was thinking you wanted me here for the sheer delight of my company.'

'You've got some sauce!' she retorted. 'I let you stay on because I'm an old fool, and because those blue eyes could lure all the birds right down from the trees! But you take care, Quin MacKenna. Pride cometh before a fall and all that! You might not be quite so cocky one day.'

'I thought you liked my cocky ways, that they helped to bring in your spiritualist trade, tempting all the old biddies in through the door.'

Old Riley let out a lewd cackle, plump cheeks stretched so wide I saw gappy black holes where some teeth used to be. 'Well, where's the harm, if it sets their hearts pitter-pattering, their lips sighing into the pillow at night.' And

343

touching a hand to red curls, she was suddenly far more serious. 'Anyway, Quin MacKenna, I've read your palm . . . there'll be time enough for you to pay. You and Eddie are destined for great success. I've been feeling it in my bones for months.'

Mr Collins looked a little alarmed, no doubt fearing that such premonitions might venture to matrimonial realms, especially now with Maud Turner gone. But after what my father had said I wondered if Mr Collins was simply a wonderful actor himself, and whether he'd ever cared for Maud or was only pretending to form an attachment, secretly one of those 'double agents'; the sort that you read about in penny dreadfuls.

Quin spoke up on his friend's behalf. 'I'm inclined to have a little more faith in the here and now. Mr Collins' future has little to do with those lines on his palms, far more with his skill on the ivories.'

Meanwhile, Mr Collins was looking at me. 'It's Phoebe's future we're thinking of here. She must consider things carefully.'

'And, of course,' Old Riley intervened, 'she may choose to live with her father instead.'

'I can't! I can't do that.' My heart fluttered fast as a bird in my breast. 'There would be gossip. They'd call me his bastard, call Cissy his whore. I only want to live with you.'

I might have gone on, if not for Old Riley's hushing, her hand gently resting on mine. 'Oh dearie, you shouldn't be bitter like this, not when he's trying to make things right. Give it some time and you might come round.'

A few sniffs and some watery nose-blowings later, I managed to find my tongue. 'I won't change my mind. I'm quite sure of that. But, if you wanted . . . if it helped,

I could let out the house in Tredegar Square, use any money to pay you some rent . . . if you were still willing to have me here.'

Mr Collins dabbed a cloth to his mouth, his whiskers all greasy with mutton fat, coughing a little before his response. 'That house was bought for Cissy. Now, with her gone it's rightfully yours and, somewhat more self-ishly, I dare say we should be more comfortable there. But,' he smiled, 'I have one condition. No more of your cooking, young lady. I can still taste that stew you once made!'

'Oh, that salt!' Old Riley threw up her hands. 'My mouth was so parched I thought I should die, or turn into Lot's wife! No wonder Maud gulped down the brandy that night and . . .'

Halted by Mr Collins' stern glance, Old Riley shut up and let him go on. 'If we *do* come to Bow, perhaps I could make a small proposition. While playing the halls these past months, Quin and I have achieved some degree of success. We've had approaches to print up our songs. But we're planning a little investment ourselves, venturing into the publishing trade and, if we do, we'll be needing an artist to work on the covers and, having seen what you sent to Maud . . . well, I think you might prove very useful indeed, combining your talents with ours, as it were.'

46

Old Riley brought along her stuffed monkey and set it on top of Cissy's piano, still there in Tredegar Square, not gone to the mission hall. She arranged some little glass stars on the mantels, saying they would bring us luck. But most of her crystals were left behind in that midnight blue room in Paradise Mews, where the black netted tent had been taken down, carefully folded and stored away – in case she ever felt the need to take up the soothsaying game again. Anyway, she kept herself busy enough, combining her talents with ours, as it were, rattling away on her sewing machine, tailoring suits for Collins & Mac-Kenna; making up several new dresses for me.

Galatea's costume was stored upstairs with the rest of Cissy's things. When we first opened her bedroom door, I was glad, if not a little surprised, to find her jewellery box still there and all of its treasures still untouched. Perhaps Maud saw those jewels as ill-gotten gains, that to handle those stones might taint her with sin. But Old Riley had no such qualms. She was thrilled when I gave her the emerald choker; the one Cissy wore on that last night at Wilton's. I took her old bottle of Hammam Bouquet, dabbing what remained on my pillow at night, sleeping while breathing the fragrance of Cissy – which was also that of Nathaniel Samuels.

As to Maud, whatever possessions she'd left behind, I

hadn't the heart to throw them out. Everything was stored in her room, and the door was locked up, out of sight, out of mind. The ache in my heart – of her absence – was less distressing that way.

But not everything from the past had been lost, and soon after moving back into the house an enormous trunk was delivered, and in that was Cissy's scrapbook. There was also the walnut box that contained all my papers and brushes and paints, along with those clothes that were given to me when I first arrived in Herefordshire. When everything had been unpacked, I looked through the paintings I'd made while there and though my time in Dinwood Court had been no more than a few short months and in the strangest of circumstances, I pined for the beauty and peace of that place – and for other things that I must forget.

Opening Cissy's scrapbook, I looked through every single page, and when the very last was turned my fingers reached into a pocket, formed from the back inside cover. I was searching for Esther's rosebud, for that was the place where I'd kept it, but when touching silk petals I dislodged something else, something secreted much lower down.

It was another old photograph, probably taken by one of those itinerants who set up their cameras in public spaces, hoping to gain some speculative trade. I recognised Victoria Park, a place where Cissy and I often walked. There I was, in front of the boating lake, the pagoda and great arching fountain behind, and I couldn't have been more than four or five. At my side was a boy – much taller, much older. His hair was as pale as mine was dark. And though I was smiling up at him, looking like the cat that got the cream, he was clearly intent on ignoring me, staring straight into the camera lens. Such a sullen, arrogant, beautiful face.

A fragment of memory sprang into mind – *Going home from Victoria Park one day, Cissy too quiet, walking too fast, my hands grabbing onto her skirts as I ask, 'Who was that boy, Cissy? Who was that man? Do you think we'll ever see them again?'*

'Maybe, if you're good. But let's not tell Mama about today. Let's keep this as our special secret, and then . . . who knows . . . if you're good . . . if you manage to keep your promise, then perhaps we might see them again one day.'

'Do I have to keep it a secret for ever?'

'Yes, for ever and ever.'

'Cross my heart and hope to die?'

Cissy laughs and stops walking, stooping forward to kiss the tip of my nose. 'Crossing your heart will be quite enough.'

Crossing my fingers instead, I close my eyes and make a wish, that one day I might have a brother, a brother just like that boy in the park – the boy with the father with black, black hair, who made Cissy smile, who smiled at me.

The day after finding that photograph I woke in a state of exhaustion. Looking into the mirror I saw the grey pallor and sore red eyes, and I knew how easy it could be to go back to bed, to pull the sheets up over my head and sink into the slough of despair. But I wouldn't do that again. I would not drown in grief and guilt. I would not do what Cissy had done. Squeezing my hands into tight, fisting balls, determined to hold back the threatening tears, I resolved to forget all about Joseph Samuels, to make an entirely new life of my own.

That very morning, I started to work. Mr Collins and I cleared Mama's desk and then dragged it into the music room, and under his watchful direction I sketched out some scenes for his musical covers – with maidens reclining in bowers of bliss, with young men serenading below balconies. And within the month, he and Quin had made their arrangements with printers, and then they took out the lease on a shop. In Museum Street, it was, right in the middle of Bloomsbury, and hanging outside was a green and gilt sign.

Collins, MacKenna & Co, *Music Publishers*

As well as having their own songs printed up, the shop shelves were heaving with all sorts of music, books on all aspects of stage entertainment. A boy was hired to serve at the counter, another to work in the back, packing up orders requested by mail in response to the press advertisements. And soon there were even accountants employed, dealing with all of the profits made – though I did find myself sometimes thinking of Maud, quite sure she could have managed that.

I missed her around the house, even her tempers and biblical quotes. But to tell you the truth, that following year I felt myself slipping out of a bondage, like rising up from a watery grave and starting to breathe all over again. Every morning, I drew back the curtains and looked over the garden square, observing the bustle and life below. Whenever I made my way downstairs I always stopped at a certain point, to glance at that empty space on the wall, to wonder what Cissy would think of me now. *If* she could see me I felt sure she would smile. I felt sure she would say, 'Why not give it a go?' much as she had at Wilton's Hall, when the show was almost about to begin, when Bill Wright appeared in the dressing room and asked me to act as a shepherdess, and said that the theatre was in my blood.

And, do you know, he was right all along. My first appearance on the stage might have resulted in failure, but now I was ready to try again. Not that I took to the singing. I could never compare with Cissy, even though Mr Collins and Quin were always coaxing and urging me on, insisting my voice was pretty enough. But I wouldn't give in. It didn't seem right. Instead, I played the silent part in the Collins & MacKenna musical act, which proved to be just as successful as Old Riley had foretold.

With everything taking off so well, my own share in the earnings seemed a small fortune, and I was determined to be independent, to run the big house in Tredegar Square without any resort to my father's funds. Still, at every performance we made, I looked out for him in the audience, always to be secretly disappointed when Nathaniel Samuels wasn't there.

We did a stint at the Alhambra, the finest variety theatre in town, but I loved the Hoxton Victoria best. It was where I first started, where we were so often booked to go back, where the decoration was rumoured to be as grand as the Paris Opera House. There were three enormous balconies, curving round to three rows of boxes in front, all reds and golds and exquisite relief. There were classical statues and fancy lights, a domed ceiling that looked like the night-time sky, a painted firmament of stars.

That decor fitted our act to perfection, for there was one song so popular the punters came back time after time. And while Mr Collins played the piano, with notes swirling round the hall, Quin – welcomed on by the ladies' sighs, dressed in his elegant evening attire, a white tie at his throat, a top hat on his head and holding a silver-topped cane in his hand – would stand beneath the proscenium arch, serenading the box in which I sat, and whenever it came to the final verse he would reach up and hand me a single white rose.

When we first did it I felt so self-conscious. Honestly, I thought I might faint or be sick. But Old Riley said my quivering nerves only helped to enhance the effect of young love; that the way my cheek flushed then paled so white ensured that the audience really *believed*. As time went by, I got used to it all, smiling sweetly whenever I lifted that rose, and then, whoosh, dropping down from above, there came a thousand fluttering stars, all twinkling silver and gold in the limes while the audience sang along with Quin . . .

> *There's a star shining brightly above.*
> *And now that I've seen her my heart is beguiled.*
> *Cupid has sent out his glistening dart,*
> *Drawn by the lure of my Phoebe's smile.*
>
> *When night falls and the silver moon shines,*
> *When the lamps throw out golden puddles of light,*
> *I dream of drowning in those dark eyes,*
> *Lying next to my angel, my heart's delight.*
>
> *When night falls and the silver moon shines,*
> *When the lamps throw out golden puddles of light,*
> *I dream that one day she'll gaze back into mine,*
> *And she'll call me her angel, her heart's sweet delight.*

When Quin wrote those sentimental words, I didn't mind at all, not as I had when Peter Faulkener was spouting his nonsense at Dinwood Court. Years later, 'Phoebe' became 'Phoebus' with such luminaries as Marie Lloyd taking it up as a part of their acts. But then, at the start, it was all about Quin, who gazed up as light glinted on stars in my hair, where a few coils fell loose to my shoulders, the black powdered with glittering dust. My lips were painted a silvery white. My eyelids were darkened, enhanced with the kohl. My white gown was embroidered with silvery threads, and where Cissy's filigree locket hung, the lace at my breast was spun gossamer.

Old Riley had truly excelled herself, literally turning me into a 'star', though her own appearance grew yet more eccentric – a continuing penchant for wearing hats as individual statements of theatre, with long feathers, stuffed birds and waxed fruits. I wondered she didn't steal the act then heading up the Victoria's bill; I think that performing Russian cat would have happily sat there, purring on top.

After the shows, she'd sometimes go off cavorting with a dubious crowd, a lot of old friends from her Wilton's days. There was Champagne Charlie. There was Lord Crumpet, with his black mustachios and yellow wig, and his habit of going out and about in carpet slippers and dressing gown. And even Bill Wright rolled up once or twice, and then she stayed out until morning, coming home very bleary and reeking of whisky, oyster juice staining the front of her gown.

Mr Collins, the steadier influence by far, was my ever attentive chaperon, never failing to see me home after a show, except – well, except for that one time . . .

He and I almost always dined late with Quin, before Quin went on home to Stepney Green. And everyone thought Quin and I were a pair, saying we made the most glamorous couple, that whenever we walked into a room we glistened, we shone, like the stars and the moon. He was very fine with his piercing blue eyes, made even brighter with smudgings of paint, and every night when he stood on the stage I felt myself falling under his spell, an affair so public, performed before thousands, although, in reality, we'd never so much as come close to a kiss. If we touched, it was all a part of the act.

On those nights when we were free, Quin would come round to Tredegar Square, where he and Mr Collins spent hours with the writing and rehearsing of songs. And when it grew late, when I went on to bed, I could still hear Quin's voice floating up through the house, just as I used to hear Cissy's, when she was still alive.

But how could I trust any man again, after what Joseph Samuels had done to me? Hadn't he once been charming and kind? Hadn't I once been too naive, seduced when I should have resisted, when I should have been moral and righteous, and then The Thing would never have happened: the terrible sin that had damned my soul.

No, the spectre of Joseph was always there.

47

Mr Collins had been distracted for weeks. When I asked why, he only replied, 'I have something rather special in mind. Patience and discretion is all part of the game. I wouldn't want to raise anyone's hopes only to have them dashed back down.'

But it was very soon after that when Phineas Burbidge, the famous New York impresario, came calling to see us backstage. The other artistes on the bill must surely have known that something was up, being edgy and nervous for most of the night, and when the gavel banged down the last time, when the limelights and gaseliers all died, even those who generally scurried off, heading straight to the George and Dragon pub, stayed on to loiter round dressing room doors.

The Man Serpent sat on a crate of Bass ale, sharing it round with the Miniature Mings – the troupe of Chinese acrobats who performed in spangled tights and tops. Dan Leno, a 'Lion Comique', was still wearing his Beefeater uniform – a grand affair that Old Riley ran up – and, as usual, those two were having a laugh. But they shut up when Mr Burbidge arrived, puffing away on a big cigar, shaking hands with one and all and practically oozing with confident charm. He must have been seventy years at least – but very burly, very robust, one might even say agricultural-looking with that broad, balding pate sprouting springy brown curls, a kindly round face with a bulbous, squashed nose.

'Miss Turner,' he boomed before kissing my hand. 'Phineas Burbidge at your command . . . delighted to make your acquaintance.'

From the corner of my eye I saw Mr Collins sidling near, beaming he was, looking happy as Larry, and greeting that Mr Burbidge as if they were long-lost friends.

'Phoebe,' he said, 'Mr Burbidge is visiting London, seeking new talent for his productions. He's very impressed by our act. He thinks we should visit New York some day.'

'Would you like to do that, Miss Turner?' our new American friend enquired. 'Would you care to sit in a balcony there, perhaps even singing a little yourself, performing to halls of six thousand or more? With the punters paying five dollars a head, imagine the sound of *that* much applause. I've always said, every crowd has a silver lining!'

I smiled demurely, shaking my head. 'I never have thought of going to New York . . . and certainly not of singing myself.'

In truth, the prospect appalled me, thinking of William Turner and Maud marching outside all the theatres and bars, calling them dens of depravity.

Mr Collins looked owlish, shifting his spectacled gaze between Mr Burbidge and me. I was glad when Quin appeared; his hair damp and ruffled, his face scrubbed and shiny and looking almost boyish that night, though he was a good nine years older than me – a year older than Joseph Samuels.

He draped an arm over my shoulder which drew envious looks from the chorus girls who gathered around, cadging cigarettes, which he lit as they held them in their mouths: lips puckered up like a kiss. I tried to ignore all that flirting, surprised at such prickings of jealousy. Meanwhile, Mr Collins was nodding for Quin to come forward and shake Mr Burbidge's hand and, as usual, Quin was smiling his charm, and who could have said if they'd met before.

Very soon Quin was back at my side, murmuring low in my ear. 'Shall we go somewhere else . . . leave the others to do all the schmoozing round here?' He turned back to Mr Collins. 'Phoebe's a little tired tonight. If you like I'll make sure she gets safely home.'

I didn't object to Quin's lie. I don't think Old Riley could have heard, and Mr Collins was much too distracted, accepting an invitation himself, dining at Claridges with Mr Burbidge. And when Mr Burbidge reached for my hand, kissing my fingertips again, I still thought it a matter of wooing, never suspecting a deal had been struck, the tour dates already inked into a diary, first-class berths on a steamship already booked up.

It was late December, and snowing again. The year before, when the snows began, I thought of the day of The Ritual. Not that I went to the docks any more, though I did lay some flowers on Cissy's grave, and I wept for my mother for days on end.

But that night when I left the theatre with Quin I confess I was thinking of nothing but him, and once the stage boy had whistled a cab, once Quin had a quick word with the driver, when he helped me in and slammed the door, when enclosed in our barely lit box of a world, I lost all my fear, all reserve and pride, forgetting about Joseph Samuels for once, forgetting those dancers who huddled round Quin, their bodies pressed close when he stood in the wings, forgetting those letters and gifts from his fans who sat in the audience night after night, sighing and swooning whenever he winked – as he'd once winked at me in Wilton's Hall.

Every detail remains fixed in my mind. How the driver pulled up at Stepney Green rather than heading on to Bow. How I made no complaint, though I knew I should, patiently waiting while Quin paid the fare, my feet in thin slippers grown numb on the pavement, stamping to try and keep warm. The horses snorted trails of white that looked like cobwebs spun out on the air. A gentleman edged down some icy front steps, tipping his hat in greeting. Somewhere in the distance church bells were chiming as Quin and I headed across the green, arms linked like a regular Darby and Joan, with ice crystals circling round us like tinsel – until a blistering wind got up, rushing through leafless branches of trees, spitting its warning into my eyes. Not that I took any notice of that, only shivered and lowered my head. And soon Quin was fumbling to open the door, and then he was taking my coat and my gloves, blowing hot breath on my freezing hands, saying, 'Go on through to the kitchen . . . wait by the range where it's warm.'

Ignoring a faint whiff of cabbagy drains, I was happy to make myself at home, opening up the oven door and sitting in front with my skirts hitched high, damp shoes and stockings kicked to one side as toes toasted and tingled back to life.

Quin came in with a tumbler of whisky, and though I coughed and spluttered at first, my breath quite taken away by the burn, it soon warmed the cockles, as they say. I felt safe. I trusted Quin, smiling back when he took my hand, to lead me on through to the room at the front where the fire he'd lit was now roaring away, where I stood very still, cocooned in its warmth while he loosened my gown, as waves of white silk were dropping like foam at my naked feet. He didn't ask if I'd done it before. I didn't question how practised his touch, or how very plain it was to see that he had contrived to turn that room into his very own bower of bliss – with its firelight and candles and shimmering stars, its daybeds spread with cushions and throws. And when I saw our reflections caught in the lustre of a glass, I heard Quin MacKenna's honeyed tongue. 'Look at that picture. It's perfect. You're perfect.'

I looked and I saw how pale my flesh, breasts sparkling, still dusty with all the stage glitter, and the silvery glint of my locket there. Quin's sparseness was darker, lit up like gold from the flames below – flames as red and as hot as the fires of Hell. But, to me, that room was a miniature Heaven, surrounded by all those glistening stars, and surely it was only a moment I thought again of a thundery night, and a cave that had once seemed sacred too. But Paradise Mews was aptly named, and when Quin kneeled down I did the same, only too willing to worship with him, the words of his song still fixed in my mind. *I dream of drowning in those dark eyes . . . Lying next to my angel, my heart's sweet delight.*

I sighed at the heat of his breath on my cheek, the touch of his lips on my shoulders, how he lifted the hair away from my breasts, caressing and cupping the flesh beneath, the way he murmured so soft in my ear, 'A long time since you looked in here at me . . . since you caught me naked and sleeping.'

'And now, you've caught me.'

'Have I?'

Cradling my face in his palms he drew his own much closer. His fringe fell forward over his eyes. His breath smelled of whisky and cigarettes. His mouth tasted salty and hot, and I sighed again at the touch of his fingers as they stroked their slow patterns over my skin. My eyes grew moist with an aching desire when he lowered his mouth to nuzzle and suck, as his fingers probed between my thighs, taking me into some dark dreaming place before lifting me up onto one of the beds where, still kneeling before me, his hands gently prised my knees apart and he stared a long time at what he exposed. But I felt no shame or self-disgust, and when Quin MacKenna and I made love, it was true what he said – it was perfect. Every moment stretched out with my wanting as I panted and grabbed at his hair and moaned with the pleasure, so sweet, so intense; an exquisite small shuddering agony. I'd never known that sensation before, filled with regret when it dulled and died, when I was finally released. But that little moment had been Quin's enchantment, the spell that would set me free from the past; the past which had claimed my heart too long.

Hours later, when the fire had burned down low, he lay at my side on that narrow bed, his head on my shoulder, his arm on my belly, one of his palms moulded soft to my breast. When I shivered, he reached for a quilt, drawing it over our nakedness and then, while he slept, I stared at his face through the dimming red light, as perfect as any angel's could be. And when he stirred, when he gave me that lazy grin and asked if I might have any regrets, I laughed. I said no. I kissed him again.

It was barely six in the morning when I stood in the hall at Tredegar Square, hearing a rustling sound from the landing, seeing Old Riley's face staring down, her sleep-puffy features curious, anxious, her voice deep and croaky when she called, 'Oh, Phoebe, it's you! Thank goodness, you're back. I've been fretting all night . . . when Eddie went off with that Mr Burbidge he told me that Quin was bringing you home!'

My face cracked wide in a smile. I was practically fizzing with all the excitement. 'I've been with Quin in Paradise Mews.'

'You've been with Quin MacKenna . . . all night?'

'Yes! And he's asked me to marry him . . . in the cab, when he brought me home!'

She whooped before rushing down the stairs, both of us hugging, Old Riley laughing, 'Well, well, Quin Mac-Kenna set to be married! I hoped you two would wake up in the end. But then, I've seen it coming for months. I think you'll be perfect together.' *And wasn't that what he'd said?*

With no maid coming in until seven o'clock we went on downstairs to the kitchen where I lit the jets while Old Riley made toast and brewed up a fresh pot of coffee. All the while she was prattling on about bridesmaids and dresses and flowers. But I fear those prophetic powers of hers must still have been dozing in bed, her crystal ball's powers too sluggish that day because, in the end, that part of my life – being in the act with Quin, living with Mr Collins and Old Riley in Bow – it was all about to come to an end.

Still, for then I was happy enough, ignorant of what any future might hold, only glad to have thrown off the curse of my past, though I was more than a little embarrassed when Old Riley's nose gave a sniff and a twitch, and suddenly conscious of how I must reek, of sweat and sex and cigarettes, after gulping my coffee I hurried upstairs to get myself washed and changed.

In the bedroom I stripped off my crumpled stage costume, thinking it lucky we had two to spare. I rubbed dollops of rose cream all over my face where the kohl had left streaks of black on my cheeks, like a Cinderella come back from the ball. I gave myself a quick top and bottom, using the sponge from the washing bowl where last night's water was icy cold. Was it that made me tremble, or was it the thought of what Quin and I had done last night? No blood, no pain, nothing stinging or sore. I wanted to do it all over again, longing for the night ahead when Quin would sing 'Phoebe's Song' to me – the charming Quin MacKenna who'd asked me to be his wife, with whom every girl was a little in love.

Was I in love? I lifted my hand and stared at the scar, still there, but so small, barely noticeable now.

Later on, when I came back downstairs, Old Riley said I looked tired and wan, in need of some warming sustenance, and after a lunch of stewed beef and carrots we both sat by the fire and fell soundly asleep – and might well have missed that evening's performance, for the maid had gone and hurried off home without even thinking to give us a nudge. We were only roused when the cabman arrived, and alarmed by his sudden loud knock at the door I felt muddled, disorientated, overcome by the room's fuggy atmosphere. But the hallway's cool air was reviving enough and we'd soon dragged on our hats and coats, though I could have cried at the state of my hair which had dried in the most peculiar fashion. And yet, it was more than that. I couldn't say how, but I didn't feel myself at all.

*

We'd never had such a send-off before. I saw one old woman with tears streaming down over wrinkled cheeks. But then, some of those punters knew more than me, having seen the front page of the *Standard* that night, with its pictures of Mr Collins and Quin, alongside Mr Phineas Burbidge.

What a racket there was. Two encores, and the audience still calling for more, with stampings of feet, with whistles and shouts, and the last time Quin reached up to offer his rose, when his lips kissed the tips of my fingers again, when more of those paper stars dropped down, I fancied they looked like confetti.

Such romantic musings were soon interrupted when *bang!* went the chairman's gavel, his whiskers gleaming red in the limes, his forehead glistening, shiny with sweat as a deep and melodious voice rang out, 'Ladies and gentlemen, lend us an ear.'

Someone started to heckle: 'Get on with it then. We ain't got all night. I've paid to see Lord Crumpet. Where's he got to? Let's 'ave him on.'

While others were hushing, the chairman replied, 'His Lordship will bless us with his refined presence but, before that, I'm sure he'll be happy to join with me now, in being both proud and sad to announce what many of you will already have heard . . .'

At that point, I still hadn't cottoned on, wondering – could it be – could Quin have told him about our news, our engagement now to be announced, and so very publicly? But then the chairman came to his point, putting me out of my misery – or rather, making it start.

'Won't you join me in wishing Messrs Collins & MacKenna and, of course, the beautiful Phoebe, the best of British luck in New York . . . though Mr Burbidge's gain is our loss. Join hands, ladies and gentlemen, in wishing our friends a "bon voyage", though we all hope to see them come back again soon.'

What was he talking about? I twisted round, looking for Old Riley who stood at her post inside the box door. She looked about as surprised as me, her mouth gawping open, her face flushed as red as the curtains that she was about to draw round, to give me the chance to escape backstage.

Bang went the gavel again. *Bang* went something inside my head. Something snapped – and so loud I could no longer hear the noise of applause. All sounds were distorted and muffled and strange and despite the steamy heat in that hall, the thick stench of sweat and perfume and muck, my fingers were tingling, cold as ice.

The lanterns dipped low and, standing beneath the proscenium arch, Quin lifted his hat and waved back at the crowd; Mr Collins, still seated at his piano, was smiling and bowing his head, until both men were hidden from view, the great curtain falling, gold fringes reflecting across the dark boards. Only a thin beam of light was remaining to flicker across the plaster relief, all the gilt pillars and velvet-draped boxes – around which some tinsel still fell, like snow – through which I saw him, staring at me.

In one year he'd aged more than ten. Black eyes looked out from bruised hollows. The flesh of his face was sallow and thin, the bones much too prominent beneath. Meanwhile, as the curtain was rising again, I think Quin MacKenna was calling my name, and – after that briefest distraction – when I looked back at the opposite box, my father had gone, vanished into thin air.

Running out through the side passage door, I scurried

down the backstage stairs, making my way to the dressing rooms. Surely, that's where he would be. But he was nowhere to be seen, and perhaps I had only imagined him there, because of my guilty conscience, because I'd not seen him in such a long time, and perhaps I never would again, if I was to go to America.

I was panicking, turning in circles, pushing past all the other artistes, the prop men and dressers who kissed my cheek, all eager to hear any news of our trip. And there in the midst of it all was Old Riley, calling out for champagne, hugging Dan Leno and then every Miniature Ming in turn.

'Oh good Lord.' She looked up, starting to chuckle the moment Mr Collins appeared. 'I was hoping, well, of course I was but, Eddie, you are a rogue . . . how on earth did you keep that a secret so long?'

'Phoebe, my dear,' Mr Collins looked as proud as a peacock, 'what do you think of my surprise? Quin told me yours this morning. He's asked me to be best man.'

Quin was now making his way from the stage, and he didn't look much like a man set to wed, two dancers hung on his every word, flirting and laughing, their arms twined through his. He was gallant enough to shake them off, reaching for a glass of champagne, coming close to my side to make his toast – to the trip – to the act – to our engagement.

I noticed the order of that. Suddenly, I felt suffocated by all the congratulations and kisses, the questions about when we'd marry and whether in London or New York.

Old Riley could not have been more delighted, eagerly asking, 'When are we going?'

'Next Wednesday,' Mr Collins replied. 'We'll be leaving at dawn, from Southampton docks. Mr Burbidge has organised everything. We're booked on *The Midnight Star*. Was any ship more auspiciously named?'

Next Wednesday. Less than a week away.

I was struggling to draw breath into my lungs, turning to Quin, asking, 'Did you know? Did you know about this last night?'

'He certainly did!' Mr Collins went on, oblivious to my growing distress. 'But then I'm sure everyone must have guessed, when Mr Burbidge turned up like that.'

'I had no idea it was all done and dusted.' My head was beginning to pound.

'Time's certainly tight.' Old Riley was musing. 'I wonder, should I make up new costumes? Should Phoebe have wings do you think? Could she hover a bit across the stage? They say everything's more spectacular there . . . and not least the wages. Dan was telling me only last night, about that Jenny Lind. When Mr Burbidge hired her for a stint, and a good forty years ago it was now, she was earning a thousand dollars a night. Well, Eddie Collins, fancy that!'

Mr Collins was coy, refusing to be drawn on financial arrangements. 'I don't know about such things, but I do know that Mr Burbidge is keen on keeping the act exactly the way it is right now.'

I found myself backing away from the group, feeling hemmed in and much too hot, still staring at Quin while accusing, 'You didn't tell me the truth. You lied.'

The room fell silent. Quin looked shocked, answering me in a low slow voice. 'Nobody lied.'

'You may not have lied, but you tricked me. All of my life I've been deceived. I won't go on living that way any more. And, what if I don't want to go to New York?

What about my father? He was here tonight. He was watching the show and—'

'Nathaniel Samuels, here tonight?' Mr Collins frowned. 'Oh, I very much doubt that, my dear . . . not with the troubles going on.'

'What troubles? What are you talking about?'

'Why, those riots.' Stepping nearer, his voice dropped to a murmur. 'All those demonstrations against the Jews. I presumed you would have known . . . that you'd seen the reports in the newspapers.'

'You should *not* have presumed!' My interruption was stark and rude, but all I could see was my father's face, looking so thin, looking so ill, staring out through those swirling paper stars.

Quin took a step nearer. 'Phoebe, don't be like this. There's a party arranged—'

'Indeed there is,' Mr Collins broke in. 'Mr Burbidge is waiting at Claridges now, with photographers . . . with reporters.'

'Oh, you must be there!' said Old Riley. 'When it's known you and Quin are to wed, what a lure that story will be in New York. There's nothing the public likes any more than a genuine bit of romance.'

With tears stinging my eyes I stared back at Quin. 'Is *this* a genuine romance, or is it another charade to drum up some more publicity, for the sake of a thousand dollars a night? Is that why you asked me to marry you? Is that why you—'

'Phoebe.' Quin's voice was strained. 'I said nothing last night because I wasn't sure. I wanted it to be a surprise, but we still had to secure our release . . . negate the Victoria's contract, though it seems Mr Burbidge has dealt with all that, compensating the hall for the loss of the act and . . .'

'I'm sorry. Forgive me.' I mumbled excuses, glancing round at the crowd of embarrassed and shocked faces. 'I must sound ungrateful. I can't seem to think clearly. I'm tired. I want to go home.'

'Phoebe, don't go,' Quin called out as I ran from the room, along the dark warren of passageways, past light men and prop men and carpenters. The stage boy was nowhere in sight. I cursed with frustration at that, grunting and straining to open the door, my face streaming with tears by the time that stubborn latch worked free, allowing a rush of iced air to gust in. Outside on the pavement, skidding and slipping through snow and slush, I was frantically waving my arms for a cab and, thankfully, there was one waiting, and the driver was quick to recognise me, and as we headed down the road I had to cover my ears with my hands to block out the sound of Quin as he shouted my name from the backstage door.

I sat in that cab in a shivering daze, staring at dark and shabby streets where yesterday's snow had been virginal white. But I had not been a virgin. My soul was as black as the melting slime now running down into gutters and drains. My forehead pressed hard against cold glass and the eyes I saw reflected back were not mine, they were those of my father, still watching, still waiting for me to return – in case I should ever change my mind.

When Old Riley came back to the house, I was sitting in front of the parlour hearth, so close that my skirts had scorched to brown. A wonder I hadn't gone up in flames.

'Come away from that fire!' She tugged at my arm, and then, 'Dearie, are you feeling all right? Why did you go running off like that? Quin thought you'd be thrilled . . . never dreamed that you'd go and take it like this. He wanted to come back here with me. But I told him to wait until morning, when you've had a chance to sleep on things. I hope I've gone and done the right thing. You mean the world to that boy, you know . . . more than any amount of money or fame.'

'You say that, but I know he'll still go to New York . . . whether I board that ship or not.'

She didn't reply. We both knew it was true.

I sniffed and then wiped at my eyes with white silk, that charred cloth now also blackened with kohl. I thought about Joseph Samuels, and how he'd once soiled a lovely white gown. I thought about Quin and how he'd tenderly dabbed at my tears with Old Riley's worn bed sheet in Paradise Mews.

Standing and walking towards the door, I looked back, I tried my best to smile. 'Old Riley, I'm happy for you. Really I am . . . for Mr Collins and Quin as well. But I wish . . . well, I'm really not sure if I . . .' And then, with more certainty, 'I'll go and see him, first thing in the morning.'

'Oh dearie,' she grinned, 'I am relieved. I know Quin will be ever so pleased.'

'Not Quin. Nathaniel Samuels. I'm going to see my father.'

48

Very early next morning I made the journey to Hyde Park Gate. Later on, at the house in Tredegar Square, when she got my note, when a carriage was sent, Old Riley packed my things in a trunk, all to be sent on to Herefordshire. And, something else was carried there too – though I didn't know until it was too late, and my father was kind, never judging me. But then, what right did he have? I believe he felt guilty, blaming himself, because everything would have been different, if he hadn't turned up at the theatre that night, if I'd married Quin and gone to New York, instead of remaining in England with him.

Without giving Turnbull the chance to announce me, I walked straight on past him and entered the room where my father was sitting at his desk. On the opposite wall, the doors of the black lacquered cupboard were open. It was such a shock to see what was inside it, almost as if an invisible fist had punched every ounce of air from my lungs.

'Cissy!' I gasped her name. She looked so fragile. She looked so lost, much as she had that last day at the docks.

'Phoebe!' My father turned in alarm, staring back through bloodshot eyes. His chair almost tipped to the ground as he stood, pushing past it, walking towards me. I noticed how one of his legs seemed to drag, and how when his hand reached out for mine, I felt a slight tremor, not there before.

But his voice remained strong as he tried to explain. 'The Millais had been a gift . . . from me. Maud Turner had no right to sell it, to have strangers owning that picture of Cissy.'

'How did you know what Maud planned to do?'

'Mr Collins informed me.'

'Ah yes, Mr Collins. Your faithful spy. Was he also your accomplice in crime? I had my suspicions, even then . . . but,' my voice faltered, 'I don't understand. He said he was helping with finding a dealer.'

'All a pretence. He helped with the theft, though we preferred to call it safe keeping.'

'But it was *your* fault Maud needed to sell it. What choice did she have? We had nothing left . . . we were soon to be homeless, thrown out on the streets.'

'I would never have let it come to that. I was simply trying to force her hand, to allow me to have some contact with you. She *always* had a choice, whatever she said to the contrary.'

'Was Old Riley in on this scheme as well?' I didn't know what to think any more, who could be trusted, who to believe – very relieved when my father said, 'No, only Mr Collins, and with your best interests at heart.'

'Was it him or you in the kitchen that night? I'm sure someone came into my room. I thought I was dreaming . . . a face looking down. Can you imagine how defiled I felt when I woke the next morning, when Mama told me the painting was gone? It was like losing Cissy all over again.'

Looking back at the Millais, I started to cry. 'I missed her so much. I still do.'

'Phoebe, I'm sorry.' He touched my arm. 'And yes, I did come to your room. I should never have taken such a risk, but I wanted to see you and—'

'How many more games? How many more tricks? You stole our painting. You hired your own daughter to be a companion to your wife . . . deceiving me, deceiving her!'

'I know that was wrong, but when Maud wrote to ask for help, it seemed so easy . . . the perfect solution, to hide you away, to keep you safe. Please, won't you say you forgive me?'

'Safe! Safe from what?' I laughed, and then took a deep breath as I tried to think clearly enough to go on. 'Last night, in the theatre, why didn't you wait? Why didn't you write to say you were coming? You look ill. Are you ill? Why didn't you tell me? Mr Collins mentioned some trouble . . . what trouble?'

'The shop was looted and almost burned down. One night, some intruders broke into this house. Little damage was done, but the doctors say I had a mild seizure . . . though with every chance of recovery.' His eyes lowered. He murmured, 'I know of others who've suffered worse fates.'

'But why? Why are people doing these things?'

He smiled sadly. His words cut to my heart, thinking again of Maud Turner's resentment, all of that spite, all of those accusations. 'Because I'm a Jew. Because I'm successful. Because . . . to them, I'm nothing but filth. You were right to keep your distance. I don't want you to suffer this prejudice, to be tainted by any connection with me. I don't want you to come here out of obligation.'

Obligation? I stared back into eyes that were glassed with tears. I preferred to think of affection. Surely he'd suffered and lost enough, with Esther, and Cissy, and

Lydia all dead, with Joseph now living in India – if he still did – if he hadn't come home. And, if I was honest, was that another cause for my visit, hoping to hear some news of my brother?

My father rang for some coffee. We went to sit in the drawing room, where blue-panelled walls were gloomy, where outside the gardens glistened with frost. The light that shone in was cruel, exposing each line on his gaunt, grey face. It glinted over the mantel top, and a half-empty tumbler of whisky, and a half-empty bottle at its side. That spirit smell made me nauseous, though no such effect two nights before when I'd managed to swallow a whole glass down. And, perhaps I should have been thinking of that and of what had happened afterwards, when I lay in the starry room with Quin – instead of which, I asked, 'Have you any word from Joseph?'

My father's answer was brusque. 'He and Caroline are settled in India. They have a child . . . a son, called Charles.'

'Oh.' I felt a sharp pang of remorse. *What does he look like – this nephew of mine? This child I will never see or hold?*

My father's voice interrupted my thoughts. 'I was hoping to go and visit them, but the doctors insist I convalesce.' His expression was wry. 'I mean to spend some time in the country, well away from any unrest here in town.'

'I may be travelling too . . . to New York.' I gave my falsely bright reply.

'Yes,' he sighed. 'Not that Mr Collins informs me of how you go on any more – only means to steal you away from me. That's why I came to the theatre last night, having read those reports in the papers. I wanted to see you, before you left. And, you know . . .' *that beautiful, mournful smile*, 'you looked so like Cissy, sitting there. You looked like a ghost slipping in from my past.'

'I wish you'd stayed. I would have told you about New York. But you have to believe, I didn't even know myself . . . not until that announcement was made.'

'Well, I'm glad you've come to me now, to give us this chance to say goodbye and . . .' He trailed off and when speaking again, his tone was brisk and businesslike. 'I can tell you in person of Lydia's will. Probate should be ratified early next year, at which point the details are to be published, becoming a matter of public knowledge . . . as will the fact that you are a nominated heir.'

'What does that mean?'

'It means that you own Dinwood Court.'

I was struck dumb, and barely able to make any sense when my father continued to explain. 'Most have assumed that Joseph's wife will inherit the house. You see, with regard to Dinwood, as far as the issues of descent and distribution are concerned, the property's ownership is entailed, always being passed to the nearest female family member, whether by bond of marriage or blood. But, some weeks before her death, Lydia had an addendum drawn up, formally acknowledging you as her stepdaughter . . . taking precedence over her daughter-in-law.'

He looked at me intently. 'Joseph may choose to object, seeking to have the entailment revoked, perhaps citing his mother's mental state at the time when such alteration was made.'

I felt as if Joseph was there in the room, so clearly did I hear his words. *I warn you, Miss Turner, while there's breath in my lungs, I would rather see Dinwood razed to the ground than see* you *take my mother's place. I would rather see my father dead . . .*

'Joseph's bound to object. He'll hate me for this. How can I forfeit such a bequest?'

My father's reply was measured. 'I know this must come as a shock. But Joseph will hardly be left empty-handed. He has shares in the shop. He inherits his mother's financial investments . . . enough wealth to buy ten Dinwood Courts if he wants.'

'But I don't want it.' I stood up. I was shaking, my fingers snatching at my gown. 'I don't want to steal what is his . . . his wife's. I *have* to refuse it. How can this addendum be nullified without him ever finding out, without him knowing who I am?'

As his dark eyes stared back through sagging lids, my father's voice was tired and gruff. 'We would need to take legal advice and that may delay matters considerably. Phoebe, you should think very carefully. Think about what *you* want.'

What I wanted was to feel safe, to be with someone I trusted – which is why I stayed with my father that day, returning with him to Dinwood Court. And a strange and waiting time it was, while he convalesced, while we both hid away from the rest of the world.

When we first arrived, I was afraid of finding more than one ghost in the house. And yet, from the moment we walked through the door, that palpable veil of grief and regret that had hung over Lydia Samuels' world, that before I could have almost reached out and touched, had completely disappeared.

We spent all our time in the library, avoiding the orangery and drawing room where old memories hung from gilt frames on the walls – though I did once explore some upper rooms where the children's nurseries had been, accessed from the end of the passage that led on to Lydia's bedroom. But those rooms were all bare, completely cleared, nothing left but some faded fraying drapes.

I often walked alone to the grave where Lydia's ashes were scattered, where her name was now carved into the stone beneath that of her daughter. And, once – only once – I caught a drifting lavender scent, and then chided myself because it was summer, the gardens all dusted with swathes of blue flowers, and that perfume had surely been blown on a breeze. But it was a shock to notice the bundle of faded stems, because I could have sworn they hadn't been there when I laid my roses on the slab.

I hoped to see my sister again, but Esther never came back to me. I did see the fox – rust-coloured fur, sharp snout, pointed ears, dark eyes staring out through bracken ferns – but the fox never called again at night. Even so, the last time I went to the Look Out, I became quite convinced it was following me, hearing cracking twigs and rustling leaves, a fluid dark shape melting through the trees. But imagination, that's all it was. At least that's what I told myself as I climbed all the way to the ridge, remembering young Jim Meldicott, who'd sprouted some wings and flown away, having gone off to Cheltenham to work at a stables, training to ride as a jockey there; flying as fast and as free as the wind.

Jim's wish had come true. But not mine. My chance to be free was gone, and I never ventured there again, not with it being so near to the cave. How could I gaze at the whole world below when I'd once held a wish in the palm of my hand – when I could have flown away with Quin?

As that summer drew on, I kept more to the house, sitting with my father for hours on end, reading or sketching or playing the piano, more attuned to the rhythm of life in our bodies than that of the gardens or woods around. We seemed to be waiting for something unknown, much as I'd felt when I'd first arrived to be with Mrs Samuels. And, just as she'd cared for me then, Meg, who still worked as a maid at the house, as loyal and true as the dearest of friends, fussed over us both like a mother hen.

Turnbull, who'd come with his master from London, was always professionally taciturn. But as far as Stephens was concerned, Meg said he'd returned with my father when they'd brought his mistress's ashes back home, that he saw them scattered on Esther's grave and then simply disappeared, leaving no clue to his whereabouts.

As for the rest of the servants in Dinwood – even Mr Meldicott, who used to tease and chatter away – all of them sought to avoid my eye, or stared with barely concealed contempt. Whatever Lydia Samuels had willed, I knew they would never accept my claim, even if I had wished to exert it.

If I happened to venture in public, a walk to the village of Bodlington, or a drive to the town of Leominster, I found myself increasingly shunned, my position at Dinwood generally viewed as something sordid and sinful. Heads would be turned. Hands lifted to mouths. But I heard all the whispers. I heard what they said: *She's the Jew's bastard child.* *She's his mistress you know.* Well, I dare say that some of them thought I was both. And perhaps others prayed for my soul in church. But, I never went. And, as for my father, he held to no faith whatsoever.

Nevertheless, some god watched over him. By the following spring his health was improved, his limp barely noticeable any more, only occasionally needing a stick. He started to go up to London again, sitting on charitable committees, funding aid for impoverished Jews, those displaced in Russia and Hungary. I guessed there were other diversions in town, perhaps even women he visited there, though I never felt jealous. I knew it meant nothing. I knew he would always come back to me.

Not so my friends who had moved to New York, who had left such a gaping place in my heart – and how I looked forward to Old Riley's letters.

She told me about when they'd first arrived, when she'd made great efforts to contact Maud, even finding the Hallelujah hall. But the only news she was able to glean was that William Turner had headed out west, setting up his own mission in San Francisco, working amongst the prostitutes. Anyway, to cut a long story short, she took the notion that those Hallelujahs didn't much approve of him, and they offered no forwarding address, and the only thing of which she was sure was that San Francisco was far away and known as the Paris of the West: a place of much drinking and decadence.

I worried for Maud in such a town. I hoped she was safe and happy there. I hoped her truth had set her free. She never did get that gift of mine; the money Old Riley had hoped to pass on in case Maud had wanted to leave, to come back to England again, to me.

Regarding herself, Old Riley had happier tales to recount, and very vivid they were as well. I wished I could have gone along when she visited Burbidge's Museum on Broadway, where a band played high up on the balcony, while crowds battled in through the turnstiles below, where she said there were thousands of wonders to see, not least what purported to be a real mermaid, that Old Riley claimed was hideously ugly; a mummified monkey stuck onto the carcass of some giant fish. There was even a fragment of wormy old wood that was labelled as stemming from 'The True Cross' – and casually propped next to Robbie Burns' bed! I wondered if Maud had chanced to see that.

Whenever I read those letters, I used to close my eyes, imagining myself to be there as well, and always with Quin creeping into my thoughts – his blue eyes, his dark hair, his long legs strolling down the wide avenues, past shop fronts resembling palaces, with glamorous restaurants and bars and hotels. And then, of course, there were the halls – the stages on which he sang my name. *But did he ever think of me?*

You see, though Old Riley described a great deal, I sensed she did not confide it all and I came to regret my stubborn pride, for refusing to see him before he left, for returning the letters in which he'd begged for me to relent. I chose to believe that if Quin really cared, if he'd really loved me as he professed then he would have delayed that trip to New York. He would have come to find me instead.

But he didn't.

At dawn on that Wednesday morning, he set sail on *The Midnight Star.* And he never wrote to me again. The weeks became months, and the months counted down – first one, then two, then three – and then one morning I woke to see Meg, standing there in the bedroom door with an envelope on a breakfast tray, as if nothing had happened or changed at all since my very first day in Dinwood Court.

But, four years had gone by since Cissy's death, almost two since I'd fled the Victoria's stage doors. Many things had changed.

I got up and went to the window seat and opened Old Riley's new letter which was folded around a newspaper cutting. My head started buzzing, my heart started thumping when reading the news that the following spring she was set on returning to London again. She said that 'the boys' would be following on, probably nearer to Easter time – the act booked for a run at the Leicester Square Empire.

A curious Meg came to stand very near, peering over my shoulder and heaving a sigh when she looked at what was held in my hands.

'Oh . . . to be with someone as handsome as that. You must have dreamed and then woke up in Heaven. What I'd give to meet Quin MacKenna one day. I would have gone to New York with him. If he asked me, I'd go to Timbuktu.'

She was very starry about it all. She knew every Collins & MacKenna song. Well, almost everyone did in those days and sometimes, if she thought I wasn't around, I might catch a drift of the words she sang . . . *Lying next to my angel . . . my heart's delight.* But seeing that cutting I felt no delight, quite convinced that Old Riley was sending a warning.

It showed Quin and Mr Collins standing at the door of a restaurant, a white-aproned waiter on either side. They were both smiling brightly, in top hats and tails, and I have to confess, even Mr Collins looked dapper and younger, his face leaner, his beard all shaved. Between them there stood a young woman, and that scrap might have been very grainy and grey but it was quite clear enough to see how attractive she was, with her hair so fair it appeared to be white – with her smile all for Quin MacKenna.

I felt sad. I felt angry and jealous when I read the rest of the article. This was the new 'Phoebe'. This was the imposter who sat in a box while Quin offered up his gift of a rose, while he serenaded of love and loss.

I doubted he even knew what loss was. Not with that face. Not with those eyes.

Our third winter in Dinwood came early, too cold to go out and about very much, and Nathaniel Samuels was restless and bored as he prowled through the dark panelled corridors that suddenly seemed too narrow, too cramped. I suppose I wasn't surprised when he started to plan for India.

I didn't say I would miss him. How could I stop him from going away to visit the grandchild he'd never met? And I had some plans of my own, to return to Tredegar Square, for Lydia Samuels' legacy had all but been surrendered, the legal papers drafted and signed, with provisos that Joseph should never know of any addendum to the will.

But before we even departed the house, I felt such nostalgia for Dinwood Court, staring out from the windows – east, west, north and south – staring over the drive with its black iron gates, the skeletal trees which grew there like guards; sharp branches glinting, silvered with frost. I made several sketches to keep for remembrance: the walled gardens, the fountain at that time quite frozen, its stone nymph plumply sculpted in snow, her head crowned in jagged icicles, and all around were the white-crusted hedges, the winding mazes of gravel paths where tiny stones sparkled, like splinters of glass. And there was what lay beyond – the thing I knew I would miss the most – the sleeping leviathan of the woods and the grave at its edge to which, even then, I felt myself constantly drawn.

It was the beginning of February, a few days before we were set to leave. It was that heavy silent time between dusk and the night, which in winter draws down so thick and fast. The sky was an ominous bruising of grey, but not yet so dark that I couldn't make out the figure that lurked beneath shadows of trees. At first, I thought – *Is it her? Has she come? Is it Esther?* But as I drew nearer the shape became clearer; it was no ghost, it was only a man, and somehow I knew he was waiting for me. Suddenly wary, I turned to leave. But too late, he had seen me and called out my name, 'Miss Turner. Miss Turner . . . don't go!'

I recognised his voice at once, the soft rhythmic cadence of his Welsh accent, the yearning brown eyes that stared out from beneath the wide brim of his hat. The pitted marks that had marred one cheek were now hidden beneath a thick grey beard, and his dress, which had once been immaculate, was as tattered as any vagrant who begged on the Mile End Road.

'Mr Stephens.' My feet crossed the ice-packed snow. 'I hadn't expected to see you here.'

'I see where *you* go, what you do. Have you come to give thanks to the dead again?'

'To give thanks?'

'For all this!' One of his arms swept back to the house. 'For what was bequeathed to you when she died.'

'You know about that?' I was taken aback. But then, he and his mistress had always been close.

'Oh, she never once doubted who *you* were . . . the other child. *His* secret guilt.'

'Then I wonder she didn't despise me. I know she was sometimes confused in her mind. But why would she favour me over her son?'

At that, he became strangely animated, walking back and forth at the side of the grave, his hands making small jerking movements, only stilled when he started to speak again. 'There was no logic to Lydia's desire. Even when she was carrying Joseph, all those months she fretted over that man, clinging to any hope she could find, clinging onto his fickle affections. But he didn't want her . . . and neither did Esther.'

One of his hands touched the snow-covered stone. His voice, much like his movements before, was irregular, oddly staccato. 'A high price she paid for that painting of yours, that little picture you made of this grave. I brought it back when she died. I burned it. More ashes. All blown to the wind.'

My voice was unsteady, conciliatory. I sensed danger, though still not quite comprehending how dreadful this interlude might be. 'Mr Stephens, forgive me. I know you and Mrs Samuels were close, more so than most servants and . . .'

I was unable to find the right words, though he had no such dilemma, coming straight to the point. 'You mean more like a husband and wife . . . isn't that what the other servants said, all of them laughing behind my back. Because I was the husband without any rights, the same as the child she has now dispossessed.'

'You mean Joseph?'

'Yes. Dinwood should have been his . . . his wife's.' His expression unnerved me, cold and sly. 'You turned up here, casting your spell . . . and it wasn't only her you trapped. I followed you, that night of the storm. I saw you luring him up to the cave. I saw what went on inside. Not enough that you should come here, trying to usurp his sister's place. You had to take what was mine as well. And all the while you were spinning your web, contriving to steal his inheritance.'

There *had* been someone watching, someone outside the cave. My skin was crawling. I felt sick to the pit of my stomach, to think of what Stephens had seen.

Had Joseph known he was there all along? Is that why he kept looking back at the entrance? Is that why he said, 'It's no one. It's nothing'?

My answer was thick with contempt. 'How dare you spy on us like that! I'm not surprised Joseph despised you.'

'Oh yes. He despises me now. But it was different once . . . when he was younger, before Esther died, before he was sent away to school.'

Stephens' eyes were as hard as flint, as Joseph's had been when he spat in my face, when he called me a whore and – thinking of that – cocooned in the chill of my disbelief, I finally summoned the courage to ask, desperately wanting to believe that Joseph might not be my brother at all, to think that I might forget what we'd done, forget the past and be absolved.

'Are you Joseph's father?'

'I watched out for him. I loved him. Nathaniel Samuels was always too busy whoring in town, breaking his wife's heart in the getting of you.'

Again, his fingers stroked over the stone, and what was

now inscribed there: *Esther. Lydia.* One had owned Dinwood. One might have done, taking precedence over Caroline's claim, had Esther Samuels still been alive. Still staring down at those names on the grave, my next question was barely audible. 'What happened to Esther? Do you know?'

Somehow, I felt sure he did.

Stephens caught me unawares, stepping towards me, his hands pressing hard on my shoulders, one of them lifting, gripping my chin as he lowered his face, so close that his whiskers were scratching my skin, through which his breath came hot and rank. 'Do you think I murdered her . . . that now I'm going to murder you?'

'I don't know. I don't know.' I wanted to retch. The rush of fear was filling my ears as he grabbed at the muffler wound at my throat, twisting it tighter and tighter until I saw nothing but flashing white lights, swiftly losing the strength to fight any more, until all resistance was gone. I was free. I was flying backwards, sprawled in the snow at the side of the grave, gasping and coughing, struggling to stand, pushing back hair fallen over my eyes, desperately trying to see where he was; trying to prepare for his next assault.

But Stephens had edged away from the stone and now he stood completely still. If anything, he looked afraid of me. All of his passion and fire was spent, and almost an act of contrition he made when he took off his hat, touched a hand to his brow, looking down, looking cowed as he scrunched the felt brim between his hands. 'It's time the truth was known. What's left for me now? Joseph has gone. Lydia's dead.'

I followed his gaze to look back at the house where plumes of smoke curled up from the chimneys, the roofs below them gauzy with white, some windows exuding an orange glow. And I knew I should have been there, with the living – the living I loved, who also loved me. I shouldn't have been at that grave with the dead; that place of obsessive pilgrimage.

But Stephens still thought about ghosts, of the past, reliving the night of Esther's death. Turning back I heard him say, 'You could have been her, lying there in the snow. Her hair was black against the white. She wore a white gown . . . white against white . . . except for the blood, where the trap's teeth had bitten into her flesh. All those scattered little pocks in the ice, the red steaming, melting, dissolving . . .'

Lifting his eyes, he looked over the meadow. 'I saw Joseph, running back to the house.' His voice broke. 'I loved him. I loved that boy.'

'You wanted your son to have Dinwood.'

He was shaking his head. 'Joseph's not my son. What was I to Lydia? She had no eyes for any but *him*, her blessed Nathaniel Samuels. But when Joseph was born, he was so like his mother . . . such a beautiful, golden boy. I used to go to his room at night, to sit at his cradle, inhaling her perfume on his skin, the scent of her milk on his lips. When he was older, sometimes when he slept, I would lie at his side touching his softness, feeling his fluttering breaths on my face.'

What was this? Something colder than ice gripped my bowels, but the shock and the anger gave strength to my voice. 'He wasn't *her*! He wasn't Lydia. He was an innocent child. Did he know? But he must . . . he must have done.'

'I used to give him laudanum. Lydia always had so much. She would never have noticed a few drops gone. It was too little to do any harm. If he opened his eyes, if he saw me there, the next day I would say he'd been dreaming.' He smiled wistfully. 'My dreaming boy.'

All at once, his tone hardened. 'The night Esther died, she came to his room. She and Lydia had been arguing, screeching at each other like creatures possessed. Esther was saying she wanted to leave . . . to go back to her father in London. Naturally, Joseph had been upset and later, with everyone else gone to bed, I went in to see him, to comfort the child. But he was already sleeping, so I took off my clothes and lay down at his side . . . I just wanted the warmth of his flesh against mine. And that's when I sensed someone else in the room, looking up to see Esther staring down.

'I guessed she must have been sleepwalking. She'd done it before. But I couldn't be sure. I didn't dare move, desperate not to wake her, hoping she wouldn't wake Joseph. And then, when she turned and left the room, at first I felt nothing but relief . . . before the panic set in. What if she woke and remembered me there? What if she told her mother? I couldn't take that risk, don't you see, of being disgraced, losing everything . . . losing Joseph, Lydia, my place in the house.'

'What did you do?' I had to know.

'I dressed. I followed her out to the passage. I heard her walking downstairs to the hall . . . the scraping of bolts, the rattle of chains as she opened up the big front door. That must have been what disturbed Joseph. He woke and went through to her room. I saw him stand at her window . . . watching his sister walk out through the snow.'

My words were thick and slurred. 'Joseph told me that he'd gone after her. Did you go after him?'

'I kept my distance, concealed in the trees. He was calling for her to go back to the house. But she didn't hear. She was still in her trance, pointing at something and walking on, and then came that horrible crunching thud. Anyone might have stepped there. It might have been Joseph. It might have been me.'

'Didn't you try to help?'

'At first, I wasn't sure what had happened. When Joseph ran off, I went closer. I knelt in the snow at her side, but she was already as cold as a corpse . . . but still awake, her black eyes open, staring up into mine. Her lips were so pale they were almost blue. They were opening, closing, but there were no words. I did try . . . I scraped at the bloody slush, trying to wrench her leg free of the trap. But who knows how old it was. The metal was rusted, locked like a vice. Her leg was horribly mutilated, the flesh severed away from the bone. I couldn't bear to look any more. I placed a hand over her mouth and nose, and—'

'Oh God, no. You didn't go for help? You killed her?'

'It didn't take long, though she fought hard enough. She scratched like a cat. By the time I got back to the house, I couldn't believe what she'd done to my face. When morning came and we went to search, I managed to hide the wound with a scarf. Then later on, I said that I'd fallen while out in the woods. But I still saw the proof of my guilt every day, whenever I looked in the mirror and shaved, whenever I saw my reflection. And what was it for?' He touched a hand to his cheek, those puckered marks hidden beneath his beard. 'Joseph never let me come near him again. He said he was frightened. He called me a monster. Even when the scars had faded, his loathing only intensified.'

On his forehead a vein was pulsing. I'd seen it like that before, on the morning we found Esther's dress in my room, the event that unnerved him as much as me. He looked directly into my eyes. 'Can you imagine how that feels, to have damned your own soul for someone you love . . . to be treated as nothing, as no one?'

A shudder ran through me to hear those words, and staring down at the scar on my hand, the sign of my own secret shame, I said, 'I might try.'

I don't know how I restrained myself, filled with such loathing, wanting to strike him, to tear at his flesh as Esther had done. But instead I only asked, 'How much more would Joseph hate you now, to know what really happened that night? He has carried the guilt of his sister's death . . . the guilt that consumed his mother's life . . . that spread out to ruin so many more.' My words were almost incoherent. 'Can't you see what you've done, the cost to us all? And what was it for . . . for the sake of your unnatural desire, your perversion; your vile depravity? For *that* you killed Esther, my own flesh and blood.'

'As Joseph is too! And *you* accuse *me* of perverted desire? Does he know? Well, he will soon enough, when he discovers who owns Dinwood Court . . . when he finds out who *you* really are.'

Losing control, I began to screech, 'Shut up! Shut up. I won't listen to any more of this. You kept quiet before. You should do the same now. Not because I care anything for you . . . your pathetic motives, your warped explanations, the sin for which you will rot in Hell—'

'Then I'll see you there,' he broke in again.

'Oh yes, you're right. I am surely damned. But you're wrong about me owning this house. Joseph knows nothing of Lydia's gift, and I have ensured that he never will.

Dinwood belongs to his wife, Caroline, and one day they might even come back here again. But *you* . . . you should leave and never return. If you do, I'll make sure to see you hang.'

'Why would you let me go free? This is what I want . . . for my sins to be known, to be punished.'

'If your sins are known they will taint Joseph's life. He didn't know what you did to him. Neither one of us knew the gravity of the sin we committed in that cave, and I mean to make sure he *never* does. My life has been nothing but secrets, secrets that should never have been revealed, but' – how plaintive I must have sounded then, my face running wet with snot and tears – 'I don't ever want him to know the truth, and if you cared you'd feel the same. You should leave him to live in ignorance. You *must* realise, after all of these years, some secrets are better left buried . . . some claims left unrecognised.'

For a moment, Stephens turned away, staring up through the darkness and gloom of the trees, cringing like a frightened dog when some snow dropped from one of the branches above, a dull clomping thump as it hit the hard ground. A long time he looked at that now empty branch, and when speaking again his voice held such a note of despair. 'How can I ever leave this place? Dinwood has been my whole life, my home. I have nothing. I have no one . . . nowhere to go.'

Later that evening, I bathed and changed. I was wearing a high-necked gown to conceal any bruising marks on my neck. Less easy to hide were my bloodshot eyes.

Meg stood behind me, a brush in her hand, teasing the tangles out of my hair, pulling back strands stuck to tear-dampened cheeks and suddenly asking irritably, 'Won't you give me an answer for once?'

'Answer what?' I hadn't heard her previous words, lost as I was in my private thoughts.

'I *said* you should get on and write to him. Stop all of this crying and moping around, wasting your life in daydreams and sighs . . . walking out in that snow for hours on end. No surprise if you don't go and catch your death.'

'Write to him. No, I could never do that.'

Meg and I had grown very familiar. There were some days we bickered like two old women, and her nagging was always about the same thing. I knew she was right – about Quin that is. But I had been thinking of somebody else, and Meg didn't know what had happened that day, what terrible secrets I'd learned at the grave. Nobody would – not from my lips.

I glanced down at Cissy's scrapbook which lay on the bed at my side. I picked it up and looked again at the photograph where two children were standing in front of a lake.

Meg saw it too. She was softer then. 'I wonder if Mrs Samuels knew. It was strange how she took to you like that.'

'She wanted to please her husband. She wanted me to be Esther . . . her spirit come back from the dead.'

'Stuff and nonsense!' Meg was impatient again. 'Her and Miss Everett, meeting with all of those spiritualists . . . no good ever comes from that sort of thing. Course, the grieving drove them mad, though they say with Mrs Samuels, the illness spread to her mind, making her do those peculiar things.'

'Maybe. I'm not so sure.'

I didn't go on, distracted by footsteps outside in the passage, at which Meg made to leave the room, but not before stressing her point again, 'I'll say it once more, you should write to him. You can't go on hiding for ever.'

No, I can't go on hiding for ever. But I didn't know what else to do. And, when Meg left me there alone I went to the window and stared at the gardens, beyond to the silvery gleam of the woods. I prayed that Stephens would do the same – keeping himself well hidden away, never thinking to show his face again.

49

Towards the end, when they were still living in Hereford-shire, one morning when making his way down the stairs, Nathaniel saw Phoebe alone in the hall. She seemed to be lost in some reverie before peering back up through the shadows to say, 'There's a letter for you. I think it's from Joseph. I suppose you'll be leaving for India soon.'

Her voice was hoarse. Her eyes were swollen and rimmed with red, as if she was starting to nurse a cold. Or had she been crying again? He knew she didn't want him to leave, but Nathaniel had been planning this jour-ney for months. Now he was well, and determined to go. It was time to make amends with his son.

'I'll only be away a short while . . . three months at the very most. Won't you change your mind and come with me? Surely Joseph should know you're his sister, rather than thinking—'

'No. Let him think what he wants. I should be more ashamed if he knew the truth.'

His daughter was stubborn, defensive and brittle whenever Joseph's name was broached – and perhaps she was right to be cautious. He recalled Joseph's callous resentment, his taunting of her when he'd come to the house, in return for which she'd been nothing but selfless, giving up every claim on Dinwood Court. If Phoebe still brooded on old injuries, what right did Nathaniel have to try and force her hand? She'd made him happy. Her care was a blessing he'd never expected, and one for which he could only give thanks. But every fairy tale comes to an end. There were other stories, other worlds in which they still had their own parts to play. It was time to leave Dinwood Court, before they were lost in its silence and shadows.

The house was decaying around them. The staff were often churlish, reluctant to do anything more than the barest minimum of work. They'd never been like that with Lydia. And what would she think if she saw her beloved orangery now, the crack in the big glass dome above, through which the rain was leaking . . . to water the one living thing that remained?

He'd gone there a few days before. Most of the plants were withered husks, the soil in the pots as dry as dust, the air grown rank with spores of mould. But there was a silver birch sapling that had somehow seeded itself in the floor, the tiles now beginning to lift and crack, already damaged by spreading roots. He hadn't the heart to tear it up. And he'd been unnerved by the little bird. It must have flown in through the broken pane, and although he had never been one for suspicion, he thought of what Lydia used to say – about birds coming into the house – about death.

Of late his dreams had been full of the dead. Phoebe, too, was obsessed with the past, always drawn to the grave at the edge of the woods. There were times when he feared she might change her mind and decide to stay on at Dinwood Court, to become as reclusive as Lydia. He wondered if that had been his wife's plan when she bequeathed the house, meaning to steal Phoebe away from him, as Maud Turner had done before.

Thank God then that Phoebe renounced the will, denying history the chance to repeat itself. Dinwood had been kind these past two years. It had offered them solace and sanctuary. But, of late, living there felt more like a penance, much as it always had in the past. Perhaps it was only because he was well, his instincts and wits restored, but Nathaniel sensed some malevolence, something lurking, hiding, biding its time.

50

Galatea, dry thy tears.
(From Handel's *Acis and Galatea*)

Old Riley would soon be returning, coming back to Tredegar Square, but the house had been empty for such a long time, boarded up against thieves, grown musty and damp. Meg and I had a great deal to do to try and make it habitable – holding our breath when we first walked in, seeing cobwebs hang down from the ceilings like lace, and dust fairies floating around in the air.

Before he left for India, my father took us to Samuels' store. Though he no longer owned it, he still held an interest, and we went there one evening when it was closed, having the run of the place to ourselves. Meg was almost beside herself with excitement, and really, I wasn't much better, laughing as we wandered through endless halls, seeing the luxurious furnishings, the exotic treasures and ornaments – like that little gold goddess I'd found before; the one my father now possessed again.

Meg chose some new linen and drapes for her room. I chose cushions and throws for Old Riley's, all gleaming reds and purples and golds. But the rest of the house remained the same. I didn't want anything to change.

Cissy's piano was polished and tuned and, upstairs, her clothes were brought out to air. Many were spotted with mould, smelled dank, and the lingering perfume of Hammam Bouquet had been dulled by the camphor in mothballs. But some things remained unmarred by time and in the hallway, halfway up the stairs, *The Somnambulist* painting was back on the wall, as if she had never been away.

In Dinwood, she'd looked out from over my bed – Cissy, my guardian angel, warding off spirits who walked in the night, false mothers who tried to claim me as their own, or a sister who wanted the truth to be told.

That last morning when sitting in front of the glass, surrounded by yellow patterned walls with their oriental flowers and birds, as if with the eyes of a stranger I gazed at the mirror's reflection where, between the bed's barley-twist posts, *The Somnambulist*'s eyes stared back at mine. I felt myself spinning through spirals of time, thinking of a night at Wilton's Hall when Cissy looked into her dim, spotted glass, when I'd stood behind like her shadowy ghost. I could almost hear all of the clattering sounds coming from backstage corridors – instruments being tuned, voices trilling through scales, and Bill Wright's fist drumming a beat on the door. If I closed my eyes, I could still smell the odour of greasepaint, and the smoky perfume of burning wood. But in Dinwood, Cissy was the ghost, walking too close to the edge of that cliff, without any light to guide her path, without any hope of being saved.

And yet I was wrong about that, much as I'd been about so many things because, when we returned to Tredegar Square and fixed the picture back on the wall, when my father was helping to straighten the frame, my eye was drawn to the far right-hand corner where the shadowy silhouettes of two men were following at a distance, as if fearing to wake her in case she fell. But, I suddenly knew there must be a third man, and I couldn't believe I'd not noticed before, not even thinking to question the source of the radiance over her face. The candle she held was unlit. The sky was clouded, the moon far behind her. But a second shadow fell over the path, right next to her own, thrown down by the light someone else must be holding, towards which she steadily progressed, and in two or three steps she would surely be saved by whoever was waiting, just out of the frame – just where my father was standing then.

When I told him, he touched a hand to the painting. 'Sometimes, I think she's the one with the light . . . that she's waiting . . .'

He broke off and turned to me. 'You know I'll be leaving tomorrow. Are you sure you won't change your mind? Are you sure that you're going to be all right?'

'I have Meg. And Old Riley will soon be home.'

'And what about Quin MacKenna?'

I was shocked to hear his name spoken. *Has Meg been gossiping?*

'Life's rarely perfect,' my father continued. 'We all make mistakes. The thing is to forgive, and . . .' he paused at the sound of some high, muffled laughter, the splashing of water, 'and never forget.'

When he squeezed past me to go on up, I tried not to hear that voice from the past, the nagging, whispering ghost that said, *'You should never let anyone cross on the stairs. It brings bad luck. It conjures the Devil.'* But then to Maud Turner, Nathaniel Samuels had always been the Devil incarnate.

So, in a way, I suppose she was right.

Later that evening, when he'd said goodbye, when

everyone slept, the house quiet and dark, I went to lie on Cissy's bed. By the light of the street lamp outside, I opened my locket and looked at the strands of hair inside – not two, as I'd always presumed, but three, because mine had been woven into his. There was also the little white feather he gave me, and perhaps that was a sign of surrender because, before leaving England, Nathaniel Samuels had written to Quin. While I remained in ignorance, my father had given me away.

A fresh spring day. When I looked over the garden square the air was so clear that it glistened like glass, not even a tarry factory smell, and only the pollen from lilac blossom causing my nose to twitch.

Old Riley had sent a telegram. She'd docked in Southampton the morning before and was due to be with us the next afternoon – and that time had now come, and already the waiting was making me anxious, eager to see her face again, frightened of what her reaction might be when she saw that things were no longer the same.

A carriage drew up outside the house. She was the first to clamber out, and clutching a big striped box to her breast she might as well be a present herself, wearing a hat with a purple bow, silk flowers and feathers and butterflies.

Mr Collins was next, which was a surprise. I hadn't expected anyone else. He looked quite the dandy in that checked suit, with a large diamond pin in his yellow cravat, and reaching an arm back into the cab, he might almost be a magician when – *ta-da!* – he drew a white rabbit out of his hat.

My heart sank as heavy as lead to see that young woman with hair like spun gold. I knew I'd seen her face before, in the newspaper cutting Old Riley had sent. But surely Quin wouldn't taunt me like that. Surely he wouldn't bring her to the house? But he would – for as I heard the shrill ring of the bell, to which every nerve in my body responded as if shocked by a jolt of lightning, there he was, the next one to descend to the pavement.

I panicked. I thought to call Meg. She could say I was out. She could ask them to come back later on, when I might be more calm and collected. But Meg was already there at the door, and shouting back up the stairs at me, 'Hurry, Miss Phoebe . . . They're here. They're here.'

I couldn't speak. I couldn't move, and still there at the window, still staring down, I watched Quin MacKenna paying the driver, the sunlight glinting off his hair, as dark as before but grown longer now, reaching right down to his collar.

Mr Collins was taking a cloth from his pocket, dabbing a mark from the young woman's cheek and, once he'd finished doing that, he kissed her lips – and she kissed him back – and Old Riley was grumbling, 'Can't you two lovebirds stop all that spooning? I don't care if it is your honeymoon. You've been going at it hammer and tongs. It gets on my nerves, it's . . .'

She stopped short as a handkerchief dropped from my hand, wafting down past her nose, almost catching on one of those butterflies. She looked up, and she smiled and she started to wave, until her arm froze midway in the air, her mouth gaping open, no sound coming out. Then Quin MacKenna was close at her side, and he was gazing up as well, and I tried to imagine what they must see: a window with the sash half raised; light dazzling white against dark panes; a young woman who held a child in her arms, whose dimpled fists were tapping on glass, so excited to see the visitors there.

Quin raised a hand to his brow, shielding his eyes from the glare of the sun. Did he see how blue the ones staring back down – as blue as the sea, as sapphires?

My own eyes were suddenly filling with tears and, backing away, it was all I could do to walk round the room in small circles, my feet beating time with the thump of my heart, soon echoed by those ascending the stairs.

When Quin appeared in the open door, his shadow fell down on the boards next to mine. I heard those sonorous lilting tones that I'd missed so much, that I'd never thought to hear again, 'Why didn't you tell me? What's her name?'

'Cissy. I called her Cissy.' My voice was shaking. It didn't seem real. It felt like a dream, during which little Cissy was struggling and squirming in my arms, and the moment I set her feet on the floor she was trying to hide in the folds of my skirts, grown suddenly shy of this strange new man.

He knelt down beside her and struggled to smile. He drew a small box from his pocket. And then he was winding a key at the back, and when those clockwork notes trilled out Cissy started to laugh and held out her hands. But then, she knew that tune so well, with Meg singing it to her most every night and, familiarity making her brave, my little girl took a step forward, and then she took one more, and whatever the future might hold for me, I knew from the moment he lifted her up, this child would not slip through her father's hands.

51

December 14th, 1886

Dearest Father,

I wish you would send some reply to my letters. It has been six months since you last wrote. I fear it must be the news of my marriage. It was very hurried and we should have waited. But Quin was insistent we went ahead. And again, I must thank you for writing to him, since when Cissy and I have come to be blessed — were it not for the fact that I miss you so much, and she asks after you almost every night, sending her Grandpa a prayer and a kiss. I enclose a new picture, to show you how much she has grown.

I have some other news. Quin and Mr Collins have received an offer to work once again in America. The plan is to leave in June. Meanwhile, Mr Collins and his wife are setting the publishing business in order. Old Riley is selling Paradise Mews, and Meg is quite dizzy with all the excitement.

But how can I settle or look to the future without knowing how you go on? Please, won't you send me some word?

With fondest affection, from your loving daughter,
Phoebe

February 2nd, 1887

Dear Phoebe,

It is with the deepest regret that I write to inform you of the death of your father, Nathaniel Samuels. He suffered a seizure, soon after arriving here in Bombay. He never regained full consciousness. To my mind, it came as a blessing when he was finally released.

It was all very sudden. We were breakfasting on the veranda. Joseph was going through his post. There was a solicitor's letter, regarding his mother's butler – Mr Stephens – I think that was his name. It explained that the man had hanged himself from one of the trees in Dinwood's grounds, and a note for Joseph was found on his person.

I have no idea what that note contained. Joseph read it and turned very pale before passing it on to his father. Whatever it said, Mr Samuels looked terribly shocked, asking at once to be excused, and it was shortly afterwards a servant came out to inform us that he had been found collapsed.

During the following months, Joseph dealt with his father's business correspondence, but those letters clearly of a more private nature were set aside, awaiting Mr Samuels' recovery. You see, right up until the end, Joseph simply refused to accept the doctor's prognosis. I wish now that I had been firmer. We would have discovered your bond all the sooner. I might have read your words to your father. I read to him from the papers each day, and there were times when I felt quite sure that he could hear me, when he squeezed my hand, or made a slight sound.

Today, I have pondered much on that visit I once made to Dinwood Court. With hindsight, we all behaved oddly that night. I blamed my brother's outrageous behaviour, and the tense atmosphere that was caused by the storm. But I wonder if, even back then, Joseph had guessed who you really were. Months later, when our son was born, he told me about a sister who'd died. And he mentioned how, seeing you next to her portrait, he'd been struck by such an uncanny resemblance.

I do regret his decision in professing no wish to meet you again. I hold to the hope that in time he may change, embracing his sister still living. For apart from myself and Charles, what family has he left? And, with that in mind, I hope that you will not object if I keep the picture you sent to your father – the one of yourself and your daughter. How pretty she is! In return, I send you one of Charles. You will see that he is very fair, very like Joseph and Lydia.

We plan to return to England next spring. Joseph hopes to arrange for his sister's remains to be reinterred at Bodlington church, along with a memorial stone for his mother. It is our intention to sell Dinwood Court, even though I had hoped to live there one day. But Joseph is adamant, insisting the place is cursed and full of too many bad memories.

There is one final matter. It is of a rather delicate nature, and I trust it is the right thing to do. Mr Samuels was cremated here, but Joseph insists that his father's remains should be sent back to England, to you. Turnbull is entrusted with their care and will bring them along with this letter. He will also deliver some personal effects, including a little gold goddess which, I believe, may hold some sentimental value.

I send them with my condolences, and also my sincerest regrets.

Caroline Samuels

April 4th, 1887

Dear Caroline,

Your news left me greatly saddened and shocked. But I am forever indebted for your kindness and consideration in writing.

As you may have construed from the letters I sent, Quin and I are to travel to America. It may be that we choose to make it our home. It is where our next child is due to be born. It is where I may once have been raised myself, had fate worked out differently.

I understand Joseph's sentiments with regard to the sale of Dinwood Court, though the house will always have a place in my heart — as will Lydia Samuels, as will Joseph.

I enclose another photograph, and I leave it to your discretion as to whether or not it should be passed on. It shows two children, Joseph and myself, on a visit to Victoria Park where, I can only presume, our father had wished us to meet. I had no idea who Joseph was and, I am sure, he knew nothing of me. Even so, I hope he will believe when I say that, after that day, I longed to have a brother like him. I think I loved him even then, and although we will never meet again, in time perhaps he will look on that love as something untainted, and good, and pure.

I send you my thanks and sincerest regards,
Phoebe
(Mrs Quin MacKenna)

52

We went for a walk, Old Riley and me. She carried some flowers from the garden. I carried a leather bag. Once we were in the cemetery, I opened it up and took out a trowel, and the silver box with the ashes inside. The little gold goddess remained at home, but I brought along the paper scroll, still tied with its length of white ribbon.

Inside, Cissy's writing was smeared but the words were still legible, and I read them aloud, as if a prayer:

> *Oh, didst thou know the pains of absent love,*
> *Acis would ne'er from Galatea rove.*

Now he had come back and found her, and while Old Riley fussed with the flowers, I knelt down and started to dig at the ground, meaning to bury that little scroll. As I did so, my locket fell free. Silver trailed through black earth and grey ashes.

Author's Note

The Somnambulist was first inspired when I visited Wilton's Music Hall for a production of Handel's baroque operetta, *Acis and Galatea*. During that performance, my eyes were constantly drawn to the glint of the lovely brass barley-twist pillars supporting the balcony above, and I felt such a frisson of excitement to think of all the people and stories those cold metal spirals must once have reflected.

The very next morning I woke with three distinct characters in mind – a young woman called Phoebe who lived with her mother – the puritanical widowed Maud – and Maud's unmarried sister, the glamorous singer, Cissy. Those two very different sisters provided a wonderful tension against which to set Phoebe's story, and what better place to open their tale than in the heyday of Wilton's – and what better performance to describe than *Acis and Galatea* with its tragic themes of love and loss.

From that point onwards the characters' stories rapidly began to unfold, with many acts being played out against backdrops still in existence today. But to explain what is fact and what is simply fancy, I have put together the following notes.

Wilton's Music Hall

Wilton's Music Hall was built in the 1850s at the back of the Prince of Denmark bar, in Graces Alley in the East End. Sadly, the grand mahogany fittings for which the bar was once renowned have now been stripped away and the hall is much dilapidated. But it still remains a glorious venue, comprised of an intimate rectangular space with a floor that rakes gently down to a stage – and that stage quite low enough for everyone in the audience to fully engage with performers. The walls have arched niches which used to hold mirrors and the high vaulted ceiling once housed an enormous gas chandelier that dripped with thousands of crystals.

If you visit the hall today, at the very back of the balcony you will see three murals of Indian women. I have included them in Phoebe's story, even though they are anachronistic, painted as part of the scenery for a recent dramatic production based on an East India Company general. But with the East India Company's trade being based in the nearby docks, and with *The Somnambulist* having characters linked to the selling of tea and cloth, those exotic paintings of singers and dancers fitted my story to perfection.

Although I have taken some liberties with his dates and characterisation, John Wilton did indeed exist. After building his 'temple of Apollo' he produced a variety of shows, and often crammed a thousand souls into a hall which, these days, is licensed to hold three hundred. It must have been quite an experience to visit in its glory days, seeing circus acts, ventriloquists and dancers and, of course, the opera singers who graced his 'shrine of gentle music'. But sadly, after his death (which actually occurred in 1880, despite his appearance in *The Somnambulist* in 1881), the hall very soon deteriorated, becoming the haunt of prostitutes, sailors, dockers and thieves. By 1888 it had been closed down, used as a gospel mission instead, and during the dockers' strike of 1889 it provided two thousand meals a day for the many starving workers. In 1936, Wilton's was involved in history again when used as a base for those demonstrators who stood against Mosley and his fascists in the famous Battle of Cable Street.

Today, this magical, crumbling hall has been given Grade II* listed status and hopefully it will be preserved. Many events are produced, and there are regular open days when you can take a tour of the building and learn more about its history. For information, please visit the official website: www.wiltons.org.uk.

Of those other theatres referred to in the later parts of the novel, the 'Victoria in Hoxton' is imaginary. But should you wish to discover more about the real Victorian halls there is a wealth of material online, of which *The Arthur Lloyd Music Hall and Theatre History Site* is a wonderful resource. www.arthurlloyd.co.uk.

Tredegar Square in Bow

Tredegar Square has hardly changed since it was built in the mid-nineteenth century. Only a five-minute walk from the Mile End Underground station in Bow, this beautiful garden square is surrounded by grand houses that would not be out of place in the most affluent parts of London. The square was indeed once home to the notorious murderer Henry Wainwright. It was also in close proximity to the Bryant and May match factory, which has since been converted into the 'Bow Quarter', a complex of residential apartments.

Victoria Park

Now often used as a venue for music festivals, Victoria Park was opened in 1845. It covers 218 acres which are bounded on two sides by the Regent's and the Hertford Union canals. This little-known 'People's Park' in east London was originally envisioned as being a sort of Regent's Park for London's poorer residents; somewhere to exercise in the fresh air. It is still a spectacular oasis, with wide tree-lined drives and hidden paths, a deer park, and sports fields, a lake and magnificent fountains.

Bow cemetery

The graveyard described in Bow is actually called Tower Hamlets cemetery and again, it is but a short walk from the Mile End Underground station. Though not used for burials since 1966, these twenty-seven acres of consecrated ground are preserved as a natural wilderness, creating a hidden gem in the middle of the bustling East End. Some of the monuments are listed with English Heritage, and many of the stone obelisks and angels bear the scars of shrapnel, the cemetery having been bombed five times during the Second World War.

The Docks

In *The Somnambulist* I have been suggestive rather than specific about the exact dockland location. Isaac's store is fictional, as is the Dolphin Bar, but I hope that both capture a particular essence of what was a unique time and place in London's social and mercantile history. I must give special thanks for information gleaned from the

Museum of London Docklands, and also to the writer Lee Jackson for his fascinating historical online resource, The Victorian Dictionary: www.VictorianLondon.org.

Paradise Row

Although Stepney Green does exist, located just off the Mile End Road, Old Riley's cottage in Paradise Row is entirely fictional. However, since writing this novel, I have discovered a terrace of that very name situated in nearby Bethnal Green.

Hyde Park Gate in Kensington

Hyde Park Gate is a prestigious address situated almost opposite the gates to Kensington Gardens. It is peculiar in that its name is actually shared by two neighbouring roads. The one referred to in the novel is that which forms a cul-de-sac with circular gardens at one end around which any traffic can turn. A very short walk away is the Royal Albert Hall, the Albert Memorial, the Victoria and Albert Museum and the department store of Harrods in Knightsbridge – the history of which formed the basis for Samuels' Emporium. And, like the fictional Nathaniel Samuels, the real Charles Henry Harrod once had a business in London's East End before moving on 'up' to Kensington where he did very well from the trade brought in by the vast numbers of visitors who attended the Great Exhibition of 1851.

Dinwood Court

Dinwood Court is my fictional name for Hampton Court in Herefordshire; a magnificent castellated dwelling that was built in the fifteenth century. Ever since I was a child, whenever travelling past in the car, seeing the great arched iron gates and the long straight drive that led to the house, I have tried to imagine the lives of those who inhabited such a place. My first chance to look inside arose when I was employed as a cleaner, spending the university holidays roaming around with a duster in hand, getting lost in a warren of passageways, and finding some of the upstairs rooms to be decidedly eerie.

Only when *The Somnambulist* was complete did I come to discover that Hampton Court's orangery had been designed by Joseph Paxton, architect of the Crystal Palace, erected in Hyde Park for the Great Exhibition of 1851. I was pleased at the symmetry of that, with the Samuels living in Hyde Park Gate and Nathaniel's business supposedly based on trade from that event.

In *The Somnambulist*, Dinwood Court's internal structure and decor is a combination of Hampton Court and Croft Castle, another nearby castellated house that is currently owned by the National Trust. But the exterior appearance of Hampton Court, along with the great swathes of woodland behind, form the true inspiration for Phoebe's visits to the house. Queenswood Arboretum – always known to my family as Dinmore (probably after Dinmore Manor, another historic house nearby) – was very well known to me in my youth. The woods have a disused quarry, and also a spectacular 'Look Out', but any cave is imaginary. Even so, I possess some stalactites discovered there when my stepfather, a civil engineer, was rebuilding the road that cuts through the wood, below which lies the railway tunnel, through which the Great Western line still runs.

For information about Hampton Court: www. hamptoncourt.org.uk.

For details of Croft Castle: www.nationaltrust.org.uk.

Music Hall Acts

The main characters in *The Somnambulist* are all entirely fictional, but some of the music hall characters have been drawn from real artistes.

John Wilton has already been discussed, but perhaps the most famous act he booked was the singer George Leybourne, who became known as Champagne Charlie following the success of his popular song which appears in the novel's early scenes.

Victor Maurel, with whom Cissy appears in a photograph, was a famous French opera singer, renowned for his flamboyant stage presence.

Lord Crumpet and Dan Leno were both character comedians. Leno was a cockney 'Lion Comique' who dressed in outrageous costumes and was often booked for pantomimes where Marie Lloyd played the principal girl. He was known as 'the funniest man on earth' but sadly died when very young, at only forty-three years old.

Mr Burbidge, the American impresario, is based on P. T. Barnum who travelled the world with his spectacular shows, signing up the best variety or circus acts, and sourcing curiosities to exhibit in his New York 'American Museum'. The singer Jenny Lind, who was known as the Swedish Nightingale, did indeed owe much of her fame to Barnum, who arranged a run of concerts to rival today's stadium events, and which earned the soprano $250,000 – a staggering amount when translated into modern currency.

The Hallelujah Army

The Hallelujah Army, a Christian mission led by the Browns, exists only within the pages of *The Somnambulist*. There are superficial similarities to the Salvation Army which was active in the East End at the time. My Hallelujah Army is also a quasi-military organisation where men and women followers march through the streets with banners and flags, campaigning for theatres and bars to be closed, leading the war against 'Satan and Sin'. I have also stolen the fact that when General Booth, the Salvation Army leader, heard so many people out on the street singing the Champagne Charlie song, he decided to use the melody on which to base the hymn, 'Bless His Name, He Sets Me Free'. When questioned why he had done such a thing, Booth gave what became his famous reply: 'Why should the Devil have all the best tunes?'

I sincerely hope that my fictional representations cause no offence to current Church members, for as Phoebe Turner says in the novel, 'the Hallelujahs do a great deal of good'. And the Salvation Army still does today, working all over the world to provide shelter for those lost or homeless.

Mrs Beeton

Being the owner of a very old copy of Mrs Beeton's *Book of Household Management*, I was amazed to find that Isabella Beeton was not the bustling middle-aged dragon I'd always had in mind. In fact, the 'Victorian household bible', which numbers over a thousand pages, was completed when its author was only twenty-five years old – a wonderful cut and paste affair, compiled as a regular supplement for her publisher husband's magazine: *The Englishwoman's Domestic*.

Despite very little expertise – Isabella's first recipe for a Victoria sponge cake made no mention of using eggs! – her pages were very popular, and soon converted into a book with lavish colour illustrations. As well as the art of cookery, Isabella gave advice on matters such as the choosing of friends, the administration of medicines, and the hiring of staff and childcare. She even expressed views on science and religion and, of course, she wrote several pages on fashion, which proved of such interest to Phoebe.

Spiritualism

The Victorian era saw an enormous upsurge in the interest for all things 'spiritual' though such 'dabblings' were viewed as sacrilegious to many devout Christians. The mania for 'table-tapping', in which Old Riley is involved, seems to have started in America where the three Fox sisters of New York claimed to communicate with ghosts by means of clicking and knocking sounds. Over the years they performed many public séances and, whether charlatans or not, they initiated quite a craze. When Prince Albert died so suddenly, the heartbroken Queen Victoria sought the services of mediums and attempted to contact her husband's soul. Lewis Carroll, the writer and mathematician, was also a 'believer' and a founder member of the Society for Psychical Research.

For those of us today who might tend to be more sceptical, it is important to recall all the technological advances developed in the nineteenth century. The 'invention' of electricity and the telegraph produced what then seemed near 'miraculous' feats of light and communication, as if some invisible 'essence' was moving through the ether. Many Victorians genuinely believed that scientific study would eventually discover other dimensions in space and time, enabling the living to speak with the dead.

Civil Unrest against Jews

Maud Turner's attitude to Nathaniel Samuels may seem offensive in the extreme, but the shocking fact is that her views about Jews would have been very widely shared. There was even an anti-Semitic tradition of associating Jews with vampires, creating a myth of 'bogeymen' who sought to destroy all things Christian.

During the 1880s, following an influx of immigrants who fled from persecution in Russia, Poland and Lithuania, many Jewish businesses grew up, resulting in riots and looting attacks from those resentful Londoners who feared the loss of their homes and jobs, despising customs they did not understand.

LAST, BUT BY NO MEANS LEAST

The Somnambulist by Millais

The Somnambulist is a painting by Millais.

I love Millais' art, and this particular work has been a great inspiration to me. Not only did it provide a striking image for Cissy, but it also raised the concept of living a life as false as a dream and, of course, the perils of sleepwalking with all the ensuing occult implications of 'blindness' and 'hallucination'.

It is true that many considered the painting to be based on Wilkie Collins' sensational novel, *The Woman in White*. But others presumed it to be inspired by Bellini's

La Sonnambula, which was one of the century's most popular operas.

Hammam Bouquet

When writing *The Somnambulist* I wanted to introduce a perfume that Nathaniel Samuels might actually wear; something that would typify the era. My research led me to discover Penhaligon's Hammam Bouquet which was actually created in 1872, though I hope the reader will allow me the liberty to claim that it might have existed before, at the time when Nathaniel and Cissy first met.

William Penhaligon's creation was based on aromas of amber and rose, sandalwood, musk, orris and jasmine. It was inspired by the odours to be found inside 'hammams' or Turkish baths, such as those in London's Jermyn Street.

The idea of such a decadent fragrance being worn by respectable Victorian gentlemen was appealing to me on several counts, not least because it personified everything that would have attracted the young Cissy to the glamorous Nathaniel – which would have been the very same lure that Maud Turner would find so unnerving, conjuring visions of naked sultans reclining in steamy baths, of harems, and boudoirs that reeked of sex.

And finally – by happy accident, and only when this novel was done – my editor, Kate Mills, discovered that Hammam Bouquet is still produced by Penhaligon's today – and what a relief to find that the fragrance is as intoxicating and sensual as I had imagined it to be.

You can find more detail on my research, including many other Victorian 'Facts, Fabrications and Fancies' at my blog: www.virtualvictorian.blogspot.com.

And, for more information about me and my writing, and specifically *The Somnambulist*, please visit my website: www.essiefox.com.

E.F.

Reading Group Notes

For Discussion

How has the author created an immediate impression of the East End in *The Somnambulist*?

How are images of decay and dirt used in the novel?

'Wasn't pretence his wife's forte?' Is this true of Lydia?

How is the image of red against white used in the novel?

'We all cling to what we know the best.' Always true, do you think?

How is the contrast between real flowers and silk ones used in *The Somnambulist*?

Is 'all of life an illusion'?

How does the author contrast the rural Dinwood with the East End?

To what extent is the novel about salvation?

'Though you can never escape your fate.' True, do you think?

Does wealth help?

'Things aren't always black and white.' Has Maud any redeeming features?

'Truth was a tyrant.' Why?

'People believe what they want to believe. They see what they want to see.' To what extent is the *The Somnambulist* about this theme?

To what extent are age, and the passage of time, themes of the novel?

In Conversation with Essie Fox

Before taking up writing, Essie worked as an illustrator – designing greetings cards, gift wrap and decorative ceramics. Before that she worked in a Dickensian office in Bloomsbury's Museum Street, employed as an editorial assistant. So, in a way, it almost feels as if she has come full circle, returning to her very first love, which is the world of books.

Essie is currently researching her second Victorian novel. She also writes the popular blog, *The Virtual Victorian*.

Born and raised in Herefordshire, Essie now divides her time between Bow in east London and Windsor. She is married with one daughter.

Q: **Which character in *The Somnambulist* are you most like?**

A: Because the novel is narrated in the first person by Phoebe Turner, I suppose I empathise most closely with her character – and many people who know me have said that they thought of 'me' all the time while reading Phoebe's words – which I find slightly disconcerting. But, there are similarities. I also grew up in a matriarchal family, where some of the women were staunchly religious while others were, well, quite theatrical, loving nothing more than to act, sing and dance. But perhaps more significantly, just like Phoebe, I saw very little of my father while growing up, although we did have the chance to meet again shortly before he died, for which I shall always be grateful. For that reason, the scenes between Phoebe and Nathaniel Samuels remain very poignant and true to my heart.

Q: **How important do you think historical accuracy is to a novel set in the past?**

A: When writing historical fiction, I think it is important to do as much research as you can, especially if a novel draws heavily on actual events, people or places. But, even if confined to one room with entirely imaginary characters, it is still important to understand the influence of the time that has 'made them'; the styles of décor, the styles of speech, the opportunities that would have been available to colour the characters' perception of their world. But, having said that, the best novels wear their research lightly, allowing the story and characters to live and breathe 'naturally' without being over-encumbered with the minutia of too much detail.

Q: How did you physically write *The Somnambulist* and why?

A: I write on a laptop and edit the structure as I go along. There's something about seeing words on a screen that makes the whole process of writing more immediate and real for me. It always feels very exciting, whereas if I write in longhand, the page soon becomes such a muddle of scribbles and crossing outs that I don't have a clue what's going on.

Q: What comes first for you – plot or character?

A: In the case of *The Somnambulist*, apart from knowing that the story would open up in Wilton's music hall with a production of Handel's operetta, *Acis and Galatea*, the rest of the novel was very much driven by character. The 'voice' of Phoebe was very strong, as was the knowledge that she would be an only child who lived with her religious, widowed mother and her glamorous, semi-reclusive aunt who had once had a singing career on the stage. But the only thing I *really* knew was that I wanted to develop the tension between the two sisters, with the sense of Phoebe being emotionally trapped in their midst. Everything – and everyone else – led on from that starting point.

Q: Have you always written?

A: When I first learned to write I did nothing but compose little poems, and I loved to read poetry too – the Puffin edition of '*A Child's Garden of Verses*' was a well-worn favourite. As an adult, I often played out little dramas and daydreams in my head, but any 'creative' bent was taken up with my career as an illustrator – telling tales with pictures instead of words. However, that all changed a few years ago when I found myself at one of those junctures in life when I stood back and asked myself – *what would I do differently if I could start my life over again?* The answer was immediate. *I would like to write* – and I'm so glad I plucked up the courage to try.

Q: What authors do you admire and why?

A: They say you should write what you love and although I read quite widely and across many genres, I've always adored the classic Victorian novelists, especially those with a gothic edge, such as the Brontës, Wilkie Collins, Bram Stoker, Robert Louis Stevenson or H.G. Wells – not forgetting Edgar Allen Poe. Of the contemporary writers who have set novels in the nineteenth century, my favourites are Sarah Waters *(Fingersmith)*, Angela Carter *(Nights at the Circus)*, Charles Palliser *(The Quincunx)*, Michael Cox *(The Meaning of Night)* and Michel Faber *(The Crimson Petal and the White).*

Q: What's your most treasured possession?

A: I have a lovely Victorian chain and locket that inspired the use of one in *The Somnambulist*. It belonged to my great-great-grandmother, and contains some fine twisted strands of hair. I have no idea who that hair belonged to, but I think it may have been a baby.

Q: Silence or music while you write? If music – who do you listen to?

A: Silence. I find music distracting.

Q: What draws you to the world of the Victorians?

A: Sometimes, I think it must have been all the old black-and-white films that I used to watch with my family on wet Sunday afternoons – films like *Great Expectations*, *Wuthering Heights* or *Fanny by Gaslight*. There was something so alluring about those murky candlelit worlds. And later, when studying English literature, I was increasingly drawn to the Victorian Sensation novels, such as *The Woman in White* by Wilkie Collins – novels with intricate scandalous plots that kept me on the edge of my seat.

The Victorian era was such an exciting one. I love all the research I do for my blog, *The Virtual Victorian*, discovering more and more about the art and literature, and important advances in social reform, science and industry – not to mention the larger-than-life characters. And, of course, it is the earliest point in history where we can look back and actually 'see' the people then – because of the development of photography. I find old photographs incredibly inspiring.

Q: **What single thing about you would surprise us the most?**

A: I think the answer is probably the fact that I am an avid football fan and hold a season ticket for every Arsenal home game. Football is quite a passion.

Q: **What's your most vivid memory?**

A: One of the most vivid, and also one of the earliest, memories I have is of sitting on a beach on a hot sunny day with foamy white waves lapping round my legs – the still, quiet sense of pure happiness; the contentment of existing in that one perfect moment.

Q: **Any clues about your next book – any snippets for us?**

A: Well, there are more beaches and waves!

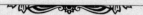

The novel is called *Elijah's Mermaid* and it is set in a Chelsea brothel with exotic mermaid-muralled walls, a crumbling vine-clad country house and another built on the banks of the Thames, full of *objets d'art* and eerie automata, where the air is always festering with the stench of drains and waste – as foul as the secrets that house conceals.

The action takes place in a shadowy demi-monde revolving around the 'respectable' worlds of Victorian literature and art, peopled by writers and publishers, by lost or abandoned children, and a black-veiled syphilitic madam who has an unnerving dandy pimp. But none of these characters are quite what they seem, and every one is drawn into the life of a man on the verge of madness – an artist obsessed with water and with painting his muse as a mermaid.

Suggested Further Reading

Bleak House by Charles Dickens

The Fall of the House of Usher by Edgar Allan Poe

The Castle of Otranto by Horace Walpole

The Woman in White by Wilkie Collins

Strange Case of Dr Jekyll and Mr Hyde
by Robert Louis Stevenson

Wuthering Heights by Emily Brontë

The Turn of the Screw by Henry James

Not
The End

Go to channel4.com/tvbookclub for more great reads,
brought to you by Specsavers.

Enjoy a good read with